IMPERIAL WINDS

IMPERIAL WINDS

PRISCILLA NAPIER

Coward, McCann & Geoghegan
New York

Library of Congress Cataloging in Publication Data

Napier, Priscilla Hayter, date.
  Imperial winds.

  I. Title.
PR6064.A5814   823′.914   81-5448
ISBN 0-698-11108-7   AACR2

PRINTED IN THE UNITED STATES OF AMERICA

To CAMILLA and ZOE
with love

Acknowledgements

For the background to Misha's adventures in Manchuria, I am indebted to Stella Gibbons' fascinating book *Tobit Transplanted*; for the fighting in the Don basin to Sir Hugh Boustead's delightful *The Wind of Morning*. For descriptions of Russia, to more Russian authors, all dead, than there is room to mention. Harvey Pitcher's charming book *When Miss Emmie Was in Russia* came out when the first draft of this book had been made; I was pleased and cheered to have many facts confirmed by it.

I am grateful to my brother, Sir William Hayter, for reading the typescript and correcting some faults of history, to my cousin Commander Sir Michael Culme-Seymour for permission to quote from his father's letters, and am most grateful to a very old friend, Admiral Lord Ashbourne, who, with my husband, as a midshipman in the *Emperor of India* in the Black Sea Squadron in 1920, was present at Novorossisk and able to confirm most of my secondhand recollections and to deny others.

*

All Russian royalties, statesmen and generals mentioned herein are real. So are all British admirals, and Florence Farmborough, the British nurse. Everyone else is imaginary.

IMPERIAL WINDS

Chapter 1

Lights shone out from the long Georgian windows and lay warmly across the snow in the gathering dusk. It was as if the people inside the house could not bear to curtain off the scenery—the white hills in the distance, the enormous stark trees in the foreground above their spread of snow. The thirty or forty children from the village who slid, scuffed up the snow or ran after Daisy along the back drive across the park were, on the other hand, anxious to get out of the scenery as quickly as possible and into the Christmas party at the Hall. Daisy, though just turned nineteen, was as enthusiastic as any. She was quite certain she was in love with Richard Kettle, and only so slightly uncertain of his love for her as to lend spice to the evening.

The Kettle family had made a fortune in jute during the war against Napoleon and by the early 1830s had bought Smetherton Hall, well set in the rolling hills of Leicestershire. Here they were soon comfortably established by a series of wise marriages, much solid but unpretentious hospitality and a certain verve and prowess in the hunting field. They had acquired the house and its four thousand acres from the declining Lynne family, who had never been financially the same since the South Sea Bubble, and who had lost their only son at Salamanca. By keeping up the ancient Lynne tombs in the village church, sitting on the Bench and on County committees, subscribing generously to the local hunt, and surviving the agricultural depression of the 1870s, the Kettles had succeeded, by the end of Queen Victoria's reign, in convincing themselves and indeed several of their neighbours, that they had lived at Smetherton for hundreds and hundreds of years.

Daisy thought them all nearly perfect. Lady Kettle was impeccably handsome and a wonderful giver of parties, Sir Reginald, red face and all, the jolliest elderly soul imaginable since the days of old King Cole, Irene and Claire models of sophisticated charm. Their glow was derived from Richard, the only son of the house, with whom Daisy intended, any day now, to start living happily ever afterwards.

The party for the village children was an episode of the Christmas season that Sir Reggie really enjoyed. He was in his dressing room, painting his jaw with spirit gum, adjusting his white beard and whiskers with real care, making certain that his Father Christmas hood and robe concealed all clues to his real identity. His father had always entrusted this task to his bailiff, but Sir Reggie moved with the times and his benevolent paternalism was laced with a dash of democracy. Hoping to convince the younger children that he had indeed travelled through snow, he had put on his cricket boots.

The Lynnes, when building the house's early Georgian wings, had found themselves too short of money to continue the work of modernisation, so that the great hall with its huge open fireplace had remained unaltered. In his youth Sir Reggie had been a keen participant in amateur theatricals, and every Christmas he hoped to discover a means by which Father Christmas could really come down the chimney. A descent through an actual medieval chimney, bearing an actual sack of toys, would have nicely combined the dramatic and the benign. But the technical difficulties seemed insuperable, and he feared to become lightly toasted.

The children poured in over the threshold, treading on the feet of Collins, the august butler, and too often failing to remove their caps. They treasured the Christmas party for the food, the glittering, lavish lights and the chance it afforded to run about shouting in unlimited indoor space. The presents provided by Father Christmas often seemed to the boys too young for their age, and failed to include pistols with caps. The girls, too, felt that they were being "improved," by the needlework and the storybooks with a strong moral basis. They longed for something grown up. But Father Christmas went on obstinately regarding them as children.

Daisy looked round eagerly. There, sure enough, was Richard, bent over the bran tub at which he was officiating. Looking up, he rewarded her with a dazzling smile. To an impartial observer he would have seemed a mildly handsome young man, well set up and with a quantity of glossy brown hair. In conversation they would have found him no fool, though with a tendency, not always acceptable in twenty-one-year-olds, to know rather too much about everything. His mother shared Daisy's glowing view of him and had never taken any pains to conceal it.

To Lady Kettle, the whole afternoon was a penance, but it was part of the job and she did it, counting the moments until the parting orange and bag of sweets could be pressed into each sticky hand, the front door could close on the cold evening air, and gentle voices and comparative peace could reign; till next morning should renew the feud between Mrs. Collins and Edna, the head housemaid, and Lady Kettle's obligation to take up her task of permanent house umpire. She was fond of Reggie, doted on Richard, and quite liked her daughters, but the parts of her life she really enjoyed were the planning of the herbaceous border, listening to Richard's tales of his life at Oxford, entertaining her friends and keeping a weather eye lifted for suitable husbands for Irene and Claire.

The long lines of children swayed backwards and forwards and Daisy swayed with them.

"Here we come gathering nuts in May,
Nuts in May, nuts in May,

Here we come gathering nuts in May,
On a cold and frosty morning."

Even Collins and Thomas had been swept in; Edward, the second foot-man, had blushed so appallingly all over his face and down his neck that he had been excused. At the piano, Irene was belting out the tune. Why can't it always be as it is at Christmas, Daisy wondered rapturously, her youthful idealism dismissing the difficulties, everybody joining in, everybody doing things together?

At tea the trestle tables were crammed with good things. Lady Kettle believed in what she called making a "do" of it: silver candlesticks gleamed, crackers and cakes and ham, sausage rolls and trifle, sandwiches and jellies were piled on silver dishes. There was a real, if momentary, flash of "All that I have is yours." For this one season, no one at Smetherton went cold or hungry; a load of coal and eight pounds of beef had been delivered to every cottage on the estate. *God rest you merry, gentlemen, let nothing you dismay*—not even Lloyd George and his unspeakable Land Tax.

Aided by Richard in the distribution, Father Christmas now delivered the goods. Daisy watched entranced, though a tiny doubt flickered somewhere across her mind. Wasn't Richard a little bit too pleased with his gracious air of knowing the name of every tenant-farmer's child, of every last baby of every employee? He had done his homework marvellously, but wasn't he too emphatic in showing that he had? Irene and Claire had unobtrusively escaped. Mr. Pelham, Daisy's father, who did not believe in the kind of rector who stood around looking benign but serving no useful purpose at this kind of gathering, had departed with Sir Reggie to the library to discuss who was responsible for cutting the churchyard hedge. The party now underwent a slight sagging, since many of the brighter spirits had fled upstairs to run races along the splendidly long and wide passages, knowing full well that the redoubtable Edna, head housemaid, was too busy playing The Farmer's in His Den to come and stop them.

The two hours after tea were the really taxing ones. The party ranged from sticky babies of a year old on their mothers' laps to hefty fourteen-year-olds who could hardly be expected to rejoice in even one round of musical bumps. It was at such moments that Lady Kettle excelled. At once bossy and exhilarating, she infused the shy, the recalcitrant and the overenthusiastic with her own determination to make the party go, suggesting game after game, making sure that everybody had a turn and that everybody enjoyed it. Her voice grew hoarse, her back started to ache, but her appearance of zest never left her.

A noisy Hunt the Slipper was followed by a still noisier Blind Man's Buff. "Old Roger is dead and he's laid in his grave," they sang, with the peculiar zest that this macabre game always evokes. Mafeking Rogers, with his usual combination of luck and skill, won the Musical Chairs.

At last, at last, came the magic hour of a quarter to seven, when the festivities would be concluded by the dancing of Sir Roger de Coverley. Sarah Jane Stubbs was bawling already, and the hair of Tommy Savage was inextricably clotted with meringue, but Lady Kettle swept both of them into her set of the dance and departed to rout out her daughters, who were having a soothing cigarette in the morning room. This was a practise of which their mother disapproved even at the best of times.

"And in any case, Irene, you must play for 'Sir Roger'."

"Must I? Can't Daisy? She plays much better. And, Mamma, I am pulled in *half* after that last Oranges and Lemons."

"Come, Irene, don't be absurd. I need Daisy to dance in one of the sets. The children get in such a muddle if they have to do it on their own. And I need you, too, Claire. Please put out that cigarette and come at once."

Her daughters, who knew when they were beaten, followed her meekly back to the drawing room.

Lady Kettle gathered her second wind for the last lap.

"Right hand, Tommy! Now your left, Susan. Now *both* hands. Now round each other, back to back. *Bow*, now, Tommy. You should have curtsied, Susan. Now lead off and make an arch—surely you remember from last year?" Sir Reggie, breathless but beaming, accompanied her in the dance. At the piano the boring tune banged on bravely; on the floor, the clapping and the stamping and the humming kept time. "Now, Sidney, it's us," Daisy told her partner. "We're coming to join your set, ours isn't big enough," Richard announced suddenly from behind her, and Daisy's heart leapt. "Right hand, Sidney; now your left." The swinging and the stamping and the clapping became appreciably wilder. No doubt now that the party, in its closing moments, was going with real gusto.

The last small boy executed the last slide over the polished floor. "Hobnail boots, too, I shouldn't wonder," Collins reflected gloomily. Irene, her wrists exhausted by the repetitive chords of the dance, was fetching out the boxes of sweets and oranges from the deep windowseats behind the hall curtains, and bending to distribute them, in a final burst of seasonal bonhomie.

"Goodbye then, Grace," Lady Kettle said. "I'm so glad. And how is your mother, Sidney? And the new baby?" Her husband, with the spirit gum still faintly in evidence, was by her side, pressing oranges upon children to whom an orange was still a rare treat. "Goodbye, Martin. Goodbye, Sylvia. Have you got your sweets? Irene! Sylvia hasn't got her sweets. Goodbye, Heather." So it always had been, and always would be. The rich man in his castle, the poor man at his gate. "Goodbye, Beryl. Goodnight, Gladys. Take care going across the Park, Bobby, it may be slippery. Is the wagonette there, for the Slobury children, Collins? Goodnight, Teddy. Goodnight, Blanche."

The stars had pricked out, and there was a faint moon. The children bounced and slithered home across the park. As always, when under the influence of a sharp frost, they ran faster, shouted louder and fell down harder. They were followed at a distance by Daisy, and by Richard, anxiously scanning the starry sky and talking happily of nothing much. How well we get on together, Daisy thought, as they went on in companionable silence. Her heart was full of feeling. Would he say something now, in this soft starlight, with their cloudy breath going before them?

Sure enough, he did. "I hope to God there's a thaw before Boxing Day," he pronounced. "Not a hope of hunting if this holds." Daisy looked at him a little sadly; with an effort he dismissed the thought of hunting from his mind. "You were splendid," he told her, as they reached the wicket gate of the park. "Good of you to come and help. I really enjoyed that last 'Sir Roger.' " They embraced warmly, and Daisy trembled with joy. That's the fourth, she told herself. Once when we were looking for that tennis ball, once after the Harvest Supper, and then the night before he went back to Oxford. The evening glowed, and she was able to respond with amiability to her mother's complaint that she was spoiling her new shoes and would catch cold by going out in the snow without galoshes.

Her mother noted Daisy's flushed face and sparkling eyes, her general look of alarming exaltation. Had they been giving her champagne up at the House? It did not occur to Mrs. Pelham that that nice, pompous Richard, whom Daisy had known since she could walk, was the Midas whose touch had suddenly turned her daughter's world to gold.

Obligingly, the snow was still crisp and even, if not very deep, on Christmas Eve, lying smooth along the distant hills, and crunching underfoot in the road. Daisy went about the Christmas preparations in a haze of joy—the final wrapping of parcels and decorating of the church, surveying with a kindly eye even Mrs. Morrison still jealously guarding both the font and the pulpit as her kingdoms, even Miss Benson still trailing ivy round the pillars. How nice they both are, really, thought Daisy, and she even forgave Mrs. Morrison for taking her aside and expressing the hope that their mother was not going to allow anything like tinsel or paper chains or Japanese lanterns to be employed as decorations in the Rectory. "There should *only* be evergreens," she insisted. "They are the symbol of everlasting life, and all these modern ideas of what is nice are only *commercial*, and to my mind, very vulgar." Poor old thing, what did it matter? Daisy pricked herself on some holly and was able to mutter a noncommittal reply.

There were eggs for tea, because of the coming two hours of carol singing—all the family and half the church choir moving, in hats and mufflers and thick coats, round the village and down to Hall Farm, on to outlying Ridge Farm and Mill Lane and finally across the park to the Hall. The lanterns flickered, illuminating the wide mouths of singing faces and Ben Robson's fingers in red mittens as he accompanied on his flute. The lanterns swung in cold gloved hands, and the Christmas bells rang through the darkness from every steeple in villages all along the valley, round and clear, an affirmation of joy, a falling together of communal enthusiasm. The frost held and the night was so clear and still that you could hear the bells coming faintly from far away down the valley, as much as ten miles, perhaps. The familiar magic wrought in Daisy's heart. If Richard could be with her, holding her hand, listening with her to these enchanted sounds!

At the Hall her spirits were slightly dashed. A large party of Kettles and their guests were gathered in their dinner jackets, and among the elderly aunts, uncles and cousins, she caught sight of a very pretty girl with cloudy dark hair and an air of sophistication. Perhaps she was just another cousin to whom they were being kind? Richard was too busy handing round rum punch and mince pies and being affable to all and sundry to have time for more than a word, and the dark girl, floating in the background in a dress of sombre blue velvet, gave Daisy a feeling of faint unease.

Joy mounted in Daisy throughout Christmas Eve. Apart from love, she was still young enough to rejoice in the whole succession that next day would bring forth. All passed in a rose-wreathed dream—early-morning stockings, presents at breakfast, her father hurrying in and out between services, church at eleven with always the same three hymns: "O Come All Ye Faithful," "While Shepherds Watched," "Hark the Herald Angels Sing." Communion, and her father's head bent as he administered the sacrament. A sober lunch, and washing up afterwards, because the servants were having their Christmas dinner now. More present opening, and the brief rush out into the stinging air to exercise the dogs, and oneself, and to make sure that Mouse, her horse, was all right in her stable. Everything sparkled, just as the sun on the snow sparkled; a squabble between Virginia and Jenny over the toboggan seemed remote and unimportant, as if it had happened long ago and were forgotten. Then there came tea, cake and crackers, her younger sisters ecstatic again in their paper hats, calling out the idiotic riddles, Papa departing to light the candles on the tree, and everyone, cook and Elsie and Broadbent the gardener and Mrs. Wilson, all singing "Good King Wenceslas" round the tree. More presents from under its branches, and Mrs. Wilson not altogether pleased with hers and making this clear enough; Virginia and Jenny were rather unenthusiastic as well. Whatever you gave Broadbent he always said that he had plenty of *them* already, and this year was no exception, but even that seemed funny and endearing to Daisy. There was a brief lull and a clearing up, and Papa going off to take the evening service, and Mamma to visit two lonely old women in the village, before the final gala of Christmas dinner—clear soup, turkey, plum pudding, mince pies, nuts and fruit and wine. Jenny for the first time was allowed to stay up for dinner, and Colonel Riggs, an old bachelor from the next village joined in, and two couples of neighbours with no children of their own. The ritual never varied, and Daisy would have been the first to complain if it had. She wanted everything to remain exactly the same and yet to include Richard. He had pressed her hand as she left after the carols, in a long warm clasp. The glow of it still suffused her being. And his, no doubt, as well.

On Boxing Day, the day of giving Christmas boxes, or tips, to tradesmen, the ground held like iron and there was no hunting, so that there had to be an impromptu shoot with all available children roped in as beaters. Virginia and Jenny returned scratched to pieces and radiantly cheerful. "We like that girl, Pamela something, that's staying there," they reported. "She's *so* funny; she made everybody roar with laughter while we were having lunch in the barn." A perceptible pang returned to Daisy.

For the next three days westerly gales blew, and every time Mrs. Pelham opened a window the Christmas cards all fell into the grate, and the despised Japanese lanterns in the hall swung madly. The snow melted, and the ground softened under steady rain, till even the most dedicated pessimist could no longer complain that it still had a bone in it. But, alas, on the vital morning, Mouse was discovered to be lame, and thus not available for the Smetherton lawn meet.

Daisy was horribly disappointed. She loved hunting, and was well aware that she cut a dash in the field, attracting admiring glances from all those male members able to deflect their attention for a moment from the way hounds were running. Colonel Riggs took her and Virginia out in his dogcart, swinging round the corners of the lanes, while his Irish groom, up behind, clung on for dear life and shouted encouragement, laced with imprecations fortunately inaudible to his master. But it was far from being the same thing as riding. Richard looked particularly handsome on a sparky chestnut horse, gleaming with fitness. "Why aren't you out?" he called, but had no time to listen for the answer. Daisy noted with slight dismay that the dark girl, close beside him, rode unmistakably well.

There was still the Hunt Ball, to be held this year at Smetherton, and Daisy looked forward to it with undimmed pleasure. She even had a new dress, pale blue moiré, the gift of Aunt Emmeline, and very pretty. The Kettles were sending their carriage to pick up her and her parents and another girl called Hilary Wilson who lived at the other end of the village, and they were all to join the Hall party for dinner. Surely the dark girl wasn't staying forever? Apart from her, there was not a cloud to be found in the sky.

The band had already arrived and could be heard twanging in the grand salon, so lately the scene of the children's party's more earthy revellings. There were bright lights everywhere, though the age of flower decoration had not yet arrived in force, and the potted palm still reigned supreme in hall and bower. Collins looked alert and proud, and there was a general sense of revelry and anticipation. Ivy trailed from stag's antlers, and holly crowned the heavy gold frames of such ancestors as the Kettles had been able to accumulate in barely a couple of generations. There were red coats and red faces and not a few red noses as well, as people came in from the winter night. Some pioneering figures had even arrived by a novel method: "In motorcars, at night, can you imagine it! The Doughtys have come twenty-five miles! And are hoping to get back tonight! All that way!"

It was the familiar local atmosphere; innocent, coarse, jovial, standoffish, friendly, unimaginative and set upon enjoyment—a scene scarcely changed, except for the two motorcars, since the days of Trollope or even of Miss Austen. Plentiful diamonds and plentiful gossip amongst the ladies, of whom there were as many old as young, since all girls must be chaperoned. And in any case, they asked each other, is one *ever* too old for dancing? "Come on, Louisa! You can manage this polka! It's none of this tango or foxtrot nonsense!" "No, really, Reggie; dance with Cynthia instead." "Come on, Lou, for old times' sake!" and off Lou would twirl, her eyes dancing, young again as ever she had been. "The three supper dances?" "Truly, Leo, I'm booked, I promise you." "You're foxing me; where's your programme?" Laughter, flirtations, family gossip, hunt gossip, horse gossip, hound gossip, game gossip; gossip from the bench and from the county council; an incessant unwearied "Do you know? Have you heard? No, it's simply not true? *It can't* be! You must have made it up! But how extra*ord*inary! People are *too* odd!"

People might be odd, but to Cousin Imogen they seemed pleasant as well as interesting. She was drowning memories of a sad youth in the enjoyments of a rollicking old age. Her head swayed gently to the sound of the music. Born another girl instead of another boy, she had been received with minimum enthusiasm. Her father never spoke to her until she was ten years old, after which he had begun taking her to Tattersalls on Saturday mornings to teach her the points of the Horse. She had not been allowed to meet any of her first cousins, because their parents were Evangelicals; her own father was emphatically not. Diptheria had swept away her two sisters, and her one brother, a charming lazy colonel, had died of enteric in the Boer War. The shock and sorrow of this was hardly over before her parents had followed suit. For a few weeks she had been ashamed of her feeling of relief, but their deaths had left her, at sixty years old, independent at last, able to decide how to spend the day, not at the beck and call of anyone, and very well off. The unknown Evangelical cousins had rallied round and discovered her to be jolly as well as rich. They had all become rather less Evangelical over the years, and Cousin Imogen now knew scarcely a dull moment. She sat happily, near the band, dressed in violet velvet, surveying the scene with sparkling eyes and beating time with feet encased in pointed shoes thickly embroidered with bronze beads.

Conversation flowed over Daisy, swept round her; she listened to it all with keen interest. The Fieldings have turned over from Shorthorns to Herefords. The Martins have turned over from Church of England to Christian Science. The Wrights have turned over to electricity from acetylene gas.

Round and round and round went Daisy, fleetingly aware of being a round peg in a round hole. A Landseer portrait of two improbably large dogs swam before her eyes. Laughter floated past her, and she laughed with it. "Who is that pretty girl dancing with Richard?" Cousin Imogen asked her hostess. "Is he at all *épris*, do you think?" "Oh no, she's far too"—Lady Kettle sought for the right, the harmless adjective—"*young*, little Daisy Pelham from the Rectory." "You are making a mistake to discourage it," Cousin Imogen thought, but her long years of thraldom to her parents had taught her to keep her thoughts to herself.

This is my second dance with him, and he's booked me for a third, thought Daisy. Glory, glory, alleluia. A waltz is really my favourite thing. But I wish, she thought, whirling past the ballroom door, that someone would dance with that tall pale girl, she looks so haunted.

Serena Doughty hated dances, especially Hunt Balls, but her taste was never consulted. Her mother was an invalid and her father was a good shot. He had brought her over in his motorcar and was certain not to leave the house until the last card had been played and the echo of the last dance tune had faded into the rafters. He had introduced Serena to a young man he knew, who had politely but unenthusiastically asked her to dance number nineteen. A well-meaning cousin with his eyes fixed elsewhere had booked her for number twenty-three. Since tradition and good manners compelled the young men who had sat on either side of her at dinner to dance at least once with her, she was booked also for numbers six and seven. But how to fill in the time during the remaining twenty-two dances?

Various alternatives presented themselves to Serena, since she was unlucky enough not to pass muster under the ruthless judgement of the ballroom. One could, she knew, retire to the ladies' cloakroom in one of the bedrooms upstairs and pretend to the maids there that one had torn one's frock and was in need of a needle and thread to mend it. Diligently stitching, one could fill in, with luck, one dance. Later in the evening one might plead a similar accident; this harmless deception, which deceived no one, might carry one through a second dance. Or one could simply sit in the lavatory, hoping that no one would come and compel eventual exit by rattling the door handle or by sighing heavily. When the band started up again for the next dance, one could return to the hall with an expectant and hopeful look and here one might meet with a late arrival whose favourite girls would be already booked. Simply in order to get onto the dance floor and exchange chat with his favourites, he might be prepared to ask Serena to partner him. As a fourth alternative, and one requiring the most courage of all, one could stand right in the forefront of the battle, near the ballroom door, tapping one's foot, wearing a slight frown and a look of impatience. "Bother that sickening Freddy!" one would cry, "I believe he's cut my dance!" so that anyone treated likewise by *his* partner might engage one out of sheer pique. Never for one moment did it occur either to Sir Fane or Lady Doughty that there was cruelty in subjecting their daughter to this process. She had acquaintances in the neighbourhood, but no friends; the evening stretched interminably ahead. Why didn't one have the luck of that pretty girl in blue, Daisy whatever-it-was? Serena was an agreeable girl and by no means ill-looking. But clearly something was lacking, and her large mouth drooped.

"Richard, couldn't you?"

"No, Mamma, I'm sitting this one out with Cousin Imogen."

"You couldn't lure Roy Ingram out of the dining room?"

"In his present state, I wouldn't wish Roy on my worst female enemy."

By the fireplace in the great hall they were discussing matters of real moment. The two elderly Miss Nosworthys were now refusing to allow the Hunt over their land because one of the joint masters had been involved in a divorce case. Some of the best of the Tuesday country, too. One understood their feelings, of course, about a divorced woman, but . . . Surely if *only* Major Todd hunted the hounds when they were over that side? He was the husband of one wife, sure enough. But no, it seemed that the Miss Nosworthys had banned the Hunt from their land altogether. A serious business.

" 'You should see me dance the Polka' ", Toby sang tunelessly into Daisy's ear. " 'You should see me cover the ground!' " There was something deeply satisfying to her in that thump and twirl, in the slight shaking of the floor beneath all those rhythmically descending feet. Why must this glorious blissful ball ever stop? " 'You should see my coattails flying, as I whirl my partner round!' How about the next polka, too, Daisy?"

"Gwen, have you heard about Colonel Longmore?"

"No. Nothing. Only that he broke his neck last month."

"October, actually." To break one's neck in hot blood with hounds in full cry was one thing, and as good a way to go as any other, but this had happened on the way to a cubbing meet, skylarking about on a fresh horse, and before hunting proper had even begun.

"They say she's left with almost nothing to live on."

"Freddie was so distressed when we heard that. He sent her a brace of pheasants last week."

Too many sympathizers, it seemed, had had the same idea. "They say she's now sighing for a good plain mutton chop." Gwen, the speaker, appeared to be of indeterminate sex, but had clinched the matter by dressing in pale mauve satin and tulle, with a blaze of diamonds.

Halted near this group on her way back to the dance floor with Rupert, by the crowd, Daisy wondered why older people seemed to dwell so lovingly upon disaster. Poor old things! Long past love and its joys! Long past secretly looking round the room, whenever one entered, to see where Richard was! They seemed to exist on a kind of negative pride in disaster's not having yet befallen *them*. To have to eke out one's life on that!

"I wonder," Gwen said, "how many people will send Alice Longmore a brace of pheasants this time next year?"

But this gloomy consideration was frowned upon by the group. On with the dance! The last thing old Algy Longmore would want would be to have people moaning and groaning on about him. "Come on, Maggie, you know you always love a waltz!" Bouncing round the room with reckless jollity, the old couple, who were both, in fact, still on the right side of fifty, cannoned violently into Rupert's back, nearly bringing him and Daisy to the ground. "Now then, young fellow!" As if it hadn't been the old boy's fault. "Mind how you go!" But who cared anyway? The thing about Rupert was that he was gloriously unpompous and never made a fuss. Or, come to that, ever took a stand. Perhaps he was simply lazy. Who cared? There, cutting across the other dancers with his usual skill, was Richard, coming in a beeline to make a joke, smile, talk to her, as if he couldn't even wait for the next dance! As if they were quite alone together in the middle of the room, and as if Rupert, and whatever girl Richard was dancing with, simply didn't exist. I am so happy, thought Daisy, that I don't even know I'm happy. And I no longer care who sees how gloriously happy I am! Not even a rosy-faced married couple in their early forties, twirling together in an oblivious enjoyment of their great night out of the year, and kicking her sharply in the ankle, disturbed this sensation of floating joy.

Serena was sitting on the mahogany edge of the bath, the bathroom being a moderately warm place where no one came unless they had a nosebleed or were feeling sick. Serena prayed that good health would prevail. There was a twisted crack in the plaster over the bath, and if you used a bit of imagination you could make it seem like a map of Italy. Should she have a bath? But there seemed to be no bath towels, since in this epoch everyone kept his own on a mahogany towel-horse in his bedroom. She contemplated using the bathmat, but dismissed the idea. The awful thing was that she had lost count, and was now uncertain whether the dance in progress was seventeen or eighteen. Father would be furious if she missed his friend who had booked her for nineteen. Whether to venture down, and ask, very casually, What dance have we got to?

Below her, the music thrummed violently and then stopped. Some enthusiast was putting on the gramophone; it sounded tinny and ineffective. The supper dances! The band had gone to refresh themselves, and with a deep sigh Serena realised that there were three more dances to go before number nineteen.

"Mummy, no more Strauss waltzes please! Irene and I do so want a tango! No, it's not some vulgar American dance; everybody is doing it. I don't mind *what* the Committee has organised, I'm going to ask the band . . . No, really, Mummy, we can't have the Lancers, it's *too* stuffy! Well, of course, if Cousin Imogen particularly asked, but you'll see, *nobody* will do it. And after supper let's really have some proper dances, two-steps, turkey trot. When all the old fogies have gone home."

The old fogies, for the most part, show a dogged determination never to go home. They twirl, and hop, and swing their coattails or skirts with the best.

The dresses seemed to Reggie and his contemporaries particularly ugly, but the girls did not. "Who is that stunning little thing in blue?" Reggie was pleased to be able to tell them that it was Pelham's daughter—"our rector, you know"—as if he had given him the living entirely so that his daughter should delight the eye of his own old friends. "Robin Wilson is tight already; see to him, Richard, will you, or get Thomas and Edward? Collins is too old for this sort of thing . . . Who's for supper? Come on, Rose. Stop flirting, Willy, and get your feet in the trough . . ." "If Asquith seriously thinks—oh, there you are, Reggie! Do you want me to rustle up Colonel Riggs to take Cousin Imogen in to supper? Is she still staying the course?" "More or less: I've suggested bed and some hot milk, but she's not having it" . . . "What's this in aspic? . . . Lobster mayonnaise . . . Chaudfroid of *what?* Here, Archie, you're a bright fellow, what's this in English? Quails? Not for me, thanks; they taste like mice. Isn't there any salmon?" . . . "The champagne the Hunt Committee lay on gets worse every year . . ."

Whirling round with Richard, with his friends, with neighbours, Daisy had forgotten the dark girl, who was still present, and very attractive, in deep red of an unfamiliar cut and fashion. Daisy was aware only of being a pretty girl having a glorious time. Even the Wilson twins seemed witty, even freckled Sam Orme not without charm. "I say, Daisy, you waltz uncommonly well! Do you really think so? You're not so bad yourself, Rupert." "Ripping band, isn't it . . . Have you had supper?" "Well, two suppers actually, but I didn't eat anything at either. I can't bear to miss much of the dancing, can you?"

Too soon it was midnight, and the dowagers were departing, with their diamonds and their weary backs, held upright too long in stiff chairs. Tough chaperoning mothers propped up their eyelids and stayed on, slightly vexed with husbands who had long since disappeared with Reggie Kettle into his library to drink brandy and smoke cigars, seeming not to care whether their daughters had partners or not.

Mr. Pelham had departed to cheer the bell-ringers, ringing the New Year in. Walking across the park in the starlight, he felt suddenly overwhelmingly happy: blessed in his job, his home, his life, and for a moment untroubled by the idea that he had done nothing to deserve it all. Reaching home, he looked in on his younger daughters, asleep and breathing peacefully.

"Oh dear, I've lost one of my gloves! You're not sitting on it, are you, Toby?" For Daisy, the fun had not flagged. "Actually, I never have smoked. I'm longing to, but not exactly here, with Mamma's eye upon me . . . Oh, shall we? No, the band's just starting again. Another waltz! I'm sorry, but I'm doing it with Richard."

Round and round and round. Everything was a dream, giddy and delicious. The time and the place and the loved one. "People used to think it was bad form to reverse," Richard told her, "but everyone does it now." How else stop becoming unbearably giddy, certainly if one whirls at this pace? . . . "I'm sorry, was that your heel? Well, my dear fellow . . ." "Richard," his father interrupted, "Guy Wilson is out, now, too; can you deal with it? They can't hold it, those two, proper menaces they are, horse and foot, and a famous blowing-up they'll get from the old man tomorrow."

The hem of Daisy's dress had been mutilated in the last polka, and she went upstairs to the Chinese bedroom for a quick stitch. Lucy, the third housemaid, vigorously plying her needle, caught a glow of reflected joy, as if Daisy had brought in the whole exciting party with her, as if its fireworks were now fizzing and sparkling within the Chinese Bedroom, floating through the air towards the Chinese wallpaper and ricocheting off the Chinese Chipendale chairs. Glancing round from her sad seat at the end of the bed, Serena bent over, as if concerned with the state of the heel of her shoe. So she, unrecognised in a new hairdo, had been the tall, pale wallflower.

Daisy, flown with the dance, with the music, with discovered love, and also with her first glass of champagne, was in no condition to focus upon anybody else, even urging the patient and careful Lucy to make haste—"it doesn't matter *how* it looks so long as I can't fall over it"—and even attempting to pull away, impatiently, after the first couple of stitches. But when she did, for a moment, focus, she was aware with a heightened perception. Serena was known to her but slightly, but what she knew she liked, and there was something in the droop of those bent shoulders that held her attention.

"Don't lose me," she begged, "if your shoe is really all right again. I do want you to meet Toby Fox. And Rupert, or do you know him? He lives more or less over your side of the country. He really dances so divinely!" Lucy, observing all this, and aware of how little had been the trouble with Serena's shoe, at once forgave Daisy for her impatience and remembered her warm thanks. Speculations as to the Richard and Daisy possibilities were already rife in the lower echelons of the servants' hall.

For the next hour and a half all went well with Serena. Enthusiastically introduced by Daisy, she danced with Rupert, with Toby, and with two or three other young men who had left the later dances on their programmes unfilled in case of hopeful developments, or who wished to stand well with Daisy. After that, things seemed to go flat, but Serena, never expecting much, was content. Her father, emerging briefly from the card room on some errand of his own, had seen her twirling successfully in the middle of the dance floor, and would report favourably. And she would have enough to tell her mother for herself. Serena had found by experience that if she reported sadly or complainingly upon a dance her mother became scornful, making odious comparisons by reverting to tales of her own brilliant youth. Had she really ever been, Serena sometimes wondered, such a *femme fatale* as all that? On the other hand, if she had had a good time, and came in next morning full of the glow of it, to see her mother, as she lay on her chaise longue by the window, her mother would grow jealous and restless, and become desperately wistful about her own incapacity for further enjoyment. "You've managed to upset your mother again," her father would say, coming in from his shooting of a winter evening; and a glum silence would fall; and tentative enquiries as to whether he had had a good day would evoke no response. On the whole Serena found it safest to have had only a *rather* good time. Rupert and Toby would be safe cards to play, coming from respected neighbourhood families, but without anything special or glamorous about them. Even the cousin who had booked number twenty-three in the near certainty that Serena would have gone home by then, had faithfully turned up to claim his dance. Altogether, things could have been much, much worse; and Serena could contemplate, almost with relief, a switching off of the effort, and an honourable retreat to the Chinese Bedroom.

For Daisy, the evening roared on far too quickly, glowing with sound and colour and the quickening of love. Even the older generation had got to the point where they very easily made jokes and very heartily laughed at them. Thank goodness for wine, that maketh glad the heart of man! Distressing incidents in the hunting field had been forgotten, bad language given and exchanged in the heat and excitement of the chase had faded away as if it had never been uttered. A shared sport that in its varied forms had enlivened the countryside for at least the past thousand years, and whose rightness and necessity had not yet been seriously questioned, held the company together like glue. All native dourness had melted into a warmth of neighbourly good feeling. "Auld Lang Syne," when it came, would be sung from the heart. The Wilson twins had been safely put to bed in the Bachelors' Wing.

The evening roared on, far too quickly. "Archie is going great guns on his hunting horn!" No one seemed able, or indeed, willing, to stop him.

The band was tuning up for the final gallop, and what were the bandsmen thinking, behind those sweating foreheads, or feeling, underneath those wilting shirtfronts? Pleasure, envy, boredom, or simply fatigue? Off they went, anyway— "Do you ken John Peel in his coat so grey, Do you ken John Peel at the break of day?" Serena Doughty had given up, and was in the bedroom among the fur coats, happily listening to Lucy, the third housemaid, telling the lurid tale of her little brother's accident in the hopper.

"No!" the dark girl in red declared. "I've ruined too many dresses doing Hunt Ball gallops; I'm not spoiling another. People hang on like grim death or else trample all over your skirt. Why not find that dear little thing in pale blue who's so sweet on you?" Daisy, seated with Toby on a sofa behind the door, wondered whom she could be talking to. Or about.

The voice of Richard, slow and slightly blurred, answered her. "You mean Daisy, the local talent?"

The voice of the girl in red went on. "I'm quite jealous, if that's who I *do* mean. In a pale blue dress that looks as if it's Mamma's cut down?" Richard's voice came again, in a caressing drawl that Daisy had never before heard. "I can't be with you in London all the time, darling. Must have a little local amusement. And don't be bitchy about her. She's sweet. I really like Daisy."

"What you really like . . . is teasing." Her voice, low, intimate, caressing as Richard's, went on inaudibly.

Daisy doubted her ability to get up and walk across the room. The voice of Toby came from a distance. Rupert, appearing to claim her for the gallop, seemed to hover and dip before her eyes. From some lost recess in her throat she managed to retrieve her voice, to utter false words.

"Do you mind, Rupert? I think I must go. I suddenly am rather tired."

"But you can't miss the gallop, Daisy! And 'Auld Lang Syne.'"

"It's just that I can't dance another step . . . Oh, thank you. Thank you . . ." Mercifully, Mrs. Pelham was close at hand, mercifully, the light in the hall was dim. It was possible to slip through, half hidden by her mother in her fur cloak, her heart empty. By the great open fire, Sir Reggie, with his back turned, was holding forth to some cigar-smoking colleagues, on the eve of departure. "Amazin' how time flies! Obvious—but it does, don't it? Getting on into the twentieth century, aren't we? All but a hundred years since Waterloo. And that centenary will be worth celebratin'!"

Daisy and her mother were through the hall, through without being seen, stopped and well-wished. Her mother might fuss about galoshes, but in a crisis, she could see there was something grievously the matter and could whisk one away without delay or question. Sir Reggie's voice floated after them. "Fireworks! Balls! Dinners! Nineteen-fifteen is going to be *the* year. Lucky they thought of fighting the battle in June! Good month for celebratin'!"

"Happy New Year!" one of the colleagues answered. "Nineteen fourteen, by gum. Nineteen bloody fourteen!"

Chapter 2

The Pelhams were distressed by the appearance of their eldest daughter at breakfast next morning. She looked feverish, exhausted, resolute. Their concern increased when she started to read a letter aloud to them, speaking in high-pitched staccato tones. Did they remember Amelia Lynch, she demanded, who had been a friend at school? They remembered her distinctly, and without enthusiasm. Miss Lynch's father, it

appeared, had lost all his money, and Amelia had taken a job as a governess. In Russia, and this letter was from her. She had heard of another
family, a very charming one, who wanted an English governess: could
Daisy think of someone who would come?

"I would like to go myself," Daisy concluded, eyeing her parents with
nervous defiance.

"Oh, darling!" her mother objected. "It's too *far!*"

"That's the point."

"Besides, your father hasn't lost his money."

"It's time I did something practical and useful," Daisy continued, still
with the same dangerous glint in her eye. "That at least you'll agree to, I
know, Daddy."

Mr. Pelham groped for logical reasons to advance against a plan
against which every instinct rebelled. He had a vision of a lot of poor
people lying dead in the snow outside the Winter Palace in St. Petersburg, shot by the Imperial Guards, with a priest carrying the cross at
their head; people who had simply come, unarmed, to beg for reform. The
Czar admittedly had not been there—but that an officer of his should
have issued such an order! Some people were now saying that the priest in
question had been an *agent provocateur*. One didn't know what to believe.
It was widely rumoured that if the Russians hadn't taken such a beating
in the sea battle of Tsushima, their next objective would have been the
conquest of India. Besides, they were Jew-baiters, baiters of Poles, Lithuanians and goodness knew who else; and unless we ourselves looked
pretty sharp they would hop the Pamirs and start baiting the Indians.
The Czar was said to be a good man. But as he was still in complete
control, what was the fellow up to, pushing on into Chinese Turkestan,
running his railways right up to the frontiers of India? No good, you
might be very sure, Mr. Pelham brooded. Russia sounded an unsafe and
unsavoury place altogether, and his daughter had much better keep well
out of it. He began, "Apart from anything else, what qualifications have
you to teach children?"

"It isn't like that! Amelia says it's quite different in Russia. The children have tutors who come in and teach them all the regular subjects.
They just want a reasonably nice girl to be *with* the children, and talk
English to them, and read them English books, and play tennis with
them, and that sort of thing."

"Oh, no, darling," Mrs. Pelham pleaded, "it really is too far. And too
wild. Savage, really. Look how wickedly they behave on the Frontier in
India, always inciting the tribesmen. And there are anarchists everywhere, who keep trying to assassinate the Czar."

"Mummy," Daisy explained patiently, "I wouldn't be on any frontier,
and I am not the Czar."

"The winters, I believe, are hideously cold and—"

With chalk-faced determination Daisy allowed the tide of her mother's
protests to flow round her. Mummy would be certain to hate the idea at

first. But only by going so far, and to such a strange remote place where no one knew her, could Daisy begin to forget Richard, and the family at Smetherton, and having made such an utter fool of herself. Only far away could she grow into a woman—tough, sophisticated—able to hold her own in the world. What was there to be learnt among these green fields, in the lapping comfort of home? Her mother would be plaintive and regretful, but could in time be overridden. But Mr. Pelham had a glint about him, a sense of danger and of hidden steel that compelled deference. Unless he were to agree to her going to Russia she knew that she would be unable to go.

Mr. Pelham went on brooding uneasily. He had gathered that all this had something to do with Richard. How had Daisy failed to learn the extreme lightness of young men in love? Surely these were matters in which mothers should instruct and caution their daughters. An element of self-blame clouded his brow. Was he not himself at fault, in having allowed his daughter to grow up a bit of a goose? All this riding and tennis, and staying at school until eighteen—wasn't it overdone? Thousands of girls of Daisy's age had to stand on their own feet in factory and workshop, accept rudeness, and long hours and loneliness, far from home, in comfortless quarters. They had also to learn how to repel unwanted advances from foreman or boss without getting themselves the sack; to take the knocks and rubs of life and survive them. And here was his dearly loved Daisy, green as grass, taken in by the first pair of flashing eyes that had flashed in her direction. Nothing but a few hurried kisses, he suspected, a few sweet words taken as gospel, and here she was, carrying on as if she were Dido bereft of Aeneas. One couldn't particularly blame Richard, confound him. In spite of himself he suddenly felt on Daisy's side. If she wanted to go to Russia, she should.

Daisy fixed him with her large stricken blue eyes; he suffered a revulsion of feeling. Confusion take young Richard! Why should Daisy, the light of his eyes, be driven from her home? And to Russia of all outlandish places, a crusted absolute monarchy suicidally resisting any real reform! A phrase from Mrs. Gaskell came to his mind. Going as a governess to Russia was, she had said, "the equivalent of taking the veil or a ladylike form of suicide." To his mind it was behaving like those men who felt called upon, when jilted, to go off to Africa or India and shoot big game, a practise he had always considered melodramatic and overdone. A governess! His young and pretty daughter—the idea was hateful. And to some Godforsaken Russian barbarian, about whom no one knew a single thing! There were times when Mr. Pelham was rather more of an Englishman than a man of God, and moments when he was rather more of an earl's son than either.

Daisy interrupted his thoughts before he could begin to speak. "And Amelia says, and I know you didn't like her very much, Papa, but she is very sensible, anyone would tell you that, she says there is a very nice Mr. Taylor and his wife, who's the English rector in Moscow and there's a place called St. Andrew's Hostel, which is a sort of place where you can stay for very little, if you are between jobs, or want a holiday, or don't like your job and want to stay until you get another, and they have a sort of club room there, and all the English girls go there on their days out, so you can't feel lonely, and you can have tea there, and other meals too, I think. And Amelia says it's really quite *totally* different from being a governess in England, because you really *are* one of the family."

"But what sort of family?"

"Amelia was always a bit of a fusspot, and touchy and everything, so if *she* says people are treated all right they must be. Just *read* the letter, all but the first page anyway, which she says is private, and just *see* anyway what she says, and don't, don't go on saying no without even thinking about it, because if you don't let me—" Here Daisy disconcerted herself as much as everyone else by bursting into tears. They fell heavily into her porridge, which, since her mother was a Scot, was quite salty enough already. As the sound of her young sisters' voices was heard in the hall, Daisy left the dining room abruptly by the pantry door, colliding with Edith, whose morning it was for doing the silver, and cannoning off her and up the back stairs, leaving her parents in a scarcely less disturbed state than her own, which had, after all, to some extent been the point. "Storm in a tea-cup," Mr. Pelham endeavoured to mutter, but his heart was not in it.

Daisy belonged to a generation and a way of life that induced in its young women a unique and peculiar innocence. She had led a life without setbacks, and for the first seven years has been an adored only child. Just when this was beginning to seem a little boring, a pair of young sisters had appeared in rapid succession, too small to be her rivals. At school she had been intelligent enough to escape worry over lessons, pretty enough to escape anxiety over her future. She had been admired for her skill at hockey and tennis, and praised for her singing voice. The headmistress, a progressive woman, had encouraged political discussion, against the day, surely soon to dawn, when all her pupils could vote and indeed become members of Parliament. Daisy had been encouraged to write long and very boring essays, beginning "Superficially, Philip Augustus . . . but fundamentally . . ." These were generally marked $A+$, thus giving Daisy a general and erroneous impression that she was highly intelligent and very well educated.

At home, in a friendly neighbourhood, she had grown up as the well-liked child of admired and popular parents. She had no brothers to prick the balloon in which she so ignorantly floated, no male cousins whose comments might have kept her feet on the ground. Leaving school in July, she had found Richard Kettle at home, in lively frame after a virtuous three weeks spent with an all-male reading party in Cornwall. She fell in love with him almost as a matter of course. As she knew from her Victorian novels, falling in love with a suitable young man could have but one ending, and that a happy one. During the autumn, with nothing very much to do but to practise her singing, help her mamma, and shop once a fortnight in Leicester, and with no rival excitement except an occasional day's hunting or a stodgy dinner party with the parents of Toby or Rupert, she had thought so continually of Richard that she had managed to work up a mild fancy into what she seriously supposed to be a *grande passion*. How could such feeling not be reciprocated? To find that it was not had been a searing blow.

"I suppose," Mr. Pelham said later in the day to his wife, "that I could at any rate write to this fellow Taylor. He'll probably play down the idea, and agree she's far too young, and unsuitable for a governess, but I can't get an answer for weeks and it'll give the poor girl a chance to come to her senses, and meanwhile she won't be feeling that we are determined to throw a spoke in her wheel."

Mrs. Pelham, much as she would have preferred the outright veto, was obliged to admit the wisdom of his words. "Going to Ian and Isabel at Inverness would have been so much more *suitable*. Ian of course knows everybody, and—"

"That's the trouble," her sensible spouse cautioned her. "Scotland seems now to Daisy much too safe and humdrum. And familiar. She wants wolves and forests and beards and assassins, and away with the entire British Isles and its squires and their sons. One can't blame her. I much more blame myself for letting her grow up such a ninny. She's got about as much sense in these matters as Kitty and Lydia Bennet."

"Lydia who? Oh, *them*." Here Mrs. Pelham was able to lodge a well-founded protest. "No, she has not. I mean she has far *more* sense. She never runs after *any* young man."

"Follows too easily perhaps."

"All the more reason," Mrs. Pelham triumphed, "for not letting her go to Russia. Who's to help her if she loses her head there!"

As this was a matter upon which Mr. Pelham preferred not to let his mind dwell, he set out upon his Thursday visits, listening patiently in stuffy cottages whilst arthritic parishioners recounted to him the oft-told tales of their ill health and the besetting nature of their misfortunes. He had a charming way with him; by lunch time he was sad and tired and much in need of recharging his batteries in prayer; and his arthritic parishioners were all as merry as grigs.

Mr. Pelham is his heart respected Daisy's independence because in this they thought alike. He himself had declined the family living and left his own part of the country because, much as he loved his elder brother in whose gift the living lay, he wanted to make a life of his own, and liked direct contact with the country people whom he loved.

Reading the answer to his letter, a fortnight later, Mr. Pelham felt as one who in the midst of battle has his only horse shot from under him. Pausing only to point out that he and Mr. Pelham had several mutual friends, Mr. Taylor proceeded to endorse every word that the mistrusted Amelia had written. Yes, St. Andrew's Hostel existed, next door to him and his wife, and was a cheerful centre for the English girls in Moscow, and of some who came from St. Petersburg. There were plenty of them, and many were delightful. Of course, he and his wife would keep a particular eye on Miss Pelham, in case of illness or difficulty, but he begged the Pelhams on no account to distress themselves at the prospect of Moscow. He had not personally met either Prince or Princess Andrei Dubelsky, but they were said to be charming, happily married and devout. They were well off, and altogether *comme il faut*. Russian families took their English governesses everywhere and seemed to delight in giving them a good time. Daisy would meet plenty of people, could hardly help improving her French, and would broaden her mind by contact with such a very different culture. She would be taken to opera and ballet; and to hear Russian opera and see Russian ballet was worth coming much further and faring far worse.

There must, Mr. Pelham reflected, be some serpents in this Eden, and turning the next page, he found that there were. Mrs. Taylor had chipped in, informing him in firm round handwriting that the cold of a Russian winter was *punishing*; if his daughter had the least tendency to chest weakness, she had better not come. The houses were hot enough, but then one went out into these unbelievably low temperatures. The other danger was that girls so far from home and made so welcome by their Russian families were too often known to stay in Russia for a lifetime, but this, of course, applied only to girls who had not, like Daisy, a happy home waiting for their return. "How does *she* know?" muttered Mr. Pelham.

He felt bewildered and uncertain, and Daisy rushed in upon him at just this moment and pressed home her victory. Her looks had come back with the plan of foreign travel, and her eyes sparkled with hope and anticipation. Her chin, and indeed her whole bearing, looked more determined than ever.

For another few days, Mrs. Pelham went about with a look of worry and reproach, and Mr. Pelham fought a stubborn rearguard action. He would send Daisy to Perugia for six months to learn Italian; to Vienna to train her voice. Would she care for a longer spell in Tours to perfect her French? How about the Monro cousins in Gibraltar, from whence she would be able to visit southern Spain, perhaps be in Seville for the Easter celebrations? Was there anything she would like to do in London—study art, the piano? "It's simply," Daisy pleaded, "that I like the *idea* of Russia. I know it may be very different when you really get there, but I love Borodin, and that translation Aunt Louisa had of Pushkin."

There was something about her pleading fresh face, about her courage, the way in which she had refused to sit at home moping and hoping, but was so determined to cut her losses and start anew, that touched her father deeply. With a sigh, he yielded; sitting down to write the necessary letters, to open the essential communication with Thomas Cook and Son. With a look of tearful resignation Mrs. Pelham set forth for Leicester where she bought Daisy a quantity of thick woollen underclothes which they both of them knew in their hearts that she would never wear. Lady Kettle, more perspicacious, brought back from London a present for Daisy of a very becoming fur hat. Whether this action were more of a generous gesture or more of an offering to the kindly fates who were moving Daisy so far from the ambience of her son, Richard, who could say? Ethel gave her a pair of red mittens, and Mrs. Wilson an outstandingly hideous scarf. Nelly came up with a maidenhair fern in a pot. "Something fresh, out there in all that snow," she suggested. "The green of it will cheer you up." Daisy had a sudden sensation, brief but sharp, that she was abandoning love and embracing an icy coldness.

On the last night before Daisy left home Mr. Pelham was beset by qualms. Did his daughter really know enough to venture into a foreign world alone? He now felt morally certain that she did not. Like many men with pretty little daughters, he had been more than content, at the end of a long day's work, simply to bask in her existence. After gloomy sessions with old women in cottages, with cases of mental deterioration, with wives chained to cruel or indifferent husbands, with drunken young men, with a curate in the next village suffering from Doubt, it had been blissful to come home to a comfortable house and an affectionate wife, and above all to that enchanting little face with its enormous blue eyes, so easily lit with laughter, the lively mind, the eager dancing small body, the readiness to be amused. She had never posed problems, never been difficult. Doctors notoriously neglect the health of their children, and he as a parson had neglected the spiritual health of his. He had simply and contentedly loved her, and thanked his lucky stars.

He was vaguely aware that some things were amiss, but by the time they became definite enough to put one's finger on, his daughter had grown past the stage where they could easily be corrected. And so he had gone on basking in Daisy's liveliness and prettiness and let things slide. Everybody had faults, and Daisy would grow out of hers. She was too sensible not to. And yet he could sometimes, from the other end of the dinner table, hear her being very irritating indeed. She asked too many questions, persistent questions, never seeming to notice the offence they sometimes caused or the reluctance to answer displayed by those questioned. She pronounced didactic judgements on subjects she had hardly begun to understand. Had the lively mind, somewhere along its route, turned into a carping and self-righteous one? Looking back, Mr. Pelham could not remember that any of his sisters or their friends at Daisy's age had ever so persistently demanded answers or so determinedly stated views. But then she would come to say goodnight with a smile that enchanted him, and make a joke, and for the next few days be as carefree, silly and lively as any other eighteen-year-old. She was helpful, competent, apparently contented. And if, in the distance, he was sometimes aware of Daisy in argument with her mother, their voices were never raised in annoyance, and the arguments never seemed to continue. She was different from his own generation, but this was the twentieth century, and one must make allowances. Throughout recorded history young girls had generally been silly; and their parents, to escape the consequence, had always kept them under close surveillance. Now that this method had (rightly, thought Mr. Pelham) been generally abandoned, there was nothing for it but to accept the risks that such freedom involved.

His daughter was gazing out of the window at the Essex countryside, flat and unlovely in the dimming light. She was a comical mixture of the trustful and the brash, unworldy as a kitten but outspoken and enquiring. How could she fare without discomfort in the Russian world of formal good manners, where, he understood, fathers still reigned supreme over daughters who were not expected to have views and theories and to hold forth upon them, in and out of season?

Oh, well. It was only for a few months, and then she would be back again, happy once more, he hoped, and even, conceivably, a little wiser. With a sigh he decided that she and the Russian family must all fend for themselves.

Nor did the view from the deck of the ship at Tilbury afford Mr. Pelham any reassurance. Daisy was travelling under the chaperonage of a Mrs. Disbrowe, wife of an English timber merchant in Moscow, but this lady had already laid herself flat in her cabin, pleading *mal de mer*, although the ship had not yet left the quayside, and a number of young men, few of whom looked at all reliable, were eyeing Daisy's flushed and excited face in a way that her father much mistrusted. He was letting her go, against his better judgement, into a far country, a strange land, knowing nothing of life, nothing of the world, and still more dangerously, nothing of herself, of the power of love to seize on the heart and lead it whither it would not go. Why do we teach them Latin and algebra and not that? Mr. Pelham wondered, a little late in the day.

Daisy read his thought. She met the glances of the young men with equanimity, sweeping them with a detached gaze, as if they were deck chairs or ventilators. The wind of January, blowing off the Thames estuary, failed to chill her spirits or even to make her look cold. She was suffused with the excitement of high adventure. "It's all right," she told him, through a warm embrace. "I am thoroughly innoculated. That won't happen again."

"No?"

"*No.* Once bitten, twice shy."

It was a comfort to him that she could talk about it, even smile about it.

"I am sad leaving you all, but if you knew how glad I am to be going! . . . I say, isn't Mrs. Disbrowe a joke! Being ill in harbour! Golly, she'll be dead by the Hook!"

A steamer hooted mournfully out of the misty darkness, and Mr. Pelham, stumbling down the gangway, uttered a heartfelt prayer. A girl, not yet twenty, setting out virtually on her own, for darkest Muscovy!

The journey across Europe seemed to Daisy very long and very dark, rather like a dream. Mrs. Disbrowe, though calm and experienced as a traveller once on shore, was not the jolliest of companions; seeming to think that all foreigners had been invented expressly to plague her. The scenery never ceased to consist monotonously of pine forests and wide plains. Once across the frontier and changed into Russia's broader-gauged railroad carriages, the forest seemed even more dense and the snowy plains still more interminable. Never compare, her father had urged her; the beauty of travel is not to let oneself make odious comparisons, but to accept each country for what it is and rejoice in its difference. And though this was in what Daisy privately thought of as his sermon vein, it was true, all the same; one only had to listen to Mrs. Disbrowe discoursing upon Russian lavatories as against English ones to realise the wisdom of it. Stepping out of the train during one of its long halts, she found that her own thick woollen English coat, which had seemed extravagantly heavy at home, was in reality not nearly thick enough. The cold went through it as if it were a shift.

What would this mysterious country really be like? She sought in her mind for old impressions. Ivan the Terrible—why was he "terrible?" Everyone admired Peter the Great, who had built an immense and beautiful city where once there had been nothing but marsh. Then there was Catherine the Great, really a German, and a bit of a murderess, and fairly shocking altogether. Then Alexander I, a mystic and an idealist. All the same, at the defeat of Napoleon he had had six hundred thousand men under arms, so that nobody at the peace treaty could argue with him or get a fair deal for Poland. Had not the climate, more than Alexander's soldiers, defeated Napoleon's Grande Armée? Perhaps that wasn't being quite fair. But Alexander had allowed his soldiers to cut off the heads of prisoners of war, and his officers had been in the habit of pissing all over people's drawing rooms in Paris, so perhaps he wasn't such a *preux chevalier* after all. An aroma of that long-used Western European phrase—the beastly Muscovite—still hung about. I wish I knew more, Daisy thought, but that's about it. People say that Russian novels are marvellous, and I wish they would translate them into English so that one could tell for oneself. I miss half the point reading them in French.

The night deepened in flurries of snow that blurred the windowpanes, and had scarcely been melted off by the heat of the train before a new flurry succeeded. At Smolensk the day was just breaking; the engine steamed in the icy air, distant wagons shunted with a melancholy clanging, instructions were issued in harsh voices through a heavy fog of breath. On the platform, half turned away, stood a young man whose fair hair and lounging way of standing reminded Daisy sharply of Richard, and her heart raced. Could he have come after her? Had he suddenly decided that he couldn't do without her, that he really loved her after all? Half-awake, Daisy sprang to her feet with his name on her lips. Hearing her cry, the young man turned round, presenting her with an ordinary, dull, unfamiliar face, staring blankly at the steaming window. Surprised to find herself still so vulnerable, Daisy sank back with a sharp pang of sorrow and defeat. From the opposite bunk Mrs. Disbrowe continued to snore comfortably.

The sun shone redly through the trees over more interminable fields of snow. Bearing a huge jug of hot coffee, an attendant knocked on their door. "Better not drink any, dear," Mrs. Disbrowe counselled, inopportunely awakening. "Better be sure than sorry. Where's the teabasket got to? Start the spirit lamp up, will you, dear? I'll make us a nice cup of tea in a jiffy." But Daisy, finally rebellious, indulged herself in the invigorating Russian brew, muttering something about doing as the Romans did. She and Mrs. Disbrowe seemed incapable of communicating except in clichés, as though engaged in some boring and life-long parlour game.

For all that, as the day passed and the strange enormous country unfolded before her gaze, Daisy felt a mounting glow of excitement. She seemed unable to sit still, hastening out into the corridor for a glimpse of a passing village or back into the sleeper compartment for fear of missing some new sight on the other side. "Couldn't you," Mrs. Disbrowe suggested mildly, "settle down for a quiet read, dear? You don't want to tire yourself out before we even get there." Like a restless child reproved by its nanny, Daisy opened her travel literature.

A Frenchman, she read, voyaging through Russia in the 1830s, had called the Russians "inept for everything, except the conquest of the world." On the other hand, the young and rich Lady Londonderry, travelling with her husband in Russia at about the same time, and having a considerable social success there, after a bad political setdown in London, had thought them not only delightful, but good. "The colossal scale of everything strikes the mind with wonder." It surely does, Daisy agreed. "Their friendly hospitality warms the heart, they are the most intelligent, agreeable, distingués, clever persons imaginable." "Fleas, bugs, and vermin abound," Daisy read on: The women were "hideous in face and form . . . and all are encrusted in dirt"; but the men were "a fine, tall, wild-looking race, well and warmly clothed" and every peasant seemed to own four or five horses. "It is dirt and barbarism that shocks one for there is no squalid misery and want as in Ireland." The post houses where Lady

Londonderry and her husband spent their nights in travel between the great towns, though filthy, had lofty rooms, parquet floors, and Italian ceilings.

The contrasts were extraordinary. Lady Londonderry had been spellbound by the effect of the immense palaces, enormous squares and wide streets "that made people look like pygmies and the carriages shrink to nutshells," and before the bright blue and green domes covered with gold, gilt spires and white houses. All of that sounded to Daisy smashing indeed; and so did the "gems and treasures like the Arabian Nights" of the Hermitage, and the sun striking brightly on all the bright colours and glittering domes echoed Kubla Khan. "Dirty strange coachmen drive their wild steeds at a wonderful pace." Whatever else, Russia didn't sound dull.

Then there were the churches, which also sounded as if they came out of some fable. The Cathedral at Zagorsk, Daisy read, was lined with gold and painting and had singing monks and an open screen behind which was the Host, priests in robes of gold and silver, rich velvets of bright colours, embroidery, thick wax tapers burning, and incense thrown into the furthest corners. The Host was brought round, prince and peasant standing together in a dense mass, continually crossing themselves or falling down to kiss the ground. Distribution of the blessed bread was made by priests with long hair parted in the middle. It all sounded a bit of a pantomime, but interesting to watch, all the same.

Perhaps Lady Londonderry's enormous social success had a little gone to her head; perhaps on the other hand, she told the simple truth. The Orphanage in Moscow had seemed to her "a model of cleanliness, comfort and good organisation," so some bits of Russia were hygienic, anyway. And she had called the hospitals of Moscow "marvellous." She had stressed that there was "a great deal of charity and benevolence, relief of the poor also; in spite of the proud aristocratic feeling in Russia, in no country are illegitimate children so well received." Daisy was reassured to learn that the Russian nation were particularly kind to suffering people, and hoped greatly that the Dubelsky family would share this quality. As for music, Rossini had said that just to hear the singers of the Imperial Court was "a sufficient reward for the journey to St. Petersburg." That, too, sounded beautiful and promising.

And yet, Daisy wondered how to reconcile the characterization of the Russians as "inept for everything, except the conquest of the world" with Lady Londonderry's phrase: "these refined, sensitive people whom we, in all the pride of our own vanity and ignorance, call barbarians and uncivilised beings."

Daisy laid down her book. Darkness was beginning to gather already; the forests had a black and sinister look about them. Maybe the Frenchman hadn't had an enormous social success; maybe, like most Frenchmen, he was firmly convinced that all civilisation was encompassed within the frontiers of France. Better believe Lady Londonderry; but more probably the truth lay somewhere between these extremes. Or perhaps Russia was simply an extreme place?

The drone of Mrs. Disbrowe's voice, lasting, it seemed, without a break from Minsk onwards, could not distract Daisy from her interest in the passengers seen waiting or descending at railway stations. The Russians really *did* wear long boots, fur hats, beards and skirted coats: she had feared that the illustrated books must be a hoax. It only remained for a sleigh to drive past, with three horses under a high yoke, or for a large bear to come lumbering out of the wood, a gypsy playing a balalaika to roll drunkenly down the road.

The bear had become unlikely, as they were now slowing down through the Moscow suburbs. A huge church spire loomed up distantly into a heavy grey sky. "The Church of Christ the Saviour, built in thankfulness after the defeat of Napoleon," Mrs. Disbrowe informed her sententiously; she feared that Daisy's insatiable curiosity would soon cause her to outstrip her chaperone in knowledge, and sought to impress whilst there was yet time.

With a hiss and a clang the long train drew up beneath the roof of an enormous station whose lights were hung from a dark distant roof of cathedral-like proportions. Bearded characters whose boots appeared to be bound on with string advanced towards the train in a horde, with cries that seemed to mingle the triumph of an invading army with the jovial bellow of long lost friends greeting one another. Foreign indeed! With a delighted curiosity that, for the moment, swallowed up apprehension and sadness, Daisy stepped down from the train.

Chapter 3

On the platform was Amelia, her colourless pussycat face screwed up in amusement and pleasure. She gave Daisy her usual welcome—warmth shot through with an underlying vein of mockery—and expressed unqualified admiration and envy of Daisy's new beaver fur hat. Different, she approved, different; not like every other bloody fur hat.

Daisy was delighted to see her among all the strange words and faces, a familiar figure, well remembered in attitude and gesture. Amelia's greeting held an equal warmth, but the usual mocking gleam soon appeared uppermost in her eye, and above the shouting of the crowds of people and the hiss and roar of escaping steam from the engine, she administered her customary splash of cold water.

"So you're really here? I never dreamed you would actually come, when it came to the minute of goodbye. The proud and successful Daisy Pelham, down to earth at last, signing on as a gov! Who'd have *believed* it?" Daisy could at least be thankful that her friend made no attempt to explore the wherefore or the why of her arrival, simply drawing an arm through hers and pulling her down the platform with her usual bounce and zest, barely leaving time for farewells and expressions of gratitude to Mrs. Disbrowe, who was being embraced in a gingerly and apologetic manner by a stout husband in an Astrakhan fur hat. "That's all right, dear," Mrs. Disbrowe told Daisy abstractedly, for the embrace, however careful, had disturbed the angle of her hat. "It was quite a pleasure. Ta-ta, now."

Amelia detached Daisy from the handshake of Mr. Disbrowe, almost before he had had time to doff his Astrakhan, and bore her off to St. Andrew's Hostel, through streets whose bleak snowy spaciousness and offsetting of coloured sugarcake buildings induced in Daisy an ever more powerful sense of unreality. Could any city really look like this, outside of a Christmas pageant? A group of elderly women in shawls were brushing the snow along the pavement. They looked unbelievably like the sort of wooden dolls which spring persistently up again every time you push them over.

St. Andrew's Hostel turned out to be all that Amelia had cried it up to be—warm, cheerful, buzzing with gossip and laughter, and steaming with tea from a great samovar. Daisy's sense of being a new girl soon evaporated; though she was perforce held silent through knowing nothing of all the people under discussion. Names whirled in and out of the talk—who was Prince Kyril, who were B. and Lordy? Who was Serafima? Would one ever learn, or indeed, get a word in edgewise to ask?

The general conversation left her divided between irritation at finding that the hostel members had simply transferred their darkest suburbia to the centre of this exotic city, and admiration for the instinctive cohesion and solidarity of the English abroad, the sense of community and understanding, however it might sometimes be laced by an undercurrent of jealousy or malice. They might be catty, but they would certainly, when it came to the crunch, rally round one. Just now they crowded about Daisy, pleased with a new face, eager to instruct, pressing her with far too many toasted scones. Her excitement was now such that she had difficulty in swallowing one. The resolute, pretty face of Florence Farmborough stood out from amongst the crowd, with its surround of curly reddish hair. She looked purposeful and different.

Russian society, Daisy was told, was divided into separate worlds, which scarcely overlapped. There were the nobles, aloof and splendid, and the intelligentsia, who were prepared and, indeed, pleased to mingle socially with English expatriates, provided they were themselves intelligent or interesting. Then there were the rich merchants in one of whose families Amelia was situated. "They are *unbelievably* rich," she told Daisy. "Ostentatiously rich, and I suppose at home one would think them rather coarse, but it's all so—what's the word?—*exotic*, it's all so different that you don't feel put off by it. But the amount that's eaten and drunk you wouldn't *believe*. At a dinner party my family had the other day the flowers all came from Nice—all that way on ice in a train—imagine it! Mimosa, tulips, all sorts."

"It must have looked gorgeous!"

"It did. But it all went on so *long*. For what felt like hours and hours before dinner we stood eating caviare on warm rolls, and reindeer tongue, and drinking vodka. And once we sat down! Wine after wine after wine. You've no idea, about twelve I should think, but I lost count. And of the courses, too—they were endless. Then there was a ballet, and some superb people playing Chopin nocturnes, and *then* there was a dance."

"Too much of everything," Daisy commented severely.

"Yes, perhaps," Amelia conceded, "but there's something so ungrudging, generous and lavish about it. But just listen to this. Do you know, in the middle of dinner there was a colonel something or other called to the telephone, and it was his mistress, saying goodbye forever, and do you know, he shot himself, right there, the receiver still in his left hand, and do you know there was such a noise no one even heard the shot! Wasn't it *awful?*" Delightedly, they all joined in declaring how awful it was, and how unlikely ever to have happened at home— "I mean, at someone's *dance*—so unmannerly."

"The children are all awfully spoiled," chimed in a pale tall girl named Kathleen, "but lovable. I *make* mine finish their food up—they were horrified first. Vegetables and fruit and all. No one has any idea of *healthy* food. And there's always an old Nyanya somewhere about and the children rush off to her if you try and discipline them in any way. And my Madame K. is divorced; have you ever heard of such a thing? She's had three husbands, and still is received, and she and all three husbands play bridge together—would you believe it?"

"Russians are allowed to divorce," Amelia pointed out.

Whatever else, thought Daisy, I am not going to gossip about the Dubelskys; that really is too housemaidish. But I wonder if I'll be able to resist it? I hope there'll be nothing to gossip about. Golly, how I hope they are nice and I shall like them! She noticed that all the English girls appeared to rival each other in being shocked: at the same time they were clearly also fascinated. But it's barbaric! they would cry, whenever anything not immediately to be accommodated within their way of thought was described. Barbarism evidently had charm.

"The world of the nobles is a small one," Amelia told her. "Small as a mouse, and just about as uncatchable. They aren't so rich as the merchants, and not nearly so ostentatious. Easier to live with in some ways, I should think. They don't throw their money about in that bewildering way. And people say that their children aren't nearly so spoilt. You may be lucky."

But will I be? Daisy wondered. I can't wait to know.

The noisy cheerful afternoon wore on. Daisy met Mr. Taylor and his wife and liked them both: here was a solid link with home. About the other girls she felt less sure. Amelia's family were taking her almost at once to St. Petersburg, and Daisy felt half inclined to accept Mrs. Disbrowe's invitation to spend her first day off with her. The gossip flowed on round her—"I went out to tea with some people who knew my uncle was a composer in England, but I suppose I wasn't up to scratch in a musical way, because they never asked me again."

"In Russia one just *goes* to people, one hasn't forever to be asked," the knowledgeable voice of Kathleen maintained.

"Do you know that old Miss Ritchie who has been such centuries with the Galitzines was once asked to marry by a Russian colonel in a Cossack regiment? And she said yes; and then she heard that the Czar would never receive her, so she broke it off, and there she still is."

"But worse, did you hear about the English girl who married Prince someone, with an estate in the Ukraine, and they had lots of children, and she had a chaplain of her own there, and christened them all Church of England. And then someone went and told the Czar this, and he banished the Prince, and all his family, right out of Russia for always? Not this Czar, but the last one."

"How awful! Don't they ever complain about their Czar?" Daisy asked.

"Never. And don't you. Russians practically think he is God."

"All the same, it must be awful to be him. All that terrific responsibility."

The talk turned to tales of St. Petersburg, to accounts of the huge frozen Neva covered in skating figures, to the Winter Palace, the golden domes, the dances at the English Club, to summer at Tsarkoe Selo in the row of houses where the nobles spent summer in attendance on the Czar, to walks in the park, full of lilac groves and heavy with their scent in spring. The Empress, Daisy gathered, disliked Moscow and rarely came there, thinking it full of revolutionaries. And besides, to increase her fear, there had been that terrible accident in their coronation year, when a stand had collapsed and hundreds of people had been killed. "The Czar is charming," they all insisted, "but people are frightened of her. She's rather stiff and blaming. Fearfully proper, you know, like the old Queen."

"What old Queen?"

"Queen Victoria, of course. Her grandmother."

"All the same, charming or not, it was the Czar who dissolved the Duma, the Parliament, in 1906, in the summer, and that was quite unconstitutional."

"Unconstitutional! You do know some topping words, Amelia. Have you ever seen the Czar?"

Daisy wanted to, very much.

"I once saw him, quite close," ventured a mousey-haired girl with a round face and round spectacles. "Here, in Moscow. It was June the year before last, I think, or the year before that. He came for some special thing, the anniversary of when his grandfather was murdered, or the Grand Duke Sergei, one or the other."

"What did he look like?"

"His face was very like our new King, George V, but not such very bright blue eyes, and he wasn't so sort of *firm* looking. Frail, and with narrow shoulders, and he looked anxious."

"You'd look anxious if you were a Czar, with all these anarchists about," Amelia said tartly.

"Not exactly that sort of anxious, not fear. More a sort of doubt. He didn't look quite up to it."

"Absolute power—who *does?*" Amelia spoke with sophisticated scorn.

"Did he just ride along?"

"That was the oddest thing of all. He came to the place where the assassination had happened, and he got off his horse and knelt down in the street and *prayed*. And then he kissed the place on the ground where it happened."

"You can't imagine King George praying in Piccadilly," Spectacles commented, "or in Whitehall, where King Charles's head was cut off."

"Nor kissing the ground either."

Daisy waited for somebody to say "How barbaric," but no one did . "I find that rather touching," she ventured.

"Oh, if you're going to fall in love with everything Russian!" the spectacled girl protested. Daisy blushed hotly.

"I saw him, too," Amelia said, kindly plunging in to cover Daisy's embarrassment. "He came for the centenary of Borodino, and it was quite different and very jolly and splendid, millions of marching troops, and the Czar's Cossack guard. Goodness, they were thrilling! Everybody cheered like mad. They looked wonderful and invincible, with all their swords and lances flashing. And their uniforms! And their horses! Bloody gorgeous!"

The tall, pale Kathleen spoke up. She seemed older than the others, with wispy hair and a long, sad face. "The Czar would have done better to have gone to pray at the Khodynka Field where the stand collapsed at his coronation and those hundreds of peasants were killed. It's never been forgotten. A bad omen, too." There was a brief silence before the company decided to ignore this gloomy note.

"That's Kathleen; she's got a Menshevik young man and feels strongly," Amelia murmured to Daisy.

"What's Menshevik?"

"A sort of Bolshevik, only less so."

"What's a Bolshevik?"

Amelia sighed. "Don't let's start on all that!"

"No, but do tell me!"

"Revolutionary. Terribly boring; young men with wild hair and mad ideas who don't shave."

"Oh. Are there many?"

"Masses, probably. They don't amount to anything. But other young men here," Amelia maintained, "are very fascinating, though of course the ones you'd like to marry are not the ones who'd think of marrying you. The eternal housemaid's trouble," she added cheerfully. "They're very sophisticated and charming; debonaire, really. Before I came I had pictured a whole lot of small-scale Ivan the Terribles."

"One might as well go to England," Daisy argued, "and expect all the young men to be Henry VIII."

"Oh, that's quite different!" Kathleen contributed. "England is so much more *civilised*."

Daisy would have liked to continue the argument, but Amelia announced with finality: "In my opinion, the Russians are good-natured, but quite immoral savages, *au fond*, that is. Don't be taken in."

Daisy blushed again. Could Amelia know why she had come to Russia?

At seven o'clock a troika came from the Dubelskys to fetch her. With a certain sinking of the heart she said goodbye to Amelia, stepping out into a night whose coldness made her gasp. The coachman wore a coat padded against the bitterness of the January night. At the back of the sleigh, on a carpeted platform, stood a footman who handled Daisy's luggage and put a thick fur rug around her. He wore a long coat with a huge fur collar. In the intense frosty air breath came from men and horses as solidly as from so many steam engines. The cold was so extreme that it seemed to Daisy almost to burn.

The drive was an enchantment, so that the cold was all but forgotten. The snow lit by clear starlight, the jingle of the sleigh bells, the crispness and dryness of the air, the strange silence of wide streets banked in snow. The icebound Moscow river was lit up like a silver thread by a faint young moon; in the Kremlin misty towers stood up, ghostly sentinels of an alien night. There was something entirely and fascinatingly foreign about the whole scene, as if it came from a play, almost from another world. There were different smells, different sounds. Figures moved mysteriously in their long felt boots. Despite the cold, there was a spice of the orient, of distant minarets, of Tartar hordes, riding over deserts to lost cities amongst stony hills. I now understand Borodin, thought Daisy hopefully.

She had accepted the long journey, the strange food, the incomprehensible shouting, the wild, bearded figures pushing past her, even the silliness and gossip of the girls who would have to be her friends. Not till the sleigh drew up at the Dubelskys' gateyard did a moment of panic assail her. One of the family! Like it or not, she was to be one of this family for perhaps many months. One could not put one's hand to the plough and then take it off again if the plough got too hot to hold or if one developed blisters. Visions of dreadful uncontrollable children assailed her, mocking her ignorance in their strange unpronounceable tongue. Of a mother and father who were aloof and didn't concern themselves. Of a family that was no family. How be one of a family who didn't like one? How anyway be one of a family when one already had a perfectly good family of one's own?

The door opened, and the doorman, Pavel Nikolaivitch, bearded and blue-uniformed, ushered her in. He wore an ornamental bandolier and looked exactly like someone from the chorus of an expensively produced opera. In the hall, Daisy jumped at the sight of a great stuffed bear, holding a silver tray for visiting cards. People had just such a thing in England, but the bears were smaller: in this huge hall the bear looked more real and menacing. Everything about the house seemed to be formed in the noble manner, grand and richly wrought yet neither crowded nor fussy; but spacious and solid, as if made for kings and near-kings to inhabit in splendour for centuries, to withstand heat and cold and the ravages of war and weather. An amazing warmth flooded over her, and an air full of faint, exotic and opulent smells, in powerful contrast to the Spartan cold without. With a sensation of having arrived in quite another world, Daisy followed Pavel up the marble stairs. His bandolier creaked as he moved.

Coming down the stairs, at full speed, were two entirely beautiful young men. The first one, very tall and splendid, had a fair, obstreperous face, with high cheek bones and light blue, very wide-set eyes. He tore past Daisy, not seeing her, as she was all but hidden by the great bulk of Pavel. A dark replica followed him, with a more sensitive and intelligent face, less prominent cheekbones and huge dark eyes. He saw Daisy when he was almost past her, sketched a bow and was gone. With a swing of long coats they clattered through the hall and into the waiting sleigh.

"Who was that?" Kolya, the dark-haired one, asked his brother.

"I didn't see. The English governess, perhaps. What was she like?" Misha asked, momentarily curious.

"Pretty," Kolya pronounced succinctly.

"Good. I am tired of seeing poor old Mademoiselle across the table at meals every day. It was better before her mole grew those long white hairs."

"Mademoiselle is with us forever, Misha," Kolya said, "however many English governesses come and go. I am fond of the old girl."

"Fond, yes," Misha agreed, "but not to look at." Their minds switched to other matters.

I suppose, Daisy thought, that a part of being a governess is not being seen. Like Thomas or Edward handing the fish at dinner at Smetherton. At home, of course, one can't help seeing Nelly, because she breathes so loud, and is rather apt to chip in to the conversation. But in a house this size full of so many people, a governess must be a sort of nonperson, like a chair or a potted palm. It's a state of not being noticed, and one must get used to it. I mean to learn Russian, however difficult it is, and to talk it to the nannies and servants and people, have a kind of companionable life there, where I am a person, and quite real.

She continued bravely across the very wide landing to a tall door, from behind which came the sound of many voices, all talking French at the top of their lungs. Oleg, an elegant figure who wore the same blue livery as Pavel, had taken over. Eyeing Daisy keenly, and not at all as if she were a chair or a potted palm, he threw open the door.

Chapter 4

To her surprise, Daisy found her duties pleasant enough. A week after her arrival, she wrote home delightedly:

The work here is very, very slight. I hardly have to teach any lessons. Just English, and I talk it to the children and they are very quick and rapidly improving, the family sometimes talks English and sometimes French, but oddly enough hardly ever Russian except to servants and people in shops. I read to the children and please send me out any books that Jenny has really grown out of, because there's not much here and it's inclined to be Dickens. *The Jungle Book* they'd like, I'm sure, and *The Princess and the Goblins* and *Jan of the Windmill* and *The Cuckoo Clock*, and *Us* and *Treasure Island*. Varya would like *The Black Arrow* too I should think as she's nine and very grown up for it.

There are twin boys, exactly alike, Nikolai and Arkady— middle syllable pronounced Card, and the stress is on it—who are six, nearly seven, and who lead me a dance pretending to be each other, and a little one of four called Ella, but really an old Russian nanny looks after her. She is pretty but rather too holy if you can imagine such a thing, always praying and she never stops crossing herself and the old Russian nanny eggs her on. But it isn't quite so odiously pious as it would seem in England because she is so natural about it and not self-conscious.

I am learning quite a lot of Russian, you'll be glad to hear, and how to manage the samovar. The houses are quite hot with a funny sort of wood stove. The cold outside really makes you jump but it's a dry cold and the snowy streets are lovely and better still lit up at nights. Moscow is beautiful, except in the terribly slummy parts which really are saddening. I make the children go for long walks which I love and they hate. Old Nyanya used to come too because she was sure I'd lose myself and all the children, but she's fat and got so out of breath that she soon gave up and stood calling after us for ages "*Vot zapomni!*" which means, "Now remember." I'll tell you in my next letter about the Kremlin and everything. But I'll tell you one thing which I find most extraordinary, which is that Sunday begins on *Saturday* after lunch and ends on Sunday after lunch, so that you never have one complete day which is Sunday, at least you do, of course, but the Russians don't think it so, and this I find very, very rum.

I will write lots more soon but this is just to say that I'm perfectly All Right. There's an old rather sad French governess as well as me, really a good soul but she started off being stiff and perhaps jealous till she realised I couldn't teach much and certainly not French. She's jolly old, quite sixty I should think, or even seventy and quite glad to have someone else to do the energetic things with the children, like building snow mountains and tobogganing down them. Masters come in every day to teach Latin and Mathematics and science and German, one's very dried-up and precise and the other very hairy and absent-minded. So, Daddy, you needn't have worried about my being such an ignoramus. If I am, it doesn't matter.

Prince Andrei, the father, is blond, blue-eyed, charming, very clever, I should think, and older than you'd expect with such young children. He is bearded and stout and very slightly like the old King. He has a jolly, shaking way of laughing. The Princess is beautiful, with raven hair and high cheekbones, staggering jewels and fur coat after fur coat, of which she has most angelically lent me one because the cold outside is quite something. She laughs a lot too and loves music and parties and doesn't interfere except to be awfully kind about my room being warm enough and she quite understood my thing about wanting to open a window—which you can't in Winter—which everybody else thought quite mad. She is mad about mysticism and strange priests float in and out with their long hair fastened back by long pins but it doesn't stop her being delightful. They *may* both have bad flaws in their characters, but they haven't appeared yet and guess what? They are taking me to the Nobles' Dance, in a pale green velvet dress belonging to the Princess's younger sister, and you must admit that it's not really a very governessy kind of life and we all have meals together the children staying up for dinner and to all hours but they are not really spoilt and have to sleep on very hard iron bedsteads for fear of becoming soft. There are masses of servants, mostly with beards (the men I mean) but they are a kind family and their grandeur is of the natural kind like Uncle Claud's and *not* like Lady Crowleigh.

Another odd thing is that though there are 50 servants, the
Princess never goes near the kitchen or the servants' hall.
They seem to get on with it all on their own.

Daisy paused. Now she was coming to the most difficult part. To
describe Misha and Kolya in anything like realistic terms would, she
knew, cause her parents immediately to start making plans for her
return. No actual lies would be told them, but surely there was no harm in
playing things down.

As well there are two older brothers who are soldiers and
hardly ever here, called Mihail and Askold, this being an ancient Russian hero rather like Hereward the Wake, I imagine.
They are the sons of the Prince by his first wife who died of
cholera in the Crimea but don't worry about cholera and other
germs because I am very very well and coming here was a
good plan though I miss you all tremendously.

What point in telling them about the bugs in these grand walls, and the
spasms of powerful loneliness? "The sunsets over the snow are simply
gourgeous," she concluded, unaware of how her father would blanch at
this spelling, and she wound up with a Russian greeting the accuracy of
whose spelling he would luckily be unable to assess.

If Russian households didn't share wealth, they certainly shared feelings; and life was conducted on an open plan. Everybody was swept into
everything, and this included the strangely intense religious life of Ella,
the pranks of the twins, the question of Varya's new dress, and whether
or not her hair should be tied back with a black bow or continue to be
confined within an Alice band. The musical passions of Kolya, which
disquieted his colonel, were examined at length, and loud cries arose over
the extravagancies and delinquencies of Misha, such as his notorious pursuit of gypsy beauties. There was no going behind closed doors and discussing such delinquencies in low voices, as parents did in England.
Everyone's views were canvassed, and everyone weighed in with advice
strongly larded with tales of dire events, from Mademoiselle down almost
to the boot boy. Voices were raised, and people dashed upstairs crying
volubly, the Prince would look stern and flash his eyes and wave his
arms, Uncle Sergei would be summoned and Uncle Georg would wander
in and volunteer his own experiences, the Princess would sigh and look
tragic and the opinion of Grandmamma would be invoked. On the back
stairs doom would be prophecied in wailing and unmeasured terms. In a
flash the mood would change and everyone would be heard roaring with
laughter.

"Misha is young," the Prince said, excusingly one evening, "and when

I was young . . . I remember . . . The gypsy dancers *are* incomparable." Uncle Sergei would sigh, and "Incomparable" Uncle Georg would echo. The Prince's eyes took on a dreamy look; he had already forgotten Misha.

"If he marries a gypsy, he marries a gypsy," Uncle George contributed briskly.

"Many of our noble families have gypsy blood in their veins," Uncle Sergei consoled.

"No sound is more sensuous, more exotic, more exciting," the Prince went on, "than the sound of gypsy music . . . The Islands in the Neva—never can I forget the sound of their music coming over the water on summer nights. The music is a sound more dangerous than opium, or women, or drink. It is a sound primitive and melancholy, as though it came from the depths of our being. It is lyrical, it is an intoxication. At the sound of those wild trumpets the walls of restraint crumble . . . The gypsy girls are very strictly guarded by their parents," he added regretfully, "never to be taken as mistresses, hardly even to be gained as wives."

"And then only upon payment of a great sum in roubles," the Princess added prosaically. "Several of our noble families have paid this sum."

Daisy found it incredible that they talked so frankly about gypsies as purchases.

"Their dancing had a wild foreign beauty in it," the Prince insisted, still in his happy sensual dream. "It was far more intoxicating than wine."

"It is not to be supposed that they dance much after marriage," his wife pointed out.

Suddenly philosophical, the Prince echoed Uncle Georg. "If Misha marries there, he marries there. He has, after all, his mother's property."

Misha had sensibly absented himself till the storm passed. The scolding prepared for him had got lost on its way and had petered out in the Prince's heart into a kind of dreamy resignation to the follies of youth and even a nostalgic longing to return to his own.

Misha was dazzling, thought Daisy; sometimes she blinked when she looked at him. He was like a statue, but a statue rubbed a while in the sea, its sharpest edges humanized. He moved always with haste, impatiently, his corn-coloured hair flapping; swinging down the marble stairs and through the enormous doors as if the gypsy dances or the party for which he was bound might evaporate before he got there. Dressed for a fancy-dress ball, in fur hat and an ancient Cossack coat, he would pass from room to room at great speed, shouting farewells to the children over his shoulder or returning suddenly to embrace them warmly with the traditional threefold kiss. He would be gone in a minute, with his long coat flying behind him, arriving back very very late, and Daisy suspected, very very drunk, judging by his looks next morning as he dashed back to his barracks. But the tonic of Moscow's sharp dry night air, Daisy was assured, did very quickly clear away the fumes from the head. The streets of Moscow, she noted, were quite lively at three or four o'clock in the morning, full of people, dancing and shouting and calling out greetings or abuse. Did Russians never go to bed?

Kolya's addictions were different, and to Daisy at least were more sympathetic. In feature he was like Misha, but no sea had rubbed off his clear-cut edges. His dark eyes seemed to light up his face when he listened to music. Even when he and Misha had been in the Corps des Pages, he had been obsessed by music. He was a pleasant pianist, though no professional; hearing music was for him an absorption, it was the elixir in which he bathed and refreshed his soul. It was not in favour of the latest nightclub or to drink champagne while listening to gypsy music that Kolya, like Misha, absented himself from the Nobles' Ball. Off duty, he would make straight for "The Bat," to hear Chaliapin sing Boris Godunoff or to listen to Gorky's rich tenor; moving less rapidly than Misha but no less purposefully. The Bat was the club attached to the Moscow Arts Theatre, whose talented secretary, Mihail Lykiadopoulos, "Lyki," was Kolya's friend, a man of various talents, part Greek, part Russian, part English, and in due course translator into Russian of H. G. Wells and Lytton Strachey. Here Kolya would stay to all hours, listening to music and to the talk of musicians, dead to all other thoughts and returning no earlier than did Misha.

His at least was a passion that could be shared with his family, and he would spend long afternoons with the children, teaching them the haunting songs of their homeland. Irresistibly drawn by the music, Daisy would step closer behind them, joining in with the gentlest of voices. Kolya instantly heard her and drew her in nearer the piano. Her voice, now rising truly and clearly, was yet lacking in the right timbre, in feeling and in melancholy, was somehow clipped and arid. She felt it to be so, and exclaimed at it; but Kolya only laughed and praised the purity of her tone. "The rest, the greater feeling, will come to you in time." He talks, thought Daisy, as though I hadn't already felt *everything*.

"Play now some of the songs of England."

"Sentimental ones or rollicking ones?"

"Some of both."

Happy to shine in some way, she played carols, sea-shanties, ballads. The children picked them up with ease. Kolya fetched his guitar and was at once improvising round the tunes. All were absorbed, and the long winter afternoon, while snow fell steadily outside, passed, at least for Daisy, delightfully. It was fun to meet people for whom even "Annie Laurie" was a novelty, even "The Twelve Days of Christmas."

Much of Moscow was puzzling to Daisy. Why did the cabdrivers always argue over what was clearly their proper fare? It turned every ride into a prolonged bargaining session. Why were they so grasping and greedy, why couldn't they be more reasonable and less bullying? And then the same cabman would disarm her harshness by pausing for a reverent obeisance to the saint whose shrine stood at the Kremlin Gate. The Prince's lavish generosity would alternate with a kind of bored hardheartedness: one beggar would receive a handful of silver and the next a scornful brushing aside.

The Dubelskys' generosity to Daisy was munificent. The children, on the other hand, were kept quite short of pocket money. Only five roubles came their way every month, which was about a pound, and most of this was expected to go in church or charity. Extravagance in dress, and any deliberate ostentation, were frowned upon as vulgar. (That, at least, Daisy thought, is like at home.) She had soon learnt enough Russian to make ordinary purchases, yet money did not seem to go very far. The widespread poverty that she saw daily in the streets was appalling.

Kolya would talk politics with his stepmother, but she teased him and called him a revolutionary and begged him to beware of the Czarist police. "But Tolstoy," he would begin, "in the last thing he wrote . . ."

"Tolstoy! He was a revolutionary to the last. He dressed to the last in peasant clothes. And how ridiculous they looked, driving out together, Countess Tolstoy dressed smartly in the latest fashion and he in his peasant blouse, seated by her side!"

"But have you read the last thing, or almost the last thing that he wrote? It is not at all revolutionary. Listen, Mamma. It comes in *The Law of Love and the Law of Violence.*"

"Violence! There is too much talk of that. Do not even speak of it, Kolya."

"He calls the organisation of government by a self-appointed and would-be enlightened minority 'the axiom by which the greatest crimes are committed.' And he adds this— 'Know this, all of you, especially the young, that to try to impose on others by violent means a regime which exists only in your imagination is not only an enormous folly, but a crime. Such work, far from benefitting humanity, is a lie, an act of almost transparent hypocrisy, hiding the lowest passions we possess.'"

"Oh, Count Tolstoy! He was a heretic, I suppose you know? And condemned by the Church. It is better, I think, not to study his philosophical works too closely."

"You do not think that in this, the Church could possibly have been mistaken?"

"No, Kolya, I do not . . . Come here to me a moment, Ella, your sash has become twisted."

Princess Dubelsky's grace of movement, the uninhibited naturalness of all that she did and said, were qualities that Daisy had never before, in her brief span of being grown up and in the world, encountered in quite so vivid a form. Before the thing with Richard, she told herself painfully, I had a character of sorts of my own. Now it seems completely flattened out, and it's almost as if I didn't exist as a person at all. She longed for Amelia's sophistication; even to have Amelia's slangy pertness would have been *something*. The courage and confidence that had borne her to Russia, the faith that things must somehow come out all right in the end, that had sustained her, had temporarily trickled away with a pang of inferiority. "One of the family" was but a figure of speech: how be one of a family so closely and totally united? In no single act or word of the Dubelskys was there any exclusion; but, of course, the nature of things excluded any outsider, and always would—she had been a fool to imagine anything different.

Everything about the Princess had a kind of elegant splendour—her clothes, the dressing of her hair, the rooms in which she sat. The stove that heated the great room, and which could so easily have been a hideous object, was covered in pretty porcelain tiles and had a gilded and decorated top, so that it seemed to chime in with the beautiful china in the cabinet, the gilded looking-glasses, the glitter of the crystal chandelier hanging from the high, moulded ceiling. Even the floor, not content with being plain polished wood, was inlaid with a marvellous selection of different woods—rosewood, teak, oak, birch—in intricate patterns of garlands and flowers, so that one almost hesitated to tread on it, as if one were doing the polka on top of a piece of Dutch marquetry. There seemed to be nothing in the room not made by skilled and artistic hands. In such a room Daisy's own prettiness, her neat, well-chosen clothes, her entire personality, seemed to dwindle into nothingness, or at least into nothing much. Rising to her feet and giving Daisy a kindly smile, the Princess swept off Ella and a slightly reluctant Kolya to pay a visit to their grandmamma.

Daisy turned doggedly to her Russian phrase book and applied herself to learning useful phrases by heart. It was hard enough to believe that one could ever sound at all sophisticated in so difficult a language. Perhaps best confine one's efforts to the servants' hall. Crossing the room, she addressed a request to Oleg in a firm voice, and was immensely encouraged when he not only understood her but obeyed.

In the doorway stood Misha, roaring with laughter. "Why? Wasn't what I said right?"

Misha continued to laugh. It was quite impossible to explain to Daisy how unbearably prissy and unreal she had made his native tongue sound. Presently, he stopped laughing and said, "Bravo, you did well." But Daisy, diminished by the extreme gusto of his laughter, was not appeased.

On their return from expeditions, as often as not, Uncle Georg and Uncle Sergei would be seated on either side of the stove, a couple of non-matching firedogs. Uncle Georg in his heyday had been a dashing and fashionable figure in Russian society, knowing everyone, known to everyone. He had travelled the world, lived for two years in Italy, and generally seen life, marrying in middle age a rich and childless widow who had left him all her money. When the family returned he would sit squarely on the sofa, viewing the scene through worldly and derisive eyes, a monument to seventy-five years of good living. Yet he was aware, with dismay, that to his young great-nieces and nephews he was scarcely distinguishable from his younger brother Sergei, whom he had always considered a poor fish. Sergei had never cut any kind of a figure and had wasted his substance, not even in riotous living; he had melted it away in support of a number of good causes, moving on from one to the next in a pique when he came to consider their organisation ineffective or corrupt. The perfect good causes continued to elude him.

Sergei had never left Russia, spoke Russian almost invariably even when everyone else was in full French or English flow, and regarded the Imperial Family with a reverence that was almost religious. All of which caused Uncle Georg to behave in a very crisp manner towards him, brusquely interrupting his boring anecdotes of their mutual childhood or calling upon all, even Daisy, to note how incorrect were Sergei's facts. He hoped thus to distance himself from his inadequate brother, but it did him no good; to the young he seemed only the more crotchety of two crotchety old uncles. They bestowed warm kisses on both alike, treating them with a casual preoccupied affection. Kolya alone sometimes directed upon the great uncles an interested glance, as if genuinely concerned to know and understand them.

Sitting on a French sofa, like a stout boulder immovable in a rushing stream, Uncle Georg would direct upon the boys in particular a sharp gleam of envy from his narrow light eyes. To be twenty-four again, to be twenty-two, with it all before one! With motorcars, and maybe even aeroplanes, in which to pursue the girls, so that even less time would be wasted, even more fun might be had! Even the twins, with their unconscious and inexhaustible energy and vitality, sometimes seemed to Uncle Georg to be objects of envy. Uncle Sergei regarded them sadly—in spite of the care of their parents, were they not growing up too materialistic, worldly, un-Russian? Despite criticisms, and occasional sharp words, all were united by a strong family bond and would never have dreamed of seeing any less of each other. Far from excluding Daisy, the uncles found her very easy to look at and invariably demanded her presence if she were not there. Even Uncle Sergei, in his melancholy way, seemed to forgive her for not being Russian, taking the charitable view that she couldn't, of course, help it.

Looking at the twins, as they pranced past him, to cast their thin young arms round their mother's jewelled neck, Uncle Georg narrowed still further his light glittering gaze, kissing them farewell with a kind of intensity, as if to suck their brilliant vitality out of them and implant it in himself.

Daisy, thin, sad, and slightly in the background, was beginning to understand how he felt.

Kolya, home again for a brief twenty minutes, came bounding up the stairs and started to play. Bathed in the music, swept away as on some calm river, Daisy forgot her sorrows, forgot, indeed, all else.

Chapter 5

On a February night, when the Princess was in bed with a bad chill, Prince Andrei took Daisy instead to their dinner party. "They live far away," the Prince explained. "On the other side of the city. Have you enough furs? I hope you will not become cold?"

I am much too thrilled by it all to feel cold, thought Daisy. Wide-eyed, she gazed up at the brilliantly starry night, at the icicles hung from the heavy cornices as they went on through the eerie silence of the snow-muffled streets. They were passing through a narrow avenue in a part of Moscow that Daisy had never visited before, when a sudden ragged crowd appeared out of a side alley, almost surrounding the sleigh, with hands held out from torn fur sleeves and a thin piercing cry for alms.

Carelessly, the Prince threw out a handful of small coins; carelessly, the coachman flicked a whip to keep the beggars clear of his horses. "Oh, stop! Please stop!" Daisy called out. "There's a woman with a tiny baby and it's crying so dreadfully and she looks so thin! Please, please stop and let me give her something!"

The Prince produced a further coin and threw it accurately to the woman with the baby, running a little apart from the others. "Drive on," he ordered firmly. "If we stop," he pointed out kindly to Daisy, "these beggars would only demand more, become violent maybe, and then that would involve the police, and their last state would be worse than their first. On, Igor Pavelevitch."

How could anything be worse? Daisy wondered. The voice of the woman with the baby came thinly after them through the sparkling, still air—"*Kristá rádi! Kristá rádi!*" For the sake of Christ! Daisy pulled out the largest coin in her purse. But the woman was now far behind, and the coin would only lose itself in the snow. "Please, please stop! Let me run back!"

"You do not understand." The Prince's voice now had something of an edge to it. "It is a well-known fact that these women deliberately starve their babies so that their terrible crying attracts the attention of the passersby, and thus the purses of the softhearted are opened. It is not a practise to encourage."

"Oh *no!* Daisy cried. "Surely not. Surely no mother could be so desperate as to do that!"

"It is, I regret to assure you, a well-established fact."

"But where do they all come from? Where do they sleep? In this cold they must surely sleep indoors or die."

"From the Khitrovka market not far from here." The Prince noted that Daisy was trembling all over from fear and pity, and sought to reassure her. "Now here is something that will interest you. A countrywoman of yours, or at least in part a countrywoman, has started to relieve the miseries of Khitrovka. She goes bravely, refusing police protection, right into the most dangerous and dirty heart of the Khitrovka. She is a beautiful princess who has become a nun."

"And she is not afraid to go among such people?"

"It seems not. She speaks Russian, though with a dreadful Anglo-German accent. I myself always spoke English or German with her. She was so beautiful . . ." He paused to sigh. "She is a sister of the Empress. She was Princess Elizabeth of Hesse, daughter of Princess Alice of England, and granddaughter to Queen Victoria. She married the Grand Duke Sergei, uncle to the Czar. Ah, she was so lovely when first she came to St. Petersburg to be married! So graceful, with so lovely a turn of the head! Always good. Always lively and charming and gay. They say that Grand Duke Sergei treated her with coldness, but that I do not believe. Who could be cold to so delightful a woman? And theirs was a love match, no affair of state. That certainly is true. So also was her conversion to our Orthodox Church, a conversion of love, made they say with great pain, for she loved her Protestant Church and her Protestant family, but under no pressure from him, save the pressure of loving him and his country."

The streets were becoming wider, lighter, the houses taller and grander. Daisy could feel the intense cold beginning to penetrate even through the furs she wore and the thick rugs covering her legs. But did the coldness come from the hardness of the frosty night, and none of it from the shock and horror of what she had just seen? "Please tell me more," she begged, desperate for something of hope to be gleaned from such a scene.

The Prince went on to tell her how this Princess Elizabeth had been reft away from a brilliant social life in St. Petersburg when her husband was made Governor of Moscow, and how Grand Duke Sergei had proved a resolute and stern repressor of left-wing activities, a persecutor of political subversives. "No half-measures," the Prince applauded, "and he was right. This is no time for half-measures."

"But in the end the anarchists got him. In February of 1905. They came to tell his wife, and she ran out into the street, and his body was scattered in a thousand pieces, there in the blood-stained snow. She made no scene, gave way to no tears. She gathered the pieces of her beloved husband together, saying that he hated untidiness and disorder. And when she had seen his body safely back home, she went to the hospital to visit the dying coachman who had been wounded with him, and told him that all was well with the Grand Duke, so that the coachman, who had been sorely troubled, died in peace."

Daisy repressed a shudder. "And then?"

"She herself had always been without interest in politics. She had always immersed herself in spiritual activities. You must know that when she was a child, her home of Hesse-Darmstadt had had great distress because the Prince had taken the side of Austria against the victorious Prussians, and she with her mother Princess Alice had done much to relieve that distress. Also when she was fourteen her mother and her infant sister died of diptheria, and she came much under the influence of her grandmother, Queen Victoria, paying long visits to England to stay with her."

How does he know all this? Daisy wondered. I suppose it's the Russian habit of people always talking to everybody about everything. "And so?"

The Prince looked kindly at Daisy. Certainly she was a good and eager listener. He had never been able to get his wife to take much interest in Grand Duchess Sergei. Could there be a dash of jealousy there?

"This part of the story you, as a Protestant, will like. This part-English, part-German Princess had always cast the gaze of her Protestant upbringing upon the poor and miserable of Moscow. We can never convert entirely from what we are, from how we are bred. We embrace new forms; inside we stay the same. Were I, by force or love, to be made a Moslem, I should forever celebrate Easter in my heart."

"But the Princess?" Daisy was entirely fascinated by her.

"She had no children. She resolved to make the most wretched people of Moscow her children. Here, you know, we regard such miseries as natural and inevitable, and indeed as a means to grace. We do what we can, which," he added candidly, "is but little. Many of us think that to be particularly stricken and desolate is a mark of God's special favour.

"Grand Duchess Sergei would have none of this. She was heart-stricken by the loss of her husband, but she believed that no one should endure needless suffering. She withdrew from the world, she gave away or sold her fabulous collection of jewels, and set about quietly founding a new sisterhood, buying land, for huge sums they tell me, on the banks of the river Moskva, planting a garden around it. For four years, I hear, she travelled all round Russia looking at religious houses, consulting with men and women who were known masters of the spiritual life. She is no scholar, but she buried herself in the study of monastic rules down the centuries." A note of regret crept into his voice. "None of this need have been necessary. Had she but borne children, she could have stayed in the world, to charm and delight us."

"But did she found an order?"

"*Enfin*, yes . . . When she came into a room, everyone felt, the women as well as the men, a particular *élan*, a lightness of heart—"

"And is it going? The sisterhood?"

"Going? Ah, you mean, in being. Yes, indeed. The force of her new-found spiritual faith drove her through all difficulties. And there were many. You must know that all nuns in Russia live under the Basilean rule, neither teaching nor nursing, strictly contemplative. Never, except in moments of dire poverty or virtual starvation, when by special permission of their bishop they are allowed out to beg, do they leave their enclosure. They fast with great rigour, rise soon after midnight and stand long hours at matins; none but the oldest nuns are permitted even to lean against the pillars.

"The Grand Duchess Sergei believed that Martha as well as Mary of Bethany has a place in the Church of God. Her order, of Martha and Mary, is one in which prayer and work are to become equal parts of a perfect whole. Since her nuns were to teach, to nurse, to visit the sick in their own homes, to rescue orphan children and to cherish the old, they must be physically strong and therefore must have reasonable amounts of food and rest. And refreshment. Every one of her community has to visit their own homes or take a rest in the country for a fortnight in every year.

"In Russian Church circles this was revolutionary. When Grand Duchess Sergei submitted her plan to the Most Holy Synod they turned it down with scarcely a second glance."

"Oh, how disappointing for her!"

"Years passed, she prayed deeply, made slight alterations, arrived nowhere," the Prince went on. "She was told that if she wished to take the veil she would be welcome in one of the Basilean nunneries. Her plan, the Synod told her, crushingly, had 'a definitely Protestant leaven.' You would think," the Prince added parenthetically, "that a leaven was supposed to be a good thing and not a bad thing. At last the Czar overrode them and himself authorised the setting up of her order, by Imperial decree."

"Bravo! Bravo the Czar!" The beggars were temporarily forgotten.

"So there it is, along the Great Ordynka, on the southern bank of the Moscow river—a great church and a little church, a hospital, dispensary, outpatients' department, a home for the old and an orphanage for the children, and a guest house, the whole set in a garden. She herself leads a life of great austerity, my cousin Marie Obolensky tells me, who joined her order. She sleeps on wooden planks in a tiny bedroom and works without pause.

"She has common sense. She did not think all at once to do away with the Khitrovka slum. An English doctor who had visited them all," the Prince told Daisy, not without pride, "has assured me that compared with the Khitrovka market the worst slums of Liverpool and Glasgow were paradise."

"Where is it?"

"Promise me never to approach it. It lies close to the southern bank of the Yauza—low-lying, undrained, fever-ridden marsh. Always above it hangs a miasma of mist. I have never been there, but they tell me there is a great irregular square, with miserable stalls in the middle, and filthy narrow alleys of broken-down hovels. There is a series of barracky buildings, where the luckier beggars sleep on tiers on wooden slats. A hundred thousand people live there in total squalor among suffocating smells— beggars, pickpockets, pimps, thieves, escaped prisoners. All the children of Khitrovka who survive their infancy become thieves. No girl of ten years old is still a virgin. I hope I frighten you from it?

"Into this inferno the Princess goes daily, rescuing children and old people, invalids, melancholics. She has caught the imagination of some of the rich Moscow merchants, funds have flowed in, other practical institutions have been set up—refuges, maternity homes, training schools."

"Oh, how I would love to see her!"

"I too, but she will never rejoice my eyes again. Do not dare to approach this terrible place, though you might still see her, entering the filthiest of houses, tending the most degraded of beings. But you are strictly forbidden to go near it. I hope I have sufficiently frightened you. There are ravening wolves in there. No policemen venture in. Only her saintliness keeps her safe and alive."

The sleigh was now slowing down, swinging round the corner into the wide street of their final destination.

The Prince's spirits rose to the thought of warmth, wine, good company. "You will enjoy this," he assured Daisy. "Delicious food, and one can never be certain whom one will meet. That I enjoy. My wife enjoys it less. She prefers the world that she knows." Laughingly, he held out his hand for Daisy to descend from the sleigh. His thoughts swung back in amusement. "They say that Queen Victoria at first objected to both marriages, the Grand Duchess's and that of her young sister to the Emperor."

"Did she not like the Czar? I thought all his cousins did? Or Grand Duke Sergei?"

"Well enough, but she feared the danger from Russian anarchists. That two such sweet, pretty grandchildren should go into such a powder keg as Russia! They would both come to a bad end!" The Prince, his teasing gaze fixed upon Daisy, laughed heartily.

He led her into the world that was now becoming familiar to her—the world of high-ceilinged rooms, lavishly swathed and decorated with plasterwork, richly gilded, the candelabra that blazed more thickly with candles than any she had known, the great gilt doors embossed with ornament, and an extraordinary beauty of marquetry flooring, as if one trod over a wooden garden permanently crowded with flowers and fruit. Even the pictures, glowing on the scarlet walls in their great gilt frames, seemed larger and more insistent in their demand for admiration than any she had known in London or Paris.

Climbing the staircase on the arm of this splendid partner, introduced to everyone as Our English Friend, Daisy glowed with excitement and pleasure. She hardly knew whether to gaze longest at the beautiful faces of the women, their blazing jewels and sweeping silk dresses, or at the keen or laughing faces of the bearded men, with their loud voices and their uninhibited glances. The long table gleamed with candelabra, crystal and silver, and was laden with dishes of fruits and sweets and with long trailing smilax and flowers.

For dinner there was caviare, salmon, roast goose and wild boar with mushrooms. Daisy had never had such exquisite food before, never seen such luxury. Next to her was a cheerful young officer with a snub nose and a flow of conversation about Paris and Biarritz, but Daisy's attention was rivetted by a very handsome bearded priest who sat opposite her, his compelling gaze closely scanning her. His brilliant eyes were full of a strange light. He was unkempt and boorish, but after a while one ceased to notice that so acutely, under the gaze of his curious mesmeric eyes.

Yet he really was behaving very oddly. He ate with his hands, disdaining knife and fork, scooped remains from his plate with a great hunk of bread, broke wind loudly and frequently, hawked and spat all over the Persian carpet. Even across the table he could be seen to be very dirty, and as dinner progressed he became very drunk. I should *not* like to meet him on a dark night, Daisy decided. But all the same, she found it difficult to take her eyes off him. In a mysterious and unforced way he compelled attention.

On the way home in the sleigh, warmed by champagne and conversation, puzzlement got the better of discretion. "I loved that glorious dinner party, and the music was divine, but why do you think they asked that strange priest—or was he a monk?"

The Prince turned on her such an alarming gaze that Daisy thought for a disconcerting moment that he was about to pounce, as Russians were generally alleged to pounce, given the chance.

Nothing was further from Prince Andrei's thoughts. "He is a very holy man," he assured Daisy emphatically.

"How is he holy? I don't understand."

"He is a healer, with very wonderful powers."

"But—"

"He does miraculous cures. He heals those of whom doctors despair."

"So do Indian fakirs, but people don't ask them to dinner."

"Perhaps," suggested the Prince, "they might learn from them if they did."

Daisy was quite unable to let it go at that. "But why does he behave so oddly?"

The Prince ignored this. "He has cured many hopeless cases. Bearers of fatal and organic diseases."

"So has Mary Baker Eddy in America," Daisy persisted, "but I don't believe she smells like a goat."

The Prince sighed. Daisy, he reflected, had very beautiful eyes, and an enchanting turn of the head, but her tongue was entirely too enquiring. She was practical and competent and they all liked her, except Misha; the children loved her, and competed to seize her hand upon every occasion. But she understood little, leapt to conclusions and in general overstepped the mark. Why did she always probe into matters she could not hope to understand? He wondered, briefly, whether he and his wife could go on putting up with it. "In Russia," he said, not unkindly, "young ladies do not ask so many questions."

Daisy blushed hotly. How could she have offended her gracious host? "I am very sorry. I only wanted to understand. Everyone else at the dinner party was so beautiful, so civilised, and he—I am sorry."

There was a coldness, a dismissiveness in the Prince's manner. Daisy became slowly aware of having trodden on sacred ground. Could it be that tonight's guest had been that mysterious monk of whom people talked, who was in such high favour with the Czarina? If so, the coldness of the Prince was understandable. The Czar was a sacred object. If he caught cold and couldn't go to a ball, no one else went either. But really, to have someone to dinner who spat on the floor and had to be cleared up after like an unhousetrained dog, by some poor footman! And who ate like a beast— I can't believe it's a true part of saintliness.

And I think the Prince, in a sort of way, hates him too. What was his name? Something like Raspberry. Oh, I remember now. Rasputin.

Daisy trod the wide stairs to her bedroom with her head in a whirl; nor was the whirl more than minimally composed of champagne. Startling and conflicting images flashed through her brain; starved subhuman faces clustering round the splendid full-fed horses, drunken priests with glittering eyes and savagely unkempt hair, banks of orchids filling whole walls, an endless flow of different wines, houses resounding to the music of private orchestras. Gold plates, gold dishes, jewels the size of pigeon's eggs, dinner guests who spat on the floor. The scattered remains of a grand duke spread over the glittering snow, wolvish women who starved their own babies in order to make money out of them, a beautiful princess who gave up rank and riches and comfort and everything desirable on earth to walk through danger and stink and squalor to succour the least regarded of God's creatures. Extreme and glowing warmth within and deadly killing cold without. Kind, laughing faces, yet all the while the sensation of walking upon the thinnest of ice, with whirling depths beneath; if one fell in, who was to throw a rope?

Could her father have been right? For the first time since she left home Daisy had a sensation of having bitten off more than she could chew. Oh, to be back at home in the schoolroom, hearing her young sisters squabbling over their stamp albums while eating baked beans for supper and drinking cocoa, with nothing more difficult or dangerous afoot than a walk down the village street with some chicken soup in a screw-top jar for old Mr. Bulstrode with flu.

Courage reasserted itself with the bright light of morning. At least as an antidote to disappointed love, Russia was a howling success. Not for days had she felt a pang for Richard; she had indeed barely given him a thought. That, at least, *was* sophisticated.

* * *

"You expect too much," Amelia told her. "Don't break your heart over things you can't help."

"But, Amelia, if you had seen that baby! And *heard* it! Out on that freezing night and half-starved as well!"

"Grow another skin; *I* would if I were you," Amelia counselled. She had been brought up in India. "You should cast a glance round Calcutta. The misery there beats cockfighting, as my dear but reckless Papa would say."

"I don't know about skins, " Daisy told her solemnly, "but since I came here I feel at least ten years older. More like twenty."

"A dashing but raddled thirty-nine-year-old," Amelia mocked. "Time to burn your boats. No—but really, Daisy, anyone would tell you that the problem of people who flock into great cities without homes or jobs is insoluble and always will be."

"You are going native. You are simply going Russian when you think like that." Would she ever become so hardened? Daisy wondered.

"Russian! Not on your nelly," Amelia replied concisely.

Chapter 6

Over the next few days Daisy was unusually thoughtful. That strange and curiously attractive monk haunted her thoughts. Was it possible that in the West we all laid too much emphasis on being clean? If you come to think of it, probably St. John the Baptist smelt like a goat, unless permanently in the Jordan baptising people. And the desert saints in their caves *must* have. But at least they hadn't emerged from their caves to get drunk at dinner parties, nor gorged masses of food whilst people virtually starved in the streets outside. It was the mixture, she decided, that really would *not* do.

Spending a day off even with dull Mrs. Disbrowe was restful. Explaining to Daisy that she never touched caviare, she had arranged a Sunday lunch of roast beef and Yorkshire pudding. At tea there were drop scones, Tiptree's Little Scarlet strawberry jam, Lyle's Golden Syrup, Huntley and Palmer's ginger nuts, and Cadbury's Tropical Chocolates—these last particularly suitable as Mrs. Disbrowe kept the temperature of her drawing room somewhere in the eighties.

The doorbell of the flat rang loudly.

"And now," Mrs. Disbrowe announced proudly, in the tones of one who had cunningly kept the best treat to the last, "you are to meet my nephew George."

Daisy's heart sank. An evening of male bromides stretched before her, couched in terms of cricket, golf and football. She felt sure that George Bennett would be the kind of young man who never really noticed that you were there until you managed to get in a word edgewise to point out that your father had kept wicket for Harrow. Upon which, after one brief glance, he would bang on interminably and with a totally false modesty, describing how badly he himself had played against Harrow in the match of 1909.

But there turned out to be something to be said for George Bennett. He was older than expected, and made no mention of athletic prowess. He had hazel eyes and a determined-looking face, a head well-thatched in crisp dark red hair. A personable young man, solidly built, he sat four-square on the sofa, eating seedcake and being patient with his rather boring aunt. His very relaxed English conversation made him seem to Daisy something of an oasis in a desert, and he was soon asking her to go sleighing with him.

He was in his uncle's firm, and was to be in Russia for some while, buying timber. He took his job very seriously, had learned Russian, and having heard that the intelligentsia were the only Russians he was at all likely to meet socially, he had read Karl Marx, understanding him to be their staple diet.

"What's it about?" Daisy instantly demanded to know.

"Well, that's rather a tall order. About reforming the world, basically."

"How fascinating! And has he got good ideas about how to do it?"

"On the surface, they sound attractive. If you don't follow up any of the implications. I should think . . . a lot of people would be taken in."

"But you weren't?"

George Bennett was flattered by this keen interest. "My brain isn't anything special," he insisted in his slow voice. "But his theory is all based on false premises, so it can't be right. It's based on bad history and bad science; so what can you expect? But it will appeal to a lot of people at odds with the world, and a lot of fatheaded idealists as well. Dangerous stuff, I'd say. Still, I'm glad to have read it. You don't want to be like those chaps who run down the Bible and have never done more than turn a few pages over."

"But Karl Marx wouldn't ever seem like the Bible to people!"

"I shouldn't wonder," George said.

Daisy was impressed. Here was a sensible, responsible man who spoke her native language. She took to going to the Opera with him, which they both loved.

The ballet he declined to go near. Daisy coaxed. "You should. You really *should*. I've been three times with the Dubelskys and it is *glorious*. Why, the Russian ballet is famous all over the world! It's unique!"

"They are getting it going in Paris. London too," George Bennett replied, doggedly factual. "I might go there some night if I've nothing better to do."

Sensible but not passionate, Daisy thought.

* * *

The Dubelskys took a keen interest in Daisy's outings with George Bennett, and smiled upon them. It's a little like Mama being pleased when Ethel and Nelly started walking out regularly, Daisy thought without rancour; it makes them feel safer. She had rashly told the Prince that George Bennett had read Karl Marx, and he had taken up this theme with great delight. "How is your anarchist friend?" he would ask. "Were many bombs thrown tonight?" The joke never seemed to lose its force and charm with him. "Miss Pelham's young man is a member of Zemlya Volya," he told the uncles, who had looked in to drink tea and would stay to drink brandy. "The specialist terror group against police spies. He's a leading member, I assure you. They believe in 'motiveless terror,' and call murder 'progressive action.'"

Even sad Uncle Sergei chuckled delightedly. "Verkhovensky?" he suggested.

"Verkhovensky to the life, I daresay. He's the man in Dostoyevsky's *The Devils*," the Prince explained kindly to Daisy. "An intellectual terrorist who says something like, 'Crime is now no longer insanity but common sense, indeed almost a duty, and at any rate a noble protest.'"

Uncle Georg gave a fat, comfortable, wicked laugh. "Best not allow the young man to embrace you," he counselled. "Take care, Miss Pelham! One of his hand grenades might go off—bang!"

Misha sat silent in the background, grinning from ear to ear.

"Let me not blush," Daisy prayed. "Oh, God, let me not blush!" But God, it appeared, was not prepared to be invoked in such a cause. Daisy could feel the hated flush spreading from cheek to neck, up over her forehead and even into her hair. Kolya rose and went to the piano, beginning to play, very softly at first, and then increasingly loudly, until general conversation became virtually impossible, and even the most gurgling great-uncle paused to listen.

The house hummed perpetually with great crowds of people. Most of the menservants had their quarters and lived with their families somewhere in the great house; all those who lived out, and those who did not, were fed and warmed by the Prince. No wonder they are happy, Daisy concluded, when one thinks what life is like outside. Dubelsky friends and relations streamed in and out of the house daily, and hospitality was freely offered. No social arrangement was calculable. In the Western World, if one asked eighteen people to dinner, or four, the same number either came or declined. In Russia, if you asked eighteen people to dinner, you might have ten arrivals, or five, or none, or more probably, twenty-seven, all of which was accepted happily and as a matter of course.

They never seem to have our English preoccupation with wanting to be alone sometimes, Daisy thought; life's absolutely communal. Do they think that my wanting privacy is just sulking? Talking incessantly, people drank wine, brandy, tea, coffee, in enormous quantities, or sat down to enormous meals. The Prince, in expansive moods, would entertain them with a seemingly endless stream of diverting *histoires*. He communicated with his children through a series of jokes and teases, in many of which he wholeheartedly involved Daisy, and of which he appeared not to mind being sometimes himself the victim.

"*Le Prince est toujours blagueur*," his wife would say adoringly. Daisy could well understand after the business with George Bennett. He always dressed with extreme elegance, but never forgot to come up and say prayers of a night with Nikolai and Arkady. He loved to dance and seemed quickly to forgive Daisy for her *bêtise* over Rasputin. He urged Daisy to join the children at their dancing classes, held in the grand salon. Of course the polka and the waltz she knew already, but she must learn the polonaise and the mazurka. "Come join this dance, miss," the dancing master would call. "Prince Nikolai lacks a partner for the mazurka!" The violinist smiled indulgently at her; the cellist indicated her position on the dance floor with his bow. Overcoming a feeling of awkwardness, she was soon stamping and twirling with the best. What music! What a dance! "It's old-fashioned, one must admit," the Princess said, "but the children should know how to dance such dances, and not be content only with these vulgar modern steps, with which people hardly *dance* at all."

Dances, music, opera, ballet. Caviare, flowing wine, the rustle of soft thick furs, the gleam of fantastic jewels. There were moments, when the sleigh rushed through the sparkling night, when home seemed very far away, small, provincial. All was just as she had dreamed it—and how quickly, in the rush and sparkle of such a life, one forgot the teeming beggars, the rags, the feet shod in broken boots, the grimy hands outstretched. What hugely wide streets they had here! Laid out by rulers who knew themselves masters of illimitable spaces. Nothing, except the dwellings of the poor, seemed cramped.

Yet there was always the invisible barrier, delicately and gracefully maintained by the Princess: You may play with George Bennett as much as you like; be happy; my children will be the happier. Enjoy—just so long as you do not smile too sweetly at the Prince, nor laugh too uproariously at his jokes, and above all, do not flirt with the young men. *Keep off the grass*, she communicated silently, never with harshness.

She little realises, thought Daisy, how hard I am trying not to tread on a quite different lawn of my own! The image of Richard still sometimes haunted her mind—his smile, the easy companionship that she had taken so much for granted for the many happy months of last year. All this whirling about is a very good thing, I know, but when it stops or I am tired I sometimes feel as if my heart were broken. She gazed hopefully in the looking glass, to see if there were dark circles under her eyes, or anything of a drawn look, but she was obliged to admit that there was really nothing of the kind. Dressing with some care, she set forth for a jaunt with George.

* * *

Coming out of the Opera into the midwinter night, the cold struck George and Daisy like a blow in the face by some vicious enemy.

"Half the fun," Daisy said between gasps, "is seeing the audience. How they enjoy it! That old couple next to us were so excited I thought they were going to have a fit. Their eyes were simply popping out at the climax of the fourth act."

"I feared they were about to rise to their feet and dance," George admitted. "Some Russians have . . . not exactly a rush of blood to the head . . . more a rush of soul to the eyes."

"They must think us awfully unmoved, and kind of . . . slow. Slow in feeling."

"Of course," George agreed happily. "Famous slowbellies."

"Surely that's not a good thing to be."

"Famous slowbellies," George repeated equably. "But slow to anger as well. Slow to violence."

And slow to love? Daisy wondered. She thought of Richard with a sudden sharp pang, looking at George doubtfully. The sleigh's runners made a whistling sound as they sped over the snow. Overhead many bright stars shone in the frosty air.

The children had often to be taken to see their grandmother, and here, in her dim and decorated room, Daisy felt herself to be indeed in a foreign land. All was sombre, save for golden ikons blazing from dark walls and the red gleam of votive lamps. A smell of incense warred with a smell of cloves and peppermint. Polite, heavily jewelled, infinitely remote, the old Princess gazed at Daisy from under her hooded lids, old hands stiff with rings patted hers gently. She dressed always in complete black, as if in perpetual mourning for the sins and heresies of the world. She looked as if she could be both lavishly kind and deliberately and immeasurably cruel. Upright and queenly, she lived surrounded by what appeared to be a considerable court of elderly and dependent relatives, who smothered the visiting children with kisses, pressed sugared almonds upon them and uttered a continuous chorus of little cooings of approval, like a wood of doves. The Princess herself was crisper with her grandchildren, but her brusque way with them inadequately concealed her adoration, her appreciation of Varya's dark Slavic good looks, of the exploits of the twins, of the solemn pronouncements of Ella.

After the first few visits the piercing gaze from the steel-blue eyes with which she confronted Daisy had softened into friendliness. Since she was gentle and sensible with the children, for these things the old Princess forgave her her foreignness, and more remarkably, her Protestantism. Her fear had been that Daisy might turn out to have Jewish blood. She had sent her nephew to St. Petersburg to consult the copy of Debretts at the English Club, and had learned with relief that this was not so. She regarded the entire Jewish race with blank hatred, with a fire and bitterness which amazed Daisy, though by now she had learned sufficient wisdom not to question one so old.

Towards Misha the old Princess expressed an almost doting love. In looks and air he was like her father, who had also, as a young man, gambled heavily and run after gypsy girls. In her eyes, Misha could do no wrong. Kolya's fancies annoyed her far more; she could not forgive him for his constant attendance at The Bat, or his friendship with the musicians who haunted the club. Of course, one must hear music, of course, one must handsomely reward musicians—but where was the need to make friends of them? In such company a young man ran the risk of learning socialism, atheism even; certainly he would become familiar with heretical views. Yet when Kolya actually appeared, her stiffness melted. "He should never have been named Askold," she told her son severely. The Prince looked wistful. "His mother," he pointed out, "was a romantic."

In time Daisy grew to enjoy the general warmth of her reception, and to accept her position. Papa warned me about this, she told herself, and I must just adjust myself to it. At times she found it far from difficult. Summoned to the Princess's bedroom of an evening for a discussion of Varya's latest wildness, Daisy would very easily and quickly succumb to her employer's native joyfulness, her charm of manner. She was dressed for dinner, in a gown of bronze gauze; opening the drawers of her little cabinet, one after another, she revealed set after set of beautiful jewels— emeralds, lapis, sapphires, rubies—each in their baize-lined and baize-covered drawer. The Princess paused, intent on her choice. "Yes, Varya is very naughty," she agreed absently. She was clearly more intent on soothing Daisy than in taking Varya's peccadilloes seriously. "I must say a special prayer for her. Father Ignatius says . . ." The jewels sparkled as she held them up one after another in the soft glow of the vigil lamp. "Emeralds," she decided finally. "They have always been my favourites. And you, Daisy?"

"Amethysts," Daisy said stoutly, having nothing other. The warmth of the room, the friendliness, gave her confidence. "Princess . . . can you tell me . . . at the old Princess's I was struck by . . . I mean, has she had some injury done to her by a Jewish person?"

"No, indeed. How should she?"

"It is only . . . I wondered, not wanting to say something foolish that might upset her . . . but she seems to hate Jews so bitterly."

"She feels only as we all do. They killed our Saviour. His blood is forever on their heads. Naturally we hate them." She spoke with the certainty of utter conviction.

The thoughts boiled in Daisy's brain. But it was they themselves who said that, not Christ. And if he could forgive them in the middle of being tortured to death, surely, after nearly two thousand years we, his followers, could too? And in any case it has nothing to do with Jewish people alive *now*.

Her silence, which was due more to an inability to express herself calmly, than to discretion, let alone persuasion, was received by the Princess with gratitude. She flashed Daisy a charming smile. "Tomorrow," she promised, "we shall go out to visit my cousins who live twenty versts from Moscow. A large family. They are delightful. You will like them."

Through the Moscow gates and over the Sparrow Hills and into the rolling countryside beyond. The wine-like air whipped Daisy's cheeks to a brilliant red and the children bounced up and down in their seats with the exhilaration of their swift sliding passage over the snow. There was a stillness and silence, no sound but of the faint jingling of the harness and of the lumps of frozen earth and snow thudding against the front of the sleigh. "I'll bet you've never seen a wolf, a *wild* wolf not in a zoo, have you, Miss Daisy?" Nikolai demanded, and Arkady, bundled in furs on her other side, rolled affectionately against her, laughing up into her face. "Just you wait!" Nikolai promised; and Daisy was quite unable to resist glancing behind her, into the darkness of the winter wood. Why do I love them? she wondered. They are both *absolute fiends*. Their flushed cherubic faces and bright eyes gave her the answer.

Since the Dubelskys did not know, or wish to know, the family for whom Amelia worked, she and Daisy confined their meetings to the St. Andrew's Hostel on their days off. "I'm away soon" Amelia announced one evening. "I don't seem cut out for nanny life, and Igor and Constantine are slowly driving me demented. The girls are worse. A bunch of spoiled brats if ever I encountered one. And my Monsieur is inclined to flirt in a boring heavyhanded way. Easy enough to brush off in the normal way, but less easy under the same roof."

"Oh, Amelia, not at once!" She was genuinely sorry to see this last link with England leave.

"No, not at once, because we are off to St. Petersburg next week and I *ache* to see that. The whole experience of Moscow has been well worth it and I wouldn't have missed it for cheese! You'll be all right, Daisy. I can see you are well dug in, in that family of yours."

Daisy felt obliged to continue the occasional visits to Mrs. Disbrowe, who seemed to become less interesting with every encounter. "Don't let her put you off George," Amelia insisted. "Why bother about people's aunts? They aren't a life sentence like a mama-in-law can be. That George of yours would pay looking into. Worth a dozen Russians of the same size and shape, in my view. I like his slow voice and that bloody calm. One longs to ruffle it."

A joint expedition was duly effected, and was not a success. George brought with him a small pale Russian friend, a passionate Menshevik who talked politics without ever once drawing breath, in rapid and incomprehensible French. Daisy, in the kindness of her heart, stayed listening to him, but Amelia, bored, and having no such scruples, drew George away with her and taught him the tango. They were on the floor for a long while. The politics poured on, and Daisy's eyes glazed with boredom. George, she noted, was far from being physically stupid. He learned the tango quickly, and was clearly enjoying himself, entering into the spirit of the dance. Amelia danced and laughed with equal zest. Daisy grew increasingly restive and impatient. Her friends returned to the table at last, pleased and thirsty, and Amelia even seemed able to make the Menshevik stop talking politics and emerge from his gloom.

"That friend of yours, that Miss Lynch, has got a tongue on her," George later commented.

"But she often is *very* funny."

"One can have too much of that," George contributed sternly.

"But you must admit that she *is* very funny? And attractive?"

Upon this subject George declined to be drawn. Which was as well; Daisy feared that he might be about to say something prosaic like Handsome is as handsome does. Yet Mrs. Disbrowe, she reflected more kindly, is only his aunt by marriage. Obvious remarks don't run in his blood.

It was obscurely gratifying that he had not been taken by Amelia's superior sophistication. Daisy intended to return to England from Moscow fully as sophisticated; but it was a little difficult to know where to begin. At home, with the Dubelskys, everyone talked so fast, and seemingly so brilliantly. They seemed able to be funny in at least four different languages, almost simultaneously. Although her French was good, Daisy was quite unable to be amusing in it, and even remarks made in English came out as amazingly naive. After a while she gave it up and simply listened, a process to which she was unaccustomed. But at least, listening, she no longer felt a fool. Native resilience asserted itself, and she began, in time, to make occasional comments at the dinner table without the feeling that she was simply exposing herself to ridicule. A feeling of familiarity, of friendship, crept in. She ran down the stairs, and even caught herself, sometimes, singing a Russian air as she brushed her hair of a morning.

The nobles, Daisy found, kept themselves to themselves. There was a great gulf fixed between those who traded and those who drew their wealth from inherited land, who were far more dutiful and much less ostentatiously rich. And yet a strong cohesion seemed to draw people together, a powerful, almost mystical love of Russia, her land, her faith, her ways. Russia was neither of the East nor wholly of the West, and so huge as to be a world unto herself. There were magical evenings of Imperial fêtes, when Daisy would lean out of her window in the stillness of a frosty night, to see huge monograms outlined in the sky, elaborate Imperial crowns, armorial designs. Although she knew that they were only made of coloured electric bulbs, it was as if the whole sky blazed with jewels, a vast display of ruby and diamond, of sapphire and amethyst, of emerald and tourmaline. Daisy would forget the cold and lean out entranced, gazing at the glowing spectacle above the snow-lined cornices of the houses opposite their own.

There were days, also, of religious festival when all the city was alive with sound. Bells from distant trams mingled with bells from Moscow's eight score of churches, a ringing and swinging of a city-wide jubilation. The breath from thousands of people in the streets rose up like an incense, hanging in clouds in the cold streets, as if the whole city were one vast temple. "Holy Russia," thought Daisy, I see what they mean. Endless patient, poor, devout people shuffling through the snow, forgetting their miseries, crowding in to pray. It was deeply moving.

In so large a household it was difficult occasionally not to find oneself overlapping or even interfering. Ella always danced enthusiastically at the dancing class and became very hot—could she not wear a lighter dress? Daisy asked Nyanya, receiving in return a glance of thunder and an unhesitating negative. She had also carelessly and unknowingly broken in on the twins' hour of French conversation and literature, sacred in the eyes of Mademoiselle. Daisy was reading them *The Jungle Book* one afternoon when a furious figure confronted her.

"*Et alors, Nikolai, qu'est que tu fais? Viens donc, Arkady, viens vite!*" Mademoiselle's pale blue gaze refused to meet Daisy's. She declined to admit that anyone was there, besides the two little boys. Her tall gaunt figure was trembling with indignation; the watch pinned to the neatly striped dress that covered her flat bosom heaved up and down with her furious breathing. She wore a high net collar, sustained all round the neck with little whalebones, and a net front decorated with little pale blue bows, all of which quivered indignantly as she spoke.

"But we're in the middle of the story, Mademoiselle," Nikolai grumbled, adding insult to injury by addressing her in English.

Mademoiselle's lips tightened. She stood bolt upright, high and stiff as a lamp post. As if any country outside France could boast of a literature, as if all other races were not steeped in backwardness and barbarism! But Daisy, with her eyes fixed on the book, seemed stupidly impervious to conviction. "May we just finish the chapter?" she rashly asked.

Mademoiselle vouchsafed no reply. She was shaking all over; even the copy of *Les Malheurs de Sophie* that she held was a-quiver under her vibrating elbow. Suddenly bending forward, she seized Arkady by the wrist and swept him away with her, knowing well that where one twin went the other would follow.

And so it proved. At the door the old woman paused for her exit line. "I think you forget, Mademoiselle," and she looked at Daisy for the first time, "that I come from *Limoges*." She shut the door with well-bred gentleness and Daisy was left alone.

She felt considerably nettled; it had been so unceremoniously done. And anyway, Daisy crossly told herself, the twins are too old for *Les Malheurs*. And what on earth has coming from Limoges to do with it? Poor old thing! But why be so rude? Whatever does she mind about so *much?*

Light slowly dawned upon Daisy. Limoges, Limoges . . . Porcelain was made there; but was it also the place where the Black Prince had misbehaved? The history came back to her. The town, a part of his inheritance, had broken promises and rebelled against him and he had retaken it and sacked it. Which was the general form in his days, Daisy reflected, but had not hitherto been his; and people had been correspondingly shocked.

But that was in 1300 and something! Daisy told herself incredulously. To mind it still now! To hold it against anyone English six hundred years later! Mademoiselle could hardly have looked more outraged if the Black Prince had personally violated her last Wednesday. What nonsense!

But in the evening Mademoiselle looked so old, and indeed so ill, that Daisy's heart smote her and she found herself apologizing for a matter that was not her fault; she was sorry, she said, to have encroached on the twins' half hour of French. Mademoiselle, Daisy recollected, had been with the Dubelsky children for twenty-five years, from Misha's babyhood onwards; of course she must resent an interloper who might turn into a rival for their love. They had become her life. She had never been back to France; perhaps now she feared a tepid welcome in Limoges from nephews and nieces who knew her only by name. Daisy suspected that the old woman really was ill, but was refusing to accept defeat, and that the Dubelskys were so well used to that long, pale, gaunt face that they had failed to notice the increased pallor of her looks. They were all fond enough of her, but how truly sad it must be to be so much alone, so bereft of kith and kin! Mademoiselle would surely die here in Russia, far from home. For this daughter of France there was to be no Retreat from Moscow.

And as Daisy dimly perceived, Mademoiselle was scarcely jealous for herself or fearful lest Daisy's bright eyes should seduce the graceless and fickle twins away from her personally. What Mademoiselle feared was that Daisy might imbue the children, *her* beloved well-taught children, with the appalling heresy that art, literature and architecture existed at all, outside the borders of France; that good manners and civilized behaviour, let alone clothes, food and drink, were present in any meaningful sense elsewhere.

"I used to love *Les Malheurs de Sophie* myself," Daisy concluded her apology. "Our copy had those fascinating Boutet de Monvel illustrations too. I specially liked that bit where Sophie—"

Mademoiselle relaxed. Her head, insofar as was possible within the whalebone casing of her neck, inclined graciously. Once Daisy had admitted, or even implied, the immeasurable superiority of French culture,

Mademoiselle was prepared to forgive. Something that could almost be called a smile creased the corners of her pale blue eyes. It might even, in time, be conceded that Rudyard Kipling, barbarous though he was, could at least tell a tale.

She and Daisy became firm friends. Daisy invariably spoke to her in French, submitting with a good grace to the asperity of Mademoiselle's corrections. She never again poached upon the preserves of the boys' sacred hour for French conversation, and grew fond of the old woman, who would even, from time to time, pat her gently on the shoulder and tell her that the hat she was wearing was not without chic. The shade of the Black Prince seemed to have ridden off elsewhere.

As the winter wore on, Mademoiselle would even invite Daisy of an evening up to her room, which held a few stiff, straight-in-the-eye photographs of formidably stern relations, but was in the main thickly plastered with oleographs of Sainte Thérèse of Lisieux in every possible or impossible attitude of piety. Here Mademoiselle would brew tisane on her spirit lamp and advise Daisy to take up knitting seriously, and to improve her knowledge of Molière. By a common consent of loyalty, they never discussed their employers, though to Mademoiselle at least they were a subject of perennial interest. She contented herself with a general repudiation of everything Russian save the Dubelskys, and to a general paean of praise for the children, although, once or twice, when the latest doings of Misha were brought to her notice, she would draw in her breath with a sharp, alarmed hiss. She would never have dreamed of codemning him, to Daisy or to anyone else. She saw him still as a charming naughty little boy in a sailor suit with a striped vest, dodging round the boles of the lime avenue whilst the streamers of his sailor cap floated out on the summer breeze. For two sad years of their lives, Mademoiselle had been the two older boys' mother-substitute: they might forget it, she never could. The numbers of photographs of Misha and of Kolya competed even with those of Sainte Thérèse.

Misha was in trouble again, and this time it was obvious and serious. He had lost a great deal of money gambling; his latest debacle had come to the ears of his father. Kolya, pacing up and down in the grand salon, was trying to beg him off, alternately flashing his dark eyes at his stepmother or turning humble and melancholy to plead with the Prince. He appeared to be getting nowhere, even to have done nothing but include himself in Misha's disgrace. The Prince was addressing him as Askold, always a dire sign. Daisy had come to ask the Princess about an alteration in Varya's piano lessons, and the Princess had detained her by a firm grip on her wrist, as if afraid that Daisy might miss one moment of this absorbing drama. One of the family, thought Daisy: in for a penny, in for a pound.

Passionate reproaches were heaped upon Misha's head. How like each

other fathers are, thought Daisy, all round the world! Any minute now
the Prince will tell Misha that it isn't the money he minds, it's the principle of the thing. Now in his full stride, the Prince was prophesying ruin
on the house of Dubelsky, ruin and disgrace, and ruin and disgrace on
Misha in particular. If a son of his couldn't learn when to stop at play,
thought of nothing but gaming and running after gypsy girls, would
neither obey his parents nor learn from experience, what fate would
befall him, would befall all of them? In a low voice Kolya intervened to
point out that they were both shortly leaving Moscow anyway, that the
summer manoeuvres would then be on, and after that the regiment might
be sent to the East, perhaps, even to the Caucusus for a spell. "There are
gypsies everywhere he goes," the Prince grumbled. "In the East, in the
Caucusus, all the way to Vladivostok, no doubt. There is weakness that
Mihail will carry with him. Are there no gambling hells but in Moscow?"

He glared reproachfully at Misha, who sat on the edge of his chair,
handsomely dressed and not notably abashed, his rebellious lower lip
pushed out like a young child's. Hopelessly spoilt, thought Daisy. But
how utterly nice Kolya is, in the way he stands up for Misha, pacing up
and down and obviously minding so much about his brother's misdoings
and his father's wrath!

Misha sat still as a rock, but as a rock that knows that the tide must at
length go out and the waves cease to beat upon him. This total silence
further incensed his father. "Mihail Andreivitch!" he demanded. "Have
you nothing to say! What have you to say? Words of sorrow and contri-
tion, I trust."

There was a timely interruption. A great dark patch was spreading
overhead on the finely moulded ceiling, and the Prince, raising his eyes
to heaven in exasperation with his firstborn, suddenly caught sight of it.
Drops began slowly to fall on the polished floor, to trickle down the candelabra.

With a cry, Daisy rushed from the room and up the wide stairs to the
floor above, where Nikolai and Arkady, aided and abetted by Varya, had
turned on the bathroom taps, overflowed the bath, and were attempting to
float the inverted nursery table along the flooded corridor, impatiently
pulling aside the sodden Persian rugs. "But it can't have," they protested.
"Water can't go through anything as solid as a floor!" The Prince
appeared with a face of thunder, followed by the Princess, throwing up
her hands. Servants poured in from all directions, uttering tumultuous
cries of distress. In the confusion, Misha was able to make another of his
swift dives out into the glittering streets and away to his chosen
haunts.

Daisy had taken off her shoes and waded through the shallows to turn
off the bathroom taps. Slowly, before it could be mopped up, the water
subsided into the floor. It occurred to neither of the Dubelskys to cause
their offspring to help mop it up. For a full ten minutes the Prince was

very very angry with them indeed; and was echoed, whenever he drew breath, by the cold and furious tones of the Princess. By the end of this time, what with the wetness and the dire penalties with which they were threatened, Varya, addressed by her full name of Varvara, was in floods of tears, Nikolai too had begun to sob, and even the stubborn defiance of Arkady was breaking down into a trembling of the lips and a heaving of the shoulders. Ella, waking up and hearing the row, started to scream lustily.

More doom was prophecied by the Prince, more dire penalties threatened, but in a slightly quieter and sadder voice. Even when enraged, Daisy noted, the Princess never ceased to look beautiful, and her sapphire eyes seemed to flash fire. The servants, unable to mop any more, had floated down to the lower floor to exclaim loudly at the damage. "After all," the Prince said suddenly, "this is naughtiness and not sin. Nikolai, cease crying. Arkasha, little one, come to me. Ella, my darling, kiss me, you are not in fault, Varya. . . ."

It was over. All too soon, in Daisy's view, they were sitting happily together in the grand salon, whose ceiling appeared liable to fall at any minute, eating crystallised fruits and laughing merrily. The water continued to drop slowly through the ruins of the moulded ceiling, falling clangily into iron basins set at strategic intervals to catch it.

"Even if the house is impossible to live in," the Prince said, "in any case we go to Jevrenskaia next month. What harm to go a few weeks sooner?"

"What harm?" agreed the Princess, "away from all this damp and this dripping. Take care, my darling Nikolai, it is now pouring down from the chandelier and you will get wet."

To Daisy, it seemed all wrong. Not the flooding, though that was bad enough, but the shameless lying about it. Nikolai had lied about the flowing taps and had been backed up by Arkady. They had meanly blamed it all on Varya, and even on Ella, who had the perfect alibi of having been asleep, with Nyanya to prove it.

Daisy tackled them next morning, after they had finished writing out their English sentences, in the library, the only room unaffected by the deluge. She felt, now, that they were fond enough of her to take a scolding. Holding a hand of each, she sought to impress them with the seriousness of their offence.

"Telling a lie is wicked, really wicked. Telling a lie that blames someone else is the depth of wickedness. Do you understand?"

The boys abstracted their gaze; Daisy began again.

"Gentlemen are truthful. Gentlemen never tell lies, however much it gets them into trouble."

Arkady looked scornful. "We," he said coldly, "are not gentlemen. We are *noblemen*."

"Princes," Nikolai emphasised.

"I mean," Daisy stumbled, "gentlemen in the *behaviour* sense. Men who are lucky enough to have advantages and who scorn to tell lies. A true gentleman never lies."

"Never?" A mocking voice sounded behind her. Misha had put in a silent and debauched appearance in the library, where he had come to fetch the morning papers. His hair was rumpled and he wore a very loud orange silk dressing gown. He was smoking a cigar and smiling broadly. The little boys, encouraged, started to smile too, and finally, to giggle.

Daisy was nettled. What was the good of trying to make the twins see the point, when the family would obscure it immediately? "What is worse than a lie, then?" she demanded, and was still more nettled to hear her voice come out squeakily and without dignity, as from one of those rubber dolls that Ella owned and squeezed. She could hear herself sounding affected and slightly hysterical.

Misha grinned more widely than ever. "What's worse? Since you ask— spiritual pride. Come, boys, apologise, and don't lie again or I'll bump your heads together." His tone of voice heightened Daisy's impression that he thought her a stupid foreigner to whom these concessions must be made in the interest of good manners. And yet, surely, truth *was* vital, *was* more than manners. Hateful, hateful young man.

Seizing their chance, the twins faded into the landscape, and Misha, departing to get dressed before lunch, said as he left, "How many seven-year-old children do you know who *always* tell the truth?"

She was thankful to be far from him at the luncheon table. At the other end, he was absorbed in a spirited discussion with his stepmother about the new opera. The twins, all sunshine after storm, were refraining from further aggression. Nikolai, in whom his sister Varya sometimes raised the devil by being so female in her reactions and fastidiousness, resisted the temptation to tug a lock of her long black hair, hanging so provocatively near him. Arkady, not to be outdone, abandoned a plan to sprinkle sugar over Uncle Sergei's salmon mousse.

What made it worse, in Daisy's view, was that Misha had succeeded, the previous evening, in winning almost all his money back. He sat on the library sofa, all smiles, virtue's self, full of genuine sympathy about the ceiling, and of cheering advice. He was spending the evening at home. Architects had come and gone, the water continued to drip steadily from the ceilings, and great dark patches to appear on the walls.

After a while, Kolya fetched his guitar and started to sing wild Caucasian songs; and all those who were not singing with him, danced. Daisy departed to her bedroom, to read a good book.

Misha's smile broadened. "Do you think," he asked kindly, "that we can have offended Miss Pelham?" Rising from the sofa, he started to dance a Cossack dance. Kolya, inspired, strummed wildly on. With a grace and agility extraordinary in one so tall and large, Misha bent and sprang, twirled and clapped. He looked handsome, wild, happy, without care. The Prince, entranced, sat gazing at him, his eyes blazing with love.

The lips of Uncle Georg parted in pleasure, his light narrow eyes gleaming golden as a cat's. It was as if he himself moved in Misha's movements, swung in that springy body. A kind of glow lit even the wan mistiness of Uncle Sergei's visage. Kolya played on, entranced; later, two friends of his came in; the music thrummed on.

Daisy, annoyed and sleepless, could hear it from her room, an echo of distant, unapproachable happiness.

A footman, arriving in the small hours to renew the piano candles, found the party all still at it.

Chapter 7

The fact that the engine was stoked with birch wood instead of coal might make the country railway journey slower, but it certainly made it less smelly and smoky, Daisy reflected, as the train rolled past wide marshes, past chestnut woods with their sticky black buds closed fast against the iron cold, past the endless clumps of birch, the plains and the dark pine forests.

At the station was gathered a welcoming crowd of peasants. There was a buzz and a hum of pleasure: Nikolai and Arkady were caught up in strong arms, tossed high, exclaimed over and embraced by a score of bearded enthusiasts. Salutes and endearments continued as they drove over the snow homewards, past mossy log cabins from whose doors roughly hewn faces looked out, smiling a greeting. Icicles hung on the eaves, and the thin wisps of smoke rising up into the still air lost themselves quickly in the cold immensity of the landscape.

Jevrenskaia, once arrived at, revealed itself as large, square, and yellow plastered, set in rolling fields and woods stretching to the horizon. Without, there were marble busts of Greek goddesses, slightly cracked by frost and set in the formal garden with its frozen fountain and great Italian wrought-iron wellhead. Within, large porcelain animals were ranged in rows along a colonnaded gallery. English chintzes covered the sofas and gilded French nineteenth century furniture adorned a great central hall, with a wealth of dark china cabinets and *bureaux plats*. In the great salon, little tables held photographs in silver frames, bearded men in uniform, swan-necked ladies in tulle; Misha and Kolya as small boys looking threatening in white sailor suits, their cap ribbons streaming in a summer breeze. Walls held a few brightly painted Dutch pictures. There were ferns in majolica pots and a quantity of sombre engravings of Napoleonic battles, full of people dying bravely in heavy snow. Great-grandpapa Dubelsky, wearing sword and side-whiskers, glowered abstractedly from an alcove in the hall, as if he were an indignant Early Father in an Italian Renaissance church and seemingly ten or twelve feet in height. The general effect was not very pretty, or even splendid, rather as if thrown together by persons with their thoughts on other things. Away from Moscow, the Princess had, perhaps, stopped bothering. The warmth, however, was delicious, and Daisy enjoyed the change of scenery.

The children poured over the house in all directions, with cries of joy; and even Ella, dashing from place to place and from one set of welcoming arms to another, forgot, momentarily, to cross herself before and after every action. Night seemed to come suddenly, and snow still fell, enhancing Daisy's sense of isolation. But within all was warmth and a pleased clustering round the samovar, a continuous hum of peasant voices and childish laughter flowed in and out of the servants' quarters. Bloused characters exactly like those seen in Chekov plays drifted in and out for comment or instruction. There was never a silent moment. Daisy observed spellbound.

Her bedroom turned out to be huge and dark, and smelt musty. On the wall was a signed photograph of Queen Victoria in late middle-age, wearing a look of settled mourning. The wood stove groaned, as if at the unusual effort of burning. Summer here might be beautiful, but the flood in the Moscow house had precipitated them too early into what was not an ideal winter house. The linen sheets smelled deliciously of herbs, but the bed sagged into a deep hollow in the middle, as if for too long the abode of some ailing and weighty ancestor. The night was clouded and very dark. Unaccustomed sounds floated from nearby woods to Daisy's sleepless ears. Dawn seemed a long time in coming, and showed a landscape still locked in frozen snow.

"We are leaving today," Arkady informed Daisy in the morning. "Going to stay at Misha's house. He wants Papa to come and shoot bears."

"But we've only just arrived!" Daisy complained to Mademoiselle, who was looking unusually pinched and old. "I've only just unpacked everything! And now it's all to be packed up again. I thought the plan was to stay here? Really, it's not rational."

"Plan! Rational!" Mademoiselle mocked. "You come to Russia and expect people to be rational! To stick to plans! Other good things, yes, friendship, affection, but to stick to plans and to be rational, no! For that you must stay further west, I fancy." Her large face lengthened, as if in mourning for those orderly *boulevards* of Limoges that she might never see again.

Misha's house was smaller, lower, far more uncomfortable, and embedded in thicker woods. A lake, overgrown but loud with the cries of wildfowl, faded into a vista of range on range of wooded hills. Beds were damp, and the food, though plentiful, seemed most unsuitable for children, consisting almost entirely of large quantities of game and lacking vegetables, fruit or puddings. The Prince and Misha were out all day, returning ravenous and jovial in the evenings. The children wandered round the lake; Daisy, mistrusting its marshy edges, went with them, oppressed by the harsh crying of the wild geese who flew round, seeming never to settle. Catkins hung on the hazel boughs, but of other signs of spring there were none; and no birds sang. Daisy found the limitless horizons oppressive, and why were there so few cottages, such sparse inhabitants?

On the far side of the lake a dead aspen tree leant over the water, at an angle melancholy to the beholder but tempting to small boys. Nikolai felt called upon to climb along it, while Daisy's attention was distracted by a complaint from Arkady. Slipping off, he fell into ice thinned by a hidden spring. The water was shallow, but he was soaked in its iciness and had to be rushed home, where he was rubbed all over with vodka to prevent rheumatic fever.

"Wouldn't it be better if I drank it?"

"No, Nikolai, it would *not*." Even the Princess was angry, for once, with her firstborn son. "You are a foolish, disobedient boy. Another hot blanket, if you please, Daisy."

The arrival of Kolya from Moscow was cheering. He tuned the piano at once, enlisted Misha's Boris to play the balalaika, and though out all day with his gun, was not too tired in the evenings to play and sing with the children. In Moscow Daisy had sometimes heard him talk of the land hunger of the peasants. It was almost mystical, he had said, their feeling for land. She felt emboldened to ask him how it could be, this hunger, when there seemed to be so much land and so few peasants?

Kolya's dark eyes kindled. "You will see," he began. "Every twelve years the land allotted to the peasants is redivided among the families, but the rural population has so increased that by the beginning of this century some young men had only half an acre as their portion, not nearly enough to live upon."

"But would it not be possible to allot them some more?"

"In some places this has been done—but in others! Here is the problem. The owners, you will believe, part with great reluctance with good land, land which they, or their forebears, have reclaimed from wilderness. But we hope, I and my friends hope, that someday . . ."

The Princess's bell-like tones interrupted, calling him to fresh exertions at the piano. "It's almost Ella's bedtime, and we still haven't had the song she chose! Please, Kolya; they so greatly prefer your playing to mine!" Charming, jewelled, scented with amber, she swam at him irresistibly.

Daisy was silenced. As the song ended, Misha, frosted and cheerful, tramped into the room, causing his usual self-congratulatory hubbub. The children crowded round him, increasing the din. "Misha! Misha! Did you get him? Did you kill him? How big was he? Huger than Papa? Huger than Uncle Vassily?" Even Ella was dancing up and down at the triumph.

Why should I mind, thought Daisy, when I don't mind foxes at home? But a bear! So large and lovely, and surely rare? Do they really kill stock, like foxes do, I wonder? She was relieved to hear that they were to return to Jevrenskaia at the end of the week. More bears, at least, would now enjoy another summer. "Can't we come with you tomorrow?" the boys pleaded.

"No. After their long sleep the bears awaken very lively and fierce!" Misha said with pleasure.

Though there was a small railway station some miles from the house, Misha announced his intention of travelling to his father's house by sleigh. "I must go by Balkursk to pick up the gun that I left there."

"Take us!" Nikolai begged. "Take me and Arkady! We've never been to Balkursk!"

"It's too far. Too cold."

"Me and Arkady are never too cold."

"Nikolai wasn't even cold when he fell in the lake, were you, Nikolai?"

"No, and we should be no trouble. All that way, Misha, you need some company."

"Very well then, you little beggars, but mind—do exactly what I say. No arguing."

"Oh no, Misha! Glory, glory, glory!"

"If the twins go," the Princess insisted, "Miss Pelham must go too. I know you, Misha; you and Kolya will spend too long with the keeper and you will forget them and they will get into mischief. But they may go if Miss Pelham goes too."

"But if Miss Pelham comes," Misha pointed out coldly, "there will be no room for Kolya in the sleigh."

"I'll ride."

"Kolya, I thought you told me that your mare was lame?"

"Very well, I'll take old Dick Turpin, if I may, Papa? Miss Pelham will like him; he's a retired English hunter."

"It's been a long hard winter," the Prince pointed out to Misha in a low voice, below the delighted shouts of the boys. "There's been no trouble . . . no sign of *them?* None have been heard of? It's a lonely way, on from Balkursk."

"None this side of the river, Papa. Not a whisper of any. Such news travels fast."

They set off early, wearing leggings, turbans, coats and fur cloaks for the open drive. They looked, Daisy thought, like a party of bears, and had in addition bearskin rugs to cover them.

"Ah, the poor bears," Misha mocked, glancing sideways at Daisy through his long and already frosted lashes. "Your guardsmen, I think, are so cruel as to wear these same skins on their heads. Not for the cold, which you do not have, but for show."

"They took them from the guardsmen of Napoleon whom they defeated at Waterloo," Daisy gasped involuntarily in the intense searing cold of the morning.

"Don't rise, Miss Pelham," Kolya laughed. "He only says these things because a little war amuses him."

The sleigh swept on through the sharp brightness of the morning. It's exhilarating, Daisy thought, whatever else. Next time, I shall not answer Misha. But if I don't he only gets worse.

The wise head of Dick Turpin kept abreast of them, cantering easily with a long tireless stride. At Balkursk, Misha disappeared abruptly into the gunsmith. "He'll be half an hour at least," Kolya said. "He may tease you about England but he cherishes those English guns as if they were holy relics." Leaving the horses at the inn, they wandered round the little town, the wooden houses set in snow, the onion-domed church.

"All of wood, you see," said Kolya. "They burn with terrible ease. If but one small house catches fire, the village is gone in a moment. Over and over again, we implore the peasants to build their houses further apart, but they like to cluster close together. And then someone is careless, and pff! Their whole village is up in smoke, church and all, and they are homeless and without shelter on a winter night!"

An occasional prosperous merchant walked the streets, but there seemed many poor and ill-clad peasants among them. Two desperately thin and ragged children begged from Kolya and went away rewarded. Daisy could see that he really minded their plight. "We do mind their poverty," he said when he noticed her expression. "And give, though little enough, to the poor who cross our path. But we do nothing real. Too much of what we do is talk."

Aware of having spent too long with the gunsmith and his guns, as his stepmother had predicted, Misha emerged impatiently and put his guns very carefully in the troika. The evening had darkened early, under heavy cloud. Daisy felt depressed by the poverty she had seen. Even the twins were quiet; they pressed on in silence for some miles. The cold gathered against them like an enemy.

"Is it much further?" Daisy asked. The iciness of the air was unlike anything she had ever dreamed of. "Twenty versts, perhaps a dozen miles. Keep rubbing your nose," Misha advised. "You don't want to get frostbitten."

There was not a house or habitation within sight, nothing but the cold plain of snow, the dark trees; it was like a country to which human beings had never penetrated. There was no sound but the swish of the runners on the snow, the faint jingle of harness. Not a breath of wind stirred.

"How does your brother know the way?" Daisy asked Arkady.

"He knows."

"I know by the lie of the land," Misha contributed tersely.

Silence fell again. There was something uncanny about this total solitude, something hostile and dangerous that seemed to affect the spirits even of the twins. What happens, Daisy wondered apprehensively, if a horse founders or a runner breaks? I should think we'd all die of cold in about twenty minutes. Now they were entering another belt of thick pine-woods, and even these, desolate though they were, felt like a kind of shelter.

The danger, when it came, came from what was to Daisy a totally unexpected quarter.

Suddenly a distant howling pierced the later afternoon. "What was that strange cry?" she asked. Misha said something to Kolya in Russian.

"They may be hunting something else," Arkady said calmly.

"Hunting what? *Who* may be hunting what?" A fear of the unknown woods gripped her.

The twins took no notice. "I think not," Nikolai said. "I heard it twice before. Getting nearer. They are on to *us*, all right."

"But who? But *what*? What is that cry? There it is again!"

Misha turned to look at her. There seemed almost to be a look of pleasure in his glance. "Can you shoot?" he asked. "Can you at least put a gun together? That sound is the sound of a pack of wolves in full cry. After us."

Daisy felt a wave of appalling panic. But this isn't true! This only happens in storybooks! But the cold, and the loneliness, and Kolya's tense profile as he rode on, told her that it was only too true, was happening to her, to the children, to Misha and Kolya, and to the four horses which, now terrified, plunged madly on, so that Misha could hardly control them. "If you can't shoot, can you ride?" he shouted back at her.

"Yes."

"Astride? You don't need a sidesaddle?"

"Yes." Thank God that I learned, however much Mummy didn't want me to, she thought through her terror.

"Can you ride hard? For your life? On a horse that will be wild with fear? Can you husband his strength?"

"I come from Leicestershire," Daisy told him through her chattering teeth.

"Shorten the stirrups as you go," Misha shouted to Kolya. "Two holes, I would think. I am going to slow them in a minute. Be ready to change. Miss Pelham can't shoot."

He held the horses. With trembling hands and shaking knees Daisy felt herself cast up by Kolya upon Dick Turpin's stalwart back, felt the horse tremble and sweat under her, endeavoured at once to soothe and control him. In the troika Kolya was loading the rifle.

The noise of the wolves now sounded horribly near.

"Ride for your life!" Misha shouted. "Don't look back. Whatever happens to us, ride on, don't look back. You can't help, so don't try. Ride on, hard. You might save your life, and Turpin's. A horse can travel faster than a wolf, though not for so long. Keep straight on, make for the gap in the next belt of forest. You'll come to a bridge at the other end, and there is a village only a couple of versts beyond. Ride steady, and God go with you!"

Daisy could feel the fear running through the whole of Dick Turpin's great body. She had ridden a nervous horse often enough, but never one consumed by panic, galloping for its life. We can't keep up this pace, she sighed almost despairingly, and he's been going all day already. Gently now, Turpin, have you forgotten English? I wonder. By now, they were in the open again. To Daisy this great space felt even more sinister and unprotected than the wood. An enormous distance of snow stretched interminably before them. The next piece of forest seemed almost beyond the horizon. She ceased to believe that they could ever reach it. Only instinct kept her hands steady, tightened her legs on the trembling flanks of the horse.

The head of the wolf pack was out of the woods already, gaining steadily upon the troika with the desperate drive of hunger. Kolya steadied the rifle on the hood of the sleigh and urged the twins to keep still. It seemed a long while before Daisy heard the crack of the first rifle shot, followed quickly by another. How good a shot was the gentle Kolya? How easy was it to take accurate aim from the back of a swinging, swiftly moving sleigh? Wolves, Daisy knew, will in their frantic hunger fall upon each other's wounded bodies. All their lives must depend upon how many Kolya could shoot, upon how big and how desperate the pack was.

Tirelessly, the wolves came on; and the horses, under this desperate pace, seemed now to be slowing down. The trees looked no nearer, and in any case, what help were the trees? Shots from Kolya's rifle rang out now continually, but the pace of the surviving wolves seemed never to slacken and their dreadful cry still rang out.

"Mother of God!" Misha shouted suddenly, and for the first time there was fear in his voice. "Another pack! Look over on the right!" Far off to the right, over the waste of snow, Daisy saw another long dark line stretched out across the white, the same tireless loping leader, the same straggle of hungry mouths spread out behind him. They must be hungry indeed, thought Misha, to intrude upon the country of another pack.

"Won't they fight each other?" Daisy shouted hopefully.

"Not while they have still got hope of us," Misha yelled back. "Keep in close, for now. We don't want them to concentrate on you. Keep in."

Kolya's shots continued. It seemed to Daisy almost as if the cry of the first pack were growing fainter. Were they falling back? But away to the right, the long new line was perceptibly nearer.

"How much further?" Daisy gasped, weakening. Out of training for such a strenuous gallop, she could feel her knees growing weaker, beginning to lose their grip. Oh God, she prayed soundlessly, save us all, but especially save the little boys. The illogic of this quite escaped her, since the hope of safety for the little boys lay entirely with Misha and Kolya.

"Only a mile to the trees now," Misha shouted. "Keep him steady. Don't give up hope." But the fresh pack was now horribly near, and the old pack seemed still to come on. Kolya switched away from them, briefly, to take aim at the leader of the new pack, now gaining steadily as the exhausted horses began, barely perceptibly, to slacken their speed. It looked as if, at the edge of the forest, there was to be a terrible convergence. Some of the new pack were down now, rolling over under Kolya's fire, to be torn in pieces with terrifying speed while the others pressed relentlessly on.

Misha now took a decision from which his heart revolted. Both little boys were shouting aloud, but whether with terror or excitement it was hard to tell. *"Be quiet,"* Misha told them. "Come nearer, Daisy, come very near. Nearer still. That is right, keep there. Take your feet out of the stirrups. Knot the reins. Let go the reins. *Do as I say.*" With a sudden violent wrench he seized Daisy out of the saddle and dumped her unceremoniously on the floor of the sleigh. "Now, Kolya, shoot him! Quick, before he gets out of range. Shoot, and be certain to kill!"

Kolya shot, once and again. The great horse wore off to the right, keeled over, kicked once, shuddered and was still.

In a terrifyingly short time, the wolves of the new pack closed over his body, a swarming, struggling wave. The old pack joined in with them, closed in a snarling tangle as the sleigh slid under the outlying trees of the forest. "Oh no!" Daisy cried. "Oh no!" The trees concealed the swarm over Turpin's body, but the horses, under Daisy's additional weight, seemed to slow down still more. But the few wolves who still came on were swiftly dealt with by Kolya, and the cry of the pack sounded ever fainter. Daisy lay gasping and trembling. Kolya's boots, as he knelt to shoot, stuck out over her and prevented her from getting up. I think I am going to faint, she thought, but if I do, this seems the best place to do it.

Their way now began to descend. "The bridge!" Nikolai shouted. "I can see the bridge!"

"And lights from the village!"

"Are you all right?" Kolya bent down to ask Daisy. "The wolves won't come down into the valley. Too many men, with too many guns. Here, let me help you up. Are you sure you are all right?"

"No, I'm not," Daisy wept, as the sleigh swept over the bridge. She was now sobbing uncontrollably. "How could you do it? How could you shoot him when he had gone so bravely, galloped so well?"

"Don't reproach me," Kolya said. "I hated to do it. I loved that old horse." The lights of the village went by. "Populated from here on," Kolya promised; but though the dreadful blood-curdling cry of pursuit was now far away, Misha would scarcely allow the horses to flag. He was in a right royal rage with himself, made no better by Daisy's inability to halt her sobs. The twins recovered their fright with amazing speed, but their excitement did not so swiftly abate. "If the wolves get you," Nikolai told Daisy delightedly, "there's nothing left of you except the toes inside your boots."

"Weep if you will," Kolya urged her kindly, "but he was an old horse, and we all must die."

"It was his *way* of dying! Killed by friends he trusted."

"You rode him bravely."

"It wasn't me, it was *him*. He was a brave, brave horse."

Kolya saw that she was all but hysterical and he attempted no further words, but took her hand and chafed it soothingly, with a kind of abstraction, as if she were a frightened puppy. His huge dark eyes regarded her with sympathy. "How will you explain this to Papa?" Arkady asked suddenly. Misha silenced him with a mild clout. He was wondering the same thing himself.

They stood in the hall, unwrapping. Misha looked thundery. He had lost a good horse and risked the lives of his three brothers. He felt shame.

But Daisy was too overwrought to leave well alone. Her teeth still chattered with an overwhelming mixture of anger and fright; she could not allow Misha to depart and make his peace with his father as best he might. "It was *you* who made Kolya shoot. It was *you* who made him do it. Couldn't you have let the horse run free? Couldn't you have given him a chance?"

Misha spoke from between clenched teeth. "To shoot him was better than to let him be torn in pieces and devoured still alive."

"He could have taken his chance! Why did you bring him from England to die like this! He could have ended his days in peace in some green field."

"You believe that the life of one old horse matters more than the life of five people, two of them young children?"

"Yes! Yes! . . . Well, perhaps—"

"I will remember that," Misha said with the level tones of deep dislike. "And next time we will throw *you* out. And leave you to run free and take your chance without shooting you. You would like that." Shaken himself by the death of the horse, Misha turned to rend this idiotic young woman. "You love animals. Think of this then. The starving wolves are now happy."

Turning on his heel, Misha went off to make his peace in the stables. His father, he learned, was out and would not return till late.

The twins had hurried towards the drawing room, arguing excitedly. "No, Nikolai, it's *my* turn to tell Mamma! You told about the frogs. No, Nikolai, let *me*."

"Be quiet, Arkady. I tell best. You take so long. And the frogs were dull compared to the wolves." Kolya followed on their heels to allay his step-mother's fears. But there was no one in the drawing room. The Princess stood in tears among the porcelain lions on the first floor. She had returned to find Mademoiselle seriously ill; the doctor was in doubt whether she could live through the night. The Princess wrung her hands, hardly able to listen to a tale of wolves or of anything else. Which was as well, thought Kolya.

In his heart Misha continued exceedingly sore about the horse Dick Turpin. He sat up late, drinking brandy and waiting for the Prince to return; his anger, seeking outlet, directed itself upon Daisy. Misha had once spent a hunting season in Northamptonshire, from whence he had gone with his friend to pass a fortnight of the term at Oxford: he regarded himself as an authority upon all things English. "A vicarage Miss," he fumed, pouring Kolya another glass of brandy. "That is what she is—a vicarage Miss." A phrase heard at Oxford,—"poor fellow, he married some silly vicarage Miss"—had obligingly presented itself to his mind. "That is her to the letter. That is exactly what she is. Simple. Her inno-cence is only silliness. She is like that Fräulein who was with the Galit-zines and who thought that babies were brought by the stork, until she was found to be with child by a footman. She is equally simple."

Kolya pointed out mildly that Daisy was still young. Varya at twenty might be just as simple.

"Varya! At eleven, at ten, at whatever age she is, she has more sense, more knowledge, more proportion. She is not a sentimental fool who would sacrifice humans to animals. Varya could never be fooled by infant tales; she is aware by instinct that babies are not brought by the stork." Misha expatiated at length upon this theme, cheering himself up at the thought of Daisy's idiocy and becoming in due course quite funny, so that Kolya started laughing too, and they both became drunk, missing the Prince's return and continuing into the small hours until Misha, return-ing to his abuse, suddenly seemed to his brother to be too offensive. Lay-ing his arm round Misha's shoulder, Kolya said authoritatively, no more. But whether Kolya referred to the brandy or to the abuse of Daisy, Misha was by this time too drunk to care.

Chapter 8

In the early hours of the morning Mademoiselle died. Daisy, still shak-en by her previous day's experience, came down to breakfast to find the whole family in tears. She stood in the doorway, gazing in amazement at this extravagant display of grief, and uncertain whether to come in or stay out.

Even the debonair and casual Misha seemed affected. He had just been told the news; his yellow head shook and heaved until at any moment Daisy expected a loud childish bellow to emerge.

Misha was stricken with remorse as much as anything else. It was years since he had addressed more than a few casual words to Mademoiselle. Now she had ceased to be a boring old woman, cadging for more affection than he could afford her, and had again become the kindly protective figure who had consoled him and Kolya in their motherless infancy, who had slapped him, cherished him, made him eat horrible food and taken him into her bed when he had nightmares. He had sobbed with fright into her bony shoulder, drummed his cold little feet into her stringy thighs. I wonder, thought Misha, it didn't put me off women for life. The admission of this thought occasioned him further grief.

Daisy felt that she should beat a retreat from this family scene, though equally sure that no one would have noticed if she had advanced into the room and danced a jig down the middle of the breakfast table, so deeply absorbed were they all in their feeling. Kolya was remembering a long ago passage of arms with Mademoiselle. As a nine-year-old he had once been so noisy and obstreperous that she had made him sit down quietly and learn a long passage from Racine's *Alceste*. With indignant determination he had made himself word perfect, recited the passage without faltering and with a wealth of dramatic gesture, and at the end, put out his tongue at Mademoiselle to the limit of its length. She had retaliated by sending him to bed for the rest of the day on bread and water. For some reason this gloomy recollection caused Kolya a fresh flood of tears.

The Princess was the first to recover. "Eat, my darlings, eat!" she cried, but ate nothing herself, and the Prince confined himself to a cup of very hot coffee. This, Misha felt, was hardly the moment to touch on Dick Turpin, and yet, if Papa went down to the stables! In the colonnade Daisy found Nyanya throwing up her hands and rocking her body in sorrow. "Aie! Aie! She was too tall for a woman," Nyanya cried. "Too tall, too long a body; how could the poor heart pump the blood so long a way? Aie! Aie!" Steadily and sometimes bitterly at odds with Mademoiselle over the twelve years they had spent under the same roof, she now wept uncontrollably at her demise. "Only yesterday, she spoke to me of summer, of the needs of Varya's clothes! Only yesterday!"

I liked Mademoiselle well enough, and I am sad, thought Daisy—she was a friend, she understood how strange it all felt to me—but this is all too much. Can it be real, and not just showing off? Even the Prince is in tears, and I hardly ever saw him even speak to Mademoiselle for more than a moment or two.

Next week, at Easter, joy seemed as unconfined as grief had been. The house filled with preparations. The children brought in armfuls of pussy willow, which flowered too soon in the warmth, so that the whole house was filled with golden dust. An immense quantity of eggs were hard-boiled and everyone set to work to colour them in brilliant and varied designs. From the kitchen came a delicious smell where huge Easter cakes were baking; they were crowned with icing and surrounded by rich concoctions of almonds. There was a peculiar sweet cheese pyramid, *pashka*, which Daisy hoped very much not to have to eat. "They seem to eat nothing much but lentils all through Holy Week," she wrote home, "and it's impressive that they make such an utter fast of it; but one of the things I find so baffling is that Easter begins at midnight and everyone starts eating *then*—a sort of midnight feast. And their Easter is a different date from ours and nobody can explain why."

The Church service appeared to Daisy to last all through Easter Even; Nikolai and Arkady, tireless and solemn, acted as altar boys. The singing rose and fell—sad, alien, mysterious; the golden robes of the priests swung and dipped. At the magic moment after midnight, when Easter had truly come, the candles were lit, held steadfastly upright beneath all those earnest faces, swaying and dripping in the hands of the very young and the very old. Ella's face was radiant; instead of nodding with sleep through the long evening, she had gone into some private world of bliss. In the cold black morning everyone streamed forth in a chorus of greeting, over the snowy ground towards the great house whose lights now blazed welcome. Every candelabrum was lit, presents were exchanged, the hand of welcome held out. Exhilarated in the general joy, Daisy found herself being presented with coloured eggs, presenting the ones from the table to later-comers. "Christ is risen!" they cried to her, and soon she had learned the reply and was calling back with equal fervour, "He is risen indeed!" The contrast between the cold and dark and sadness of Good Friday, and this blaze of light and laughter, this feast of food and joy, could hardly have been greater or more symbolic of the living truth that lay behind it.

The spread of food was great enough to have fed a thousand, the long tables seemed almost to sag under it, and Daisy feared to be confronted with smoked ham and *pashka*, with sweet cheese and almond icing, for weeks to come. But all the food melted away in the general enthusiasm and joy. Even quiet Kolya was noisy, even arrogant Misha was kind. Or fairly kind, thought Daisy, rousing from the Easter spell and seeing him spill old Nyanya's wineglass into her lap with his elbow and pass on without troubling to look back.

Next week the two young men returned to their military duties, resplendent in new uniforms. Kolya was silent again, and Misha as peremptory as ever with a luckless groom who had failed to have one of the carriage horses harnessed just so. On the steps all the family blessed one another, embraced, wept, clung, waved, and in the case of Nikolai and Arkady, ran shouting after the carriage, as if both brothers were leaving forever instead of for less than a month.

What a palaver, thought Daisy. Yet another side of her was touched by the depth of feeling in which they seemed all to live their lives. Yet, why, if they felt so deeply, could they not turn some of all this emotion upon the plight of the poor, who swarmed the land, suffering visibly, and storing up, surely, a terrible fire of resentment? Politicians did little, and priests seemed only to counsel the sufferers to submit themselves to the will of God, without seriously considering that the will of God might not exactly coincide with the preservation of the status quo.

Summer came with the rapid Russian burst, seeming to admit but a brief few days of melting snow and flooding streams between the grip of winter and its own greenness and warmth. In the mild evenings while Nyanya put the children to bed, Daisy would walk out into the woods to hear the nightingales—or what sounded like them—and wake up in the morning to the sound of the golden orioles. An incredible lavish richness of growth came forth from the dark earth, ramped and climbed in the woods, waving and leaning over the flowing streams. At evening, she noticed that the peasant women would leave their houses and gather to walk together into the woods. "What do they do?" she asked Nyanya.

"They sing together. They sing alone in the woods where no husband or child will interrupt them."

"Could I go too? Could I listen silently to them?"

Nyanya looked scornful. "Those old songs! Why should you care?"

"But would they mind?"

"Mind? No, why should they, Mamzel? Go—if you can find the secret place where they sing."

After dinner one evening, at a cautious distance, Daisy followed two women who lived behind the stable block. It was a mild dank evening, with the stillness almost of a frost. Eager, yet feeling a little frightened, she followed deep into the forest. This, she thought, is like every fairy tale one has ever read, and I shall see a cottage soon, with a witch, or two dwarfs. But no cottage obtruded, and presently, coming very faintly on the still air, she could hear the sound of singing. Creeping stealthily nearer, for fear lest her presence should disturb, she listened for an hour and more to the sad enchanted sounds, strange words, a strange rhythmical music, sometimes accompanied by the stamp of feet, sometimes with a brief burst of gaiety, a quickened tempo, sometimes by the dancing of feet or the clapping of hands.

Fearing to be found, she stole at last back onto the homeward track, moved, elated and saddened by the sounds she had heard. The setting sun had cleared the clouds, and the air was now warm and benign. The way home seemed long, and presently she heard horsemen behind her and turned to see with relief that they were Misha and Kolya, riding over from their nearby camp to spend a night at home. She was relieved that they were not strangers, but would have liked to stay uninterruptedly in her mood of enchanted melancholy. She did not wish, on this soft evening, to have to take up arms against Misha once again.

Kolya got off his horse to walk beside her. "What did you think of the singing?" he asked, when she had explained her errand.

"It was beautiful. I could have listened forever." The words sounded, and were, trite; but who could say what they felt with Misha breathing down their necks? He had stayed on his horse, but was clearly listening to every word. His look of mockery was unconcealed.

She decided to be bold. What did Misha matter? Let him listen and mock as much as he liked. Kolya was in a serious mood, really wanting to talk, and how one missed and needed the conversation of one's contemporaries, when one was deprived of it!

"It was beautiful—but so sad. Sad, sad, haunting. Why does Russian music always sound so sad, always have a melancholy note running right through it?"

"Because," Kolya said soberly, "life is sad, and especially is it sad if one is a peasant woman."

"Surely it ought not always to be sad?"

"Not always; but *au fond*, sad."

"It wasn't sad at Easter. Not for anyone."

"Ah, Easter. One day. One season. One great festival, the greatest. But in sum, life is sad, and songs are made, for the most part, by sad people."

"Hey nonny no!" Misha interrupted rudely. He swung out of the saddle and plunged into the discussion, towering over Daisy and not always being careful to lead his horse so as not to bump into her. "In England," he insisted, "you live in cloud cuckoo land and have songs which say Hey nonny no! I went there to hunt one winter and I know. You live so safely with your sea and your great navy and your wealth in trade that you know nothing of real life. It is all so safe that the young men ride like fiends out hunting because that is the only danger available to them. Small wonder that your music is not sad. Sadness comes from an understanding of life. And only one tribe, the tribe of Wales, is able to sing."

"Everybody doesn't hunt," Daisy protested.

"No. And so they have to go to India or Africa to fight the poor Afghans, or the Ashanti. You think that they go for trade. I *know* that they go for danger. They fear to grow soft in so safe a land."

"It is *not* that. We go to civilise. India and Africa are more peaceful since we went there than they were when we came. And not so many babies die," Daisy insisted doggedly. "There are fewer famines, less disease. More roads and things, less crime. People are better for our coming. And happier."

"So happy that the Indian Army mutinies and kills its officers?"

"Fifty years ago! And only a few regiments out of hundreds!"

"Don't rise," Kolya advised Daisy. "He is but teasing."

Daisy insisted upon rising. "And what of Russia? What about the Tartars? What about the Uzbegs? You have colonies, too." She would have it out with this arrogant man.

"What do you know of Tartars? Of Uzbegs? We do not cross the seas to conquer and despoil harmless tribes. We subdue such as the Tartars because for centuries they invaded our Russian homeland. What do you know of cruelty or kindness, of hardness or mercy? Speak of them when for centuries we have lived with Tartar hordes at our gates!"

"Misha," Kolya warned him.

But Daisy, with flushed face, pressed on. "My father told me about the Tartars and the Uzbegs and the Turcoman."

"Ah, the good pastor. Mr. Pelham. And how comes he to know, except in books written by ignorant or wrongheaded people, of Tartars or the Uzbegs? You are the child of England, of the British Empire, which is like some great elephant, trampling all over the globe, breaking into other countries, trampling down their princes, stealing their crops, despoiling their fields; sometimes even behaving like those great bull elephants of India that come in season and go mad, and kill, kill even their friends."

Daisy was increasingly livid, and quite unable to stop. "Indian elephants can be wise, I think. They help, they build, they are capable of learning . . . But Russia is like an African elephant, pulling off roofs and devastating forests, and, and . . . tearing up crops without even eating them, the sort you can't tame, you can't teach, the sort that knows only how to flap its great ears and destroy trees." Daisy stopped; appalled to find that she could be so rude. Not even wittily rude, or subtly rude, but rude in a kind of prep-school manner. Her face was crimson, but she no longer cared. Her rage really startled her, it seemed to have carried her past all bounds. She had had no idea that she had it in her to be so offensive. She had come within an ace of quoting, "inept for everything, except the conquest of the world," which would have been not only exceedingly disagreeable, but simply untrue of Russians, who appeared to her to be apt for a great many things. Why could not Misha go right away back to the army, and *stay* away? She could think of no one else who induced in her this choking rage.

Misha was simply laughing, like a schoolboy who had managed a successful tease. Daisy continued in a calmer voice, but one that had lost nothing of its conviction. "If it were to come to an end, if the British Empire were ever to fold up, the world would be a colder place."

"Colder for England, maybe."

"And what is your alternative? *Your* secret police, the lash, the knout, imprisonment without trial? Even left to themselves, it would be a colder place for the poor and the oppressed."

"For India? For Ireland? For Africa?"

"For India. For Ireland. And particularly for Africa. Who else, who else in the world, will take the trouble to save them from their own wild men?"

"And your own wild men?"

Daisy was still trembling with rage. She turned on Misha now the full blaze of her immense blue eyes. She managed, by a great effort to speak in level, almost quiet tones.

With total unexpectedness, Misha found himself strongly attracted by her.

"We have no wild men," Daisy said. "Other things, yes. But wild, no." Her pride was exultant.

So, thought Misha, she's got a little blood and fire in her, she's not solid milk and water, not simply Miss Prim all through. Her eyes shone like aquamarines. Her words fell on him with less of an impact than summer rain. He bent himself to provoking once again the furious flash of those blue eyes. Swiftly, his brother intervened.

"My father and my mother, how are they?" Kolya asked, seeing that Daisy was fighting speechlessly with her indignation.

"Well," she told him, "but out to dinner, having not known that you would come." In the effort of self-control, her voice came out coldly, with a hard edge, as if Kolya too were encompassed in her enmity to his brother. They had arrived at the house; the horses had been taken away. As if to prolong the argument, they seated themselves on the terrace.

Suddenly losing interest, Misha got up and went into the house. The night continued mild and beautiful, quiet but for distant farm sounds, and full of sweet smells from the garden and from the climbing roses. Kolya kept perfectly still and said nothing. In the lulling silence Daisy's indignation slowly died within her. Rude Misha had certainly been, but it was no part of a civilised English person to shout back, she thought regretfully.

After dinner, loath to leave a night in which the moon was now slowly rising behind distant forest, they lingered on the steps, and Kolya, fetching his guitar, asked Daisy to teach him another English song. "The one you have taught the children, the one of turtle doves, and Christmas."

"It's not very . . . intellectual," Daisy objected, "only traditional," but she sang it all the same. "It's better with the parts."

"Teach me the parts." He had quickly picked up the accompaniment.

Misha had listened in silence. "You see," he said triumphantly, "you have proved what I was saying of the frivolity of life in England. All this is nonsense. Whoever saw a partridge in a pear tree? And if they had, what has that to say to the birth of our Saviour? These lords, these ladies, these swans—*quelle bêtise!* You sing that in church? Even your holy songs are frivolous, meaningless."

"It's not meant to be serious. We like to laugh."

"So you laugh even in church? England is, as I tell you, cloud cuckoo land."

"Leave us," said Kolya. "We are making music. Miss Daisy will teach me another English song."

"I too love music," Misha said, seating himself firmly down on the step. "Come, Kolya, a Russian song that Miss Daisy can learn."

Kolya sang one, a beautiful, slow, sad song.

"That was lovely," Daisy said when he had ended. "Beautiful. But sad, sad, sad, Prince."

"Could you not call me Kolya? Of course it is sad, the tale of a princess and her lover and a Tartar chief who carries her away."

The warmth and the stillness, the soothing beauty of the night held them silent, induced in them a mood of solemnity, of a need to express the feelings of their hearts. Except for Misha, who principally felt randy.

"Do not expect too much of life, Daisy. It can never be without sadness," Kolya urged in a low gentle voice. "Enjoy today. Enjoy tomorrow when perhaps the children will take you to the river to find wild strawberries. Enjoy next month when Mamma has her summer ball, for her saint's day."

"I enjoy tonight," Misha said with great firmness, and when Kolya went into the house to fetch another piece of music and Daisy rose to follow him, he held her back in a sudden warm embrace and released her as suddenly with a friendly slap on her bottom. "Shall we both enjoy tonight?"

Stunned and yet excited, Daisy was aware that a dignified silence might be the most effective reply to this, but she was not capable of maintaining one. The moonlight, fortunately, concealed the colour of her face. She felt moved to point out, rashly, that she was not the French governess, but the English one.

Upon this opening, Misha moved in at once. "Ah! So you read Tolstoy? Not suitable for young girls, and especially not for young *English* girls. And what do you make of him? What do you think of the life of Anna Karenina, from whose story you must draw the tale of the French governess, since you can scarcely have drawn it from the life of our lamented Mademoiselle? Anna Karenina! When you read of her life, do you not tire of being a governess, always with the children? What brought you here, so far from home? Love, perhaps; yet who could spurn so pretty a girl? Any time you tire of the children, and want a nice establishment in Moscow, you tell me."

He is teasing again, but not altogether teasing, Daisy thought, shocked beyond words. Silence seemed the best refuge. She walked into the house with a flaming face. The niceness of Kolya, she thought, is quite undone by the horribleness of Misha. Yet I am not going to give up and go away. That would be to be defeated by him.

"Misha," Kolya said later, as they smoked a cigar and waited for their parents' return, "lay off this poor girl far from home."

"I find that narrow smugness unbearable. *Unbearable.* And her silliness. And that primness. I wish Mamma would send her home."

"What you also find unbearable is that she strongly attracts you."

Misha made no attempt to argue. "I wish Mamma would send her home," he reiterated.

"The alternative would be to leave her alone."

The gleam of Misha's eye was still dangerous, but his brother so rarely offered him advice that when it came, he would always consider it, sometimes even take it, though never without protest. "How can I never speak to her, living under the same roof?"

"You spoke rarely to poor Mademoiselle, living under the same roof."

Misha perceived that Kolya was laughing at him, and he too laughed, suddenly, his dangerous mood blown away on a gust of amusement. Kolya sighed inwardly. By the next time they came home Misha would have forgotten the entire conversation.

At least he still remembered it next morning, as they rode away, in the mist of a very early summer day. His eyes, as he turned to Kolya, were gleaming with pleasure.

"And you, brother, with your songs and your guitar, had you not also better leave her alone?"

Kolya's eyes, under his peaked cap, betrayed no change of expression. "She has taught me many new songs," he said imperturbably. "Some are rubbish, but some give me pleasure . . . And furthermore, I *like* her. There's a difference."

Chapter 9

"Do you remember," the Princess asked, "that you are not yet eleven years old?" Anchored by her hairdresser, she was for the while at Varya's mercy.

Varya tossed back her long dark locks. She had but recently discovered what a useful ploy this was, emphasising at once her independence of mind and the lustrous heaviness of her hair.

I give her mother five minutes to hold out, Daisy thought, passing the door. Ten at most.

"In Shakespeare, I think, Juliet went to dances. Juliet married when she was thirteen," Varya maintained.

"Her story had not a very happy ending, my darling! But who would dance with you, Varya? Balls are for grown women. There will be plenty for you when you are a grown woman—in six years, seven perhaps?"

"People will dance with me, I think you will find. Uncle Vassily for one. Papa, Yaroslav, maybe. And Kolya certainly. Perhaps even Misha."

"Misha! With Misha it will not be a night for little sisters, I think."

"Why should I not stay up just to see! I want to see Misha's beautiful girls from Moscow. And the friends of Kolya, that smart widow he goes round with. How shall I know how to *be*, unless I learn early how smart women *are*, how they comport themselves?"

"I think you might find some better examples than the ladies whom Misha and Kolya import from Moscow," the Princess said coldly.

"But surely, Mamma, they must be respectable women or you and Papa would never entertain them here."

"There is the respectability of the heart and the respectability of the outward seeming." The Princess felt herself to be approaching deep waters. "My darling Varusha, I tell you again that there will be many dances for you, many balls. Wait till the time is ripe."

"Suppose I were to die first? Suppose I were to die and never go to a ball? How sad you would be, Mamma!"

The Princess crossed herself and simultaneously urged her hairdresser to pile her hair a little higher at the back.

"Wouldn't you be, Mamma?"

"Oh darling, Varya, how you pursue your desires! Is it quite right, do you think, to tease Mamma so? I do not think that Papa would like to hear you, and I do not think that Papa would like you to be late at the ball. You and the boys and Ella will be there for dinner and to see the Cossacks dance—is that not enough?"

Varya's dark head drooped in silence. What persistence had not won, acquiescence still might. Her head fell lower, lower; her hands folded meekly in her lap.

"What is life that we should punish our children because they are children?" the Princess exclaimed suddenly, throwing up her handsome head, to the despair of her coiffeuse. "There, stay till midnight if you must, Varya; stay for the Bolshoi dancers. Enjoy, my darling, enjoy! Like Cinderella! Till midnight, mind, Varya, only till midnight . . . There, be careful of my hair, or you will drive poor Colette distracted." Having bestowed a warm embrace, Varya departed like lightning, lest there should be a further change of mood.

"Do you know, Arkady, that Varya is allowed to stay up for the Bolshoi dancers, and that we are not?"

"I don't mind. Who cares for the ballet? So long as we can see the Cossacks dance, and Papa says that we may."

"I do not see why we should go to bed while Varya, a girl, stays up."

"You may stay in bed, Nikolai. I have other plans."

"Tell me!"

"I will tell you later. Come now, they are laying out the tables for supper. I want also to see the band the moment they arrive."

Daisy's pleasure at the approach of the summer ball was tinged with apprehension. June was too hot for the winter's velvet frock, and how would her blue moiré measure up to the splendours of Russia's social scene? But I am not supposed to be smart, Daisy assured herself, I ought to be like Jane Eyre, wearing grey and silently absorbing myself in etchings in the background. Only that it doesn't seem to be like that, and thank God there's no Mr. Rochester here; he is quite my least favourite character in the whole of history or fiction.

But again, how about the dancing? There would be mazurkas and polonaises, because the Prince liked the old-fashioned dances of his youth: could one keep step with people who had danced them from childhood? Suppose one turned the wrong way and upset the whole figure? And who, in this strange land, would ever think of asking her to dance? Perhaps Jane Eyre had the right idea after all.

At least, she thought stoutly, I'll be in the house where I am living and I can always slip away to my own bedroom. But it was no delight at twenty to lie in bed and listen to the thrum of the music to which other and luckier girls were dancing. "I shall be glad when it's all over," Daisy assured herself, brushing out her bright hair vigorously before the looking glass. The blue moiré, newly ironed and laid out on the bed, looked hideously juvenile and unsmart.

Nothing turned out as expected, since Daisy had overlooked the power of plentiful champagne to overcome the pangs of loneliness and shyness. The Princess repeatedly introduced her to young men—"Do you know our English friend?"—and Daisy forgot about the blue moiré and became less like Jane Eyre with every passing minute. Even the mazurka seemed easy as well as glorious, and she had a waltz with Kolya and a polka with the indefatigable Prince.

"Last week," he told her, "I saw your Beatty."

"What Beatty?"

"Your Admiral Beatty. He had a fine strong face and a great presence. He wears his cap over one eye like a young *gaillard*. I met and talked to him and then I also heard him speak. He had a great success, I think, on his visit; he seemed to all to be a fine ally. He had a formidable look. There were also with him two other admirals. Brock, I think one was, and the other Halsey. They had good faces. They too seemed fine admirals. God knows, we may all have need of them soon enough. But let us not talk of these things. My wife does not care for us to talk of these things. Ah, I see with relief that the twins are being taken to bed. We need fear no more mischief from them. You are enjoying yourself?"

"Very, very much."

The Cossacks had passed in a whirl and a flash, springing and gyrating with fantastic skill and rhythm. Kolya was dancing with the smart widow whom Varya had designated as his: she was tiny, fair, exquisite, her long white neck circled with amazing diamonds. What jewels they wear! At home, she thought, so many and such huge jewels would be thought vulgar, what her mother called *arriviste*, but here, though everyone blazed with near Koh-i-nors, with rubies, emeralds and sapphires the size of pigeon's eggs, with ropes of such things as amethyst, all richly set, it seemed *not* vulgar but right and a part of the glitter and the splendour, as if everyone were a Shah or a Rajah or the Emperor and Empress of China.

Jewels blazed in high-piled hair, shone with every turn of the neck or movement of the wrist, sparkled in the folds of dresses, or girdled those exceedingly small tightly corsetted waists.

Kolya's partner leaned nearer, whispering something in his ear. Passing nearby, in the waltz, Daisy tried unsuccessfully not to entertain base feelings towards the fairy-queen figure twirling in the curve of Kolya's arm.

"Some champagne? We need to restore the forces before the polonaise! The old people have so much stamina!" By suppertime Daisy's head was in too much of a whirl to eat more than a couple of mouthfuls. But what a spread, she thought; at other times, I would have tucked in . . . Oeufs à la russe, escargots, caviare, oysters, game . . . In the early hours a new orchestra took over and the floor was cleared for the Bolshoi. As the music began, Daisy was astonished to recognise a familiar theme. Kolya, it appeared, had taken a fancy to the "Twelve Days of Christmas"; by some miracle he had in the available time induced a genius of a young friend to arrange the music and another to do the choreography, and the Bolshoi to allow some of the stars of their young company to learn it. Daisy gazed entranced; it was like some magically realised dream; there they all were, from the two turtledoves and the partridge circling round the pear tree to the ten maidens milking and the eleven lords leaping. With a great din of cymbals, the triumphant chords crashed into the finale while Daisy sat on, silent, captivated.

The Princess had seated herself beside an elderly cousin who was looking a little neglected. "Yes," she agreed, "*seemingly* our women of fashion behave better since the Czarina is so strict, but is it not only a semblance? You and I know how deep this alteration goes. You and I—"

"Mamma, come to me a minute! I want to tell you, and I want you to remember. I have quite decided whom I shall marry, so will you and Papa set about arranging it? First, Prince Sergei Obolensky. I danced the mazurka with him."

"Varya! Why are you not in bed long since!"

"No, but listen, Mamma, this is important! First Prince Sergei. Then, after a while, when we have had some happy years, I think an accident, a little accident will befall him. And then," and Varya's proud and sparkling look grew dreamy, "I shall marry Prince Alexander Galitzine. How handsome he is! It would be impossible not to fall in love with him. And then, maybe—How unlucky it is that one can have so few husbands!"

"Varya! Why are you still here?" The Princess had hastily imposed herself between the elderly cousin and her daughter's excited assertions. "Say goodnight at once to Marie Alexandrovna, and then to bed, with no more trifling. And put all such ideas at once from your head. How was I so foolish as to allow you to stay up so late?"

The darkness of the short summer night was paling, but the dancers, seemingly indefatigable, whirled on. Daisy danced another polonaise, a waltz with Kolya, was persuaded to eat a little more supper, to refuel on the champagne, and then the Princess was suddenly entreating her to dance her sword dance, as she had danced it sometimes for the children. "*Please*, dear Daisy, no one has seen it, you dance so beautifully, and it would give us all so much pleasure!" Somehow Daisy was upstairs and into her kilt and velvet jacket almost before Kolya had fetched her two swords from the hall and given the tune to the band. The Princess clapped her hands—"Behold, the Ecossaise!" In a moment there was Daisy Pelham, totally carried away, more by excitement than champagne, dancing the sword dance to a vast assembly of splendid and jewelled Russians, who clapped and cheered, until, more astonishingly still, as in a fantastic dream, she was singing, "My heart's in the Highlands, my heart is not here," to the thrilling chords of Kolya's guitar.

Her Scots mother was very much a part of her and she put feeling into her voice. But halfway through, she suddenly thought, What nonsense— my heart isn't in the Highlands, I don't even really like them much. I love Uncle Ian and I quite like Aunt Emmeline, but their house is as cold as the tomb and I don't care for fishing, I loathe going with the stalkers and almost dislike walking up grouse. Heather makes me sneeze. As for my heart, I don't know where it is, but it is certainly gloriously free of Richard. She suddenly saw him, very tiny, as through the wrong end of a telescope, walking down the oak avenue and smiling delightedly at his latest girlfriend, and good luck to him.

". . . a chasing the red deer,

"My heart's in the Highlands, my heart is not here," she concluded, and there was warm applause. She sat down beside Uncle Vassily for a breather. Nearby, Misha, with gleaming eyes, swung into a polka.

To stop at all had been a mistake. Suddenly, the champagne died within Daisy and she went out onto the terrace. Even in the darkness, her face flamed. What a donkey she had made of herself, what a downright blithering idiot! To sing, and above all to dance after something so magical as the Bolshoi ballet! She must have been perfectly mad. Or drunk—at this possibility Daisy's face flamed deeper still.

Kolya seemed to have abandoned his lady and was sitting at a small table on the terrace with his back towards Daisy, deep in conversation with a bony young man whose wild hair and high prominent cheekbones made him look like a caricature of a temperamental Slav. His white tie had taken leave of its senses and was dancing a tango under his left ear. "But the Zemstovs," Kolya was saying. "You must agree that the Zemstovs are in advance of anything of a like nature in Western Europe. A local self-governing agency, concerning itself with taxation, schools, roads, public health. And now of late every village has its school—"

"And do you know," the young man interrupted passionately, "how the literacy rate still stands, for all your schools? One million: one million can read from a people of a hundred and sixty-five million. Answer me that, Askold Andreivitch."

"Of course it is only a step on the way to parliamentary democracy,"

Kolya conceded. "But this great concession of Czar Alexander II's is a long step. Free medical care for everyone. Where else in Europe, or indeed America, will you find that?"

"Palliatives! Palliatives!" the young man cried. He thumped the little table until the glasses jumped.

"Palliatives are first aid, are better than no care," Kolya pointed out mildly. "Palliatives soothe and aid until real help comes. That, at least, you must grant. They tell me that our public health is ahead of that of the most advanced English cities."

"Why should we measure ourselves by any other people? Do not insult the poor of Russia, do not insult me, Askold Andreivitch, with talk of any such palliatives." His sweeping arms here came into play, and Kolya had only just time to snatch his champagne glass from before the flailing movement. His companion looked exactly the kind of hungry-hearted young man who would be incapable of harming a fly, but who would conceal a hand grenade in his opera hat and at the first chance fling it unhesitatingly into the royal box to explode at the feet of Czar Nicholas II and his innocent flock of muslin-clad grand duchesses.

Daisy leant silently against the house. The stars were fading, the dew would soon be falling. If Kolya failed to look up, she might perhaps steal past him and round the house to the servants' quarters and so safely up to bed.

"Do, now, Misha, dance with Miss Daisy. Please, for my sake," his stepmother pleaded, touching his arm as he swung past her.

"Kolya has been dancing with her. And plenty of others. You saw her dance a reel just now. She is a success. She is happy."

"The kindness must not always be left to Kolya. Go now, dearest Misha. I see her so sad on the terrace. After singing so charmingly, too. She rises to the occasion magnificently," the Princess added perceptively, "and then goes down like a rocket hissing damply into the sea."

Dancing with Daisy had been no part of Misha's plan for the evening: a month in and out of Moscow had cured him of a chance predilection, and damply hissing rockets had never been in his line. But he loved his stepmother, and recollected that it was, after all, her saint's day. He moved reluctantly, not even certain that Daisy would dance with him, and disinclined to give her the chance of a rebuff. He saw her walking rapidly further into the garden and away from the lights, and had a shrewd idea that this retreat had been prompted by his appearance on the terrace. Misha followed with long strides. He had promised to dance with her, and dance he would.

On the edge of the formal garden, two other figures flitted in the balmy air of the summer night. Once the Cossacks had leapt and whirled themselves offstage, the twins had allowed themselves to be put to bed with lamblike docility. But the moment Nyanya left them and stumped off

downstairs to participate in the fun and rush of the kitchen and its pur-
lieus, and to have her bite of supper, the twins had sprung out of bed and
proceeded, via the back stairs and with the aid of a good deal of hiding
and dodging, to the garden. From here, in their nightshirts, they could
gaze into the lighted house and easily conceal themselves from the couples who came to take the air or engage in more daring *amour* than was
yet permissable in the ballroom. The twins sustained themselves by an
occasional bold foray into the supper room, where, they hoped, the foot-
men would be too busy to know or care that they ought to be in bed. Well
filled with unusual delicacies such as stuffed quail and lobster, they were
now reducing themselves and each other to helpless giggles by imitating
the dancing and even the flirtations of their elders.

When Daisy thought that she caught sight of two leaping figures in
nightshirts on the edge of the grass below the terrace, she advanced rapidly nearer to make sure. The twins, seeing her silhouette against the
light, followed by the large shape of Misha, backed swiftly away, keeping
their gaze fixed upon Daisy, lest, failing to see them, she might take a
direction that would enable them to escape. They backed steadily further
into the darkness, coming into the small formal garden in whose centre a
low wellhead guarded an open well. Still moving backwards, Nikolai
came upon it, the low wall caught him behind the knees, and unable to
stop himself, he toppled backwards into the well.

Arkady set up a wild broken yelling, echoed, between plunges, by Nikolai in the well. Rushing into the darkness, the alarmed Daisy could see
little; she felt rather than saw Misha tearing past her.

"He's in the well! Save him! Save him!" Arkady continued to bawl, and
Nyanya, who had discovered their absence and come in search, joined in
with wild cries, calling on the saints, rocking herself back and forth and
holding her hands on high.

"Hold my legs!" Misha shouted to Nyanya and to Daisy. "The water is
not far down. Arkady! Stop yelling and run to the stables for all you are
worth and find the men. Tell them to bring ropes, a ladder, blankets.
Tread water, Nikolai—I will reach you in a moment."

For a few seconds Daisy had stood gasping and faint with terror at the
little boy's danger. She rallied swiftly. "We're not strong enough," she
shouted back at Misha. "*You* hold *my* legs." She flung herself down on the
wellhead's rim, felt Misha's firm grasp on her ankles, wriggled herself
over the edge.

Above, Nyanya's cries continued unabated. "Aie! Aie! Aie! Mother of
God! Mother of God! Aie! Aie! Aie!" she re-echoed, like a stuck gramophone needle.

Nikolai's dark head was invisible in the well's darkness. Where was
he? Could he have drowned already? "Let me go further," she besought
Misha, and felt the cold water rise over her hands as he lowered her
down. Groping wildly, she could feel nothing. Had the little boy gone
down for the last time? The black water came up to her elbows. Nothing

still. Above, she heard Misha give a desperate groan. "I will haul you up and go in myself," he called down. "I can dive deep and hold him up till help comes." Behind him the old woman's voice sounded fainter. "Aie! Aie! Nikolai, *babushka!* Aie! Aie!"

"Wait!" Daisy called up urgently. Suddenly Nikolai had come up, yelling faintly and forlornly, and as if for the last time. But it was long enough for Daisy to seize him by the wrist and to work with her other hand up to his shoulder, to hold up his gasping head. But then what? The water, for all the balminess of the night, had a deathly chill.

With her hands under his arms, she was able to haul him up a little way, but he slipped back; she feared to try again lest she let him slip altogether. He seemed in a bad way; great shudders ran through him. The blood had rushed to Daisy's head, she felt her strength failing; the reaction from the champagne and the excitement of the night were making her feel weak and stupid.

"Hang on, hold *on*," Misha called, and his voice echoed hollowly. "They are coming with the rope!" After which she made no further effort to haul Nikolai out but had to be contented with hanging on to the shivering little boy. But for how much longer? She felt her fingers go numb and powerless. Praying for strength, praying not to faint, she held on for what seemed an eternity.

A noise of voices drowned Nyanya's cries, there was a sound of running feet, other hands seized her ankles, and Misha on a rope was beside her and heaving Nikolai under one arm as the rope hauled them both up. At last Daisy could detach the boy's cold little hands and allow herself to be dragged to the wellhead and set upright. She sat, swaying, on its low wall, and finally collapsed, for safety, on the path.

Misha was holding Nikolai upside down and the water was coming out of him, but not fast enough. He righted him for the moment and Daisy roused herself to seize Nikolai round the waist and bend him over. He was still full of water. "Sick it up, Nikolai," she besought him, pressing his stomach.

"He could still drown," Misha warned. "Vomit, Nikolai!"

From the house the gay sounds of another mazurka floated out. The silhouette of the Princess appeared at the door to the terrace, looked into the darkness and disappeared again. "Sick it up, do, Nikolai darling," Daisy entreated. "Put your fingers down your throat and sick it up!" Nikolai obligingly complied, parting company with what seemed to be several gallons of well water, to sounds of admiration from the bystanders, who included the house steward, Anatoly, reft from his supervisory duties, who stood with a face full of consternation. Nikolai, at last, seemed safe.

"Do not disturb the Princess tonight with this tale," Misha told the men. "Say nothing of this. Anatoly, you will send Boris at once for the doctor. Let him in by the back way. And you, Nyanya, rub Nikolai with spirits, give him hot tea, watch him all night, never leave him. Send

Katinka for me if he is in distress." Frowning, he turned on Arkady, who had his hand between the blankets and was holding the cold hand of his brother. "Tomorrow morning," Misha informed the trembling twin, "you shall tell Papa of this."

A footman bore the now less waterlogged Nikolai to the house and Arkady, for once subdued, followed them meekly with his hand in Nyanya's. The helpers faded from the scene. Daisy sat on by the cold wellhead, unable to speak or move. Misha stood dripping beside her.

Indoors, where had taken him to replenish their drinks, Kolay was still held in the Ancient Mariner grip of his political friend. "You speak against violent action. Have you then forgotten the year of 1905? Do you remember how the Peasant Union in the south invaded and ransacked estates, how the police withdrew, how all the peasants rallied under the cry of "All the Land for the Peasants?" They established Soviets, initiated small republics, threatened to close all works. There was no electricity, no railways, all schools were closed. Have you never heard tell of the riots that took place everywhere, in the Baltic provinces, in Poland, where they openly displayed the White Eagle, in Siberia, amongst returning troops? In Sevastopol there was mutiny of the Fleet; also at Kronstadt. In Rostov also there was trouble, and in many parts of south Russia. And have you forgotten the seizing of the battleship *Potemkin*?"

"There was at least very little bloodshed." He was on the verge of leaving.

"No, Askold, do not leave me. This is no time for dancing. You have not heard my point. All this was repressed roughly—villages were burnt. People believed that nothing had come of it. But it had. The Duma was established. The Grand Duke Nicholas persuaded the Czar to establish it. Without violence, without a real fright administered to the government of the Czar, do you think that any of this would have happened?"

"Then this surely was enough," Kolya said, with a touch of impatience. "There is need for no more violence, only for holding to those reforms that were then won. All those first four Dumas did good work, our freedom increased, and so also did our prosperity. You must agree? Our industry became better organised, foreign capital flowed in, our democratic reforms were accepted in the West as an established fact. A few years ago the President of the Duma and leaders of several of the parties in it visited England. They were cordially received there. More capital flows in. More factories are opened. It is within all the existing framework that we can now legally and peaceably carry out reform." Impatiently, Kolya's foot on the marble floor was beating time with the music. And his poor friend, unless he were careful, would get himself into trouble with the Czar's police, such was his effervescence.

Melancholy had now taken the place of excitement in his political friend, and Kolya was at last able to escape. "We Menshiviks are but

theorists," Kolya heard him mourn to a luckless girl who had happened
to be passing and was now enlisted in the role of listener. "The Bolsheviks
may be only a handful, but they are disciplined and organised. They are
stronger. They are more ruthless," he added, his gentle countenance taking on a wistful look. "It is they who will win. We Menshiviks want to
ally the Russian Labour Movement with the reformers and socialists of
Europe who do not believe in the terrorism and the political conspiracies
of the Russian revolutionaries. But I ask myself how much longer I shall
ally my ideals with such temporising companions!"

The luckless girl, attempting to disengage her wrist, looked round wildly for Mamma.

"Well, Miss Pelham," Misha said, at length with curious formality, "if
you are strong enough, walk to the house and I will give you some brandy. You are certainly good for a crisis—good for danger." He took her by
the arm. "Come, we will go in quietly, by the back of the house."

And good for nothing else, I suppose, Daisy thought. She made an
inarticulate reply and was relieved to find that her legs were now perfectly prepared to carry her.

She is not such a Miss Prim after all, Misha thought. Steering her
carefully away from the lighted terrace, he ventured a joke. "I have
always wondered what Scotsmen wear under their kilts and now I know.
Frilly knickers." No response. He tried again. "When I am changed, will
you dance with me?"

She thanked him, but she did not seem pleased and said she really
could not dance another step. She put the glass of brandy back on the
table untasted. "I must go and see how Nikolai is doing."

Rubbing himself dry in his bedroom, Misha felt baffled. He was used to
women who shrieked in moments of danger, who fainted, who wept, who
clung to him and drooped on him and generally got underfoot, and had
long ago decided that that was their nature and it couldn't be helped. The
crisis once over, they almost invariably thanked God, danced for joy and
effected instant recovery. He understood Daisy's calmness, her cool, prag-
matic reaction to danger, because most of the English whom he had
encountered were like that. But for the most part they went on being cool,
continued in fact to make jokes throughout. Daisy, he decided, was a sad
wet blanket. With relief he heard the doctor's gig draw up in the stableyard; Boris for once had been quick.

Nyanya maintained her vigil at Nikolai's bedside. The little boy was
almost asleep, which did not prevent Misha from seizing him up in a
passionate embrace, making the sign of the cross over him and tucking
him tenderly in. Nyanya reported that the doctor had pronounced him
out of danger.

"Tomorrow, Arkady, you will tell Papa," Misha again warned the still
wide-awake twin.

Arkady glowered. "Why not Nikolai too?"

"Because he won't be well enough. Watch him, Nyanya, don't drop off."

"As if I should, Mihail Andreivitch. As if I should. Go you, now, and dance; leave them to sleep. You also, Mamzel. By the mercy of God he is safe. Leave him to sleep."

At the far end of the big bedroom Arkady lay in bed fuming, as Misha and Daisy left the room. His feelings towards his brother swung bewilderingly from love to hate and back again. While Nikolai was in the well, and even while he was being carried, chilled and white, into the house, Arkady had known that his twin was a part of his being, and an important part at that. But then had followed the concentration of fuss and attention, while he was allowed to creep into bed without a word from anyone. Then had followed, for Nikolai, hot tea from Katinka, brandy from Misha, rubbings with warm spirit by Nyanya, Daisy and Katinka combined, a soothing draft from the hastily summoned village doctor. From Nyanya had then followed a steady process of sweets, huggings, rocking in her arms, more sweets, and a succession of lullabies. There seemed to Arkady no good reason why he should miss all of this and receive the whole of Papa's wrath into the bargain.

Nikolai was the oldest; that was an inescapable fact. But why should he also *always* be the one to fall in?

Suddenly Arkady recalled that the getting out of bed and into the garden had been entirely his own idea. But for him Nikolai would never had gone near the well, nor fallen in, nor nearly been drowned. Thankfully, he felt the sense of injustice die within him and he fell instantly asleep.

Misha halted abruptly among the porcelain lions along the colonnade, perceiving that Daisy was in silent tears. He ached to get back to the dancing, but she had as good as saved his young brother's life, and he had at least the grace to listen. "What is wrong?" he asked kindly.

"It's because," Daisy spluttered, "I made such a fool of myself, dancing, singing, showing off . . . Good night. I just want to go to bed."

"Not a fool," Misha reassured her. He had been in the garden, at the time, in actual fact.

"Dancing! After the Bolshoi had danced!" Daisy continued, surprising herself by this outburst. To Misha, of all people!

"You did charmingly. And your voice is beautiful, and worthy to be heard. Why do you weep? People were delighted to hear you."

"But it's not them or what they would think. I don't care two straws for the Highlands, and I made a fool of myself, to myself. Acting a lie!"

All this was beyond Misha. "The conscience," he said. "Too tender. Or is it that you feel that the good pastor would disapprove?"

"Don't call him that!" Daisy cried furiously. "My father is a sensible, highly educated man of the world and he wouldn't care a rap either way. It is *I* who care. And my mother. She hates showing off, and especially she hates her children showing off."

Misha felt bereft of comment. This girl wouldn't dance, she wouldn't drink, she stood there tormenting herself with nonsense, forlorn and small in her crumpled blouse and absurd kilt. He said, a little lamely, "You were splendid to perform tonight, you were splendid at the well." But to his amazement this comment produced an increasingly stricken look, and even a few more slow tears.

Daisy was still staggering under the shock of the little boy's danger in the well, weak from the physical strain of hanging on to him, and generally dazed by the stress of the evening, her lowness increased by a post-champagne flatness and emptiness. Misha's large and physically overwhelming presence, his cheerful lack of care and concern over all that had happened, gave her a sense of distance, of a frightened alienation from her surroundings. Once again she found herself feeling sure that in coming to Russia, in attempting to live in this family at such close quarters, she had bitten off more than she could chew, more than she could swallow unchewed. An absurd childish longing for her mother shook her, for her father and her young sisters, for a home where she could forget loneliness and weep away her shock and be at once understood. Why do I always *think* I can manage everything perfectly all right? she wondered. Misha's unaccustomed kindness fell upon unlistening ears; all that came forth from Daisy was a muttered "I shall be all right in the morning" in tones that were the epitome of ungraciousness. All that she wanted him to do was to go right away and leave her in peace to recover her morale as best she might.

This, to the surprise of both of them, he seemed incapable of doing. Something, he felt, was needful, something to cheer this brave but tearful girl out of her sadness. But what? Words of praise had got nowhere. They stood a moment in silence, at odds with each other and unable to resolve their impasse; Daisy unable to brush past Misha to the shelter of her own room, Misha unable to go.

Impatience reasserted itself. He embraced Daisy warmly, felt a mild surprise at her lack of response, and retreated, vaguely dissatisfied both with himself and her. He moved with becoming slowness whilst still in sight, and with lightning speed when once round the corner.

Downstairs the dawn increasingly announced itself in a glow of daylight that poured in through the terrace doors. No one gave a thought to stopping the ball on that account. Misha, passing through the grand salon, found his father happy amongst his cronies, several of whom detained him with greetings and wry comments upon his wet hair. His father had been listening with pleasure to an anecdote that illustrated the boorishness and the arrogance of Kaiser Wilhelm II of Germany, to which he replied with a saga in dispraise of the Hapsburgs.

"And now more trouble will come in the Balkans," he was declaring. "That old Franz Josef! All the Hapsburgs are mad. His son Rudolph was mad. To shoot himself at Mayerling! The Empress Elizabeth, though a fine beauty, was also mad. And now this foolish Franz Ferdinand who married so foolishly is foolishly going amongst the Serbs on the anniversary of the battle of Kossova, of all moments the most wounding. Does he imagine that Slavs have no feelings, no pride? Is there no end to the stupidity of Hapsburg oppression over the Slavs?"

His audience assured him that there was none.

"And just at this dangerous time of the year they go to Serbia, when the harvest is nearly in and the roads not yet impassable with autumn mud. The most dangerous time of the year. The English know this well—where is Miss Daisy? She would tell you—and so at this season they go away and shoot grouse. Where *is* Miss Daisy?"

"I imagine she has gone to bed, Papa." As if it were that simple!

"Too early. You should have danced with her, Misha. She dances well, lightly . . . Fortunately, Sergei, our good Czar is a man of peace."

The music swung on, insistent, demanding, pushing out of mind all other concerns. Relieved now of all family burdens, Misha was at last able to enjoy himself again.

Upstairs in her bedroom, restless and overwrought, Daisy was unable to sleep. It is so idiotic to shudder about what might have happened when it hasn't happened, she assured herself, and yet I am as bad as I was after the wolves. But for all her sound reasoning, she continued to shudder. Dawn glowed through the curtains, but she trembled still with fear and even with something that was not fear. Floating through open windows, the waltzes thrummed on, the musicians sounding as tireless as the dancers.

In the intervals, the sound of laughter drifted up, carefree, untroubled. It was the laughter that lived in the moment, that soared high from danger, like the cork from a champagne bottle, the loud gusts of Misha's enjoyment clearly distinguishable among it. At times Kolya's calmer tones came up from the terrace; looking out, at seven o'clock, Daisy saw him and his partner, dancing an entranced *pas de deux* in the bright morning sunlight. Kolya was leaping as if the night had only just begun.

Daisy was awakened late next morning by a knock at her door and arose to find herself in the warm embrace of both Prince and Princess. "How brave you were!" they cried. "How quick! how clever! You saved our Nikolai, bad boy, you saved him from drowning! O my God, if you had not been there! What can we say? What can we do to thank you?"

Still exhausted, Daisy replied with that deprecating and needless honesty that is so disconcerting to the gracious. She had herself precipitated the accident, she told them, by running after the little boys in the darkness.

"But you held him up, you saved him," the Princess repeated, slightly chilled. "Misha and Kolya have left, alas, for all the summer now, we shall see them no more until it is autumn, they will be with the Czar, at St. Petersburg, and with their regiment. But before he left Misha told me all that had happened, all that you did. Ah, those twins, how they need the protection of the saints!"

"My wife and I owe a debt to your courage which nothing can ever repay."

"We will not embarrass you and perhaps hurt your feelings by a present, for something that is without price; but if ever there is anything that either of us can do—"

"Oh no!" Daisy cried, astonishing herself with yet another burst of tears, and casting herself into the arms of the Princess. "It is *you* that have been kind! It is *you* that have been generous! All, all the debt is on my side! All of it!" They have left for all the summer? she thought with a sudden pang.

By noon life had resumed its easy and pleasant routine. The hot days went by, the raspberries ripened, the children gorged themselves upon them, old Nyanya indefatigably continued making enough jam for an army. An army! The very word rasped along the nerves of some, probed the exposed feelings of others. But on the green lawns of Goodwood, in sunbaked châteaux along the Loire valley, on the polished floors of Viennese ballrooms, and far north where the flag of the Czar's royal yacht *Standart* fluttered over the gleaming waters of the Gulf of Finland, the Old World enjoyed its final blaze of summer.

Amelia, shortly to leave Russia, had been invited down in late June to Jevrenskaia for a farewell visit to Daisy. Bowling along the dusty road to return to the station, they chattered happily.

On the platform of the little local junction, at a loss for parting words, "Write" commanded Amelia, with a final amused wrinkling of her nose. "And mind your eye, and don't bloody well go all Borodin on me. Russia for the Russians, as far as I'm concerned, however dreamy St. Petersburg is with all those golden domes and sugarcake houses and that ripping great river."

"When will you be back? Come back soon, *do*, Amelia."

"Maybe not ever. My pa has scraped together a few pence again and put them all in steel. He says there's a war coming, and he has a nose for that kind of thing."

"But if it did, would you *leave* Igor and Constantine and all of them?"

"Like hell I would! I'd go like a scalded cat. I'd be out through Finland

and across the North Sea and walking down Bond Street before anyone
had time to load the first gun. We haven't had a proper war, not to call it
a war, for a hundred years, and I wouldn't miss it for chalks . . . Don't
look so glum. What did you expect? You know I've never set up to be
Grace Darling, nor yet Florence Nightingale. I've always been in love
with *me*."

"But, Amelia—"

The train drew out. Amelia sat down in her seat, with a final mocking
grimace.

Walking soberly away down the platform, Daisy felt this idol tottering
very slightly on its pedestal. Perhaps Amelia's wasn't the final word on
everything? Yet better to be as she was, candidly and breezily selfish,
then a sort of humbug goody-goody. Certainly Moscow would feel lonelier
without her jokey company. Amelia's rugged unscrupulous high spirits
made her fun to be with. For a long moment Daisy wished very much
that she too could be walking down Bond Street with Amelia, giggling
irresponsibly over imaginary purchases from Aspreys and hearing sharp
cheerful cockney voices. She longed to see her parents and her home
again, and if a war were to break out—

As if in answer to her mood, Ella appeared suddenly from nowhere. "I
love you very much indeed," she insisted, clasping Daisy firmly round
the waist and impressing a warm kiss into her waist. "Stay here always
with us and don't ever go away again. And also," Ella added, cashing in
on the moment, "please tell me again about the Little Princes in the tower, tonight. That is my favourite one of all your stories." A wild gleam lit
her eye. "Suppose they'd been Nikolai and Arkady! Squashed dead with
pillows!" Ella bit her lip with pleasure.

Such affection was engaging, but Daisy was all the same restless after
Amelia's departure. It had unsettled the easy routine of the days. As the
heat of the summer increased, an uneasy languor invaded Daisy's spirits.
Why did life, and the plains of Russia, seem so flat, so landlocked? She
longed now for a change, for release from these vast dusty plains, for the
freshness of home. The days were long and wholly child-oriented. She
reflected that she had only undertaken to come to the Dubelskys for six
months. Fond of them all as she had become, the six months were now up.
And if, as Amelia had prophesied, there really was to be a war, surely
home was the place to be? Richard was back in his place as merely an old
friend; she no longer even resented him. Her heart was whole. Or was it?
After a long, warm, restless night, she took a firm decision.

The Princess, appraised of Daisy's wish to return home, expressed horror. Almost with tears in her eyes, and speaking in tones of strong emotion, she begged Daisy to stay on. Or at least to stay on till after Christmas. Or at least, she entreated, to think over her decision for another day
or two. Did she realize how much the children loved her, how sad they
were at losing Mademoiselle, how pleased both she and her husband were
with her way with their children?

There was no resisting those shining eyes, the gracious persuasion, the eagerly clasped hands; Daisy promised to think it over. Secretly her mind was made up. She feared her own vulnerability; she would go while the going was good. She feared the whole Russian assault upon the emotions. They set up in her a kind of defensive counterfeeling. Anyone at home, she felt, to whom one gave a notice of leaving which they did not wish to hear, would simply have said, with a faint tightening of the lips, "Very well, my dear; and now, about your train tickets?" Pride had its uses, and so had indifference; either of them would have been likelier to persuade Daisy to stay. Moreover, her father's last letter had been urgent for her return home. She knew her own mind. It was settled. She would leave Jevrenskaia at the end of July.

Two days later, most unexpectedly, a letter arrived for her from Serena Doughty, due now in Russia. After the Hunt Ball, Daisy had had Serena to stay for a couple of nights at her home and had been told the troubles and difficulties of her home life in full measure. Daisy's sympathies had been fully engaged. Now some friends of her mother's at the St. Petersburg Embassy, Serena wrote, had asked her to stay; and her parents insisted that she accept.

> I hardly know the Hudsons and I hate the whole idea and I'm sure it's only because Mr. Hudson likes coming here to shoot, and I'm terrified of formal dinner-parties, and having to talk to foreigners, and the only thing that makes it *at all* bearable is that there's going to be a month in Moscow for some conference or something in October, so *do* stay on just till then, I do beg you. It would completely save my life to have you there to talk to about how awful it all is. Do *please*, Daisy, be there. You are always so kind to me and make me feel better. You always cheer me up. Even to feel you were in the same town would be a help.

It was emotional blackmail from the opposite direction, but Daisy felt more inclined to yield to this naked appeal. One might resist the happy Dubelskys, but one could not help feeling really sorry for Serena, with her impossibly demanding and dominating parents. It would hardly hurt her, Daisy, to stay on in Russia over October. And it would be nice to be able to concede, even if only temporarily, to the Princess. At the back of it all, a faint pleased excitement crept into her heart. Why be hesitant and fearful? Especially when there was such an undoubted good deed in the offing. Once one had taken on the Serenas of the world, there was no escaping from them.

"Yes, I am delighted," the Princess told her husband later, after they learned Daisy was staying. "I very much need her for the children . . . But . . . there *are* your sons. I could wish that Miss Pelham were not quite so pretty. Fortunately, she is still remarkably young and gauche for her age."

"Do not alarm yourself, my darling. Kolya is under the spell of Countess Katya, Katarina Mihailovna. For the time, she holds him fast, though he is not so green as to marry her. And as for Misha, he never addresses a word to Miss Daisy or so much as looks at her. She is far too unsophisticated to take the fancy of either. At heart, they are reasonable young men."

"No young man is reasonable, where his fancy is caught." The Princess continued to look doubtful. "Simplicity," she mused, "is not without its charms."

"But you like her? If that is so, the boys must look after themselves. If their fancy were to be caught, it would have been caught by now."

"Oh yes. I like her well enough. I am pleased to have her. And she is splendid with the children. Never have we had an English girl who played with them so well, with such zest, and fun, and taught them at the same time. With small eyes and a lumpy figure, she'd be a treasure. The children's English is very much better. And she is without vulgarity. How rare that is!" To herself, the Princess thought a little differently. Daisy is like a gun loaded with ammunition and never firing, she felt, but she decided that the thought behind this confused simile was not one to transfer to a young-hearted and attractive husband living under the same roof with its subject.

"Under all this music, and his fancy for the theatre," the Prince said, "there is a hard ground of good sense in Kolya, and of what is right and suitable. There is no need to alarm ourselves." But the Prince too had thoughts of his own. For Misha he had no fears. His eldest son was like his own father had been: a cheerful, resilient rascal who would get himself into every kind of trouble and emerge from it all to land on his feet. But Kolya was too like his mother, physically so like her that it sometimes pierced the Prince's heart to look at him. Loving her steadily and admiring her deeply, he was happy with his second wife; but Marie Sergeievna had been the passion of his life, as he had known she would be from the first moment he laid eyes on her, on a sparkling day in St. Petersburg a quarter of a century ago, spinning over the ice like a bird on the wing, with her bright downy hair and eyes like stars. She had been an enchanting impulsive romantic, whom his good fortune and her own had steered into his arms, and their marriage had been six years of continuous delight.

But he never felt quite certain of what her son Kolya was up to: he was, his father feared, also subject to romantic impulses. Romantic impulses were wonderful, and dangerous, and could land one in heaven, and just as easily land one in hell. Might the holy saints keep Kolya! Romance, what dynamite! Where was Kaiser Wilhelm's romantic notion of his own infallibility and his own glorious destiny leading Europe? And that very different person, the Czarina, with her increasing hold over her husband, where was her romantic faith in that ruffian of a monk leading Russia? The Prince shook his head. The thought that he had once been something of a romantic himself had faded from his mind.

Chapter 10

In central Russia, summer storms lashed the countryside night after night. It was as if the Four Horsemen were already at the gallop. Sleep was restless for all; and though in the mornings the sun flooded into Jevrenskaia, long before noon sudden gusts would prelude another storm: wind bent the poplars double, and the great grey Percheron farm horses tore round the meadows in alarm, their stalwart little foals straining to keep beside them. The wild flowers of later summer, so like the English ones—hawkweed, thistle, willow-herb, Good King Henry—were tossed and broken. Green rowan berries shook to the ground. Clouds of rose petals blew from the roses, scudding across the sandy paths which two peasant girls were raking, clutching their head scarves against the rising wind. All afternoon the thunder would crash and boom over the woods, with a noise like splitting wood; lightning would start fires, which the torrential rain would as quickly dowse. Farmers went long-faced; there seemed almost to be a purposeful malignity about the weather, and great acres of maize lay flattened.

At the end of June the Archduke Franz Ferdinand of Austria was assassinated by Gavril Princip at Sarajevo.

"This will indeed mean trouble," the Prince said. He sat on the steps in the brief hot sunlight, leaning moodily over hands clasped on the nob of his malacca cane.

"No more than usual, I fancy," the Princess told him. "But that poor old Emperor! His son makes away with himself, his wife is assassinated by some fanatic, and now this! His nephew and heir, and the poor wife as well. What a dreadful thing!"

"Let us hope it does not send him mad. He might do mad things to the Serbs." Worriedly, the Prince kept putting on his panama hat and taking it off again, gazing into its hatband as if there lay the solution to Europe's problems.

"Oh no! He's too fat. Fat people don't go mad," the Princess asserted comfortably. She swept away before her husband could think up instances of fat people who had.

In the cool of the shady side of the house the children were dancing with an unusual slow stateliness, to the sounds of a wheezy gramophone. Varya twirled alone, her arms waving gracefully; her dark heavy locks, crowned by a wide straw hat with roses on it, swung to the music. Arkady, absorbed, his feet stamping, his body bending, was circling round

Nyanya, pleased and plump and far too hot in her innumerable petticoats. A lizard skittered round the corner of a stone urn and stood transfixed, its throat working. There was a faint smell of hot cow and late
lime-blossom, a sound of bees hard at work.

A burst of loud laughter came from the distant stableyard. Suddenly
bored, Nikolai stopped dancing and stood on his head. Ella leant back in a
wicker chair, far away in some dream of her own, her round innocent
brow beaded with sweat. The Princess stood contemplating them all in
silence, feeling that strange and lulling sense of peace that comes from an
ordered and settled world. Her heart glowed with the richness of life;
unmoving, she basked in a sun of contentment. Nothing should disrupt or
spoil all this, *nothing*. After all, why should it? The Prince, following her
round the corner of the house, demanded to know what had happened to
his copy of *The Field*. One could forget even Franz Josef if one looked long
enough at photographs of clumber spaniels.

Confronted by Austria's might and force, the Serbs offered to make any
concession short of the loss of their dearly won independence. Russia
counselled the Emperor Franz Josef to act with moderation. Other voices,
and the old man's wrathful sorrow, spoke louder. "The Slavs were not
born to rule but to serve," Kaiser Wilhelm told Austria. "This they must
be taught . . . I stand behind you and am ready to draw the sword when
necessary." He declared he would tolerate interference from no other power. Encouraged, Franz Josef issued his impossible ultimatum to the Serbs.
Futile telegrams flashed hither and yon, while, in a trance of ignorance,
an intoxication of pride and of national self-esteem, Czar, Emperor and
Kaiser drove steadily towards their doom, taking with them the flower of
Europe's youth and manhood.

Men of all ages were reft from the harvest; armies mobilised and rolled
towards the frontiers. Clouds of dust from the feet of marching men lay
over the roads of Europe. She had known, more or less, a hundred years of
peace; now she seemed bent on committing suicide, as if her rulers were
inhabited by an irresistible death wish. The storms of wild weather, as if
their attention were rivetted by this extraordinary behaviour, suddenly
ceased. A blazing, unclouded August sun shone down.

The Dubelskys trembled for their sons, but educated opinion on the
whole in Russia was in favour of the war. Listening to the French conversations held around the dinner table, Daisy gathered that the German
economic hold on so many industries and positions in Russia was widely
resented. People in general seemed to rally to the watchwords of defence
of the Slavs and the Orthodox of the Balkans; these claims appealed to
everybody and touched a deep chord within them, a mystical dream of
gathering all Slavs under the mantle of Russia. Soon the German name
St. Petersburg was changed to the Russian Petrograd. The Princess read
out at breakfast a letter from her sister in that northern capital, reporting

that when the Czar had come out on to the balcony of the Winter Palace enormous crowds had cheered him, and nearly all of them had fallen on their knees. A wave of religious patriotism had taken over, and great crowds cheered the departing troops.

Meanwhile, Misha and Kolya, warned of mobilisation, appeared briefly at the estate, to collect their shotguns and say farewell. It seemed to Daisy as if thousands of people had gathered outside the house to greet them, bless them, weep for them as they went on their way. Even Nikolai and Arkady were affected, their white linen Sunday suits splashed with tears. Varya was sobbing without restraint; Ella prayed, her lips moving silently. Wailings, blessings, cheering rose from the assembled crowd. No one attempted to keep a stiff upper lip or indeed had ever heard of such a thing.

I almost wish that I *could* cry like that, felt Daisy, and not just feel miserable and awful, for them, and for all the other hundreds and hundreds of families. It's the first time I've ever felt glad not to have a brother. How splendid they both do look, one can't help thinking. Oh God, bring them back safe!

Kolya was serious, talking to everyone, patting backs, calling people Mother, shaking old men by the hand. Misha looked excited, bursting with life, as if he were bound for some particularly enjoyable party where all his friends would be met together, as if at any moment he might break into a Cossack dance or start singing at the pitch of his lungs.

Unbelievably, he's liking it! Daisy regarded his flushed face with amazement: could he be drunk at ten in the morning?

Catching her eye, he advanced, kissed her warmly, and advised her to practise her reels and entertain the local garrison—"They've never seen such Scottish dancing!" His eyes shone with elation. "Let bygones be bygones," he said grandly, pleased with this idiomatic phrase though not positive as to its meaning. He kissed her again with friendly warmth, seized up Nyanya and whirled her round him, and was away down the line of servants, embracing, laughing, planting loud kisses on all alike.

They must go, the Prince pointed out, if they were to catch the train. There was a sudden pause in the noise, a silence for prayer, for recollection, and then both young men were caught up in peasant arms and borne to the waiting carriage. In a moment they were gone, with a crack of the whip and a rumble of wheels on the sandy gravel. There was nothing but a cloud of dust, a noise of household sobbing, a scattering of sad peasants drifting away and the Prince and Princess with their arms about each other and their faces streaked with tears.

"Should we, later on, have a picnic?" Daisy suggested; but the children looked at her in horror at this facile suggestion.

"A picnic, on the very day that Misha and Kolya have left us, perhaps forever?" Varya cried. To the Russian soul, Daisy suddenly perceived, grief was a luxury of feeling to be tasted as deeply as joy.

"Today," said Ella, her firm little face setting in gravity, "is for prayer." All the same, an hour later, she and Nikolai were bowling their hoops down the drive with undiminished vigour.

The zest of life had gone, it seemed to Daisy. Rumours of battle floated back, but it all seemed very far away. Where exactly was the Vistula? Daisy wondered. She couldn't read the names in Cyrillic letters on the Russian atlas. She half expected a telegram calling her home, but none came.

"You can't leave us now, Daisy," the Princess pleaded, as if reading her thoughts. "The children love you very much and the seas are so dangerous."

Picnics were allowed to resume; they wandered in the damp autumn woods, picking mushrooms and bringing home great basketfuls to be sautéed in butter and eaten in a sauce made of sour cream. The deep and secret woods kept their peaceful beauty, smelling of damp moss and decaying trees, and the variety of the mushrooms, their different shapes and colours, fascinated Daisy. "Which do you like best, which are the most delicious?" the children clamoured. But even the mushrooms had somehow lost their taste.

From Moscow, where the Dubelskys returned in late September, long troop trains for the front left every day. Taking the children to see the departure of a young cousin, Daisy watched the troops grey with dust from their long marches, as they were packed into cattle cars. There were huge crowds on the platform of the Alexandrovski Station—the bearded fathers, the wives and mothers with their farewell gifts of flowers and cigarettes and cakes, the priests giving their blessings. There were tears, cries, hysteria, incense, laughter, faintings. Slowly the train departed into the twilight, groaningly, as if in complaint at its overloading, its whistle shrill and imperious. The huge crowd waited quite still and silently, craning their ears until the sounds of the singing men faded away. It seemed impossible that so much patriotism, such depth of feeling, could ever meet defeat and disintegration.

Yet the refusal to listen to real grievances remained. The Imperial Family had come to Moscow, and Daisy watched them walk in glittering splendour through the Kremlin to the Cathedral of the Assumption, for a solemn service of Mass where the Czar would pray for victory. Daisy was thrilled to see them, but somewhere along the way, an old peasant had tried to present a petition to the Czar. The peasant had been brushed aside, surrounded by armed men and arrested.

"What will happen to him?" Daisy asked nervously.

"Imprisonment. Hard labour probably. He knew the customary punishment," the Princess answered. "He should never have dared to interrupt the Emperor at a sacred moment like this, when his spirit is set on prayer." Like a fly, brushed off by an impatient hand, the old peasant disappeared.

Wild cheers greeted the news of Russian advances all along the line. The streets rang with the national anthem, were brilliant with flags. The

Princess waltzed both the little boys round the grand salon, now restored to all its preflood grandeur. On September 10 there was a gala performance at the theatre in Moscow in honour of the capture of Lemberg by the advanced Russian forces; never mind that the German armies were by now on the Marne and that the fate of Paris itself hung in the balance. The play was a Russian adaptation of Rostand's *l'Aiglon,* and at the end of it a telegram from Joffre at French headquarters was read out, announcing victory on all fronts. Its words were spoken by an angelic-faced girl, very young, with a touching vibrant voice; she was the daughter, Daisy learned, of the President of the French Chamber of Commerce. On hearing her news the orchestra struck up the *Marseillaise,* and from the gallery four hundred French reservists, who were leaving for France next day, took up the refrain, their voices ringing with pride and love. The audience was full of bearded men kissing each other; women smiled and wept at the same time.

All seemed to be victory and hope. From England Daisy's father reported just such another surge of patriotism: he rejoiced in its hope but doubted the endurance of such emotions. But in the shouting, laughing, crying Moscow theatre, Daisy felt no room for doubt. War *must* be glorious after all, she thought, if it could stir such a tempest of joyful pride and fellow-feeling.

Was it conceivable that those impossible militaristic Germans, for all their industrial might, could be utterly defeated, and that right could triumph, and that all could return again to the joys of peace and of family life? In the glow of Lemberg the defeat of Tannenberg faded, and for at least forty-eight hours even Uncle Georg ceased to grumble about the shortage of Havana cigars.

As autumn deepened, shreds of doubt crept into Moscow's crowded streets. Had that enormous Russian sacrifice in the northern marshes, which had saved Paris, gained no more than a breathing space? Life in Daisy's world continued much as ever. Theatres flourished, and smart gentlemen to whom fighting was really distasteful inserted themselves into jobs with the Red Cross. Uncle Sergei existed blissfully in a whirl of good causes. Vodka was still available on permit, except to the poor; in restaurants wine and spirits were poured from teapots instead of bottles, the lucky recipients making no demur. Brave men continued to depart in thousands for the Front, and the courageous Florence Farmborough, true to her name, completed her hospital training in Princess Golitzin's hospital, and departed for the Front. Nursing the patient, ungrumbling wounded men, this robust country girl from Buckinghamshire wrote in her diary that she had "never before seen a sick adult in bed." She would see all too many before she was through.

Daisy's job scarcely altered. Customary work went on, teachers arrived punctually, dancing classes were held, the same young limbs twirled and stamped to the music of the muzurka. But austerity curtailed at least some of the children's usual activities. It had become a point of honour not to hold parties. The Princess, absorbed in her war work, seemed to have less and less time for her children. She lived in a daze of energetic patriotism, always at the hospital, rising early, working late. Furred and beautiful, she would rush in to say goodnight, rush out again. "Beastly meeting, beastly hospital!" Arkady would cry. An inexplicable menace seemed to hang in the air, caused perhaps by the daily and terrible lists of casualties from the Prussian front.

Why do I stay? Daisy wondered. There is no need to be enslaved, just because the children need me and their mother charms me. I could be doing war work at home, and I'm totally cured of Richard, so why stay? The Prince, too, was away, recalled to the army and training recruits somewhere near the Urals. No stout and smiling figure arrived every night to say their prayers with the twins. He returned sometimes, thinner, less ebullient. "How is your Beatty?" he would ask Daisy, with a flash of his old laughter, but Daisy couldn't tell him. Letters from home came slowly, contained no news of the war. Perhaps it wasn't allowed. Then this came:

> Your mother and I are both very anxious that you should return. But for the moment, stay where you are. There have been a great many sinkings by German submarines. When these have been brought under control, I will arrange your passage. I can, I think, pay for it from London. After the winter . . .

People led a kind of suspended life. Everything was for tomorrow. Everything was to happen soon. After the war, the front door will be repainted. Uncle Sergei will have a new coat. After the war we shall be able to get Cadbury's chocolate again. And Lyle's Golden Syrup, in that green and golden tin. After the war there will be Huntley and Palmer's biscuits again. Don't you remember, Ella, they had that blue and red tin? Uncle Georg, stumping up the marble stairs, complained furiously that the supplies of Cooper's Oxford Marmalade had run out. After the war, there will be plenty. After the war, we will stay longer in the country, make a tennis court, plant more lilac trees. Every pleasure was distanced. Even Nikolai and Arkady suffered a dimunition of spirits. *After the war—*

Germany had decided to strike westward first, and neared Paris: at the earnest request of the hard-pressed Allies, Russia took the offensive against East Prussia. Successful at first, they had been driven from the terrible East Prussian marshes by the German General Hindenburg, with appalling losses in men and guns at his Tannenberg victory. But the Austrians, advancing into Russian Poland, were defeated, and by a right decision taken by Grand Duke Nicholas at a critical moment, were driven away back. The Poles, promised independence, fought sturdily on the Russian side; Hindenburg was driven from Warsaw. The Russian army crossed the Vistula under fire, and by October was reaching into Silesia.

But as hard fighting went on in Poland through November and December and the Russians were cheered by their successes under Ruzsky and Plehve, the fatal lack of support or supplies began to make itself felt. There were nothing like enough big guns. Man for man, the Russians felt themselves better fighters than the Austrians—but of what use were men without guns? The bodies piled up upon each other in the now steadily falling snow.

Once, Kolya returned on leave, followed a day later by Misha. Daisy had been away, taking Ella to stay with the old Princess. She minded missing the men, and the rejoicings that would have been held. Rejoicing with two Russian soldiers would have made her feel the least bit nearer being part of the Allied effort; insisting that Arkady cleaned his teeth didn't. Were they altered? Older? What had this terrible war done to them?

Both looked shabby, Varya reported. Misha's greatcoat was frayed round the bottom—Misha, of all people, to wear a frayed coat! "And Kolya looks very sad and thin, but Misha is exactly the same. He broke the stove in his room on purpose," she added.

"Broke the stove! How! Whatever for!"

But Varya was still child enough to volunteer a piece of dramatic information and then entirely lose interest. "He gave me a German helmet. Have you seen it? He gave it to *me*, not the boys. He says they can wait until next time."

Nikolai explained later. "Misha *shot* the stove. It made such a crash, you should have heard it! A pity you were away, Miss Pelham; you've never heard such a crash as it made. Why? Because it had written on it MADE IN GERMANY. So he shot it with his revolver and broke it. You should have seen how many pieces it broke into, but I'm afraid it's all cleared up now." It seemed that even Misha was not unchanged by the horrors and stresses of the battles.

But it was the sadness of Kolya and not the madness of Misha that Daisy longed to cheer. "Did Kolya play anything new?"

"Nothing new. Not anything much. Actually he hardly played the piano at all," Varya said. "Often we wanted him to and he wouldn't. He said he didn't *dare* play. But that must have been a tease. Why should he not dare, a brave soldier like him? Kolya has a medal, did you know? And, of course, Misha will have one soon. And after the war, Mamma says she will have a party, just especially for me. A real party, with dancing and music. After the war . . ."

Winter gathered itself, a hard white enemy, hungry to slay both friend and foe alike. Daisy dreaded to drive through the poorer quarters of Moscow, to see the beggars in the street, the raised beseeching hands, faint voices asking in the name of God, the look of long-endured hardship upon pale, pinched faces. After the war, she told herself, things *must* be made better, in this great rich land, full of food and fuel. The kopeks, falling sadly into the snow, seemed a miserable response. After the war . . .

There were fewer faces at the English Club, the young were all disappearing—all but George Bennett, who had but one lung. I should go, if I were you, he advised, while the going's good. I should miss you, but, after the war . . .

Waiting for her at the Dubelskys' house was a querulous letter from her mother. So many things were in short supply:

> Muriel is getting more and more unsatisfactory and I need you very much. Derek Parsons has been killed, and the eldest Brown boy, and the youngest one terribly wounded. It all seems so dreadful and this time last year we were all having such a happy Christmas, and this year one can't even get currants for the cake and puddings.

Outside, the wind howled sharply, vindictively. It is of no use to keep thinking of Misha and Kolya and a million others, out in it, trying to kill each other. Where now was Richard? Freckled Sam Orme? Toby, with his cheerful, tuneless songs? Rupert, who was such a beautiful dancer? Even the tiresome Wilson brothers seemed now able to be regretted. Why didn't any of her family write and tell her about *everybody,* not just snippets about a few?

One person at least was finding pleasure in the situation. Amelia wrote delightedly from Brighton, where she was learning to drive an ambulance.

> I enjoy myself like billy-oh! So long as nobody asks me to drag any wounded bods into it. At first I crashed the gears with a noise you could hear a mile off, but I'm getting smoother—now I only carry about twenty yards. All the boys, even the weediest and toothiest, look better in uniform, and I can't wait to get to France. Be good. Fondest love, A.

The letter took long to arrive, but its exhilaration communicated itself to Daisy and made even Christmas, spent in the melancholy discomfort of its being the wrong day, feel more cheerful.

Every part of the Empire, from Fiji to Canada, had joined Britain in the war, Mr. Pelham reported happily, and without prodding or pressure, spontaneously. This was a real slap in the eye for the radicals in Parliament who were always denouncing the Empire as unpopular and oppressive. Oh, that Misha were here to be told this! Daisy exulted: how would he laugh *this* away? The Americans, her father went on, were showing no signs of life, "but there are many good fellows over there, and they will talk down their Irish and see daylight in due course." The Irish in Ireland were volunteering in great numbers—bravo for them. There was a warmth of feeling that seemed to unite everyone, he told Daisy, and the only fear of the young men was that the war would be over before they could get to the Front.

Reading his letter, thinking of her father's kind, lined face bent over his desk, Daisy found even the desire to triumph over Misha die within her. All Allies were at one now.

Chapter 11

The spring, when it came, did not allay the anxieties of Mr. Pelham over Daisy's sea journey and the menace of the German submarine campaign. Impossible now, of course, to travel through France; this meant the long sea passage from Petrograd, through the Baltic and across the North Sea. I will write the very moment I consider it to be reasonably safe, Mr. Pelham promised.

> Your mother stood the winter remarkably well, thank God, and Virginia talks of training to be a V.A.D.; you know she has always been interested in nursing. Fred has volunteered and has gone; Broadbent is managing the garden alone, but I fear it's getting rather too much for him, specially as we've dug up the tennis court to grow additional vegetables. Hard luck on Virginia and Jenny, but it had to be. The price of hay and oats has leapt up but you'll be pleased to hear that Mouse is going well: Jenny hunted her at the last meet of the season.
>
> The Church is full every Sunday: peril has opened all our eyes to reality. Parochial things go on in a sort of muted way, but there have been some terrible losses in the village. People are so *good*. Young Watson was the latest. Not the farm Watsons, the ones who live beyond the mill. An only son. You see such a lot of real heartbreak. It's sometimes dreadful to be old and alive when so many young men are dying. I miss you, darling, very much. I wonder sometimes how we came to let you go to Russia, though I know you are doing a good work there, and with sons at the Front the Dubelskys must be so very glad to have you and I am sure you are a comfort to all the family. God keep you.

There were times when Daisy felt anything but a comfort. *Nothing is happening*, she felt, in a mood of melancholy self-absorption. I'm standing still and soon I'll be twenty-one, and my time of being *young* will be completely over. This is a crisis, a world crisis, and all I've done is learn better French and not nearly good enough Russian. Why am I not like

Florence, nursing the wounded at the Front? All this is safe, pointless, *futile*.

As Misha and Kolya knew, quite a lot was happening, if not to Daisy. Morale in the Russian Army was still high; Kolya wrote home happily about the undiminished courage of his men. As far as the river San the Ukrainian population had welcomed the Russian soldiers as liberators, he reported proudly, since most of the regiments on this front came from the Kiev area. But he did not report that in February 1915, the German forces, in some furious fighting, had driven the Russians back to Grodno, despite stubborn Russian resistance, fighting almost from tree to tree through the forest of Augustovo. At least the Duma had insisted on the provision of machine guns, but in other matters their equipment was hopelessly inadequate. There were still not nearly enough heavy guns, few shells with which to fire them. There were plenty of priests, but no adequate medical service, though the few doctors and nurses did their brave best.

Transport was chaotic and the food supply very erratic. These dire facts Kolya kept to himself. Misha's letters, like a schoolboy's, generally demanding that something should be sent to him, were very brief, and always ended by saying, Kolya will have told you all the news. He was very well, he added, and the last lot of Beluga caviare had arrived in prime condition. How about risking a couple of York hams?

How can he go on thinking that war is a picnic, or does he just pretend? I'm not too sure, Daisy reflected, with a dawning of shrewdness, that his spoilt darling attitude isn't at least partly an act. But if the Front, if the war in general, sets so open and natural a character as Misha acting, what can be really going on?

The Russian war effort was now concentrated upon the weaker of the Central Powers. Through the late winter and early spring Misha and Kolya with the Russian troops were slowly fighting their way through the Carpathian mountains. With lamentably small artillery support, and therefore with appallingly high casualties, the regiments stormed hill after hill, until by March they were triumphantly over the crest of the mountain, had a foothold in Hungary. Surely now, thought Misha, ever optimistic, Austria must crumble, and Germany of necessity capitulate without her. Leaning on a tree, at the day's weary end, he thought contentedly of the sweets of Buda Pesth, through whose streets, he hoped, his troops would shortly ride in triumph. He had been there in peacetime, and happily contemplated looking up old friends. Erstwhile enemies, they could soon be won round to having a good party again. But the more thoughtful Kolya wondered how much longer his men could possibly endure such conditions, could tackle their enemies at such a disadvantage in supply and equipment. They were not fools: how long would they stand the inhuman callousness of those responsible for such deprivation? Could

not the Czar himself, fully informed, see that there were at least enough
rifles to go round, enough greatcoats, enough food for the men fighting on
these icy heights? It's like Tsushima over again, Kolya thought, magnificent courage, obsolete ships, bitter defeat. A shudder of apprehension ran
through him. He felt empty and heartstricken by the loss of so many of
his men, of beloved jovial friends. What were cavalry doing in the mountains, where the need was for mules and artillery?

Misha, joining him where he sat by a fire in a woodman's hut, said
nothing, but put an arm round his shoulders.

"It is not for myself I shiver, but for Russia. Why are there no more
guns?" Kolya demanded of him. "It is eight months since the war
began."

"Napoleon was triumphant," Misha told him, "for a while. Have you
forgotten that Moscow itself was evacuated? Was burnt? And here we
stand, on Hungarian soil, scorching the pants off Franz Josef. Here,
drink up. There is no lasting defeat for a Russian army."

I don't believe Misha even sees the dead bodies piled up, his brother
thought, frozen stiff in the attitude of death, bundled into carts like so
much rubbish, as little regarded as worn-out cattle. So best. Such as he
win wars. He regarded his rumpled and half-drunk brother with love. His
presence in the same regiment did at least make the war tolerable. But
why could Kolya himself feel no exhilaration in the winning of these
Carpathian heights for which they had fought so hard?

In Moscow the Grand Duchess Sergei, with her usual practical thor-
oughness, had gathered great quantities of medical supplies for despatch
to the Western Front, where they were desperately needed. But harrassed
railway officials had despatched the whole lot to the far southeast, where
nothing was happening and where no one knew what on earth to do with
them. Learning this, the Grand Duchess's Anglo-German blood came to
the boil. Saint or no, she made a right royal row. *What* had happened to
these twenty-five wagonloads? *Who* was to blame? In vain was it explained to her that the freight clerk concerned was terribly worried about
his sick wife, that another who had signed the despatch was mourning
the death of his mother. Hundreds of lives were involved, she stormed,
the recovery or death of thousands of brave men. The stationmaster
stared at her blankly. What a carry-on, and in a German accent as well!
These aristocrats seemed to have no notion of how a man was doing his
best, in particularly trying circumstances too, with all his best men called
to the Front.

Prince Andrei, hearing this tale through his cousin, was consumed
with admiration for the Grand Duchess's efforts and her anger. If she
had but stayed in the world, he sighed, what might have been accomplished by her rank and her organising ability! But in his heart he wished
desperately that she would bring all her guns to bear, all her spiritual

powers, all her skill at persuasion, on the task of separating her younger sister from the influence of the sinister and rascally priest who was threatening to dominate not only her life, and the life of the Czar, but all of Russia, in this hour of her terrible danger.

In May of 1915, the Germans mounted a strong offensive under General Mackensen. It was supported by overwhelming barrages of artillery against which the Russians had no reply, since they still had few guns and almost no shells.

To Kolya it had seemed that the German spring offensive broke with appalling suddenness—the Austrian civilian population streaming for cover in their battered houses while the great German guns gathered thunder. At night the sky was filled with their rockets and mortars, and the countryside with the lurid light of the fires they had kindled. At Gorlitse the Red Cross had been ordered to abandon their wounded, and all along the road by which the Russian cavalry retreated there were men with outstretched arms praying the soldiers to remain, to take them up with them on their horses, men crawling beside them as they cantered past, imploring them, cursing them. Other men, exhausted, lay flat in the mud roads that were a chaos of retreating men in vehicles. Munition carriages and artillery took up the full space of the road, crowding out the luckless wounded who fought to accompany them. To Kolya it was a nightmare of heartbreak and disregard.

There was a kind of bewildered disbelief in the faces gazing up at him. At the small railway stations the luckier among the wounded were lain in rows all along the rough wooden platforms, waiting for trains that would perhaps never come. "Oh God," they would cry, "why is this happening to *me?*" Why should they, their own unique, valuable selves, lie thus deserted and in pain, while their luckier fellows marched by to safety? Amongst the cries and the curses Kolya was moved to hear the voice of a single soldier singing the ancient Russian funeral chant above the body of a dead comrade, *Vachnaya Pamyat* ("Eternal Memory").

The Third Army was decimated. At morning, in woods full of singing birds, the shouts of men saddling their horses mingled in Kolya's ears with the hiss of falling shrapnel. Dark clouds of smoke covered the sunlit morning air. As dusk came on, the nightingales set up their pure, clear song, ringing out above the groans of the wounded and the creaking of the wooden carts along the dust-filled roads. Always the orders came for retreat, further retreat, continued retreat.

Storks were now nesting on top of the whitewashed thatched cottages and from the deep woods the smell of wild lilies of the valley came wafting on a warm evening breeze. Waking at dawn in encampments in the sandy forest and hearing the innumerable birds begin their chorus, Kolya was able to believe for a moment that this was the real world and that the nightmare scenes of the previous day were the fantasy.

Sometimes their horses floundered through deep sand, retreating, always retreating. Yet it was a retreat that had lost nothing of its stubborn quality: whenever able to engage the German soldiers with the bayonet the Russians drove them back.

The price of such counterattacks was a terrible one. With a stony face Kolya stood by the common grave and saw the hundreds of sheeted bodies, heard the unceasing cries of wounded men racked by pain or mutilation: Oh God, is it possible that *I* am left to die? By the end of May, the Russians had been forced back across the silver windings of the river San and the Germans had crossed it after them, renewing their advance. There were no Russian bullets to stop them, and scarcely a shell for the guns.

It was June now, the wild strawberries ripening in the woods, fields of corn turning slowly to gold under the midsummer sun and coloured by the scarlet of poppies and the deep-sea blue of the cornflowers. Still more wounded men creaked by in their carts along the dark roads at night and the retreat continued. Herds of cattle were driven eastward, churning the dusty roads and disappearing into the clouds of their passag' Lemberg had fallen, and behind the armies rose the smoke of hay and corn stores set alight, their smoke darkening the summer sky.

Soldiers of the 62nd Division, using only the butts of their rifles, held up the Germans for days at Yaroslav. Of heroism there was no lack, only of the means to fight effectively. By the end of June the total Russian war losses amounted to 3,800,000 men.

Leaving the road one hot sweet evening in early July, Kolya heard singing. Riding at their quick trot, a *sotnya* (hundred) of Cossacks were pounding down the forest track. Faces, horses, accoutrements: all were covered in the thick dust of passage. Yet every man had his lance fixed, his throat wide in song. A single rich voice sang the verses, and then the refrain would burst from a hundred throats, wholeheartedly, a musical thunder. Hearing them, Kolya felt his faith renewed in the indestructibility of his people.

By July, a large consignment of Japanese cartridges had reached the Russian Army, and hopes rose high. Now at last, the Germans would be met shot for shot. They proved unusable in Russian rifles. The soldiers, undiscouraged, hewed themselves clubs from the forest trees and fought on.

An endless stream of refugees now crowded the roads, travelling by day and night. Sometimes at noon, they slept under hedges before rising to plod doggedly eastward, their carts piled high with household goods, along the dusty roads under the August sun. Behind them their homesteads burned, and all the crops of a rich area. Carts creaked, children cried pitifully, sometimes an exhausted horse lay down and died across the road, or a gun carriage ran over a stumbled old man. Always the cry went up, "My God, what will become of me?" A curly-haired young soldier, with the look of a student, caught at Kolya's stirrup. "Autocracy has us by the throat," he cried through parched lips, "and we are being slowly strangled. Why do you ride by as if none of this mattered?" On the Russian frontier the Cossacks had seized young Polish boys for the war; they

rode, tearstained and bewildered, behind their captors. Kolya was aware
of all the terrible suffering, but in a numb way, as if some power within
him refused to accept its reality.

At the end of the day he came upon Misha, washing the dust of the day
from his face and hair in a tin basin. With his yellow locks darkened by
the water, he emerged as Kolya came up. His servant had just told him a
funny story and Misha threw back his head and roared with laughter, a
true belly roar, as if such a thing as war, death and sickness had never
been invented. Misha and the Cossacks, Kolya thought, they are as one.

Becoming serious, Misha told him that the woods all round them were
known to be full of Uhlans, German cavalry; and having seen what they
had done to the local peasants, he was more than ever anxious to go out
after them. But always the orders came to retreat, and again retreat. Did
the higher command know what it was at? Kolya wondered. This was no
rout, yet it could hardly be part of a planned retreat—to bring the war
into Russia proper and involve the destruction of food supplies in a whole
rich countryside. But of course, he reflected, one couldn't see the whole
picture.

Less and less could he discuss matters with his brother. Misha had
built himself in, into a kind of devil-may-care world in which serious
thought was to be eschewed; and in this perhaps he was right. All
thoughts, all energies, should be confined to the matter in hand.

"Nothing can defeat them! Nothing! Nothing!" the Princess cried
when she heard of the fight in the woods of Yaroslav. Her eyes flashed
fire; she looked as if she might at any moment kindle the hair of Ella,
who sat on her lap. Daisy could not but be moved by such a rush of soul to
the eyes. But at the same time, Daisy saw, the Princess clutched Ella
suffocatingly close, as if afraid to let her out of her arms.

By August 22, the whole of Russian Poland was lost. Yet for all the
retreats and the slaughter of their finest officers and men, a splendid
fighting spirit endured, and the defence was still stubborn. Defeat was to
arrive from elsewhere. And winter, at least, put a stop to active campaigning.

The War Minister, Sukhomlinov, did nothing to remedy the now notorious lack of munitions, even refusing offers of supply from private factories. And now, twice saving the life of the Czarevitch Alexis, the menacing figure of Grigory Yefimovitch Rasputin stalked slowly into absolute power, and the agony of Russia, as in a Greek tragedy on an
undreamed-of scale, moved inexorably to its climax.

Summer had brought the Dubelskys as usual back to Jevrenskaia, but
the Princess, full as ever of restless energy and purpose, was soon preparing her own return to Moscow. In case Andrei should return and need me,
she told Daisy, bending over her bureau in the blue salon and locking and

unlocking its innumerable little drawers. "You won't, you won't think of leaving the children?"

Daisy reassured her. "I must anyway wait till I hear from Father, and he seems to feel that the submarine menace is still too great. It doesn't seem certain I could even get a passage now, and there would be sure to be great delays, so would you like me to go on with the children's routine as usual?"

"Routine," the Princess echoed abstractedly, continuing to rummage through her little drawers and speaking the word with a slight shadow of disdain. "Routine, yes, I suppose so. Here are the children's passports, if ever—but that's unthinkable."

The July sun shone hotly outside; the shutters made a coolness in the beautiful room. Outside came the sounds of Arkady, being chased by an indignant Ella through the stone pots of hydrangeas along the terrace. A smell of raspberry jam-making floated in on the hot air. Unthinkable indeed that anything should disturb this lavish peace. But that nearly four million Russians were dead in less than a year was unthinkable too. The wailing of the bereaved was a common sound now in every village. Old men and old women moved through their tasks bowed by an unassailable grief; a grief before which even priestly consolation seemed to trickle down into the warm dust. Terrible tales had spread round. And why had there been no guns, no shells to counter the dreadful destruction of the German barrage? The summer wore on, rumours swirling over the countryside like summer dust.

At least, for the wounded, the Zemstvo Union of the Red Cross did much, even organising food and transport. The efforts of women like Princess Andrei Dubelsky seemed to bear fruit; a kind of order prevailed in the hospitals where the thousands of wounded men were nursed. On June 25, in the summer of 1915, the hated Sukhomlinov was at last dismissed from office, and the popular delight was very great. All had been disgusted at his neglecting to supply an army that was still Russia's pride and delight. The Progressive Bloc in the Duma put forward a detailed and reasonable programme of reforms, and asked for a uniform Ministry which would hold the confidence of the Duma.

Fitful gleams of light continued. But in July of 1915 the Czar had spent two months with his wife at Tsarkoe Selo and the dark shadow moved a step nearer. She persuaded her husband to remove the Grand Duke Nicholas from his post as Commander in Chief, which he had occupied with some distinction at a critical time, continuing to command strong popular support. On August 24, the ministers were summoned and were told that the Czar himself would take command in the field. The Empress had persuaded him that he must not let himself be overshadowed by his uncle.

There was consternation. Everyone in authority with any influence tried to dissuade Nicholas from such a course, but against his adored and dominating wife they were powerless. During his absence at the Front, the Czarina, and hence Rasputin, came to enjoy absolute power. She had succeeded in persuading her husband that he had not limited his powers by his October 30 manifesto in the revolutionary year of 1905; and he delegated those powers to her.

"That man!" the Princess exclaimed to her husband in the privacy of their bedroom. "Oh God! That man! Vile! Drunken! False to his vows! And a monstrous seducer of women and young girls! How can she trust him? Make almost an intimate of him? Believe nothing of the truth about him?"

The Prince shook his head wearily. It was a mystery past his comprehension. More mysterious still that the Czar himself should tolerate this strange magnetic man who strode through the Imperial palaces as though he owned them, coming and going at will where few could obtain so much as a brief audience.

He laid an arm along his wife's shoulders, burying his worried face in her soft hair. For now, the spark had gone out of him. "We can only pray," he murmured, "that the Empress's eyes should be opened to know that monk as he is."

Rasputin regarded the Duma, and the Minister Gurhkov in particular, with peculiar animosity, since this minister had exposed some of Rasputin's more unsavoury activities before the war. Rasputin also violently opposed any lessening of the autocracy: if the Czar were obliged to listen to constitutional advice, the first stipulation of his advisors would be for the removal of Rasputin. He rapidly induced the Czarina to get rid of liberal ministers. On September 16 the Duma was prorogued. The Czar declined to see any delegates. Gradually, all the hopeful or useful characters in Church and State who dared to argue in any way with Rasputin's arbitrary rule were dismissed by the Czar, or in his name. All slowly became chaos. The vital Minister of Agriculture had swiftly been dismissed; and Samarin, Procurator of the Holy Synod, soon followed him. With a sharp twist of the knife in the wound, General Kitchener, sent from Britain to help to organise the production and supply of Russian munitions, was drowned off the Orkney Islands, going down in an evening of storm in the torpedoed cruiser *Hampshire.*

Rasputin continued in triumph, as if he had conjured up the torpedo and the storm himself. He interfered in every department—finance, food supply, movements at the Front. He demanded that plans of operations be sent to him in advance, dictated messages to the Kings of Greece and Serbia. In February of 1916 he appointed a man named Sturmer, one of his stooges, and no more than a court official, to be Prime Minister.

What next? the Prince demanded of his wife, on a rare visit to Moscow. His eyes glittered, as if with fever. He could hardly believe the deadly events happening to Russia. All was outside the compass of his comfortable imagination.

The next blow was not slow to fall. In a curious, fey, and unseeing mixture of religious fervour, fear for her son, and refusal to hear anything she did not want to hear, the infatuated Czarina on April 2 dismissed the efficient Polivanov, whom she suspected of liberalism because of his close cooperation with the public in the work of the Munitions Committee. Afraid where no fear was, she was blind to the real and dreadful perils of the situation. Affectionate, loving, devout, obstinate, silly, she went on determinedly cutting off every branch on which the Imperial Family sat, for fear lest it might infect the whole grand tree.

Against this terrible tide the brave and the efficient continued to strive. Behind the front line the waiting Russian soldiers built themselves an altar of ice in the open air, because the small wooden chapels would not hold them. Laboriously they erected a great cross of ice, which stood for months unmelted in the bitter air. As much as was possible they celebrated Easter, praying and worshipping and calling *Khristos voskres— Voystinu Voskrece* to one another across the frozen ground. They knelt in the snow, when Mass was celebrated, and still prayed for the Imperial Family and sang "God Save the Czar" as lustily as ever.

Amongst the officers the Siberian monk was now openly abused. "Rasputin by name and *rasputnie* (licentious) by nature!" they said, and loudly condemned him to perdition. In the March and April offensive around Lake Naroch the Russian Army met with great initial success. At home the Union of Cities as well as the Union of Zemstovs continued to do good work in providing the army with a network of hospitals and factories, thus staving off the inevitable collapse. But, because these organisations were honeycombed by the ever dreaded liberalism, the government of the Czarina did its best to hamper and curtail these helpful activities. The Czar was unable to take such public organisations into his confidence, owing to the Czarina's obsessive ambition to hand down the autocracy unimpaired to her son. The Czar's loyalty to his allies was unshaken, but he failed to harness the deep loyalty of his own people—the classic example of a good man trapped in a situation he was too weak to handle.

In July the Czarina had Sazonov dismissed because he had worked out a detailed scheme for the autonomy of Poland. Beloved Alexis must not inherit a diminished empire. Foreign affairs were now entrusted nominally to Sturmer, so that these also came wholly under the control of Rasputin. England and France were now making feverish efforts to arm the indomitable Russian soldiers. But Rasputin remained as he always had been—bitterly opposed to the war.

"Have you heard the story that's going round?" the visiting Sonya Dokansky asked Daisy. "It's going all round the country. A general leaving after an audience finds the Czarevitch crying in the corridor of the Winter Palace.

" 'What is wrong?'

" 'When the Russians are beaten, Papa cries. When the Germans are beaten, Mama cries. When am *I* to cry?' Did you hear that the people are referring to her now as 'the German woman'?"

"Don't!" the Princess cried. "Don't! Don't! *Don't!* Don't, Sonya, *repeat* such tales. Think what harm they must do!"

"My dear! You are out of the world down here! That story's gone the round everywhere. You hear workers and peasants and everyone repeating it!"

"They should never have learnt it. Oh, the folly of repeating such tales, inventing them, as this of course is invented by malicious tongues. How can they not do harm? How can anyone be so cruel to the soldiers fighting for us all?"

In June and July on the Southwest Front, the Russian Army, under General Brusilov, broke the Austrian line. Hundreds of Austria's Slav troops, including many of the Czechs, came over to the Russian side. Once again, this time in summer weather, the Russian troops took hill after hill, storming through the Carpathians, this time from the eastern side. But the Lake Naroch effort ended, with heavy losses, and the Carpathian list of casualties seemed to have no end. Here Kolya was missing for several days, finally staggering back late one evening to rejoin his troop. He was wounded in the leg, exhausted and nearly starving; he clutched the stirrup of his foundered horse, his face pale as paper. Misha was so relieved to see him that he sepnt the first ten minutes scolding him up hill and down dale, like a mother with a too adventurous child.

For two months Kolya was in hospital, before being sent home to convalesce for three weeks. Everyone came and wept over him, and tempted him with enough goodies to feed a battalion. His pallor remained, he spent the first few days in the silent abstraction of extreme spiritual exhaustion, trying in vain to eat the food with which he was lovingly pressed. His soulful eyes seemed to be fixed upon some scene he could not bear to see, yet from which he was unable to withdraw his gaze.

"Leave him," the Princess told the twins. "He is very tired."

"But we want him to do things!"

"Why won't he ride? Why won't he play? He says his leg is better."

"Leave him. He will do these things again. One day."

At the end of August 1916, Romania came in on the Allied side. Her men were so untrained that to the Russian soldier they seemed more liability than asset. Despite their enormous losses, Russian courage and hope were still high. In Germany, Hindenburg admitted that what he most feared in 1917 was another Russian offensive—"one of our chief dangers."

Chapter 12

Kolya had become very thin. Though he had recovered from his wound, his dark eyes blazed in a face older and leaner; they held a look more wary, less dreaming. But he seemed more serene than of late. Once again he could lose himself in music: the sound of it floated out all day over the grass of Jevrenskaia (grass which Daisy had mentally decided that one couldn't really call a lawn), over the climbing roses and the sandy paths, the great blue blooms of the hydrangeas in their stone pots and the marble statues hot to the touch in the summer sun; even over the lime-tree avenue in full flower, alive with the hum of bees and intoxicating in the sweetness of its smell. During his three weeks of convalescence, Kolya slowly became less thin, the drawn lines of his face became less deep. He was stronger, did not so soon tire. He would drive them all out into the woods in the wagonette, to picnic in their mossy stillness or to fish by the slow river. Every evening the children's clear voices rose round him at the piano. He had started to read again, even expressed a wish to buy a motor and take his family for longer expeditions. He was quiet enough, but seemed to have lost his earlier silence, though he refused entirely to talk about the war. Like a child unhappy at boarding school, he would answer no questions, as if obliged to cut himself off from all that side of life.

But one evening when the children were in bed and the Princess closeted in a domestic conference with Nyanya, Kolya began in low-voiced fervour to tell Daisy about his hopes for Russia after the war was won. Things must be different now that under the strains of war, the inefficiency and corruption of its government had been made clear for all to see, so that the demands for constitutional government must now be nearly universal. Out of all the horrors of the war would come a unanimous feeling for reform, for an *agreed* reform. It could be brought about without violence, without bloodshed, now that people were ready for it. No great revolution, no sudden upheaval, so that the framework and foundations of life were removed and simple people left bewildered and afraid—but a steady, irresistible process of root and branch reform. He would have nothing to do with those who demanded violent action. What harm revolutionary violence had done to Russia! Only increasing the vigilance of the secret police, setting Russian against Russian, settling nothing, improving nothing. His arms, his whole active body, as he paced the terrace in the failing light, emphasised the folly and the wickedness of revolutionary violence. But through the appalling miseries, the unbelievable suffering and universal sorrows of the war, the revelation of a better and more just way of life must surely come.

"I and my friends, we used only to talk, but now we will do. This war has been the spur we needed." He turned on Daisy the extreme direct clarity of his gaze, a gaze that had some strange luminous quality about it.

Daisy was silent, her eyes fixed on his face. No one else, thought Daisy, no one but Russians could contrive that sudden rush of soul to the eyes. The effect they had was remarkable.

"Papa and Mamma will hear of no change. Nor need their lives be greatly changed. It is not such as Papa and Mamma who oppress the poor, it is those who are corrupt, ambitious, greedy for power or wealth who deny the people their just rights. But you"—he went on, taking Daisy's hand and looking deeply into her eyes as if to search her soul—"but you *do* understand. You are young and you see as I do."

The evening sun's mellow rays shone on the terrace, everything was hushed with dusk, the scent of the limes came across in waves of over-powering sweetness. The air breathed romance.

He is in love with something that is not me, Daisy thought. Not even with some other person, but with an idea, a dream. I am just a human hand to hold while he expounds it. All the same, he must be a little fond of me or he wouldn't talk about something so dear to him. He doesn't realise how terribly attractive he is, how easily he draws love out of one. Her hand trembled in his, her lips parted in eagerness.

Daisy's head had become a thought more level since the days when she had so easily persuaded herself that Richard Kettle loved her, but none of this prevented her from being carried away by Kolya's words and his nearness, from leaning forward and listening to him, her lips parted in eagerness.

So! Vassily, the stallion man, passing the end of the house with a cap-ful of wild strawberries for the young woman who worked in the scullery, paused briefly to look upon Kolya and Daisy with approval. It was time, in his opinion, that both young Princes were put out to stud. Two such fine young men! What did such as they want with fighting the Germans? A year was quite long enough to prove their mettle, they should settle now, and breed. Long before their age, their father had married and had sons. He paused, hoping not to miss the embrace.

No embrace ensued, not even a kiss. Vassily sighed. He did not care to linger too long. Prince Kolya was not as fierce as Prince Misha, if crossed, but Vassily had no wish to expose himself to the cool peremptory tones of any young princeling interrupted in a love passage. These days young men seemed not to want to settle. They roamed, ranging the steppes and mounting the wild mares who galloped there, wasting their precious seed upon such kicking and biting monsters. Shaking his head, Vassily con-tinued on his errand.

Suddenly alert, as if he had felt the presence of the hopeful Vassily, Kolya became aware of Daisy as a lovely and touchingly sympathetic girl, and realised that he was holding her hand and gazing searchingly into her eyes. He kissed her hand and let it go.

To cover a mutual wave of feeling and a certain alarming shyness that she felt at its intensity, Daisy asked him what Misha thought about such things.

"Misha! He doesn't think. He lives. He lives from day to day; in time of war perhaps that is best. He will think hard enough when the task is done. He thinks now only of the matter at hand; when he has thought, he acts. Misha is a natural soldier. Some of the war, I think, he enjoys. To survive, one must be as he is."

"Must one?"

"One must, I think. In a less vivid way than Misha, I can be like that also, living only for the day, rejoicing at the end of it still to be alive, to be whole. But in hospital I had much time to listen and much time to think."

"And you thought?"

"Ideas not always pleasant would float in my mind. Of the mistakes, of the confusions. Of the waste of life. Of the fearful wounds endured by peasant boys who had had almost no life at all, boys scarcely grown up. But present always also was the feeling, the *certainty*, that Russia would live."

Daisy strove for calm. Her heart was suddenly racing, her voice refusing to function. To switch one's mind to oneself might be a good device. "Though . . . though . . . I love my country, I don't believe I feel as you do, with such a deep feeling, such a religious feeling really."

"Yes," Kolya admitted soberly, "with me it is like that." He was suddenly acutely aware that his emotion, mustered in the cause of Russia, had transferred itself to the trembling figure who sat beside him. His recovery of feeling over the last few weeks had led up to this. For all her awkward corners, there was a powerful sweetness about Daisy that had wrought upon Kolya's warworn heart. What a time, what a place, what problems! What huge differences in thought and feeling barred him from this wide-eyed girl, who, very evidently, felt as he did. And how little did such considerations matter, straws in the torrent that now, to his astonishment, swept over him. "Daisy," he began, "I . . . we . . . if it were not the middle of the war, when all is so uncertain—"

Up in her bedroom above the terrace, hearing familiar voices, the Princess had glanced out, and seeing what was toward, impatiently rattled the silver-topped bottles on her dressing table, startling Daisy out of her trance. I must go down, the Princess thought, gently smoothing back her still lustrous hair. I am, after all, responsible for this girl to her mother. The thought wearied her. Daisy is really *too* simple a girl, but even she surely cannot imagine that Kolya would ever marry her. A governess, a heretic! It would be quite impossible. Yet impossible things did happen in wartime. Kolya is an innocent in some ways; he has no notion of how attractive he is, indeed how beautiful. Or if he has, he too often forgets it. The rashness of young men! The follies they could commit on a summer evening, or on a sparkling winter day, uttering idiotic words that would tie them forever to impossible girls of whom they would tire in six months. Daisy's heart might be a little narrow, but it must not be broken. For her sake and for ours: we need her too much.

Leaning from the window, the Princess called in her clear mellow voice, "How lovely an evening! I will be with you in a minute—let us have dinner early and some music. Varya has a little headache and I have put her to bed. The boys are still out fishing with Oleg. They have their supper, we will not wait for them."

The sun was now disappearing behind the lime trees, whose long dense shadows lay across the grass. Sounds of lowing cattle came faintly from the farm, the despairing bellow of a cow parted from her calf. A few rooks were beginning to fly home from the fields, lumbering slowly overhead in ones and twos.

The voice of the Princess could be heard in the hall, commanding an instant dinner. Daisy was both irritated and relieved to be snapped out of her trance.

Kolya, who was not in truth quite without worldly wisdom, rose to his feet and moved further away, standing to face Daisy with the sun behind him; she could no longer see the expression on his face. With difficulty, he had mastered his rush of feeling: the time for love was not yet, though certain words must, should, *would* be said. Later in the evening. He wore a look of gravity, a serious and distant expression, continuing the previous conversation in a low impassioned voice.

"I used to worry bitterly for the fate of Russia," he told Daisy. "At times, at the Front, when things went wrong, when no rifles came, when men died sheerly through muddle, I could be almost frantic with concern, all but mad with revolt and bitterness, fuming with anger. Now, no more. Since I was in hospital, and could think calmly, I leave it to the long term. What do you suppose the men of Russia thought when so many died at Borodino, when still the French troops came on, when they saw Moscow burning, and Napoleon's troops everywhere, killing and destroying? They knew that it was not the end of Russia, and I know that this is not the end of Russia. Greater armies were raised then, will be raised now . . . I leave it to God, who will bless us again in time, after this terrible sacrifice, this grief . . . and pain . . . this loss of friends."

Again involuntarily, he came nearer. "Do you remember the saying, I cannot remember who wrote it—I should know, but I forget—'To love with all one's heart and leave the rest to fate?' "

He stopped, seeming not to need an answer. Daisy was silent; her silence was answer enough. She felt calm again, locked in a long calm moment. The whole evening seemed to breathe an unbreakable peace.

"The midges will be upon us in a minute," the Princess said, stepping out onto the terrace in a rustle of silks. "Shall we go in? Your last night, dear Kolya, but we won't think of that. Some music after dinner, perhaps?" With her habitual graceful bustle, charming and quite irresistible, she swept them into the salon, where the lamps were lit and the moths already immuring themselves upon them. "Varya was so charming just now; do you know what she was telling me? She said, 'The rooks fly awkwardly, as if they were souls newly made angels!' Wasn't that delicious?"

Daisy, inwardly reflecting on some of the less roseate things which Varya said from time to time, agreed civilly that it was. Were all mothers very slightly daft about their children? Yes, and I will be equally daft about mine. Her heart was still racing.

The Princess took Daisy's arm and led her gently away from the window and across the room. Kolya followed them in silence, his dark head bent, as if in prayer or at the sealing of some solemn contract.

"Oh you noisy boys," the Princess cried, "to interrupt our music! And how late you are! And you have caught nothing? Nikolasha, you are so hot, was it still warm by the river? Good night, my darlings. Miss Pelham, I know, will see you into bed. And Nyanya will bring you up some soup. No, nothing more, Arkasha, you took mountains of food with you. And ate it all, I do not doubt. Good night, my beloved children. Go quietly, Varya is perhaps sleeping. Good night, Daisy, sweet repose." The Princess's face lit with a charming, warmhearted smile. She had the grace to make even so definite a dismissal sound kindly. She sighed when Daisy had left; it cut short the music, and the evening felt flat and disjointed. Kolya was silent. How tiresome, sometimes, it was, to do one's duty, to act responsibly by two young people! Many a mother, let alone a stepmother, would simply have let things rip and made a good *histoire* out of it.

Early next morning, in the misty, pearly dawn of a fine summer's day, the unsleeping Daisy heard the wheels of the carriage turning on the gravel, the neighing of a horse fresh with morning. Her heart sank. The carriage was to bear Kolya to the station, and back to the war, the war that for all its horrors he believed would bring Russia's salvation. In a long white dressing gown, elegant as always, the Princess was waving Kolya goodbye from the portico, with Varya beside her. At the last possible moment the twins, still in their nightshirts, sped over the gravel in their bare feet and cast themselves upon their brother. "Wait, wait, Kolya, wait! We haven't told you! The foal is born! Catriona's foal is born! Come down and see it! Come quickly! A filly foal!" Kolya shook his head.

Self-pity seized on Daisy. I have not even the right, she thought, to get up and say goodbye to him. I am the background, never to be obtruded, with not even the right of a freed serf or a servant to stand weeping in the hall; a stranger, a sojourner, having no part here, no abiding city. Seizing on the general emotion as the focus for her distress, she refused, with unconscious determination, to acknowledge the particular: once bitten, twice shy was still her ruling maxim. Denying the knowledge of what this departure meant to her personally, she believed herself excluded simply by her foreignness from the warmth and the tears. Was she to be forever left behind, a slave in this far country, victim of a sense of responsibility, of a promise exacted from her by one who in like circumstances would not dream of being bound by it?

Kolya's voice, calling out his farewells, rebuked her for these low thoughts. The sound of his wheels died away down the long drive, cocks crew stridently from the farm, through the gentler sounds of cows being milked. The sun, defeating the mists, rose golden and glorious upon another hot day.

Only once during this long summer did any sign of the times manifest itself, though the Princess grew thoughtful as she read her husband's letters. Kolya's gravity had deepened as the time approached for his return to his regiment. Before the war he would have laughed more, he would at any rate have smiled at his own seriousness. But now he is so much in earnest. Too serious, really. The Princess almost found herself wishing for the return of Kolya's pretty widow.

Late at night, Daisy would kneel by her bed, sleepless with love. Oh God, keep him! she prayed. Let it end! Let it all end! The blame of the world should not fall on such as Kolya, so beautiful, so gentle, so grave in his endeavours. A sad inner voice of apprehension told her that it is upon such that punishment will always fall.

The Princess had planned a consolatory drive with the children in the wagonette one August evening after Kolya left, to the distant fields to see the harvest, and accompany the singing peasants back to the great barns. They had barely caught up with the tail of the procession when a man sprang out from among its ranks, seized the reins of the nearside horse and brought the cart to a standstill. "Why do you ride when we must trudge like this, at the end of the long day of toil?" he demanded furiously. "Tell me that. By what right do you own these lands, which should be the property of all?" He jabbed the horse's mouth violently, shaking the bit; his voice rose to a throaty cry. "By what right do you lead idle lives, do you sit in the shade whilst we toil in the sun, do you feed full on our labour, while so many starve? It is not God who commands you to keep warm while so many of us must freeze! It is not your sons who are sent to the war to die in the army!"

"Leave the horse," the Princess said coolly. There was an icy, cutting edge to her voice as she held the horses in check. Her colour was high, and she sat bolt upright. "And hear me. My sons, as you can see, are but eight years old. My husband's sons are both at the war. No one starves at Jevrenskaia. The wood of the forests is there for all. These lands, which you hate us for owning, feed us all. Leave go, I tell you. Do you not see that you frighten the children by your violence?"

With a curse and a look of extreme bitterness, the man complied. The Princess's voice, with centuries of unquestioned authority behind it, had been too much for his brief burst of defiance. He ran from them, disappearing amongst the singing peasants, whose ranks, Daisy noted, opened to conceal him. They were at the tail end of the singing column, and perhaps scarcely anyone had seen what had happened.

"A stranger," the Princess commented, "not one of our own. A stranger from beyond the river no doubt, brought over for the harvest. No one at

Jevrenskaia would speak thus. Before the war, I would not even have answered him."

"What would you have done, Mamma?"

"Had him beaten like a dog, Arkady. The horses could have bolted when he sprang at them like that. He risked all our lives. And then," she added, "I would have prayed for his soul. Let us forget about him, children. His mind is perhaps deranged, poor soul." The colour was still high in her cheeks and she still held herself tautly erect. "Hark, children, they are beginning the harvest song! How beautiful it sounds!"

But after the children were in bed, the Princess returned again to the incident, as if to convince herself of its unimportance. "Assuredly he was no peasant of our estate," she repeated to Daisy. "No one from Jevrenskaia. Some recalcitrant fellow dismissed from a farm beyond the river. He may have crossed in the ferry to escape from trouble. There are many such, set loose by the war."

Since the Princess had herself opened the subject, Daisy ventured to ask whether none of the peasants owned their own land.

"Assuredly not all, but many do; many neglect and misuse it. There are some intelligent and hardworking men who are able to buy farms, but they are hardly peasants, though of peasant stock."

"What would happen if they did own their own farms?" Daisy persisted, emboldened by the look of desperation on the man's face, his untended beard, his naked dirty feet. Bare feet in stubble, as she knew from childish experience at home, were far from comfortable.

"Ah, you've been listening to Kolya's foolish talk! He sees himself as one of those young nobles who tried in 1825 to make the Czar Nicholas a constitutional monarch. He will soon grow out of these ideas! Russia needs an autocracy. She is too huge for lesser methods."

The Princess had reconciled herself to the event, which now seemed remote and unimportant as a horsefly bite, irritating enough at the moment. But Daisy, unable as ever to let well alone, persisted. "Have they ever had a chance to work their own land?"

"Yes, yes, many have, and many do. And very often it is disastrous. You see the peasants laughing and merry and singing their songs, and it is all what you call 'picturesque.' But they are feckless and drunken. They do not *want* to think, or plan, or be responsible. Unless we led them by the hand like children they would eat the seed corn, they would neglect the beasts, and ruin the machinery, and they would starve and die in their thousands. The peasants! When a peasant farms his own land, all perhaps might go well for a few months. After that all would go awry. The farms would fail, and, having no one responsible for him, that peasant and his family would starve. Our peasants are not, as yours are, *industrious*." Again there was that faint note of disdain, as if industry were something vulgar, materialistic, not in tune with the soul of Holy Russia. "Our peasants live for the day, and must be cared for. When duties become disagreeable, the work is neglected. The Russian peasant is not capable of sustained effort. Anyone of experience would tell you that."

Then what, Daisy wondered, were they making at the Front, unsustained by guns, ammunition, or regular food supplies?

But the Princess, as if reading her thoughts, told her, "You may speak of the war. There they fight long, they fight bravely. There are no soldiers braver than our peasants fighting for their fatherland. But there they are led by their officers, by the Mishas and Kolyas of their regiments, high-hearted men to cheer them along, check them when they stray, carry them to victory. That is very different." There was a clear clipped certainty in her speech which caused even the argumentative Daisy to fall silent.

Earlier than they were wont to, the family returned in autumn to a disturbed and restless Moscow, to be welcomed by a harrassed but still urbane Prince, dressed in yet another new suit. "How about your Beatty?" he mocked Daisy. "He met the German Fleet on the high seas in June, but he is not, I fear, another Nelson. Many of his ships exploded; and for all that dashing cap, cocked over one eye, the Germans, I rather think, came off best."

"My father says they won't come out again. Our supplies are safe."

"Maybe, but what good can your Beatty do if they don't?"

"Andrei Mihailovitch, don't tease her," the Princess told him.

But her husband, unabashed, went on to laugh at Daisy over Beatty and the angle of his cap—"Too rakish for an Englishman; he should be more serious, he should not allow his ships to be exploded." Both his sons, he told them, were well, but Misha had a flesh wound which he declared was but a scratch. "Lying dog," the Prince added dotingly.

Moscow was duller and quieter this autumn, seemingly steeped in a kind of sullen resignation. Faces were more drawn, the black clothes of mourning everywhere to be seen. Beautiful young widows moved in a trance of grief, their long black gauze veils floating out behind them. The liveliness of the city seemed to have taken wing; people shuffled along with no spring in their gait. Daisy found that even the reliable George Bennett had gone, despatched by his timber firm to some Black Sea town near the Caucasus. He had been made a vice-consul, he wrote Daisy, and was studying Russian history with a view to understanding better the Russian people with whom he had to deal. It was impossible for Daisy to find either of these pieces of information breathtakingly interesting.

One missed George, all the same: the solid unmoved compatriot to whom one could speak one's mind. Everything was a curious mixture— ominous but dull. "No, Nikolai," she told him crossly. "It's be*gan*, not be*ginned*; you know that perfectly well. Perhaps you'd better write the whole sentence out again." It was increasingly difficult to believe that the correctness of Nikolai's English was really a matter of moment. The distant thunder in the hills was too clearly coming nearer.

Unimportant it might be to correct Nikolai, but it was at least better than sitting around and brooding, with nothing to do. She was trapped, for the duration of the war, in this far country, far from home, and it was better to work than to be sulky with the children or to indulge in an agony of longing for what might never be.

Even the Moscow winter, that had seemed before so sparkling, so softly lit by starlight and glistening snow across its generous open spaces, was changed now by war and menace. It was dull, monochrome, a deadliness of dark trees and blank white spaces, black towers and domes against a heavy laden sky, locked in an unchanging greyness; where hurrying, muffled figures had no time to turn their heads, no heart for smiles or laughter.

Chapter 13

Hindenburg need not have feared—there could be no new Russian offensive. From the chaos caused by Rasputin the rot had really set in in the rear of the Russian armies.

The western provinces had held much of the railway system; their loss meant difficulties in the food supply, and especially in the Petrograd area.

The Russian railway system had never been good. Now it worsened with a speed that could have been due to sabotage. Trains of food for the cities, drawn from the illimitable rich fields of Siberia and the southern steppes, broke down, failed to be repaired, lay abandoned in sidings. In the great towns of grain-rich Russia the people were brought near to starvation. The cry of *izmiena,* treachery, began to be heard, poisoning minds and undermining morale and loyalty. Rumours ran unchecked through the long food queues—Russia had been sold to the Germans by her German-born Empress! Elizabeth, the Grand Duchess, who had travelled from Moscow to beseech her young sister not to entrust so much power to Rasputin, but whose advice had been disregarded in favour of "Our Friend," now began, for all her goodness, to have her name coupled with her sister's in the cry of *izmiena.* They were two of a pair, German, working for Germany, they were the "Hessian witches." On an icy day in Moscow Elizabeth's windows were stoned.

Parts of the country were now slipping out of control. Misha and Kolya found that food supplies were no longer regularly reaching the Front. The army was obliged to forage for food, with consequent distress to peasants and farmers. To the general agony of the war was now added the hateful need to conduct a minor conflict against defenceless countrymen. The Cossacks foraged ruthlessly; the cry of "Kazakis!" was no longer one of hope and pride but of deadly fear. "If you live with wolves, you must howl like a wolf," was their grim rejoinder when disciplined. Typhoid, typhus, cholera and smallpox were now added to the general miseries, and still the wounded in their carts groaned along the dark roads through the night, or were laid out in cowbarns or in tents in the sandy forests, waiting relief, with their faces set in pallid hopelessness. Remote areas of Russia were being combed for reinforcements; fur-hatted nomads from the Kirghiz steppes in Turkestan were recruited, raked off from God knew what distant impoverished mountainsides or dusty camel-tracked plains to die under the merciless efficiency of the German guns.

Yet even by 1917 the Russians had lost very little in proportion to the hugeness of their land. In the summer of 1916 the whole of the Austrian Front was giving way; the fortified Austrian escarpments, with their many lines, destroyed by Russian guns. Ah, thought Misha, if Russia herself had had such fortifications! Why must we always play the Scythian war game, luring an enemy on to destroy him? We are no longer mobile Scythians with flocks and herds to take with us—it is a game that lays waste a whole countryside! In August a Russian victory near Tarnopol in Galicia left them with ten thousand Austrian prisoners.

At home Protopopov was put in charge of the Ministry of the Interior, which meant that the pro-German faction, part of a peace movement, enjoyed access to the Czarina. Discontent, and fear of the supposedly pro-German woman now at the head of the State, became general. Why had she received Protopopov, straight back from Sweden where he had seen the German peace emissaries? What was being engineered over their heads, behind the backs of the still desperately fighting army? If she was not a traitress, she must be a fool! Must the destinies of Russia, at so desperate a moment, be entrusted to such a one? In October of 1916 the general discontent provoked a strike; the soldiers sent to disperse the strikers joined in on their side.

At last, on November 14, the Duma was summoned: all its members denounced the government and its conduct of the war. But the ministers it elected were dismissed, the Czarina insisting that Protopopov must stay on in charge. On December 14 the whole of the rest of the Imperial Family, all the Czar's oldest and closest friends, and the Ambassadors of England and France, besought the Emperor for a constitution. On the last day but one of the old year the inevitable happened. Rasputin was assassinated by Prince Yousupov and his friends. His powerful body, refusing to die, floated horribly, bobbing up and down, beneath the Neva ice, its once brilliant eyes still wide open.

To the Czarina, desperate with anxiety for her haemophiliac son, the monk's death was an agony. To many Russians it brought intense relief, mingled with feelings of superstitious dread. Even the most rational feared that no joy could come of cold-blooded murder. The army greeted the news with undisguised pleasure. "The world is well rid of this treacherous man," the officer who brought the news to Misha and Kolya's regiment had insisted.

At the Winter Palace Czar Nicholas sat in a state of complete apathy, refusing to listen to any advice, deaf to all warnings. The Empress would see only Protopopov, who divided his time between forming plans for repression of the strikers and spiritualist conversations with a ghostly Rasputin. It was as if no death could exorcise his evil spell. All the while, in factories and barracks, the revolutionaries were at work.

In this dark hour, golden news was announced.

In their desperate fear that Russia would crumble, the Western Allies now made a helpful move. Over the years they had come to take a more heartening and less critical view of Russia. Influential Englishmen and Frenchmen had read Tolstoy and Dostoievsky, Turgenev and Chekov, had heard Russian music, had seen Pavlova dance. Here, they had realised, was a people of exceptional and varied gifts. The image of barbarism had faded. Meeting Russians in the flesh, Englishmen at all levels had found that they got on well with them and liked them. It had become abundantly clear that the Russian armies, by their enormous sacrifices in the early months of the war, had relieved the pressure on the Western Front and saved France.

Some huge prize must be offered to keep the Russians in the fight, and aged prejudices had therefore to be jettisoned. For more than a century both France and England had been haunted by the spectre of Russian power let loose in the Mediterranean and brought to bear on the Near East; much effort had been expended in shoring up the crumbling edifice of the Ottoman Empire to act as a continuing stopper upon Russian expansion. But now that the Turks had carelessly come in on the wrong side and were fighting alongside the German armies, their interests could be disregarded By the end of 1916 the Allies had agreed that Russia's reward in victory was to be Constantinople, eastern Thrace and the Dardanelles. She was also to hold Erzerum and Trebizond, which she had already conquered from the Turks—"if the war were brought to a successful conclusion."

In December of 1916 the Russian Prime Minister publicly announced from Petrograd that these were to be the prizes of continued and successful war. Russia was to realise "the immemorial and sacred dream of the Russian people." They had but to hold on and hold firm, and once more the holy bells would ring out over the Golden Horn, and the great cathedral of Saint Sofia be reconsecrated to the worship of Christ; the Czar of all the Russias would reign in Byzantium, imperial Czargrad, spiritual parent of Russia, the sacred city of Constantine the Great.

Even from the throats of the starving came cries of joy at such news; bereaved parents lifted their drooping heads. Folk such as the Dubelskys were beside themselves with happiness and hope. Even Misha and Kolya, driven ever eastwards with the Russian armies in their desperate struggle, shared in the moment of exultation, drinking far into the night. Misha was soon asleep, but Kolya, who had drunk less, lay long awake in the dangerous darkness, his eyes glowing. All this sorrow and agony was here made purposeful, even right, set in such a balance. Every misery became acceptable with Byzantium as prize.

* * *

All the while a force had been gathering itself together in the rear of the Russian armies: a body of men who cared nothing for treaties with the Allies, who would repudiate them all, who cared nothing for Byzantium or for the Russian people's immemorial dream. They cherished newer and more potent dreams of their own.

Although nothing overtly revolutionary occurred in Moscow within Daisy's cognizance, the atmosphere seemed to thicken, as with thunder. The imminence of danger seemed to hang in the air like a dark cloud, to move in the footsteps of all those famished figures who padded through the snow across the vast open square where stood the fantastic dreamlike towers of the Cathedral of St. Basil, and crossed the wide streets to scuttle back into the narrow alleys of the older town. St. Basil's Cathedral itself, which had once wholly enchanted Daisy by its joyful and nearly comic oddness and richness, now seemed too like Russia itself in its wild asymmetric exuberance. Imagination had here run riot in shape and colour and intricacy of design: it was daring, splendid, miraculous—and very slightly mad. Even the sombre golden splendours of the Kremlin, the arresting mingling of darkness and mystery within and painted and gilded lightness and brightness without, seemed now bizarre and alien, altogether inside out, as if the gloom and darkness and danger of the times had translated the glory and majesty into something sinister and wizard-haunted, a meeting place of demons. Could it be these dark interiors that made Czarist Russia so deeply addicted to secret police? Had native secretiveness bred those dim churches where daylight never came, or vice-versa?

Menace lived in the whispers and shudders of the older servants—the younger men had all long since gone. It announced itself in lines of anxiety on the Prince's cheerful face, on his rare appearances in Moscow, in his murmured conversations with his wife. And all these fears found themselves solid foundations in the supply shortages, the talk in the bread queues, and the endless tramp of marching men, many of whom were no men but young halfgrown boys with innocent bewildered faces and uniforms too large for them. With increasing apprehension, Daisy tucked the twins into their beds at night. Might the war end before they too grew into participation!

From Misha, and more surprisingly from Kolya, came no news at all. If he loved me, if he meant anything by such words and looks, surely he would find means to write, to send some message through to me? But even if he did, how, by what possible means, could I send my feelings back to him, tell him even a little of what I feel for him? Like a dark curtain, the war, the upheavals and uncertainties, was drawn across the hopeful blaze of love.

Early in 1917 events gathered a horrible momentum. Of the Allies,

France had mutinous troubles of her own, England was in appalling danger from the success of the German submarine campaign, reaching its climax in the April sinkings, Italy was the victim of defeat, and America only a message of hope in the distance. The meeting of the Duma was postponed until February 27th, and although there was still food in plenty, its distribution was so incompetent that the shortages grew, and with them all remaining faith in the government. On March 8 the bread queues broke ranks and stormed the bakers' shops, carrying away in their desperate hunger more bread than they could want or eat. On March 9 the police fired on the crowds. Next day all factories closed, all schools were shut down. Everyone in Petrograd was on the streets. Soldiers took the side of the people. There was open fighting near the Town Hall and Zuamensky Square. From his headquarters the Czar ordered the immediate suppression of the disorders, and the Military Governor of the capital accordingly announced that he would fire upon all demonstrators.

March 11 was a Sunday, and through the wide street of Czar Peter's great city, huge crowds collected under their flags, demanding food, rights, peace. Police patrols rode through them, firing at random; machine guns crackled from police posted in the houses. More and more soldiers joined the crowd, and on the next day the Guards Regiment of the Volkynian also joined, to be followed by nearly the whole of the Petrograd garrison. Troops offered support to the Duma, where Kerensky had taken charge. But the crowd was now truly out of control, seizing the Arsenal, distributing weapons, throwing open the prisons, setting fire to the headquarters of the political police. By noon a few troops loyal to the government appeared on the streets, but they were powerless to stop a river of revolt now in full spate.

At three in the afternoon the Duma appointed a representative Provisional Committee, which now had its first meeting with a Soviet (or Council of Delegates) hastily elected from factories and barracks. By nightfall this Provisional Committee had received a telephone message from the Grand Duke Cyril and the officers of the Preobrazhensky Guards regiment, asking it to assume power and putting themselves at its service. The president of the Committee, Rodzyanko, telegraphed to the Czar this same day, repeating his request of the previous day that the Czar should not delay in appointing a Prime Minister who had the confidence of the country, long forfeited by Protopopov.

On the 12th he sent: THE LAST HOUR HAS COME, WHEN THE DESTINY OF THE COUNTRY AND OF THE DYNASTY IS BEING DECIDED. But it seemed as if the dying Rasputin had laid upon his master and patron the terrible curse of inaction. No reply was received to either message.

On March 14 the members of the Provisional Government appointed Kerensky as Minister of Justice. On the 15th the Soviet agreed its support. A Constituent Assembly was to be summoned on universal suffrage; all local governing bodies were to be reelected likewise. Civil rights were to be shared by the soldiers, but discipline was to be maintained at the

Front. But while the Duma talked, disorder broke out. By Order Number 1 of the Soviet of Workers, all ranks were abolished in the army, thus removing all control from its officers. The government did not sign this order, but the Soviet circulated it just the same, throughout the army, and in the name of the new government. The dissolution of all morale and discipline set in. Thousands of men poured back from the Front and conditions became anarchical. People endeavouring to leave Petrograd found that they could draw no more than ten roubles a day (about five dollars) from the bank.

The situation could still perhaps have been saved. All the generals in the army and the principal grand dukes supported the formation of a Ministry responsible to the Duma. And, at long last, Czar Nicholas sent for Rodzyanko. But it was too late: the Czar's train to Petrograd was halted, and he agreed abdication, leaving his son out of account because of his ill-health. He confirmed the new Ministry in power and asked all to support it, and to fight on until victory. His similar appeal addressed to the troops were never allowed to reach them. Now where courage and decision was too late to help him, the spell had been lifted. The last chance for the dynasty was lost when Grand Duke Michael decided not to accept the throne unless asked to do so by the Constituent Assembly due to meet on the 16th.

Prince Andrei, on a hasty visit to his mother to try once again to persuade her to leave Moscow and take refuge at Jevrenskaia, told her the terrible news. Though stunned himself, Prince Andrei's loyalty to the luckless Emperor died hard; he sought excuses for Nicholas II. The old, still brilliant gaze of the Princess looked back at him unflinchingly, her chin held high. All her long life she too had felt love for the Czar and loyalty to his sovereignty as a part of her being. Now he had failed, had given up the throne of his own will, had abused and abandoned that mighty gift of God. Her glance held nothing of pity or compassion. Something of the cruelty of old Muscovy gleamed from her hooded eyes. The gnarled jewelled hands on the top of her ebony stick did not tremble.

"The Evil One," she told her son, "can work his will through a man's weakness as easily as through the worst of wickedness. None are beyond the forgiveness of God, but he will now receive no mercy from men. His once Imperial Majesty will receive no reverence, no compassion now."

"He must leave the country," the Prince said. "They must all leave Russia now, at once, through this season of madness."

"Why did he marry that foolish, foolish woman, with her narrow morality that has left her with so few friends, and none to whom she would listen? Why does he yield to her? For myself, I stay in Moscow. No, Andrei, no more. I will hear no more."

Her eyes gazed into her son, gazed through him, with that distant, formidable, end-of-life look that has nothing in it of scorn or dismissal, but only of impatience with flesh that still thinly veils the bright, still impact of ultimate reality; a gaze before which the facile tide of optimism fades like spray along dry rocks. From dark corners of the sombre room the Prince could hear the muffled sobs of the dependent cousins, quick to capitalise on disaster as any Greek chorus of the ancients.

In one staggering week the Romanovs had fallen. They were not brought low by the Duma, whose powers they had so much mistrusted, nor by Lenin, still in Switzerland, nor by Trotsky, who had not yet left New York, nor by the few Petrograd Bolsheviks. The weakness of a good devout man, the rule of the Czarina and of Rasputin, had sent the 300-year-old dynasty, the 900-year-old princedom of Muscovy, crashing to the ground. Almost singlehandedly, one tragic self-willed woman, with all the besotted fervour of the convert, obsessed by dread for her handsome ailing young son and his inheritance, and one priest, shamelessly exploiting her fear and her religious madness in the interests of his own greed and power, had done the deed.

Nothing now remained for this once happy family but the drawn-out agony of imprisonment, ending in the murder at Ekaterinburg. Under this trial both the Czar and his wife displayed a moral courage that, if exercised earlier, might have saved them all.

"To the country, all of you," the Princess cried, sweeping into the schoolroom with a telegram in her hand. "Now, today, while the trains are still running. It's the Prince's command that the children must go to Jevrenskaia." Her voice was as wild as if she could anticipate the fate of the Czar's children. "Pack as much as you can, Daisy—their books, their toys, winter clothes, everything. God knows when we shall return!"

"And the Prince?"

"He will follow. With his mother, if he can persuade her to come. But she is too old to move! It will kill her! Oh God, that it should come to this! Only the Preobrazensky Guards! The Czar abdicated! Who would have believed it! Mother of God, help and deliver us all!" Hugging her little girls she fell briefly into a fit of tears. Whilst these horrors were enacted in distant Petrograd she had been able not quite to believe in them. Now they had struck home: into her own life, her husband's life, the life of her children.

Daisy stood by, dumbfounded. The twins, never disagreeably surprised at the thought of a change of scene, hurried from the room to make sure that their goldfish were not left behind in the rush. In the passage Nyanya, sobbing noisily, clasped Ella to her bosom. Varya, with a brow of thunder, insisted that all her best dresses should be taken with them. The great house in Moscow was full of wailing voices, hurrying feet. Daisy, flinging her own things together, felt her heart tremble.

Chapter 14

At Jevrenskaia nothing was changed. Spring came with its usual precipitation, an annual miracle whose startling suddenness never failed to fascinate Daisy, bred to the slow, advance-and-retreat springs of home. One night the land was still locked in winter, next morning rain was falling, and the snow dissolving in a thin cold mist rising through the trees. There was a week of flooding rivers, of great ice blocks grinding on the rocks as they sped past, of fields reduced to swamps and roads impassable with mud. Snowy blocks of ice, like whipped white of egg awash on a dark custard, floated unceasingly down the great rivers.

And then, as if by magic, the hot sun shone, the buds burst open, the birds sang as if intoxicated. Flowers opened overnight, and cuckoos, appearing as if from nowhere, called from every copse. The nightingales sang in the woods at dusk as if they had never known what winter was. Less agreeably, there was a great and grand burgeoning in the insect world, and lizards, which Daisy disliked, sat perkily all over the stone terrace, their supple bodies twitching alertly or suddenly held in stillness, lifted heads gazing around with their lordly archaic stare.

That spring, more than ever, Jevrenskaia was cut off from the world. The post was erratic to the point of vanishing altogether: Daisy ceased hearing from home and continued to write without any strong feeling that her letters would ever arrive in England. When at last a message from the Princess was brought by hand, it held no news of her coming. Her mother-in-law was refusing even to consider leaving her Moscow house. In any case, the old Princess insisted, if she left Moscow she would not come to Jevrenskaia, but to her own estate in eastern Russia, the property that was to be Kolya's. It was impossible to make her understand that the danger was not from advancing German armies. She refused to believe that the danger came from the Russian people themselves. She prayed nearly all the day. Her entourage of elderly cousins were now all abysmally terrified; she alone remained calm. Too calm, her daughter-in-law feared. The old Princess had given the whole of her fabulous jewels to be sold in aid of the field hospitals; the fact that these were scarcely now operative had not deterred her. She was giving to some holy, compassionate Russia of her dream. But move from Moscow she would not.

Uncle Georg, on the other hand, with his faithful servant Ambrose, had left Moscow for his Crimean villa, complaining indignantly at the inconvenience of the whole thing, and threatening to return at once if the Crimean weather turned sour. Uncle Sergei, deeply involved in yet another Good Cause, was starry-eyed once again, would not talk or even listen in anything but the Russian language, and declined to leave the committee rooms even to go home to sleep, thereby greatly putting out the other

members. He too would stay in Moscow, rage the heathen never so fiercely.

Days passed, bringing no ill tidings, but the very absence of news was
frightening. To Daisy, her life at this crisis seemed ever more futile and
frustrating. The servants whispered together; their loud clear laughter
was muted and rare. The steward Anatoly announced one morning that
his mother in Odessa was very ill; he must go to her at once. At noon he
departed with all his family. Such an event, in the busy summertime and
in the absence of the Prince, caused alarm and dismay. Of what use, felt
Daisy, to insist on table manners with the children, on piano practise, on
the repetition of Latin irregular verbs? Yet equally of what use was it to
sit around idle, with one's heart racing in anticipation of the worst?

Most worrying was the continued absence of communication from the
Prince and Princess. The children had been promised by their mother
that she would follow them in a few days, and six or seven weeks had now
passed. It was beginning to be high summer; the lime flowers, with their
intoxicatingly sweet smell, were opening on the trees. What could have
happened? Even Ella's small composed face looked drawn and anxious.
Where now was Kolya? There was a tale that the army had mutinied—
how was Misha facing that?

The village was rife with rumour. It was said that men had laid down
their arms and were streaming home; how was it, then, that none had
reached Jevrenskaia? It was variously declared that the Germans were in
Petrograd, were in Moscow, had imprisoned the Czar. The Allies, it was
believed, had sued for peace, leaving Russia to face Germany alone. All
the old latent fears, the obsessional suspicions felt by Russians for Western Europe had come to the surface again—not surprisingly in this
remote part of the country, since even a genius like Tolstoy had written
the whole of *War and Peace* without ever acknowledging that the British
too were effectively fighting Napoleon, had been from the start, and continued even when the Russians made peace with him and fought for two
years on his side. For the first time Daisy noted scowls and suspicious
looks directed at her as she walked through the village. The word *Angli-
chanka* came out with a tone of menace.

German armies, it was said, were coming, they had almost come, they
would be in the village tomorrow, or, at latest, on Wednesday. Everything
was believed, and no one had the least idea what to do about it. Take to the
woods now, later, between the hay harvest and the corn? Sit tight and
hope?

June was well advanced when Daisy, crossing the lawn one late warm
afternoon saw a figure moving cautiously through the trees. He paused to
look at the house, listening intently. He was on crutches, and when he
moved again, swinging his head round in the direction of the stables,
Daisy saw that the hair sticking out underneath the bandage round his
head was fair as straw. It was Misha! With excitement, she ran to meet

him. What news would he have—of Russia, of his family, of Kolya?

Seizing her arm, he drew her back into the shadow of the box trees. "Don't speak loud," he said, "don't cry out. Go slowly back into the house, and if you can, come out again with something to drink and a little food. Or send one of the children. You must all leave at dawn tomorrow."

The children seemed happily preoccupied. They had turned on the old gramophone and put on an immensely aged record; to its wheezing sound Nyanya and all the four children were peacefully gyrating. It seemed wiser to leave them where they were or the whole party would rush across the lawn to Misha before she could stop them, all doubtless yelling for joy at the pitch of their lungs. Daisy quietly got him food, her heart racing.

"There's this little house," Misha said, laying into a great hunk of rare cold beef as if he were a wolf. The Dubelskys, it appeared, owned a villa on the Black Sea, near Novorossisk. At least for the moment, Daisy and the children would be safe there. *If* they could get there. The children must travel in peasant clothes, speaking only Russian, taking small bundles only. As an Englishwoman with a British passport, Daisy would be, he hoped, reasonably safe. Had she her passport? The children's? In case they had to leave Russia for a while altogether? This Misha did not anticipate, but it might happen, since it must take some while before the present trouble was dealt with. And so much had happened already that no one had anticipated. Bands of Red soldiers were on the rampage, destroying property and killing all professional men, but particularly killing landowners and aristocrats.

"Even children?" Daisy could not believe this atrocity.

Yes, Misha told her, even children, and without hesitation. They had killed, he had heard also, all the surviving officers of his regiment. Misha himself had escaped because he had been wounded and driven away in an ambulance before the revolt began. He had been a day's drive from where the Front had been, when the news came after them. They had been due in a large town next day, and the large towns held the most merciless operators. Misha had escaped that night, having no desire to be tortured to death. He had stolen some crutches and crawled into the woods, and by the mercy of God, was not sought for the next day.

"That was the bad time. I lay, and crawled, and hid and crawled again, for three days, with nothing to eat and little to drink. On the fourth morning as I lay by a track through the woods a peasant with a cart came along. There was a little shrine by the wayside, and when I saw that he stopped to pray, I dared to call out. He brought me to Balkursk, hidden under cabbages, and his brother brought me on, God reward them. They fed me, on bread, and I gave them what I had, which wasn't enough. They were good men, God keep them—

"There is so much to do and so little time to do it. They told me that there were wandering bands of Red soldiers just across the river. But that the trains from the junction were still running."

"But what will *you* do?"

"Stay here. Lie hid with old Petya's brother in the forest till I can rejoin the Imperial forces. Will you now try somehow to find peasant clothes for the children and put up their bundles? And will you tell Anatoly to come quietly out to me?"

"Anatoly and his family have left. But he paid all the wages before he went."

"Good. Send Boris and Petya then. Them I can trust. The people of the estate will be safe enough if we are all gone and they no longer feel obliged to fight for us. They must give up the cattle to the soldiers who demand them; they must put up no defence, but take all, now, bury what they can, hide what they can. Some cows in the woods perhaps, or it will be hard winter for them. Oh God!"

"There is nothing else you can do," Daisy consoled him. "One man! Wounded and on crutches. What has happened to your head?"

"A shell exploded and some shrapnel came up, under my helmet. It was nothing."

"But it *will* be something if it's not dressed. When it's dark come into the house and I'll do it. Your leg too. Do we leave everyone? What about Nyanya?" Events had taken on a strange urgent pressure in which the whole slow peaceful atmosphere of the sunny afternoon seemed as far departed as another century. Daisy's mind leapt from thought to thought and action to action without allowing her to ask the one question that burned persistently in her heart. She was like someone swept downstream in a small boat who could only fiddle desperately with the oars and rowlocks without allowing herself to think of the approaching falls. Of Kolya she dared not ask, dared not be told, instead rushing to ask of every minor matter. The action of the moment was everything, *must* be everything. Whatever horror waited must be run away from, could not be faced and known now.

"Everyone, I fear. In two minutes Nyanya would blurt it all out in a burst of tears. She would be calling Varya Princess, you may be sure. She will be safe with her married sister in the village. Two old peasants— even a revolutionary would not harm them. This house, I think, they will burn."

"But why? *Why?*"

Misha disregarded this silly question. "Tell Nyanya that the children are going only for a little while or she will die of crying. It may, after all, be true."

The name of Kolya hung unspoken, ominously, between them.

Misha seemed utterly changed, as he had been changed at the time of the wolves—serious, intent, purposeful, his face drawn by the pain and exertion of his journey. This extreme difference seemed to Daisy a part of the general unreality of these sudden happenings, the transformation of Jevrenskaia's life of peace and dignity into this scuffle of escape. Only the terrible imminence of danger could have wrought such a miracle in Misha. Beneath his mockery he had always a kind of ruthlessness; now he was ruthless in his quest for safety for his young brothers and sisters.

All else, including his own pain and danger, was an irrelevance. Dumbfounded, for the moment almost stupefied, Daisy gazed at him with wide-open eyes. "Look alive," he advised her, briskly but not unkindly. "There is enough to do."

By the last of the light, still streaming in through the long windows, Daisy searched through the Princess's desk, trying to remember in which drawer the passports were hidden. She found them at last, and with them, stamped with a blurry and hatted photograph, the passport of old Mademoiselle. Adelaide Lebfevre, she read. It could be anybody. Misha appeared behind her, limping in, refreshed by a brandy and a good meal. "Take the jewels also, and what money there is to be found in the safe. You have Mamma's keys?"

"Oh no! I can't take her money!"

"What else will you and the children live on? I have found some, but not very much, in the estate office safe, and that I want to leave to Petya and Boris, against the winter. Sew this money into the hem of your dress. One of the children must carry the jewels. Arkady, I think, is least of a talker." Opening all his stepmother's small drawers, he pulled off the chamois leather covers from each tray and rolled the glittering collection together. "These will be food for a year or so."

"Longer than that, I would think. Look, here is also Mademoiselle's passport."

"A French passport. The Princess must have forgotten to throw it away." Suddenly, Daisy came out of her nightmare of shock and fright, out of her dullness of mind. "You must come with us—you must be Mademoiselle. Mademoiselle was tall, and big. She limped a little; I even know where she left her stick. There is her passport. You speak French, really speak French, not as we all do. You can alter your voice, I have heard you, playing with the children. The other day, Nyanya and I found some summer clothes that she kept put away here. You must wear them. You must walk with her stick, not with army crutches. You must be Mademoiselle!" Misha scowled with distaste. "Don't, Misha, look at it with loathing. Think . . . think!"

"To run away in women's clothes! I would be discovered, and taken, killed shamefully, stripped even of honour."

"Hear me, hear me! This is no time to be romantic."

"Death is far to be preferred. And in the forest I might not die."

"Perhaps not, but how would you ever get back to the Imperial Army if not now, when there is at least a chance of escape to the south? And without you, how can I take four children through a huge country in chaos, on my own, speaking so little Russian? I might survive, yes, but will they? This is to save the children's lives, and also to bring you sooner to where you say the Czar's troops are still fighting. Do it, Misha! You must!"

"It is impossible. It is too great a shame."

"Oh, *pride*, Misha!" Daisy cried desperately. "What's the deadliest sin, tell me that!" She hurried from the room, to collect and roll up her own essentials. What did one take and what leave; and did it matter at all, since they might all be dead by tomorrow night?

Half an hour later, when she returned to the Princess's room, Misha had tied up gold roubles and jewels into neat little chamois leather bundles. He looked deathly tired.

"Try on these clothes," she said, peremptory in her desperation. "Surely soldiers use such ruses in war if it enables them to join their companions and fight another day? Look, masses of petticoats; you will look womanly and middle-aged. I know that the blouse won't do up across your shoulders at the back, but I can pin a shawl around you. I could make the dress three or four inches longer, to hide your boots; it would take no time to tear undone the hem. Can you bear this big straw hat over your bandages? And look, there's a motoring veil! Green gauze; you'll be almost invisible behind it. And I found these; the children had them to play with." She held up a pair of old ebony crutches with red velvet arm pads.

"Roses on this hat," Misha said disgustedly—but it was all he said.

"Your uniform. We must burn it. Or bury it, perhaps. And the silver. I once promised the Princess that in case of need I would bury the silver. She said it belonged to her grandmother. Come with me please, if you can. I know where the children keep their spades. Could Petya help?"

"Petya is to be trusted, indeed."

"And shall I now tell Nyanya? She is in bed and will not tell anyone else."

"Tell her we go to Novorossisk only for a short while or she will die with weeping to leave Ella. It may, after all, be true." Daisy noted that, without conceding, he had decided to come with them.

With a dream-like, automatic rapidity, they dragged sacks of silver, baize bags and leather cases and long trays out into the moonlight. "You shouldn't be doing this, Misha, you look done in."

"I am better since you dressed my leg. At least it chafes no longer. Under the tenth lime tree on the right. You will remember that, to tell Nikolai, when the time comes to dig it up?"

"I will remember that. But you speak as if, as if—"

"Dig hard, Petya, we have not much time."

"The ground is hard, Prince, there are roots."

"Keep at it."

The moon rose high over the lime avenue. It was a night of magical beauty. I shall wake up from this nightmare soon, Daisy hoped. Kolya's dark eyes came into her mind. The hole grew in depth. Whose grave are we digging, she thought with a shudder. The old man was beginning to tire. Misha was carefully piling the earth for replacement. He heard Petya sigh and lowered himself into the hole, taking the spade from him and hobbling into action.

"You *cannot* dig with only one leg to stand on. Please allow me to do it," Daisy begged.

Suddenly Misha's calm deserted him. He sat down on the edge of the hole and his shoulders shook with uncontrollable sobs.

While there was so much to be done, instinct had continued to hold Daisy from asking him of Kolya. The same need for concentration upon practical action had restrained Misha from speaking of him. But now his wounds, his shock, pain and fatigue gathered against him, and the bitterness of loss broke from him.

"I buried him a week ago. Under a tree. I marked the tree. I shall return and raise a monument, a great monument." Suddenly he was hysterical, beside himself. The old man, resting on the spade that he had taken from him, laid an arm round his shoulders and Misha wept without restraint. A small breeze ruffled the trees, the shadows of the lime leaves trembled against the moonlit grass. A distant bell from the stable clock struck eleven.

Dead? Kolya was dead? Unable to look at Misha, Daisy fixed her eyes upon the old man. "Not by his men? He wasn't shot by his men?"

"That, never. A German shell. We had no guns with which to confront their great guns. We were in that latest retreat—he died at once, by the mercy of God. There was no lingering, no pain, no crying. He can hardly have known . . . I buried him myself. I buried him with just such a spade, on just such a summer night. I prayed by him. Not for long enough, but I prayed by him. There was no priest. Many have been killed, I think. And next day, another shell, splintering nearby, caught me. Almost despite the pain, I was glad to be hit. It made me feel one with Kolya, though that perhaps was a fool's feeling." He cast himself again, in an agony of grief on Petya's shoulder.

"Aie, aie," said Petya. "The brave Prince. The brave Prince Askold Andreivitch. May the saints receive his soul!"

Daisy stood as if frozen.

Misha leant for a long while on Petya's shoulder, the old man weeping with him, until at length, with an effort, they finished the digging, pushed in the silver, wrapped in a great sack, and shovelled the earth back. Carefully replacing the sods of grass, they trod them down.

"Go to the forest, Petya, go to your brother. Forget this house and all your duties here. I would rather stay here, but of what use? Better to join the armies of the south and fight with them, and return with them when victory comes, as come it must. Who, but a few, wish to follow these wild men from the cities? And those who do will soon regret it . . . Yet I cannot protect you, and there may even be enemies of the Czar hidden here, in Jevrenskaia. All must save themselves, but let them make free of the barns, to save and hide whatever can be saved and hidden. It may be more than a day before the Red soldiers come. But let them make haste, as soon as it is dawn, sooner even, as the moon is so bright. We shall need a farm cart, at dawn, to take us to the railway. Let it come to the short cut, to the track through the woods. Out of sight of the house, and let it be a cart, no carriage. And early, early!"

Daisy stood all this while stock still, the brilliant moonlight patterning her dress with the moving shadows of the lime leaves. The flowers, just opening, gave forth the sweetest of scents. She felt, as yet, no grief, nothing except a kind of remote exaltation to think of Kolya safe, away from the Red armies, from German shells, from the destruction of his home and the scattering of his family, from all that could assault and hurt the soul or could disturb his hallowed peace. Weeping would be for later.

Chapter 15

Food, wine, a few hours of sleep and his necessary weeping had restored Misha. By dawn the essential resilience of his nature had triumphed; he had embraced, almost with enthusiasm, the fantasy of disguise and escape, for the moment fully joining in the delighted laughter of the twins.

"Do some more mincing little steps, Misha!" they entreated him. "Do some more! Do some more French in a squeaky voice! Say some more!"

"Let me put your hat on better, and the veil," Varya insisted. "You look beautiful, Misha, you look like an enormous beautiful Mademoiselle with your eyes shining through that veil."

By the end of a snatched breakfast, the whole expedition had become a picnic. At the station Misha hobbled down the platform almost jauntily, swinging himself along on the ebony crutches, his rose-trimmed hat set at a rakish angle. The role, once accepted, was to be played with gusto. Daisy greatly feared that he might become carried away by his own virtuosity and overdo it. The roses wobbled alarmingly around his bandaged head.

"At all costs," Daisy hissed to the little boys, "you are not to laugh at him. This is a dangerous adventure, a real adventure. Like the Children of the New Forest."

"What new forest?"

"You remember, I read you the book. About *our* civil war. We had troubles like this, but they ended happily. We just have to be careful and brave while they last."

"When did you last see your father?" Arkady contributed unexpectedly. "I understand. I could tell them truly it's months since I saw mine."

"*Par ici, mes enfants,*" Misha summoned in falsetto tones, hauling himself into the train with powerful arms and in a most un-Mademoiselle-like manner. Daisy closed in behind him, going through the movements of one assisting an elderly lady. Once in the train Nikolai giggled irrepressibly.

They selected a carriage that had once been a sleeping car. It was wrecked but still spacious. Everything that could be removed had been taken: mattresses, cushions, curtains, blinds. The carpet had been torn up. One of the top bunks had been wrenched clean off, but the other still stretched its wire mattress over their heads. Into this Misha swung himself, and was levered; it was felt that he would be further from scrutiny and could stretch out his leg and rest it. He leant back, his features obscured by his gauze veil.

"Does a French lady never take off her hat in the train?"

"Never. She keeps it on until she is in her own home. Tell me just once again the Russian for an old, ill Frenchwoman?"

A trying anticlimax set in: for seven hours the train stood still in the station. No one came or went, the sun baked down, flies gathered and swarmed. Husbanding the food supplies, at noon they ventured on a slight meal.

"This dress is scratchy," Ella said, wriggling. "It itches me. Can't I take it off?"

"I knew we should have brought the gramophone," Nikolai brooded gloomily. "It is not heavy; I could have carried it myself; and the horn unscrews from it and even Ella could have carried that." Varya said nothing, sitting aloofly, her pretty nose wrinkling, her dark gaze fixed on the horizon. When we arrive at the Black Sea, Misha had said, it will be time enough to tell them the news of Kolya. If we get to the Black Sea, he had added, mentally. "Don't tell anyone anything," he warned the children. "Don't trust anyone, however friendly they may seem. Remember that we two are schoolmistresses and that you are travelling to a grandmother in Taganrog. If anyone comes, speak Russian."

In the long, stifling pause he thought increasingly of Kolya, his heart sunk in sadness. Glancing across at Daisy, he saw by her blanched face and stricken look that she, too, ached with grief.

Just before five, there was a sudden fearful bustle. The platform became crowded and many more people hurled themselves into the train, and the train, as if startled, immediately started, leaving a number more on the platform. For a long while, as the train circled the wide valley, following the river, the trees of Jevrenskaia remained in sight, and the onion dome of the church spire.

Presently, from behind the trees, Daisy caught sight of smoke arising. The house! They had come already! A great flame shot up, died down, was succeeded by another, became a great blaze. With what object? Daisy mourned inwardly. She could picture the porcelain lions cracking, the picture of great-grandpapa Dubelsky curling up in its frame, beautiful mahogany doors crackling, the whole great cheerful hospitable house folding in on itself in a final debacle. The children's attention was fortunately elsewhere, though Misha, leaning on his elbow, gazed silently at the blazing ruins of his home, of his inheritance.

"Can't we play cards?" Nikolai asked, "even in this horrible train?"

The train wound slowly and jerkily through the hills and across a darkening plain. Among those who had sprung on at the last moment were a young lawyer and his wife from Balkursk. They chatted cheerfully from behind the partition, broken at the top: the wife was pretty and very young; they were only just back from their honeymoon and had been visiting a brother beyond Jevrenskaia; the wife seemed to regard the sudden journey as almost a continuation of the wedding journey and the wedding fun. She laughed, and handed sweets, and was delighted to air her French. Once or twice a man with a dark puckered face passed by, scrutinising them all closely. Daisy mistrusted his looks and instinctively drew Ella closer to her.

At length the children slept, piled wearily against each other. The train stuttered slowly over an immensely wide plain, calm in the moonlight. Murmurs came from surrounding carriages, where passengers, restless and alarmed, went on talking all night. No one came round to light the lamps, most of which were broken and none of which held any oil. Daisy stood up to stretch herself and to ease her cramped limbs.

"Do you know," Misha's voice whispered in her ear, "that I am sixty-seven years old and was born in Martinique?"

For the first time, Daisy saw that Misha's mockery could hold a note of humour and kindness.

It was nearly dawn before he whispered again, urgently this time. "You saw that man in a dark suit who came by soon after the train started?"

"Yes, I did. I noticed him particularly. He had a rather secretive sort of face."

"He is called Casimir Terensky. He worked once on my father's estate, in the forest, a woodman. Somehow he gathered some money, no one knew how, and bought a small farm. My father helped him to get it, and I think helped him later, when he was in difficulties. But now he prospers, and I expect he has sold up quickly, to escape the Reds, and is moving south, with all his wealth in gold about him."

Daisy's alarmed whisper came back. "Do you think he knew you?"

"Maybe not, but he knew the children and he looked at me for some while, searchingly. He has just crept back for another look. He is no fool, he can draw conclusions."

"And betray us?"

"I *think* not. Unless under pressure. But to save himself? To save his gold even? If you can, watch him."

"I have some water. It is so dark, now that the moon has set, that I think I should dress your wound."

"You brought bandages? Dressings?"

"There were plenty at Jevrenskaia. Can you hold this cup of water? I can't see much, I expect I will be clumsy and hurt you more than I need, in this darkness."

Misha was hauling up his petticoats. "It will spare my blushes," he said.

* * *

In the night, one big town had been safely passed, in the early hours another. At breakfast time, the train was crossing another great plain. So far, so good, thought Daisy. But the state of Misha's thigh was alarming. There was a mass of deep lacerations and some of the leg had an angry look; Daisy feared splintered bone and internal complications; the drag through the forest and the foodless three days had done him no good. By late afternoon the train shuddered to a halt at Kharkov and all the passengers were turned out of the train and told to cross a great stretch of lines, beyond which, they were told, lay the train for Rostov.

A crowd of passengers, clutching bundles, basket trunks, and little cheap cases, trailed across the lines. From the tracks, groups of railway workmen eyed the passengers with sullen and suspicious looks. Misha, with his height, so improbable for a woman, stood out horribly conspicuous. "Gather up your skirts with your free hand, please, Misha, do."

"I haven't got a free hand," Misha pointed out. His leg had been banged, getting out of the train, and he was in such pain that he feared to pass out before reaching the Rostov train.

"Then hunch your shoulders a bit. Be old and frail. And, Arkady, don't look so perky. Act. Shuffle your feet."

Beggars sprang from nowhere, surrounding the crowd of passengers. They looked desperate with hunger.

"Can't we give them something? Papa always does."

"No, no, Nikolai! Remember you are pretending to be poor. Act! Hold your head down and look ahead. Try to be a peasant. Pretend you are as hungry as they are!"

"I am, nearly," Arkady grumbled. "What's for supper?"

It was with relief that Daisy shepherded them all into the train, which was much more crowded than the last.

The lawyer and his pretty wife, as friendly as ever, were still with them. "I'll tell you a secret," she told Daisy, twirling her skirts. "Come here and I'll show you. Do you see this? It is ammunition, sewn into my skirt. Now, what do you think of that? And Vladimir has the revolver, hidden inside his waistcoat. What an adventure! It is like the wild west of America, is it not?"

Daisy noted that Casimir Terensky was also still of their company, still regarding them narrowly through his slanted half-Tartar eyes.

"Our house is all furnished," the young wife told Daisy delightedly. "In our sitting room there is even a carpet, new, from Turkey. What do you think of *that?*"

They proceeded wearily, all day, over a long hot plain. The train went very slowly, as if wary and expecting an ambush in every belt of trees. Once they saw in the distance a column of marching men, going eastward. Even at a distance, they seemed fagged and disheartened, as if they despaired of arriving anywhere where food and reinforcement were to be found. "Ours," Misha murmured grimly, but to Daisy it seemed a sign of reassurance that Czarist troops were in being, and so near at hand. They must soon be reaching the part of Russia still in the hands of the Whites.

The train stopped at a great many small stations. It was possible to buy fruit and bread, but nothing else. But at least no officials boarded the train or made enquiries, and no one molested them. Towards evening the train drew up in a wood, and the engineer descended to draw water from a stream. The passengers, unchecked, followed suit. "Bring as much as you can," Misha urged Daisy. "Mademoiselle is badly in need of a shave. Her bristles will soon be sticking through this veil like a hedgehog." Night came at last, with the children stretched out exhaustedly on the wooden slats of the seats. Even the moon, now on the wane, looked tired.

They were awakened crisply in the early morning. There were loud shouts as the train drew up at a small station. It was swarming with soldiers. They wore red armbands, and a party of them were swinging onto the train, to embark on a systematic search. They looked stupid, cheerful, and not vicious. They could be heard approaching steadily down the train, exchanging comments and laughter, provoking only an occasional high-pitched scream.

"Get out the passports," Misha told Daisy, "but for God's sake keep the children's well hidden." He felt a fear such as he had never known in battle, a fear horribly compounded by a shame at his disguise and his helplessness.

The heavy boots, the shouts, the protests came nearer. But there was still laughter. "*Angliska, Fransooska,*" Daisy insisted, holding out the passports. Her voice came out very high and artificial; her hand shook. Two rough young soldiers took the passports, held them upside down for a while, righted them, and gazed without comprehension. It was clear that they were unable to read.

The taller one laid hands on Daisy. Outraged and terrified, she managed to protest, "*Angliska, Fransookska!*" She laid a hand on Misha's arm. "My friend is lame." The soldiers proceeded to search her, rudely and thoroughly, with evident gusto, and then laid hands on Varya. "Let them," Daisy hissed in English. "Don't scream, don't cry out, whatever they do." Varya's face was set in a white mask of pride, but she was trembling uncontrollably. Of the younger children they took no notice at all. One laid a hand on Misha's arm, but the other bade him come on and not meddle with the aged. With an obscene remark about the hardness and stringiness of old Frenchwomen, the soldier clattered after him. Varya was now weeping, quietly but heartbrokenly; in the effort of calming her, Daisy's own tremblings gradually lessened. If this happens again, Daisy felt, I shall simply lose control and scream and yell and let the children scream and yell, and there will be all the hideous effects that female screaming and yelling has upon potentially cruel men. I shan't be able to help myself; I can bear no more. An example to the children? I can't even keep hold of *myself!*

Her limbs began to shake again, under the delayed shock. Her heart continued pounding. The train jerked forward, stammered and halted again. More voices were raised; shouts and protests came nearer. No! Daisy's heart cried out. *No!* She could almost feel the scream gathering within her. Any minute now it would find its shattering release. Yet the presence of Misha, helpless though he was, afforded a kind of strength. She was not entirely alone, not totally responsible for these innocent children upon whom the sins of the fathers might be visited with burning wrath and vengefulness.

The train at length started again. Three young peasants had been removed from it, but it could reasonably be hoped that this was for purposes of recruitment rather than execution.

The train seemed to have gathered speed at last, and the Don country in the blaze of summer lay peacefully under a wide blue sky. Its great spaces were beautiful in their richness. In the valleys, the many small winding rivers were fringed with thickets of silver birch, and occasional folds in the steppe were thickly wooded. Limitless fields of green wheat sighed in the soft steppe wind. It was a land of timeless fertility, and seemingly, of timeless peace; although even Daisy knew that this had not been so. Now, it was strangely empty of inhabitants. Sometimes the wood-burning train climbed slowly through thick woods; in its pauses they could hear the singing of what seemed to be hundreds of nightingales. From undisturbed water-meadows came the harsh sounds of wild geese, a noise as of some distant and angry market.

Sometimes they trundled past a little riverside village, with its white-board church, the grey onion dome standing high above its surround of dwellings. Goats grazed on tethers or were led by children; an old woman shepherded five geese home for the evening. An occasional ferryboat traversed the wide river with a load of cattle and their herdsmen. At dusk Misha lay on his face to ease the pain of his leg; a curve in the line revealed another river, where small naked boys were riding and leading the farm horses down to the water, shouting and laughing as they plunged in even deeper. Misha remembered with a sharp pang how he and Kolya had been used to do this at home with the village boys; since the men, tired after the long day's work in the fields, always left the watering and the pasturing of the horses to the boys. Brothers, he thought, if we love them, are closer than any other men can ever be— closer than a father, with his distanced outlook, closer than a son growing up in new and different ways. If a brother is a friend, everything is shared. I have no memories of which he was not a part; I had no thoughts of the future in which he did not have a share.

"What's for supper?" Nikolai asked hopefully. The good things of home were long since finished: he turned up his nose at hard-boiled eggs, black bread, sour milk. "Eat some," Daisy coaxed, "just a little." Ella's face was pinched with fatigue. It was difficult to sleep in the sun-baked box of a train. Varya sat in her corner; her eyes fixed on far horizons. Her sobs had died down. She gazed at the sunset, bright behind the bluff of a hill. She was in the high tower of her castle, her hair was set with jewels, she wore a long robe of cloth of gold. Up the valley towards the castle a knight was riding, not solitary or errant, but with a troop at his back, on fine horses, richly caparisoned. He was on his way to fetch her. They would sail together, over the sea, to his palace, set above a sunny harbour, its garden full of orange and lemon trees, singing birds and splashing water.

The train, in the still, hot evening, drew to a sudden grinding halt. There was a block across the line, and from the wood on either side Red cavalry were riding, closing in round the train. Misha looked out desperately; there was no hope or chance of escape. "Disaffected Cossacks," he said. "These will really mean business. These will indeed search." He looked wildly round for a hiding place for them all and saw none. The throbbing of his leg had increased, he felt dissolved in pain and weak as water, unable to think or act, almost dead. His disguise and his helpessness were ever more hateful to him.

"You are good at praying, Ella," Arkady said. "Pray now."

The Cossacks were moving down the train, slowly, systematically. This time there was no laughter; if there were any screams, they were quickly silenced. Armed with swords as well as rifles, the Cossacks stood ranged along the embankment; more were visible through the trees of the wood; the campfires of evening were lit.

"Couldn't we throw everything away? Can't we throw all the gold away?" Ella asked pitifully.

"Without it, darling, we couldn't buy any food. And it's too late."

The soldiers had now arrived, and what appeared to be a young lieutenant (though there were no longer any ranks in the Russian Army) stepped forward. He was very little like the popular picture of a Cossack, having a lean, fine-drawn, intelligent face; he could have been a doctor or a young professor of mathematics. His voice, however, was crisp and determined, and he looked entirely ruthless.

But he could read; and when Daisy handed him the two foreign passports his demeanour altered and he answered her halting Russian in French. The fact that they were foreigners clearly meant something to him. "To where do you travel?" he asked, and there was as yet no menace in his tones.

"Home to England. And Mademoiselle, my friend, to France."

"And why by this route?"

"Because the British consul told me that the Mediterranean would be safer than the Baltic or the North Sea. Safer from German submarines."

"Your consul was a fool," the young lieutenant said, but not roughly. "And where do you take ship?"

"From Novorossisk, we hope."

"And why do you leave Russia now? Our country will have more need than ever for teachers."

"Mademoiselle is old; she is lame. She suffers. She lives near Nice, and I have promised to travel home with her."

"And then, when things are settled, you will return?"

"I hope to return." Pleased, the young lieutenant essayed an English phrase: "I wish you good travel." He made no attempt to search either of them. "And these children?"

Daisy felt a surge of fear.

"They go to visit their grandmother. At Taganrog." Carried away by her success in the questioning, Daisy added, "Their mother entrusted them to us."

She could hardly have said anything more fatal. The lieutenant's face changed instantly; he ceased to be an intellectual, proud of his international culture, and became at once the full-blooded revolutionary. "I have heard of this!" he cried. "Bourgeois women who entrust their children to foreigners and send them out of Russia laden with the wealth of the people, the wealth they have stolen from the peasants. Stand close, Oleg." He began an intensive search of Nikolai, who was nearest to him, feeling in his armpits, running his hand up his thighs, shaking out his shoes and running his knife into their heels. Nikolai, who at first wriggled violently, was checked by a sharp blow, and stood apparently petrified. Daisy's blood ran cold with terror.

The lieutenant turned to Ella, feeling her clothes, turning her over onto her face and drawing a sharp finger through her little bottom. He unscrewed the head of her doll, Marie-Celestine, selected for the journey as being the most loved of all, and with his sharp knife slit open her stuffed body. The sawdust fell on the floor as his keen fingers probed. Ella, panic-stricken, sobbed wildly. The lieutenant turned round to Varya. The two troopers gazed unblinkingly; their shrewd callous eyes fixed on the scene.

Next to Varya sat Arkady. Although the king's ransom was fixed high under the voluminous skirts of Mademoiselle, there were, on a belt round Arkady's waist, and concealed by the bulge of the blue peasant blouse that he and Nikolai wore, little chamois leather bags, full of enough wealth in jewels to keep the four children in exile for many years. They had been placed there in case the journey should separate them from Misha. Arkady's face, under the day's grime, had gone white, his lower lip trembled. But he sat still and resolute. Daisy was thankful that Ella's continued sobs concealed the loud gasping of her breath. She was under no illusion. This spelt the end. Discovery of the jewels would mean death for all of them.

Now that it was so certain, now that there was no hope for any of them, death meant less; it could even be confronted by Daisy with a kind of fatalistic calm. And how, she found time to wonder, did Misha feel?

Neither calm, nor fatalistic, she surmised, but probably seething with inward fury. He was motionless. His previous guise of the indignant and cantankerous old Frenchwoman, the part he had earlier played with some gusto, had fallen from him. It was as if, in the shadow of death, only silence or truth were possible. Prayers, unbidden, trembled on Daisy's lips.

Tense but still as stone, Misha sat back in his corner. His large betraying hands, neatly folded in his lap, were encased in a pair of his own white kid evening gloves, now rather grubby. He was praying that Daisy's English nationality would save her from multiple rape, and that the rest of them would be shot at once. But he feared that the lieutenant was too intelligent for that. Misha would be taken, questioned, and then left for the Cossacks to have fun with. Very likely they all would. The lieutenant's skilled hands moved searchingly over Varya's trembling and terrified body. Her large, dark eyes besought Misha for help. Her lips moved soundlessly in prayer. The lieutenant felt behind her knees, bent down to start probing her shoes. In a few seconds he would set to work on Arkady.

They were saved by the lightning wits of Nikolai. The lieutenant, his back turned, was now running his hands closely once again through Varya's long and very thick hair. But the two soldiers still regarded them stolidly from the corridor.

"Look!" Nikolai suddenly shouted in Russian, pointing behind them. "A deer! Shoot quickly, you could get him!"

For a moment, the soldiers, caught by the urgency in the little boy's voice, looked round. As quickly, the lieutenant turned his head. The two little boys, standing in the middle of the carriage, were both excitedly pointing.

"Sit down," he told them icily. "Keep still. Don't move again." He gave Arkady a sharp cuff.

But it was not Arkady! Nikolai had sat down in his place. Arkady, trembling like a leaf, was now seated next to Daisy, where his already searched brother had been placed. He mastered his voice enough to say complainingly, "They could have got it, if they had been quick!" The lieutenant had now finished with Varya, and turned his attention to what he supposed was Arkady. Nikolai submitted to a second examination with quiet goodwill. "You are more sensible than your brother, young comrade," the lieutenant told him when he had done. His civilised mask was restored, and he seemed anxious to complete his task. He sketched a bow at Daisy. "Good travel," he repeated again. The two soldiers, still scowling at Arkady, tramped after.

There was a sudden appalling screaming. Dragged, pushed, clutching at everything that could arrest her passage, the gay little wife, followed by her lawyer husband, was wrestled from the train. Their revolver and ammunition had been found.

Instinctively, Daisy started to her feet. "I must go to her, help her!"

"Be still!" Misha hissed.

"But what will they do to her?"

"*Sit quiet.*" Misha spoke very low and as if through clenched teeth, but his words had a compelling, diamond-hard edge. Daisy sank back. Her words came forth in a desperate whisper.

"But I must tell her that we didn't—that it wasn't us. She'll think we betrayed her, told the soldiers about the revolver."

"She won't think anything for long. These are *Kazaki.*" Misha's voice had the same compulsion, the same ruthless cutting edge. Did this daft girl think they were all engaged in some schoolchild game of rounders? "Do you wish to die yourself? Do you wish death for the children also? *Sit quiet.*"

It seemed a long while before the screams from the wood ceased; but Daisy, frozen into stillness, dared not even cover her ears, lest one of the soldiers still on the train should look in and have his attention drawn to the panic on her chalk-white face.

Endless minutes passed. Gazing out, Daisy saw with sickening apprehension that a dozen others had been bundled out of the train, and that among them was a familiar dark-faced figure, his slant eyes flicking desperately from side to side.

"Casimir Ivanovitch Terensky," Misha said, very low.

Passing their window, Terensky shot a look of frantic supplication, as if he believed that the old order indeed prevailed, and that the Dubelskys had but to leave the train and intervene against such treatment of their property, and thus save his life with one imperious dismissive movement of the hand. Meeting this look, Misha's helplessness lay on him like lead.

"He will betray us." Daisy's whispered gasp was more a statement than a question.

"Who knows? I think not. He is not such a man. Casimir Ivanovitch is no man to betray the children of a benefactor. But who knows? If they want to kill him, no betrayal will save him. Perhaps he knows that."

Ella was still weeping, although more quietly, for the disintegration of her Marie-Celestine. The doll hung flat and limp, her sawdust stuffing strewn over the floor. She was like a horrid travesty of what was happening in the woods, and Daisy shuddered.

"We can make her a new body," she whispered to Ella.

"It won't be the *same* body," Ella wailed, suddenly loud again in her grief.

"A better body," Daisy promised her, through teeth that still obstinately chattered. "There, there, my darling."

"I want Nyanya," Ella moaned inconsolably. "I want Nyanya!" But she snuggled up to Daisy nonetheless, on the principle of any port in a storm.

The twins sat very erect, as if poised for action. Varya had sunk back with closed eyes, as if she could not bear to see any more. She opened them suddenly, seizing Misha by the arm. "He will betray us, surely Casimir Ivanovitch will betray us. What shall we do, Misha? What shall we do?"

"If I had two legs we'd make a run for it and all get shot. Probably the wisest thing to do. As it is, sit tight. And pray."

There was an interminable wait. They listened with thudding hearts whilst the distant cries and screams grew fainter as the victims were driven further into the wood.

Another long wait followed. At any moment, thought Daisy, there'll be running feet and they'll be back in the train to seize us. Hope, that had once entirely left her, had returned. Oddly, it made fear more overwhelming and self-control harder. She clasped Ella ever more tightly.

"Why are you shaking, Miss Daisy?" the little girl asked. "Haven't the wicked men gone?"

"Wait. Keep quiet. Pray." Misha's voice had a sharp commanding edge to it, and Ella, with tightened clasp, was silent. There was so long a pause that Daisy had time to wonder why, in danger, we grasp each other and hold each other tight, as if the mere closeness of another human body spelt a kind of safety and succour. Monkey ancestry? Arkady blew his nose suddenly and violently, making them all jump.

Finally a burst of shots rang out.

"What are they doing, Miss Daisy? What are they *doing?*"

"Perhaps they are shooting the deer, Ella, the deer that Nikolai saw."

Arkady looked at her with scorn.

There was another very long wait; then the train, once again, jerkily, began to move. The barriers had been removed. The Cossack troops, no longer interested, were gathered in the wood. Daisy's limbs collapsed in a heap; her heart very slowly left the place it had taken up under her uvula and returned to its normal position. Varya and Ella were still crying, but more softly.

"Oh, twins," Daisy cried, "you were *so splendid!*"

"He said I was more sensible than my brother; did you hear, Arkady?"

"You can't be more sensible than yourself," his twin retorted logically. "Better at lying, maybe you are, Nikolai."

"Gentlemen," Mademoiselle announced, in a deep voice, and speaking in English, "never tell lies."

But Daisy feared that if she laughed she would never stop crying, thinking of the cheerful little honeymooning wife and her quiet serious husband, lying out among the pinewoods, with the Cossack campfires burning nearby, and their sightless eyes staring up into the trees.

The train moved forward, rumbled slowly on, established the soothing rhythm of movement; each clickety-click adding its tiny quota of relief. For all its strangeness and its huge sweep, with every slow mile the countryside exercised its healing power; every field and tree and hill, each browsing beast or curling river seeming to be nature's quiet recompense for the cruelty and vileness of men. Soon enough, the landscape faded into dusk, and across the wide expanse of serene pale sky a great dark smudge of cloud came rolling out of the east, dull and heavy, like brown smoke disgorged by some cosmic factory chimney. The children were restless and exhausted. Misha moved heavily from time to time under the gathering pain of his leg. For a while, a dull silence held them all. A sensation of exhausted courage emptied Daisy's heart, a haunting of threat and despair hung over her as if all the country, all the future ahead lay under that dun miasma of smoking cloud. From far away across the steppe came the low growl of distant thunder.

The night descended on them. But for a long while no one slept. In an excited babble, the children talked the fear and shock out of themselves, Misha lay restless with pain, and Daisy continued her uncontrollable trembling.

Long before dawn Daisy awoke, gasping in the sharp cold air. A pale, sad, half-moon was declining over the hills. The children were unstirring; even Misha slept, his long muscular legs sprawled in the carelessness of sleep, the hated hat slumped sideways and over one eye. His unconscious face retained its youthful look, a kind of serene arrogance. He didn't care, he hardly noticed, thought Daisy, that Casimir died sooner than betray him and all of us to death. He takes it totally for granted that a peasant should die for him, that any of us should risk our lives for him or his family. To him, it's nothing but a part of the natural order of things. On one side of the great divide—Dubelskys. And on the other side—serfs.

She was alone and could think for herself now, for the first moment since she had heard Kolya had died. For the first time, in this clear cold night, freed from the distractions and the dangers of the day, she could realise and understand that he was dead, could try by some means to face this hard indestructible fact. Slowly the tears began to stream down her face, her shoulders to shake in silent heaving sobs. She gave herself up to the luxury of grief, to the simple animal pain of losing that loved flesh. She no longer deceived herself. Foolish as she had been to think of him, hopeless of fulfilment as such love had been, she knew that she had indeed grown to love him. There was no shame anywhere in this: he had at least liked her, talked to her, let her into his hopes and dreams, thought of her as a real person and not just as someone who happened to make part of the enormous Dubelsky household, who sang, and danced, was good with the children and amused Papa. From selfish thoughts her grief carried her on to the sheer unmixed bitterness of Kolya's death, his youth and hope blotted out, his intelligence and his promise blown into nothing. Even if one knew that he lived elsewhere, what agony of pain she felt for the lost flash of those dark eyes, the zest of his manly body. She could hear again his voice, singing a haunting Russian melody, and she cried his name out, with unbearable sadness: "Kolya! Oh, Kolya . . ."

Misha stirred and was immediately awake. He removed the sleeping body of Ella and levered himself across the seat towards Daisy. Aware of her muffled sobs, he put an arm round her and drew her sad head down onto his shoulder.

"All he would have done," she gasped. "All he dreamed of doing. A changed, happier Russia."

"Ah, Kolya's dreams!" Misha said. "Think, perhaps, that his heart would have been broken if none of it had come true."

"What will your father do? And the Princess? Kolya was so much her ally, with the children, in the house, with his music." And what, she thought, will you do yourself, Misha? His love for Kolya had been, she knew, Misha's polestar; without it he would go, probably, straight to the dogs. And the children, to whom he meant so much? Now Kolya would never have children of his own, and Daisy's tears flowed afresh. Why did God take those who could least be spared? But it is myself for whom I grieve. I loved him, I loved him, *I loved him*. What a baby I was, those few years ago, to think that what I felt for Richard was love. I knew nothing of him, and he knew nothing of me. But Kolya I loved. I loved. *I loved.* *Kolya, I loved you.* Soundlessly, she repeated his name without ceasing, as if the sound could somehow reach the dead ears of the young man buried in the distant sand of a Ukrainian forest. Listen, Kolya, I loved you.

The spectacle of someone, of anyone, weeping for Kolya brought Misha a kind of comfort. As an undercurrent to his overwhelming sorrow, he had hated the unimportant manner of Kolya's death, his hasty burial at nightfall under a tree, as if he had been some trusty dog, and not a soul which, to Misha, was one of shining greatness. It had been a ruthless nothingness; the very haphazardness of the shell that had struck him down, the gasping unconscious moments, the quickly covered grave in the anonymous dark sand of the pinewoods. No cross, no holy chant, only his own hands and the hands of his friends sweeping the pine needles over the grave, lest pursuing Germans should find it. He had wanted a great mourning crowd of all those who had loved his brother; every rite, every ceremony, every honour.

The intensity of Daisy's grief moved Misha to tell her something that at the time had seemed an awkwardness, a blow to the pride, even a failure in judgement on the part of beloved Kolya, making an announcement that Misha had hardly known how to answer. He bent towards Daisy, whispering close to her ear for fear of waking the sleeping children. "He loved you. Kolya loved you. He told me of it the week before he died. We sat late by the fire, at the camp, in a halt in the retreat. But even telling it, he had a face of sadness, as if he knew it could never be."

"I loved him too," Daisy gulped. "But who did not? Everyone loved him."

Misha's urgent whisper came closer to her ear. "No, you mistake me. He loved you as a man loving a woman. After the war, he hoped to marry you."

A fresh, more appalled sense of all that was lost gripped Daisy. She cried out loud, forgetting the sleeping children, aware only of all that had been unsaid, unacted, not enjoyed. "No! No! No! Oh no!" She wept now uncontrollably, uncouthly, bending in pain, casting her body from side to side. Arkady opened his eyes, gazed blankly at her, slumbered again. From next door an old woman who had been aroused from sleep by her cries came to peer curiously at Daisy, and at the still stranger spectacle of Misha, his hat back on his bandaged head, his straw-coloured hair tufting out of the bandage.

"Weep," he said, holding her as still as he could, as she turned and twisted as though to remove herself, by physical action, from the intolerable pain. Focussing her blurred eyes for a moment, Daisy saw in the last of the moonlight that the tears were also pouring down Misha's face.

Slowly, her struggles eased. They wept on, in the fading moonlight. She was held by Misha in a physical closeness far removed from sexual excitement. It was as if an extremity of sorrow had neutered them both, left them simply as two human beings, naked in an unbearable grief. The air grew colder yet as the dawn came and the train rocked them gently southwards, locked hour after hour in a silent vigil, moving on into an unknown destiny, perhaps sadder even than Kolya's had been.

Misha remembered what old Petya had said to him, as they smoothed the turf under the lime tree: "You cry out almost in complaint that he was so good; is his goodness to no purpose? He and his goodness are now with God. But in this world his goodness can only live in you."

In me, Misha thought; what a hope. I might try, but how long will I go on trying? The calm dead face of Kolya lay in his mind's eye. "I shall forget him!" he cried out loud, in a kind of agony.

"Not ever," Daisy said, in a broken voice. "Not ever." But her exhausted tears flowed anew. The sunrise ahead, glowing from behind the hills, brought them both a lull in feeling, an exhausted peace, as though some necessary tribute had been paid, some anthem sung, some holy rite performed.

They stopped, in the drowsy morning, at yet another small station. There seemed to be yet another delay. In time another uniformed figure came down the train. But this one strolled, looking in without much urgency upon the sleeping, huddled figures stirring from a restless night. The uniform that he wore bore Czarist insignia! In the hugeness of Russia there seemed to be no fixed frontier between the bands of Red or White soldiers, and trains still wandered to and fro, useful to both sides and largely unmolested. Unknowingly, they had slept their way into safety.

Misha sprang immediately to life, as if he had no idea what pain, grief or fatigue were. He tore off Mademoiselle's hat and sent it spinning across the platform. His petticoats, stripped of their precious contents, rapidly followed. "Hi!" he called to a tall youth strolling the platform with a case.

"Sell me your shirt! If you are going for a recruit you won't need that one!" The startled youth complied, taking a peasant blouse from his strapped basket trunk. Misha, renewed, shaved, and provided with a beaker of tea, gathered spirits with every mile. He had lived to fight again. Already Daisy and the children and their plight seemed to be fading from his mind. "When we get to the city," he said, "I shall have to report. If they order me to stay, can you travel on alone?"

Daisy's heart sank.

"Oh no, Misha!" Varya pleaded. "Stay with us! Travel on with us!"

"The rest will be through country that is in our hands. Only another twelve hours, perhaps less. Novocherkask, Rostov, you could be in Novorossisk by noon tomorrow. You could be in the villa by evening, bathing in the sea. Think of that!" When peeling off a final petticoat, he had revealed the smart breeches that he had, to his great danger, kept on all the while. Though grimed with mud and stained with blood they retained a certain elegance. He stretched his long arms in the clean shirt, as though flexing them to strike a further blow. He was reprieved, alive, free. Despite the pain of his leg, his face was radiant.

The heat came now with renewed strength. Scattered villages showed presently sometimes a minaret instead of a church spire. The children, shocked and exhausted, were more restless than ever. The novelty of escape and adventure had faded; they had no appetite for the monotonous food; they had been very frightened and now were very tired. The thought of a possible parting from Misha sunk their hearts. Misha's high spirits alone kept them going through this long, hot day. In the late afternoon, they drew into Novorcherkask, its many golden domes gleaming in the evening sun. The train stood, panting in the still air, and heat struck up from the platform. It was a day of *festa*, and the town was full of the sound of bells.

Novorcherkask was to become the headquarters of the White Army. Already there was a military office at the station, towards which Misha, no longer bowed and furtive, swung himself on his elegant crutches. He was seized on by a doctor and cursorily examined. "Into hospital," the doctor said, "if you do not want to lose that leg."

There seemed to be nothing else for it. The children stood, a disconsolate group, outside the door of the office. Should he, Misha wondered, take a chance on finding friends, or somewhere for them to stay, in Novorcherkask? But no, he would be away as soon as his leg mended. The sea, he decided, was the safer bet.

As so often, nothing but irrelevancies presented themselves to the mind, at this moment charged with emotion, with relief, with fatigue. "I believe the military hospitals are all very good," Daisy ventured, her voice sounding flat and almost patronising. "You'll find it all rather primitive at the villa," Misha told her. "Only old Gleb and his wife Anna to cook, and their daughter. If you don't look out, Anna will give you nothing but kebabs and sticky sweetmeats—she's got Turkish blood. We used always to take some servants down from Moscow. Better not take the children into Novorossisk. The fewer people who know they are there the better. Go as little as possible yourself. Send Gleb or take old Anna with you if you must go. And bury you know what. Halfway between the two tall cypress trees to the right of the terrace, perhaps. Gleb would never talk, but he could be forced into telling. There's a British consul in Novorossisk. Or there was. It would be as well to keep in touch. Open any letter. And tell them, tell them . . . the news . . . If the food is short, go to the Moslem farms in the mountains. We are on friendly terms, they will sell you what they can. Perhaps their mother, perhaps even my father, will find their way south."

The heat embraced them like a warm bath. There were flies everywhere. Church bells rang and jangled persistently in the hot air, a wild uncoordinated sound as if all the ringers were pleasantly drunk. Men in baggy trousers lounged in the shade of railway trucks piled high with bulging sacks and apparently going nowhere. Raggedly uniformed Plastunis, some of them slant-eyed and heavy-shouldered, strolled casually down the platform, with open tunics and cheerful interested glances. Like dream palaces, the pale golden domes of Novorcherkask's many churches revealed themselves through gaps in the station buildings.

The setting sun fell full on Daisy's face. To Misha, she had never looked less pretty. Nothing could blur the serene oval of her face, but her eyes were heavy-lidded and glazed with fatigue, her clear skin blotched and smeared with dust. Her hair clung together in a damp mat. She looked a poor little shrimp of a thing, and alarmingly young. But her patience and kindness with the children had been exemplary and her courage had not faltered. She looked plain as a pikestaff and he had never liked her so much. The fact that Kolya loved her had detached her from the general background of life, from her role of family usefulness, and had swung her slightly more into focus.

Whistles blew, there was a bustle of departure. Detaching himself from Ella's embrace, Misha bundled them into the train, and taking Daisy's hand, surprised himself as much as her by bending over it and kissing it warmly.

"Obey Miss Pelham," he told the children, suddenly stern and bracing as their tearful faces turned towards him from the train window. "May God bless you all. And pray, pray tonight and for nine days, for the soul of Casimir Terensky."

Limping resolutely away down the platform, Misha meditated for quite two minutes on the subject of Daisy. He was predominantly relieved that her love for Kolya would almost certainly keep her by the side of his brothers and sisters, until help came, as come it surely would, soon enough. Of this he felt sure. The focus of his thoughts shifted a little and he thought of Daisy herself with a kind of wonder. It was not possible, he reflected, to spend a night of deep grief in the arms of any woman, however innocently, without feeling nearer to her, more warmly concerned in her and her future. Something was owed, he felt vaguely, on Kolya's behalf, and must be paid.

Ten minutes later, as he gritted his teeth to endure what must be done to his lacerated leg, thoughts of her faded from his mind.

Climbing again slowly, the train rocked on into the night. In the general sadness at parting from Misha, Daisy was able to nurse unseen her grief for Kolya. With the release from the urgency of their danger, the immediate need for courage and a brave face was past. Distant hills, seen in the dusk, seemed in their starkness to echo her loneliness.

"We shall never see Misha again!" Varya cried out suddenly, late in the evening. "He is gone, he is lost to us . . . And Kolya, where is Kolya? Why does no one speak of him? Why did Misha avoid his name?"

In her weakness and unpreparedness, the soothing lies came haltingly to Daisy's lips. Not yet! Not yet! I must gather a little strength, a little courage, before I can tell them. The air was cold again, and the stale compartment seemed filled with sorrow, loss, and solitary pain. Sleep was the only friend to them all.

Chapter 16

The Villa Rosa looked exactly as Daisy had supposed it would. Cream-coloured plaster and green shutters gave a general Riviera-like aspect, as did a garden terraced down toward the sea and crammed with oleanders, low stone walls sprawled over by climbing roses, beds of bright annuals, and geraniums in earthenware pots. An occasional cypress tree speared up among the lesser growth; there were stone steps and a vine-shaded terrace, and a smell of honeysuckle prevailed. A servant's annexe stood empty, and a rocky path past it led down to the sea. Towards this the children, casting aside their tiredness as if by magic, streamed off with loud cries of joyful anticipation.

Around Novorossisk the coast was harsh and bleak, visited as it was by a perpetual northeast wind from off the Caucasus mountains, but to the east of the Villa Rosa a line of hills formed a sheltered enclave, sharing in the Crimean climate of warmth and lush vegetation. Across an expanse of deep and dark blue sea, faintly visible against the evening sky, were the Crimean mountains. Daisy sat down on a stone seat and allowed herself a moment of recollection, of mounting sorrow mingled with the enormous relief of safety, until Gleb, unable to believe that anyone, even so eccentric a being as an English governess, could really enjoy being alone, slippered across to embark on a long saga of his martyrdom to the whims of an exacting wife. He had hardly concluded the first canto before the children came racing back.

"Gleb! Gleb! Do you know that we heard two people shot?"

"More than two, Nikolai. Four probably."

"Six or seven maybe, Arkady."

"Shot dead by the Red soldiers, quite near the train."

"Ah, Princes, what wickedness! Twelve years ago," Gleb pointed out, determined to prove that he too had lived dangerously, "just such Godless men seized the battleship *Potemkin*. They terrorised all the ships on the Black Sea. I saw them here, off this very coast, sailing that very ship. All their officers they had killed."

"What happened then?"

"We were all full of terror. No ship dared to sail. Scarcely would the fishermen leave port, for fear that their catch would be stolen and they themselves killed."

"But what happened in the end?"

"I am telling you, Nikolai Andreivitch. In the end they sought refuge in Romania and we heard no more of these revolutionaries. Some were caught, I think, and hanged. This was in the terrible year, I do not recollect just which year, when our fleet suffered defeat far away in the east." Gleb, remembering it, waved his head from side to side.

"Tsushima," Arkady said knowledgeably.

"I know not its name, but all that was the beginning of much wickedness, of all this wickedness that we hear of now." And Gleb wandered off, shaking his head and bearing in mind that he had in fact been sent out by Anna to pick the beans.

He had played his trump card, the battleship *Potemkin*, but with these so sophisticated young princes it hardly seemed to have taken a trick. They grow up, he reflected sadly. They speak certainties in their young high voices, and ours are silenced. It is no less bitter because this was always so. How little heed I paid to the tales of my grandfather, of all that past life that was so real to him! And yet, what babes these two princes were, what beauty they had as young children! Gleb longed to be once more in command, to be able once again to pick them up in his arms and carry them down the rocky path to the seashore, to see them kick their strong little legs as they lay on the sand, and to bear them, crowing and laughing, out into the splash of the waves.

He longed to be back into the world as it had been when they last came to the Villa Rosa, the world of 1913, with its continuity and its certainties, the world of the splendour of princes and the humility of beggars and the safe accepted place for everyone in between. There were wrongs, he thought, but so there will always be. But now, no one will acknowledge any difference anymore, between Czar and pauper, between honest man and rogue, between priest and layman, even between man and woman.

Daisy felt deep thankfulness at their safe arrival; and the Villa Rosa, with its sea and sun and cool shuttered rooms was the very place for rest and recuperation. But it was no environment for a wounded heart. It was a honeymoon place, and seemed to breathe of the delights of love. At evening the gentlest of breezes rustled the arbutus trees; nights were warm and soft, filled with a delicious fragrance of flowers. Days were brilliant, clear, sun-warmed—and empty as a shell. The very waves, falling with a kind of languorous slowness on the beach, sighed out, *No more, no more, no more . . .*

They lived isolated, always a little apprehensive. Daisy longed desperately to get away, to take some real part in the war, to train as a nurse and be sent to the Western Front, to danger, discomfort and suffering. Only in ministering to real, harsh, physical pain could she forget her own anguish of heart. Scrubbing floors all day and far into the night, she might become so tired that she would perforce fall asleep and not lie dreaming of all that life with Kolya might have meant.

She began every week with the hope and belief that its end would bring the Princess, and her own release. Surely such an adoring mother would not, could not, keep away much longer from her children? But the weeks passed, and the months, and they brought no Princess, no message. Misha had vanished completely into the maelstrom of civil war that Russia had now become. Nor did any communication come from him. Daisy could only bide her time, with a sad dogged patience, thin as she had never been, and sleepless by night. There were even moments in the still, early dawns when the temptation to rise swiftly from her bed and swim out far into that dark and silent sea, never returning, was strong indeed. For a long while her prayers seemed to bounce back at her, like tennis balls off a steel door. Dogged in this, as in all else, she went on; sometimes with flashes of hope, sometimes in near despair.

"Could you, Varya, while I am helping Ella with her piano practice, go to the village to see if the shops have any coffee?"

Varya held her head high. "No Russian girl of noble family is permitted to go anywhere on her own till she is twenty-one."

"Oh, goodness! Take Gleb, then. But he has enough to do."

Now, in the midsummer, the way to the village was long, dusty and very hot. It involved a hard tramp, not only on Sundays, but on other obligatory church festivals.

"Need we go?" Nikolai demanded boldly, on one grilling forenoon.

"We need," Ella said quite firmly.

"Oh, Ella!"

"In Moscow we went always. And at Jevrenskaia."

"In Moscow we had the carriage to take us. Need we, Miss Daisy? It is so hot, and so far. And the smell is awful! No incense drowns it." Arkady kept silence, allowing Nikolai to do the talking, but his face expressed support.

I'm always dragooning them, thought Daisy, into lessons, and piano practise, and getting up in the morning, and cleaning their teeth; it's an almighty effort to go on slave-driving them over things I don't believe are vital myself, like St. Seraphim, or whatever, and the need to go to church on his or her day. If I keep them at it, won't I put them off the whole thing? But everything else has crumbled, and this is their anchor, and they *must* hang on to it.

Varya's line was more subtle. "I have a little headache coming on," she told them in faint tones.

"But would not your father and mother have wanted it, in spite of all?"

"I suppose so," Varya admitted reluctantly. "But things were so different then."

"We had better stick to what they want. Find your hat, Varya."

Ella's face, already hatted, beamed happiness, but Nikolai, leaving, was unable to resist a sharp tug at her locks. I hope, thought Daisy, that Ella at least will never have to leave Russia. What would become of her in exile? How could she live in the West? Here in Russia she would find no opposition, no terrible struggle between faith and family duty. She was completely the product of her Russian environment; with the approbation of all, she would eventually find her way into a convent where she would live happily ever after.

Meanwhile there were the pressing difficulties of education.

Daisy wrote to her father:

> Darling Daddy,
> Please send me several arithmetic books, suitable for several ages but with the *Answers* in the back! And a Latin primer, and please some children's stories the others have grown out of, and please some frivolous things like popular songs! I know they may never arrive, but please try! Not a hope of getting home at present because George Bennett, who is consul at Novorossisk now, says the British government has forbidden the transport of women and children through the Mediterranean because of German submarines sinking so many passenger ships. And anyway I couldn't leave the children alone here now. Still no news of their parents.

Gleb and his wife, though kindly disposed towards others, lived together on a steady diet of mutual recrimination. Anna Timofeyevna's Turkish blood flowed hot and strong; she had brothers in the hills with whose appalling vengeance she would threaten Gleb in moments of passion. She was the cleverer; under the lash of her tongue poor Gleb was forced in the end to fall back upon superior male strength. Sometimes he even had recourse to Daisy for support. *"Barysha"* he would say pleadingly, "Miss . . . Anna torments me . . . and my daughter has left me to live with her aunt at Novorossisk . . - as if there were not work enough *here!"* And then pride would get the better of him and he would stride back to the kitchen to silence Anna by a resounding smack on her stern, generous in width and encased in many petticoats. Anna would respond with a stream of abuse, until the rafters rang. "Do you want any more?" Gleb would demand, "do you need any more, Anna Timofeyevna, you Turkish hag?" Anna would subside into angry mutterings, banging the saucepans together as she concocted yet another sticky brew. All the same, the old grey mare was the better horse, thought Daisy, reverting to one of her father's unclerical expressions.

To Daisy's exasperation, both servants treated the children with dotingly indulgent affection as if their very tiresomenesses were a piece of rare charm. But in any dispute they came down squarely and unfailingly on the side of the little boys.

Daisy was often exasperated. "But don't you see, Anna, Nikolai was really cruel to Ella, hiding that doll she loves so much? And looking on, innocent as pussy, while we all searched high and low? Of course he must miss supper and go to bed." It was useless to talk; soon the stairs would creak beneath Anna's heavy and furtive tread as she bore a tray of dainties up to Nikolai. A growing boy, she would mutter indignantly. No supper! Mother of God, what cruelty! "Just to kiss the Prince goodnight," she would call out mendaciously to Daisy, and half an hour later she could be heard padding up to collect the telltale tray. How could I leave them, quite alone, with only Gleb and Anna? Daisy thought. But another of her father's aphorisms came into her mind: "Good servants must always be allowed their little ways."

Sometimes the responsibility of it all made her feel thin and inadequate. "I love you but you are not Mamma," Arkady would say frankly when she was kissing him goodnight; sometimes even Nikolai's spirits seemed dimmed. Varya was beginning to lose her proud certainties, and Ella's little voice, talking of Mamma and Papa and Nyanya, went quavering and shallow, as if she were no longer entirely able to believe in them. Men in their pride and in their conviction that they know what is right make war, Daisy thought—they die and are wounded almost of their own volition—but it is the very old and the women who suffer most deeply, and it is the children who suffer longest, because they have the longest to live.

Sometimes her own suffering lay on her like lead. There was no one to whom to turn for comfort, and if there had been, what help could they offer? What comfort could be found in any aspect of the death of Kolya, so full of life and promise, so full of unfulfilled dreams and hopes? Beautiful, and strong, and clever, and loved by all, why should he be sacrificed in a quarrel that was never of his making? If we had married, if we had even spoken to each other of love, I believe I could better bear it! But everything was unsaid, undone, unexpressed, a wilderness of waste and nothingness. She lay awake, tormented, through the long, long nights that were sometimes as silent as death itself, or broken only by the melancholy repeated fall of waves on the shore. Even the very dawn of day seemed dusty and tired.

If you are ever in deep trouble, her father had told Daisy, read the Psalms. They contain the whole of human experience; they rise to the heights and plumb the depths. Don't fight your grief and trouble; let it roll over you, the great sea of human grief. And of God's help for human grief. It will bring you, at least, a kind of calm, a breathing space. Resignation takes longer.

She found this true; looking back, she could now see that Kolya, on his last leave, had been one accepting his death, with however much sadness, going through it, travelling beyond it. A lover of life who could be a lover of something more. A casual, musical, lighthearted boy, who had loved speed, and dancing, who had doubled up with laughter, eaten and drunk with gusto, gone probably with women, taken little or no thought for the morrow, for all his moments of philosophy. How had he managed so steadfastly to say farewell to it all when the need arose? What had his three years of bitter war taught him, that he could take death so matter-of-factly, as if for all its horrible reality, it was, in the long run, nothing much?

Morning began, very faintly, to light her window. If he accepted, so I too must accept. But oh—I am stranded, stranded. Left forever on a waste shore.

It was a relief to see the cheerful freckled face of George Bennett. He had a little German car, which he drove with great pride, and he seemed still able to find some petrol. A port, he pointed out, makes a difference—supplies came from Baku—and he would persuade Daisy to come for a drive with him into the hills.

"Can't we take the children?" she would beg.

"Well, must we? Aren't you entitled to a day off?"

"I'm sure I am; but they have such a dull time."

"No duller than yours."

"Yes, but compared with what they had in Moscow! And I'm not a child."

"The Russian aristocracy," George said sententiously, "enslave people only too easily, after all those years of enslaving serfs."

He took the children all the same. He is really, Daisy reflected, a very very good sort, and I like him immensely. What fun to have jokes again, to talk slang English, to say silly and irresponsible things. "You save my life, George, you know," she would say impulsively at the end of the day; but this of course was a mistake. He stopped laughing and started looking grave, and pressing her hand and gazing with meaningful glances from under his motoring cap.

The little car would chug up into the hills, and they would halt under the plane trees of a Tartar village and drink sherbet or Caucasian wine. Here were prosperous and polite Moslem farmers and their veiled wives, with handsome eyes peering out curiously. The villages were small and very clean, each with its mosque and marketplace, its flat-roofed white-plastered Tartar houses, its small boys in skullcaps with whom the twins exchanged greetings in Russian, and, for all Daisy knew, less polite comments. All seemed untouched and unaffected by the war or the revolution; thick peace brooded over the sunny scene, over the horses clattering down the village streets, the melodious moans of cows being led in from the fields.

"And yet," George Bennett said, "these are the people who terrorised all Russia for hundreds of years. Even to us, in England, they were a byword of fierceness and savagery. You will hear old people say, when someone gets into a fearful row, or marries a cross wife, 'He's caught a Tartar.' "

"You can't believe it, looking at them. I think they're the most smiling and friendly villagers I've seen since I came to Russia. Look at that beaming old man leaning against the wall in the shade."

"All the same, I'll bet he's got a beaming old rifle hidden up his rafters, and knows well how to use it. And would, too, on you, or me, or the children, without scruple, if the chance came and it was worth his while."

"Oh no! He's got the most benign expression you could imagine. Can we stay until the man—is it called muezzin?—calls them to prayer from that minaret?"

"Are you a true traveller? Like one of those Victorian ladies who rose above the lice and the snakes and the bedbugs and rode on a camel all the way to Bokhara, looking clean all the way in spite of there being no water."

"Oh, I wish I were one!"

"Thank God you aren't. To us poor hardworking consuls they were nothing but a headache, specially as they were all first cousins of someone in the Cabinet, so one knew there would be hell to pay if any careless khan laid a finger on them." Daisy laughed. George really was very very nice, and after weeks and weeks of undiluted and demanding children it was good to receive a meaningful glance from any man at all, and from one of one's own countrymen, distinctly warming.

"Can't we buy a horse?" Arkady demanded. "They sell them here, very good horses off their farms. Papa would like us to buy one. Nikolai and me will soon forget how to ride."

"Yes, but darling, what with?" The hoard of gold under the cypress tree, regularly depleted under the light of each full moon, was growing smaller and smaller. And still no news from Misha.

He arrived next day, without warning, on a flying visit. Yes, he told Daisy, he had news of his parents. But the despair etched on his face boded ill. They had taken the old Princess, as she had wanted, to her house in east Russia, but she had died there, almost upon arrival, and by the time the funeral rites were accomplished the railways had stopped running and they had been cut off. They had tried to escape to the east, with a view to returning to south Russia through Asia, or by sea from Shanghai, but they had been captured, somewhere near Perm, it was thought, and were now in prison, no one knew where. Perhaps, even, they were dead.

"Oh God, if one knew *anything* for certain, even if it were the worst! Tell the children, tell them they have gone on a long journey and that we shan't see them for a long while. And that may well be true, in either sense."

His leg was mended, but he seemed still to walk with a slight limp, and to be older, thinner, more sober, even in two months. The war was not going well; there were disputes between the White generals, a lack of supplies. The Allies were said to be helping, some Scots gunnery experts had arrived. But nothing was coordinated, and only the spirit of officers and men gave hope of ultimate victory.

The children crowded round Misha delightedly. He was not only himself—he was their whole ancient world of gaiety and reassurance. His presence lifted them out of these days of monotonous food and worn-out shoes and English arithmetic books and into their familiar world of glittering chandeliers and the music of many violins, of innumerable smiling servants, of enormous polished floors stretching between those high doors picked out in gold, of great tables laden with silver and good food. For all Daisy's efforts to lighten them with stories and songs, with acting and dancing, the long evenings had been too silent and monotonous, broken only by the nightingales and the sound of the waves falling on the rocks below. Bathing in the clear water was fun, but what was truly fun without Mamma and Papa, without Misha himself? And Kolya who would come no more . . . at this thought Varya's tears fell fast. There was a splendid supper; with Anna giving of her best, with Misha singing, with the twins dancing; but even here the blank space where Kolya and their parents should have been haunted them all. The sun set behind the shadowy Crimean mountains, no longer crested in snow. The sound of waves faded slowly on the shore. At length even Varya, protesting to the last, was in bed.

Exhausted by the effort of cheerfulness, Misha and Daisy sat on the stone balustrade of the terrace in a constrained and uneasy silence. There seemed to be too much to say and no time to say it. Daisy gave a long, bewildered sigh.

Misha began to talk in a low hurried voice of the possibilities of getting the children away to France or England if the Red armies should sweep victoriously southward.

Daisy was astonished; he had never even begun to speak along such lines before.

Fishing boats were always to be hired, he told her, and they should go first to the Crimea. There seemed a reasonable hope that the White armies, supplied from the sea by the Allies, could hold out there indefinitely.

"We do not take many prisoners," he told Daisy, "but there was a young man, a student, a nephew of Gregor Mihailovitch, who was brought in the other night. He was shot, in the end, but before they took him out I heard him talk of the revolution and of his faith in it and his understanding of what it would bring to Russia. Kolya would have listened to him with real understanding. To me, it is generally a meaningless jargon, but there was so much real feeling in this young man, so much of dedication—he was more like a young priest. He saw nothing of the cruelty and waste of it all, nothing of the dangers; his eyes were fixed on some far-off wonderful vision. For the first time he made me feel afraid, afraid as they say long ago we were afraid as the first Moslem conquerors swept over Eastern Europe, with those same blazing eyes and indefatigable hope, seeing nothing, nothing but their goal, fearing nothing but their strange new God. It was fearful, a fearful thing to hear him."

Daisy sat dumbfounded. She had never heard Misha talk in this way to anybody, and that he should talk so to her was purely amazing. But of course, she told herself briskly, there's nobody else. He was different, exhausted, deflated. People live in armour, she told herself, and sometimes they loosen it and you see a little of what they are like inside. And sometimes it puts you right off them. And sometimes it melts your heart. And I don't wonder that people, men especially, don't often do it, because they never know which it is going to do. Particularly in war they have to *encrust* themselves in armour because if the feeling heart is allowed to rip, it busts them right open. Oh, horrible war! Why can't we think up a better plan?

Misha had been able, he told her, to get a message through to his mother at Perm, telling her of Kolya's death, and that the children were safe in the south. No reply had come, though he was reasonably certain that the message had arrived, sped as it had been by both gold and love. The last he had heard of his father was that the Prince had gone back to Moscow to try to rescue the uncles. But Uncle Georg, still complaining passionately at the personal inconvenience of it all, had already left Moscow again with his patient Swiss manservant, Ambrose, neglecting to tell anyone where he was going. Uncle Sergei, on the other hand, still declined to budge—certainly Moscow held no lack of good causes into which he might get his teeth. It had never seriously occurred to him that his own extermination could be a good cause into which others would like to get *their* teeth.

One rumour told Misha that Prince Andrei himself had been imprisoned and was awaiting either the hidden murder, now so common, or a farcical trial and subsequent execution. No one knew anything for sure. All was concealed, obscure, terrifying.

Daisy continued to listen in silence. Moscow, Misha reported, was said to be a chaos of frightened and starving people. One heard of once-proud soldiers selling their hard-won medals in the markets for a crust of bread. The structure of society was dissolved, and as ever, when this happens, the poor in whose aid revolution was supposed to be were those who suffered most. There were many instances in the starved countryside where peasant women had died in childbirth and the distraught husband buried the living child with the dead mother because there was no hope of its nourishment.

Misha's voice sank in total dejection. He stared blankly at the stone tiles of the terrace. For the first time since she had known him, he seemed helpless and naked, a being touchingly human. And more handsome than ever.

Misha sat on in the starlit darkness, his broad forehead clouded in melancholy. "I think too often of my father and my stepmother. Where are they? I think, too, so much of Kolya. Did he sacrifice his life for nothing? For a dream of a Russia that can never be? The time may even come when I am glad that Kolya is no longer alive to see what they will make of Russia, with their wild blank eyes and their dangerous dreams."

He was silent. In the warm still air the waves fell with a scarcely perceptible murmur on the shore. No more, no more . . .

The pause was so long that Daisy plucked up the courage to intrude on this mood of blank sorrow. "Even if, even if his death were in vain—and I don't believe such deaths ever are—even if Russia has to go through a long bad time, Kolya's *life* wasn't in vain. Not in vain for you, not in vain for . . . for all the people who loved him."

Misha shook his head. "There could have been much more. It could have been a long life, a blessed life. His power of goodness was without limit. It had no end . . . and he, *he* dies, while all the scoundrels of the world go unscathed." Misha's heavy, tearless gaze turned seaward, with a remoteness that moved Daisy to further utterance.

"Since already . . . we are talking . . . you are speaking of him, I must tell you something—a little—of something, of what he did for me." Why must I? It is madness to tell anything of this sort to Misha. And yet I know I must. Misha made no kind of answer, sitting quite still on the balustrade, his fair head drooped in his hands. He appeared to be in some trance of sorrow and disillusionment, and his very abstraction encouraged Daisy to continue. "This may seem to you a selfish thought, but even in grief one's thoughts turn to oneself . . . though perhaps only in grief does one recognise one's selfishness . . ."

Misha raised his head briefly to stare at the darkening sea, at the fireflies in the honeysuckle, with the same blank abstracted gaze.

"He set me free. Because of what you told me. Kolya set me free. I know that's not important really—a trifle in the face of his death. But to me it will make all the difference, for the rest of my life. His loving me, I mean."

Misha continued to sit stock still. Impossible to tell if he was even hearing or understanding the words she said. No matter, even being able to say them aloud was important.

"Because he loved me," Daisy went on, gazing down on to the tiled floor of the terrace, now colourless in the late dusk, "I have stopped feeling such a fool." But why on earth do I tell Misha this? Misha, of all the people in the world, who has always shown every sign of pleasure at the prosect of my being shown as a fool, who had delighted to mock my folly? I suppose, like him, I find no one else to whom to talk. Oh, Kolya, Kolya!

Misha returned abruptly from wherever he had been. "But why should you ever have felt a fool."

"Because I *was* a fool. I made a fool of myself at home. And I ran away from it, but it stayed with me just the same. It made me touchy, and diffident, and ashamed, and all those things. Kolya has freed me from that. I don't feel ashamed anymore. Or ready to be wounded about everything."

"We always supposed that so beautiful a girl as you are would not have left home without some bad blow to her pride."

"It was that I loved someone who didn't love me. And it was obvious. Everybody saw. Everybody who lived for miles around, I should think." Fool that I am, to tell him that!

"There is no great shame there. There is more shame in being hardhearted, frivolous, unable to love."

"Not for a girl."

Ah, girls, thought Misha. Through his fatigue he made a mental effort to guess at the spiritual problems of so outlandish a species. The mocking mask he wore could almost be seen readjusting itself. Yet a kind of affection remained. This girl had been Kolya's love, and so had become real. He thought how many people might have mocked Kolya for loving her— "Poor fellow, he married the English governess, and she keeps him in proper English order, I can tell you." With a shock, Misha recalled that the two among his messmates most likely to have spoken thus were both dead. But that world of sharp divisions and of cynical comments was unlikely to have died with them. Pride and scorn were neither of them characteristics that dissolved overnight.

A few years ago, thought Misha, I would have seduced this girl with great pleasure and no hesitation. I would have laughed off all the tears and reproaches, and skated round Mamma over it all. But I simply was not interested enough—she seemed such an inhuman little prig—and it is necessary, as one grows older, to love one's mistresses just a little. Now I am interested enough, and what is more I like her, and see that she has a human heart. But the situation is impossible. His thoughts flew to various alternatives at Novocherkask. It was strange, he reflected, how one grew out of some kinds of love, came to want other kinds. This girl looked lovely enough, and terribly vulnerable. What lay behind that sweet, that evidently sympathetic face? Now that the sadness of Kolya's loss had removed the roundness from her cheeks, the fine lines of her face were more clearly visible. Her youth and loneliness touched him as never before. A wave of tenderness mingled with the warmth of desire, and he moved unconsciously towards her. Her eyes in the starlight regarded him with an expression that he was unable to fathom, but dearly would have liked to.

Recalling himself, he made the boring effort of control. For the first time, to his astonishment, he saw a situation from someone else's point of view. It was almost as if Kolya had him by the elbow and were giving him a slight shake. This girl, who had been brushed off by some stupid oaf of a young man in England (who must be devoid of hearing, eyesight and everything else), this girl, who had lost Kolya and whom Kolya had loved, was not to be further bruised by him, Misha. For a moment he scarcely knew himself.

Upon this slight little girl so much depended; she must on no account lose heart. There must be no callous consolation taken at her expense.

He felt a wave of nobleness and self-congratulation. Prudence and generosity had prevailed. Yet perhaps the best move might still be a loving seduction? He toyed, pleasurably, with this thought. But no; it was all too complicated; and besides, he could hear in the road the sound of the horse and light cart which he had told old Gleb to summon at midnight for his return to the station.

Emboldened by having once begun, Daisy began again, her voice coming softly but clearly through the darkness. "Whatever my greensickness was, Kolya has cured it. That may not be important in the sum of things he did, but for me, it is everything." Daisy was half aware of Misha's feeling, and yet she did not feel vulnerable, as she had before.

Misha both loved and hated to speak of his brother, to hear others speak. Sometimes the bitterness of it was such that he forced himself into a detachment that sounded callous and uncaring. This was such a moment. But something now seemed expected of him. "He would rejoice for that," Misha said soberly. The sounds of the cart drew nearer. The need for action and movement invigorated him like a tonic.

He sprang up with a brisk change of mood, embraced Daisy with warm affection, not unmixed with the other, kissed her three times on alternate cheeks and was away up the lane almost before she had taken in his parting words: "Be comforted, you are a brave girl, and very far from being a fool." The noise of the horse's hooves and the rolling of the wheels faded slowly along the curve of the shore in the stillness of the night.

Whether brave, or a fool, or neither, Daisy found herself hating the feeling of being left behind. To be out of it all, with the world in such turmoil, and the whole of one's own generation involved! The sound of the wheels had now quite died away. Not a dog barked; the silence could be felt. In this war, Kolya had died, and horrible though it all sounded, Daisy longed for an active part of it—she must nurse, or drive, somehow risk her life, somehow *fight!*

How came she to be stranded on this alien shore, when everyone she knew was either living dangerously or dying bravely? The encounter with Misha had stirred her into revolt against the static nature of her task, into restlessness, a great desire to *do* and *be.* But how? And what?

The night reproached her with its calm and beauty. The sea below scarcely murmured, sighing imperceptibly along the shingle. The country lay quiet under this night of stars, veiled ever and again by a faint mist, a light drifting cloud. Perhaps it lay thus over all of Russia, high and serene, like a pure spirit, above the sickening stench of the thousands of dead bodies lying out unburied, above the beautiful pervasive smell of the blossoms from thousands of lime trees in full flower. The night lay quiet and still above the thousands of human hearts, filled with the feeling of freshness, of hope and renewal, the sheer joyfulness brought to many by the revolution, or heavy with the despair and desolation that it left in its wake. The dream of freedom and fulfillment flooded the souls of some Russians to the point where they were almost choking—bliss was it in that dawn to be alive! In the minds of many of the young a huge immovable stone had been rolled back, and hope and happiness were to have an everlasting resurrection.

But to others it seemed that a terrible earthquake had devastated all the land, taking with it all the careful building of the centuries, all the dear-loved landmarks, the trodden ways, the holy chants familiar since childhood, leaving only the scorched and smoking earth, the pit of hell opening unceasingly, the world heaving continually beneath their feet.

Chapter 17

Autumn came; Daisy's restlessness slowly died away. She was held fast, and in calmer moments knew it. The children's spirits rose with the cooler weather.

"Come up," they would cry. "Come up into the high valleys and the woods. There'll be mushrooms, red mushrooms, yellow mushrooms, lovely delicious mushrooms for soup!" They would toil up the lower slopes all day on foot, tirelessly, past the cypresses and the arbutus, into the hills and the cool woods, returning footsore but undefeated to lay their triumphant harvest on the kitchen table. "Come and look, Anna Timofeyevna! Just come and see!" Their eyes sparkled, their cheeks flushed; the fatigues of the day were forgotten. Nikolai seized Daisy round the waist and waltzed her round the kitchen table; Arkady followed with Anna.

"I must be turning into a serf," thought Daisy with combined dread and indulgence. "I know that I can never *ever* leave them until their parents come back."

Autumn closed in. Muffled by fog, the waves fell silently on the shingle of the beach. Chestnuts roasted on the braziers in the market square, and every day more flocks of sheep came down from the hills, running before the half-wild dogs who shepherded them. Twigs and leaves from the acacia trees scattered the paths. In the long, silent evenings Daisy sometimes felt that her whole life had been spent in autumn on the Black Sea, and always would be, with the rolling fogs and the distant savage sound of the shepherd dogs, the ever mournful fall of the sea.

The freckled face of George Bennett became extremely welcome. He brought them a large ham, but his forehead was wrinkled with worry.

Daisy was pleasingly grateful. "Oh, what a wonderful ham! The children will be blissful."

"The children! Where are all their own Russian relations? Surely they have dozens? Even this old couple could take charge—they seem perfectly reliable." Why didn't Daisy go home? It might be years before all this revolutionary war was settled and the Dubelskys returned to take charge of their children. Surely they had relations in the Crimea? He could fix up a passage home for her, any day. Everything would be different— back in England . . .

"Supposing Gleb and Anna suddenly went off?" she told him. "They've got a rather villainous-looking daughter who influences them a lot. Then what? Truly, George, I can't waltz off and trust them to luck. What would be lovely would be if we could all come out in the car with you. And I so dreadfully want to hear all the news. Here we know nothing certain. Only awful rumours of wicked Bolsheviks killing people."

"News! It's more like the crime page of the *Sunday Howl*." Disappointed but obliging, George bundled them all into his little car. As they came up the hill a cold steady wind blew off the mountains, stirring a chilly dust. The children, exhilarated by this novel form of transport, sang lustily.

"But, George, what has happened? Why no news? It's all utterly incomprehensible, and I've still no idea how any of it came about."

"Nobody really knows it all."

"But *everybody* knows more than I do!"

"It seems," George began reluctantly, "that after the Czar went there was a Provisional Government, a kind of national coalition to win the war, and this was recognized by the allies."

"I suppose it was their only hope."

"A remarkably frail one. It never really had a chance. The Czar's going left a complete vacuum, since every existing official claimed authority only in his name."

"But why didn't Grand Duke Michael, or whoever was next in the queue, take on?"

"God knows. Perhaps he funked it, not unnaturally. He was rather taken up with a morganatic wife, and such."

"What's morganatic?" Arkady asked suddenly from behind George's left ear.

"Not royal. Not suitable to be Empress."

"But why marry her, then?" Arkady demanded logically.

"I'm not in his confidence," George said clinchingly. "I don't know."

"Look, there's a heron!" Nikolai bawled in his other ear.

"You wouldn't," George asked hopefully, "care to get out here and climb the rocks at the top of that hill?"

"No, thank you. I like about the Czar and morganatic and everything. Please go on."

"There's not much more about the Czar. The Provisional Government never really ruled, and somehow the whole community broke up. Did Dubelsky not tell you?" he asked Daisy.

"I don't suppose he knew," Daisy said. "He was probably as bewildered as anybody. And he was too busy being Mademoiselle—there wasn't really time."

Nikolai laughed wildly. "Goodness, you should have seen Misha being Mademoiselle! You should have seen him all tied up in a lady's veil and a hat with roses on! You can't think how difficult it was not to laugh! He was so funny! So, so *funny!*"

George, who had no great wish to see Misha in any or no disguise, made no comment.

"And when he came the other day—" Nikolai began.

"So he came the other day?" George's heart sank.

"Only for a few hours," Daisy said, rather too quickly. "And we talked mostly about family things. Plans. His parents and so on. Do please, George, go on telling us about what happened."

"Dubelsky would have been aware anyway of the army's disruption," George continued a little stiffly. "Because emissaries of disorder reached all parts of the Front and started to make trouble."

"Spies! What were they disguised as? Ambulance drivers? Arkady, do get up. You're sitting on the end of my muffler and it's throttling me!"

"What they were disguised as I have no idea, but they told the soldiers that peace had already been signed in Stockholm, and that they had better hurry home in time for the land distribution or they'd miss their share. What they didn't say was that in actual fact four-fifths of the land already belonged to the peasants' village communes . . . Which way do you want to go, Daisy?"

"Any way. Wherever you like, but away from the sea. I find its noise sad and monotonous, day after day."

"Novorossisk?"

"No. Not Novorossisk."

"Somebody there," Arkady explained, "is sure to ask us when did we last see our father."

George had a strong feeling that it was high time that they both saw their father and that he discouraged them from constantly interrupting the conversation of adults.

"He did, Misha did say that masses of the officers had been killed and the rest were few and far between. I don't suppose he knew the rest."

George was mollified. "It was a hopeless job for them. The Front was spread out over vast distances and within two months there were said to be two million deserters."

"Two *million!* Could it be possible?"

"No," Arkady said flatly. "It could not be possible."

"So we're reliably informed," George went on, ignoring this. He had stopped the car by a small stream, and here the twins fortunately observed some tadpoles and switched off politics, tumbling out of the car to investigate and pursue. Even Varya, becoming less grand and adult than of late, rolled up her sleeves and scooped with the best.

"It looks rather pleasant under those trees," George said as Daisy too descended from the high little car. "Out of the wind; and there could be some early flowers."

It did him no good. "Two million?" Daisy asked once more, as they made for the wood.

George sighed. Since there was no help for it, since she really wanted to know, he warmed to his work, describing, not without graphic emphasis, the two million deserters flooding the rear of the Russian armies, crowding the roads and railways, preventing supplies and ammunition from being brought up, the army committees in which officers and men had equal votes and where the men voted against any further attacks on the Germans—why should more lives be spent, since peace had already been signed?

"Oh, how dreadful that there should be such a muddle when so many brave men had died to save Russia!"

Halted in full spate, George looked at Daisy gravely. She appeared to be totally engrossed in the fate of Russia and not notably interested in the fate of George Bennett. Patience must be his watchword. Then, he went on, Lenin had appeared in Petrograd on April 16, Trotsky had joined him, and armed Bolsheviks had paraded the streets. These had not been at all deterred by the far larger crowd parading next day to demand the arrest of Lenin as an agent of Germany. The chance to lead this had been missed; the march had caused only the resignation of Guchkov and other ministers on account of the failure of the government to restore order in the army.

"But what on earth was the point of giving in at such a time? Resigning, I mean, just when it was so vital for all to stand firm and stand together?" Daisy's voice vibrated with emotion, and it seemed to George that for very friendship's sake, now was the time to take her hand. It continued to tremble, but was not removed. "It seems to me," he went on, encouraged, "that Russians don't think on such lines."

"But apart from being Russians or not Russians—and after all they are as much rational beings as anyone else—why didn't Kerensky do something? Surely he had more or less complete power?"

"If I were a Russian," George said slowly, "and after a year or two in this country one drifts into seeing things their way, I would say the whole country had surrendered to the grip of the Devil."

"Can a whole country do that?"

"Seemingly a whole country did. The moderates seemed to become paralsed, powerless anyway, ans the extremists to be filled with a kind of demonic force. Prince Lvov gave up, and Kerensky, remaining on as President instead of him, *did* go to the Front, *did* do all he could to persuade the tired troops to fight on, telling them that if the Germans won the revolution would be doomed. But it seemed to the soldiers that the Bolshevik offers were better—an immediate and separate peace and an immediate seizure of all estates by the nearest peasants. Kerensky had offered an official redistribution of land."

"So why didn't they follow him?"

"Because that would have been bureaucratic and endless, and doubtless corrupt, and the men wouldn't wait for it. By December, the Bolsheviks had it their way. It might have gone differently. Kerensky did at least, in response to strong Allied pressure, launch an offensive in person on the Southwest Front, and at first it was successful; there were valiant officers and some very stalwart Czech troops."

"So?"

The same exhausted paralysis, George told her, had taken over. Kerensky had been unable to get a response from the Russian troops; they had simply had enough. Complete defeat, absolutely a rout, had happened at Tarnopol on July 15. "After that, I should think, Dubelsky's regiment revolted, and he came away to clear you out of Jevrenskaia."

"Yes, I suppose that was about when it was. He minds so much that I didn't like to ask him . . . We talked more about family things and about the children. But still, I don't understand what happened to the government in Petrograd."

George felt a strong desire to cease trying to explain the inexplicable Russians and touch on more personal matters, but Daisy pressed on.

"What did they do?"

George continued his sad tale. Why it should affect Daisy so deeply he couldn't imagine. Women did, notoriously, overreact to war, but, if so, why be so anxious to hear all about it? But clearly, Daisy was not going to let go until she had heard it all. Very well, so be it. He took breath again. They were back in the car with the children.

"Well, a day or two later the soldiers and sailors and some factory workers tried to seize Petrograd, and this was only stopped by the loyalty of the Preobrazhensky Regiment; and also, in part, by the Bolsheviks themselves, who didn't really want anyone else to gain power, workingmen or not. It was still touch and go who prevailed. But then the liberals, who were called the Cadet Party, resigned on a business that really wasn't vital, or at least not vital in the light of what came next—they thought that the Ukraine had been given too great a degree of independence."

"Fancy bothering about that!"

"All the same, all was not yet lost, and owing to their German links, Trotsky was arrested and Lenin had to go into hiding—"

"And then, surely *then*, Kerensky, or anybody else could have done something? How could they let the whole thing go by default?" Daisy's eyes filled with tears. Hateful, hateful betrayal! How could Kolya's country do this to Kolya?

George had removed his hand in order to change gear. Now he tried to take Daisy's hand again, if only to give it a reassuring squeeze, but met with no success. She took it away, covering her face with her hands.

"I think that Nikolai is getting a bad cold," Varya said in a grown-up voice from the back of the car. "He got very wet catching the tadpoles. Didn't you hear him sneezing?"

"Yes. No. I'll see to him as soon as we get home." This diversion had enabled Daisy to master her tears, and she begged the uncomprehending George to go on.

"All this while the Bolsheviks had been beavering away, gaining power in military committees set up in the army; and when somebody, General Kornilov, *did* do something, reintroducing the death penalty into the army so as to check the rout at the Front, he found himself at odds with Kerensky, who didn't want it at the rear. And then they held an enormous representative conference at Moscow late in August, which failed to agree; and quarrels increased between the generals and Kerensky, while both their troops fraternised. Kornilov was arrested and Kerensky slowly became discredited."

"But couldn't they see how vital it was to agree, and win the war, and argue later? Oh, why couldn't they see!"

"Seemingly, they couldn't. And another conference in September failed to reach an agreement, and so did a Vor Parliament in October; and then Kerensky, in a fit of near madness, set free all the arrested Bolsheviks—"

"He set them *free?* Oh, how awful! How *stupid!*"

"If *I* had been there," Arkady announced in George's ear, "I would have shot Kerensky."

"What good would that have done? There's been too much shooting already," George said reasonably.

"Not of the right people," Arkady insisted. "Why didn't Prince Lvov or someone shoot Lenin and Trotsky? They surely had pistols or rifles?"

"Mind you, there's probably a lot we don't know yet," George admitted with his usual fairness. "This is just what we hear through the Embassy. But in outline, I expect it is pretty well what did happen."

"So then what?"

George sighed. The trip was well nigh over and nothing but politics had been touched on. "Haven't your Russian friends told you all this?"

The wind was blowing colder and colder, and they must soon turn back.

"I never see any of them. Here we are completely cut off. And anyway, they somehow never tell one things directly, in a sort of logical sequence of events, like the English do. They wander off into things. Good things, often, but they wander off . . . You still haven't told me what happened next."

"Well naturally, the Bolsheviks then seized power. There was really no one to stop them. The Vor Parliament was driven out of the Palace of Mary. And the cruiser *Aurora*, from point-blank range in the Neva, *and* the garrison of the Fortress of Peter and Paul, started shelling the Winter Palace and the Admiralty. Then on the seventh of last November, I think it was, anyway about then, the Ministers of the Provisional Government were taken prisoner and put in Peter and Paul."

"But why couldn't they fight? Or get any troops to fight?" Daisy and Arkady demanded, speaking almost together.

"Kerensky became wise—too late in the day—and tried to rally some Cossack troops outside Petrograd. He failed to get anywhere with them. And in Moscow a week later the cadets—there was a remarkably brave band of military cadets defending the Kremlin—were finally defeated; and you might say that Bolshevism triumphed."

"Oh, how miserable! And then?"

"They reverted to earlier days and made Moscow the new capital, and they allotted all land to the peasants who worked on it, which legalised the peasant seizures that had happened earlier."

"I don't mind that part so much," Daisy asserted. "I mean, if there wasn't any killing involved . . ."

"I wouldn't like to take a bet on that . . . But this is the real tragedy of the revolution— the worst part. The Bolsheviks at once abrogated universal suffrage, which was what a great many of the revolutionaries had cared for above all else, *and* the power to elect councils, and voters were limited to manual workers. How long even they will be allowed to vote is anybody's guess. All opponents are being terrorised, and the Party itself is kept small and under terrific discipline. The Reds don't believe in democracy any more than the Czars did. All their talk about it is just lip service."

Varya spoke in a high cool voice from the back of the car. "I don't care to hear foreigners discussing Russia. You will please not go on. And Nikolai keeps sneezing. I think he should go in the front of the car where there is less cold wind."

"I'll rub him with camphorated oil the minute we get in. If there's any left. Varya, we are living in Russia, and of course we are interested. Please go on, George. What happened to the war?"

Privately, George agreed with Varya as to the discussion, but her intervention spurred him on to continue, because Daisy's authority, growing tenuous, must be backed up. "Russia stopped fighting. Understandably, the soldiers had had enough of battling on without adequate arms or ammunition."

"Yes, I see that. And?"

"An armistice was declared with the Central Powers. And then of course it logically followed on that the Constituent Assembly was dissolved by force. They simply brought machine guns into the Tauris Palace and invited its members to disperse. Which, not surprisingly, they did."

"And the Czar?"

"Nobody knows. There are rumours, but nobody really knows. Kerensky did at least send the Imperial Family to Tobolsk. To be safe."

The little car rattled up to the iron gates of the Villa Rosa. A twin, indistinguishable from the back, sprang out to open them. Dead tadpoles flowed in all directions from his damp handkerchief.

"It's too early," Arkady said defensively. "They would have died anyway from the cold."

George sighed, but Daisy's eyes were fixed upon the middle distance, as she continued to brood on the petty pride, the indecision, the silly quarrels and the downright villainy of the Russian Revolution's accomplishment. "If I had read all that in a history book, I simply would not have believed it. That in this whole huge country there shouldn't be anyone with the greatness of soul to rise to it all and take charge no matter what happens to themselves! No Alfred the Great. No Joan of Arc, or Montrose, or William Pitt, or George Washington. Nobody but horrible Lenin and Trotsky."

"There is much greatness of soul in Russia," Varya insisted with dignity. "At present it is being martyred."

No one seemed willing to follow her into this wide field for thought. "I am so hungry," Ella pleaded. "I saw that Mr. Bennett brought a tin of biscuits. Could we not go into the house and eat some?"

George was sadly helping Daisy out of the high little car. The afternoon had perhaps been wasted, but once launched on the subject on which Daisy had insisted, he was determined to conclude. "Perhaps the hugeness of the country was the trouble," he suggested. "Once the Czar had abdicated and the Grand Duke Michael hadn't taken on, the whole problem was too enormous for any other man. If you make an idol of a ruler, people are lost when he fails." Recovering from her distress of mind, Daisy asked him in to tea. "That at least we have still got."

He was so kind, solid and reassuring, playing cards with the children, laughing with them, teasing them. For an hour or two the whole strain of the situation was removed from Daisy's shoulders. George was so comfortingly one of her own countrymen. He did not fly off at tangents or vanish into moods. He dreamt no wild, idealistic dreams, was visited by no holy visions, was perhaps only about twenty-five percent a spiritual being. But on the other hand he was totally incapable of torturing anyone or letting them be tortured, could never kill men, women and children in cold blood, as Russian was now killing Russian, all over the desperate country. His power for good might be conventional and limited, but heavens! so also limited was his power for evil! How wonderful that kind of good faith and solidity was! And one truly valued it only when it was in short supply. It was with real sadness that she watched him go. Next morning brought a letter from her father and a further glow of reassurance.

At the end of this summer it may really be possible to get you home. The Germans launched an appalling offensive this spring, but they say it is petering out, after more dreadful casualties. It was perhaps their last throw, before the full force of the American Army arrives on the scene. The British as usual bore the brunt. How long they can stick it out, God alone knows. [Here the censor had cut out two sentences with a neat hole, but the letter enclosed a draft for a considerable sum of money.] The money I enclose in case you are cut off from the Dubelskys; we hear things in Russia are in a very bad way, and long for you to get out of it. Bring the children here, of course—no need to tell you that. Set about arranging for the journey as soon as you get this letter. Ask that young fellow who's consul in Novorossisk.

I don't think the roses have ever been better than they are this July, but one can't take the same pleasure in them.

The long winter dragged past. Daisy felt immeasurably older, and sadder, distanced as if by a generation from the green self-absorbed girl who had travelled to Moscow four years since. The revolution was accomplished, but the civil war swayed backwards and forwards, brought rumour and counter-rumour, but always ill news. Nor was there much cheer from home. The Americans had come up to her father's expectations and were on the way—but why had they left it so late? The Russians had made peace, the French were dead ducks, the English weary and depleted. But might not the Germans also be exhausted?

"It cannot continue long like this!" Varya declared, as the summer of 1918 ripened, her eyes flashing. "Soon his Imperial Majesty will return with an army and these terrible men will be made prisoners and sent to Siberia. Or shot. I myself would shoot them all. Willingly I would shoot them!"

"Varya, darling, don't talk like that."

"I would shoot them all. Traitors! Socialists!"

Nikolai and his twin had lost their rounded limbs and were growing into handsome leggy little boys. But even Nikolai's sure young voice faltered as he began, "They say . . . they say . . . Gleb says they say in the town that the Czar is dead, that the Reds have murdered him."

"Never listen to such things! Never say such things!" Varya adjured him passionately. "Servants' gossip. Pay no heed to it."

"It's what the men say in the town. Not just servants," Nikolai persisted.

"God have mercy! Lord Jesus Christ, Son of God, have mercy on us! And even if it were true, the Czarevitch would reign—Grand Duke Michael would rule in his name. God grant that it is not true. What an unspeakable thing! What punishment can be cruel enough for such men!" Rising from the table and tossing back her long locks, Varya burst into a

flood of passionate tears. "I don't believe! I don't believe! *I don't believe it!*"
She rushed from the room, could be heard tearing up the stairs to her
bedroom, crashing the door shut behind her.

"If she doesn't believe, why is she crying?" Arkady demanded logically
enough. An answer eluded Daisy, who had long suspected that the Czar
was dead. She urged Ella to finish up a rather unpalatable pudding. As
Varya's first transports died down, Daisy mounted the stairs to console
her, but her tread had somehow lost its spring. . .

My love for Kolya, she thought, has settled into part of my life. A calm
and comforting part. The grief that stayed on, to sour and sicken life, was
the grief shot through with guilt. I remember less that he died, and more
that he was once alive *here*, and is now still more alive somewhere else. It
was a comfort that did not lessen, it was like the comfort of having a
father and mother, but infinitely stronger and more reassuring, because a
father and mother loved one naturally, in the ordinary course of things,
but the Kolyas of this world did not. To be loved by him was something
special and glorifying; and when all the heartache and the bitterness of
sorrow was over, it stayed with one in a kind of internal warmth. And at
least there is something that I can still do for him, looking after these
children that he was so fond of, and that I am now fonder of because of
him.

All the same, how boring it was, how often! Daisy was twenty-four
now; she felt as if her whole youth were slipping away in music practises
and juvenile algebra and French irregular verbs, in this foreign and isolated place. How long must it go on? Another year? Two years? Five
years? Would she never see England again? Her thoughts turned to self-
reproach. How *could* anyone complain when young men all these years
were fighting and dying in the horrible trenches in France? And how
could one think of one's parents, of Kolya, as if their reality and their
importance depended only on their love for oneself? I am always selfish,
Daisy mourned, it's the root of my nature. I wouldn't have been a fit wife
for Kolya and he had a lucky escape.

"Ella, you are old enough now to keep your elbows off the table without
being told every day. Whatever would Nyanya say?" Daisy could hear
herself being terribly governessy, and yet seemed quite unable to stop
herself. From being a governess for so long, one simply became one—a
governess of the worst kind, disapproving and unloving.

"Nyanya didn't mind. Nyanya was never cross. She never made us eat
such horrible food as this."

"Couldn't we steal some chickens or something?" Arkady demanded.
"I'm sick and tired of horrible boring vegetables, morning, noon and
night. The children of the New Forest went out and trapped wild cattle
when they were in hiding like us."

After all, we are not peasants, always to eat peasant stuff," Nikolai echoed him. Silently, Varya pushed the food to the side of her plate, her elegant nose wrinkled in disdain.

Daisy could have willingly knocked all their heads together.

At other times they would fully realise the need to make the best of the situation, would munch turnips with undiminished gaiety, would carry Daisy along on the crest of their unabated high spirits. They would shout with laughter and fling their arms round her neck: "Daisy, Daisy, give me your answer do!" They had a natural predilection for dancing, in and out of season: one or other of the little boys would seize her round the waist and whirl her across the terrace. It was sometimes almost impossible to get them to settle down to work. "This morning, it's geography. Open the map of China—"

Nikolai and Arkady would immediately put inverted baskets on their heads and assume what they imagined to be a Chinese walk, with sagging knees and swinging pigtail. They ought, they really ought to go to school, and have some *firm man* teaching them, thought Daisy. Would this long time of waiting never end?

Misha had vanished as though he had never been. He made no communication until, suddenly remembering the saint's day of the twins, he sent them a picture postcard of Sebastopol with nothing on it except "Greetings and Love, M.A.D." Mad is what I sometimes think he really is, Daisy thought. Why doesn't he come, or say what is happening in the rest of Russia, or whether he has news of his parents? Or whether I should move the children to the Crimea *now*, and if so, where? Once he's away I don't believe he gives any of us a single thought. He's impossible. Better than he was, but impossible. If it weren't for Kolya, and for my promise to their mother, I would simply pack my bag, and leave all the children, and go into Novorossisk and get on board the first ship I saw that would take me to England or France. At times, late at night, thoughts of Misha crept obstinately back, as though endowed with a life of their own by Misha's own persistent vitality. He is impossible, and I do not even like him, Daisy told herself sternly.

The summer days passed pleasantly enough—the children playing long hours on the beach among the rocks and sand or in the deep clear waters of the sea. There were eggs again, and fresh vegetables from the garden, sometimes even some butter, though bread and flour were scarce from the breakdown in communications. Anna continued to cook, rather sourly, her spirits sometimes lightened by the gift of a couple of fowls from her brothers in the hills or a branch of what looked suspiciously like goat. Gleb, garrulous and apologetic, continued to dig in the garden. Their daughter, a sprightly, sharp-eyed nineteen-year-old, visited them sometimes from Novorossisk, glancing at Daisy with suspicion and sometimes eyeing the children with an expression of dislike that made Daisy uneasy. It seemed impossible in these uncertain days to have any real idea of what went on in the hearts and minds of men and women, even of the nearest neighbours.

George Bennett no longer had any petrol, but he would appear from time to time in an antiquated dogcart, looking hot and dusty, and bathing from the beach in a high-necked English bathing suit of red and white horizontal stripes that made the children laugh.

Their laughter nettled Daisy in a way she couldn't account for; and noticing this, Varya's good manners came to the surface. "Mr. Bennett is a very nice man," she insisted. "We all like him. It's just that his bathing dress isn't quite *chic.*" But Daisy remained unmollified. She regarded the innocent subject of mirth with some disfavour as he swam vigorously out into the Black Sea. But it's really the children I ought to be cross with. And am, in a sort of way, too. Was George right? And was she herself simply a rather dull Englishwoman, being suborned by foreign charm— that ordinary, *ordinary* spinster type? On the whole it was herself with whom she was angry.

Swimming in that cool, delicious sea, so clear and sparkling, Daisy could not but be happy some of the time. In the middle of so much agony and suffering, she thought, how unbelievably lucky we all are to be safe, and fed, and well. She looked at the flourishing children with deep thankfulness. And yet somehow the safety and the brilliant sunshine were not enough. It's all right for them, but I should be doing something tougher, like everyone else. I ought not to be out of it all, splashing in a warm sea. It would be just all right, perhaps, if these were my own children; but they aren't even that. I'm only someone looking after them for money— not that there's been any of that for the last year or so. It would be different, and not so shirking, if they were my own children.

And then she would remember that they were Kolya's brothers and sisters, his beloved half-brethren, and all that remained of him to cherish and help. The salt tears, running down her face, would mingle with the salt dark waters of the Black Sea.

Their food, the children pointed out often enough, was becoming increasingly dull. Certainly the dish that Anna had brought in, one hot day, looked wonderfully unappetizing—a vegetable concoction exuding a strong smell of over-vinegared beet-root, and barley covered by a thin doughy-looking pastry.

Varya's adolescent pride and temper flared up. Seizing the dish, she flung it from the table; the dish cracked on the floor and fell apart; an uninviting vegetable gravy oozed forth from it. Not content with this, Varya seized Anna by the shoulders and shook her violently.

"Stupid beast!" she cried furiously. "Do you think that because you and Gleb eat pigs' swill that *we* can eat it too? Do you imagine that we are peasants, to be fed on such stuff! Never dare to set such a disgusting dish again before us! Oh, that my father and mother were here, that you should be beaten as you deserve!"

"Varya! Be quiet! Don't speak so!" Daisy was appalled.

But Anna, much to Daisy's surprise, took the assault with surprising docility, as if it were quite to be expected. Ella looked alarmed, and the boys simply hungry and disgruntled. Humbly, as if to blame for the food shortages herself, Anna began to clear up the mess. Varya, in icy tones, continued to blame her.

The kitchen door opened to reveal the sharp narrow features of Anna's daughter. Her eyes took in the scene—the furious Varya still imperiously reproaching Anna for daring to produce such a dish, Anna's meek acquiesence, a speechless Daisy, the indifferent children waiting until such time as Anna should produce a substitute lunch, the food spread over the floor. She made no attempt to assist her mother, leaving this task to Daisy. Shooting a glance of bitter resentment and malevolence at Varya, she retired into the kitchen, closing the dining-room door in a sharp crash of contempt.

They dined silently upon bread and goat's cheese, followed by dried figs. "Varya, how *could* you?" Daisy asked her later. "How do you find it possible to treat another human being like that? It was not just undignified, and very bad-mannered; but with Anna's daughter in the house, who already dislikes us, it was terribly *dangerous*. After all, Anna is only doing what she can."

"She could do better. She needs to be treated thus. She *will* do better. You will see. We shall not be treated to such disgusting food again." Varya was unrepentant, her head held high. "My parents would think it intolerable. I also think it so." She looked at Daisy with sudden chilling scorn, as if they were two rival adults discussing some fine point in a cultural debate. "You couldn't be expected to understand. You know nothing of Russia or of our ways. Nothing, nothing, nothing!"

"I know enough to understand that your parents would both have been ashamed of such behaviour," Daisy maintained stoutly. But would they? Daisy remembered suddenly that her own grandfather, when his cook was so thoughtless as to send him up boiled potatoes, had been known to hurl the dish to the floor. Maybe, as long as there were people to clear them up, there would be people to throw their dishes to the ground. "Times change," she said aloud, briskly. But Varya had turned from her, weeping tears of mingled rage and grief, and had run out onto the terrace. "My parents! How dare you name them so to me! My parents! Martyred perhaps by these terrible Bolsheviks! How can you name them so, to *me!*"

In the kitchen, in a manner to Daisy unaccountable, Anna had burst into a loud cheerful song. Varya's torrent of abuse had flowed over a seemingly well-waterproofed spirit. Their daughter had departed, and Gleb, leaning from time to time in at the kitchen window, joined in the chorus of relief, as he fed the despised dish to the pigeons. The employers to whom they had been accoustomed from youth now and again indulged in such outbursts of rage or impatience—a natural phenomenon like thunder or lightning and to be accepted as such.

To Daisy, the danger from Novorossisk seemed sharply increased. If Gleb and Anna's daughter, through regard for her parents, had hitherto concealed the presence of the Dubelsky children at the Villa Rosa, she would almost certainly do so no longer. On her next visit Daisy endeavoured to placate the young woman by a present of one of her few remaining good dresses. It was received in a grudging silence that contained no trace of friendliness or reconciliation. Towards the passing figure of Varya a look of sullen hatred was again directed, a look at which Daisy's heart dreadfully misgave her.

With dusk a fog crept over the sea. From the distance came the melancholy bray of foghorns. But to Daisy there was a sort of comfort to be drawn from these. Out there on that shrouded sea were ships manned by people to whom faith and compassion had not yet become dead letters. To us, Daisy thought, to the British as to the ancient Greeks, the sea is a symbol of deliverance; its presence a way of escape and freedom, a safeguard against the horror of being trapped in a strange country, landlocked, immobilized.

Chapter 18

The summer lasted long into an autumn still and serene, of warm nights, warm seas, days as golden and mellow as a ripe peach. News filtered through of the continuing successes of the Allies on the Western Front. Daisy breathed great sighs of relief; Varya was still unappeased. She was growing up, and there was nobody to recognise how important and special she was. Daisy was affectionate, but seemed to pay equal attention to the twins and Ella. The continuing uncertainties over her parents' fate and her own future lay heavily upon her.

"Varya's crying again, Miss Daisy. On her bed. She won't stop. I am crying too," Ella added helpfully.

"Well don't, darling. She will be better soon. I will go and see her."

"Anna has told her about the Grand Duchess Sergei."

"Who told Anna, Nikolai?"

"Gleb did. And Igor Zakarevitch told Gleb, so it must be true. He heard it from the stationmaster at Novorossisk."

Daisy sought out Gleb, who confirmed the tale. The work that the Grand Duchess did amongst the poor of Moscow and the love that she inspired amongst them had been so great that the Tcheka had not dared to murder her in the capital. Instead, she had been taken secretly this summer to the town of Alapaevsk near Ekaterinburg, and here she and five of her cousins, some hardly more than boys, had been cast down a disused mineshaft to die of their injuries and of starvation. Frightened peasants, not daring to try a rescue, had crept to the lip of the shaft and heard the sounds of hymn and psalm being chanted faintly below. After a few days there were no more sounds. When the bodies were brought to the surface by the Whites who soon afterwards took the town, it was found that the Grand Duchess, born in a palace and granddaughter to Queen Victoria, had torn up the robe of her sisterhood to make bandages for her injured kin, as they lay dying in the near-darkness of the mine.

Varya lay on the bed face downwards, abandoned to her grief. Impatiently she shrugged off the hand which Daisy laid on her shoulder. Undeterred by this rebuff, Daisy waited patiently while the passionate sobs slowly exhausted themselves, turned to gulps and heaves and to the final indignity of sniffs. Varya was at last able to speak, gruffly, but communication had at least been established. She looked at Daisy with reproach.

"How could you understand, you, a foreigner, how we feel for our Imperial Family?"

"She was a granddaughter, and a much loved one, of our old Queen."

Varya fixed her with the familiar nobody-outside-Russia-has-any-true-feelings look. "And it is not only for them that I grieve. Where is Papa? Where is Mamma? Shall we never see them again?" Her furious dark eyes fixed Daisy, who wisely refrained from pointing out that she was not personally responsible for the Russian Revolution.

"Why should we not see them again? Because many have died, not all will die. We can always pray, and go on praying."

"How can you understand how we suffer? Your father and mother are safe, and your sisters. You have no part in this agony. And already we have lost our beloved Kolya."

Daisy bit back an answer, silently taking Varya's hand, which was not removed. "Think about him often," she suggested. "Remember them all very clearly, what they said, what they did, how loving they were."

"That only makes it worse."

"For the moment, perhaps. But not if you think of them clearly, and for long, remembering all the marvellous things about them."

Varya sniffed dubiously, crumpling her wet handkerchief up in her free hand. A thought struck her. Suddenly her face cleared; light returned to her dark eyes veiled in thick lashes, that were so like Kolya's. She rose from the bed in a sudden swift graceful movement. "Would you like me to read you something?"

"Very much," Daisy assured her.

"It was something that Princess Marie Obolensky told Mamma, and she wrote it out for me. Something that the Grand Duchess Sergei said to the sisters on the day she opened her sisterhood in Moscow."

"Read it to me. I would love to hear."

"If I can find it." Carelessly, destructively, Varya began to throw everything out of her chest of drawers and to scatter her belongings, silk petticoats, bright ribbons and scarves and flowers, all over the floor. But it seemed no moment for reproof.

"Here it is. I knew that I had it. Listen, Miss Daisy. I will read it out to you—listen carefully: it is very lovely and very important. 'We receive all things from God, and it is in God alone that our neighbour can best be loved and served. The deepest natural love, let alone philanthropy, is apt to change, and to fall victim to extravagance or disillusionment'—like Uncle Sergei's good causes," she added in parenthesis. " 'There is no such jeopardy once our love is rooted in Christ,' " Varya read on, her dark locks falling on the page, " 'once we learn to see Him alike in friend and in stranger and even in enemy. For such was His pattern when He lived among us . . .' " Varya paused. "How beautiful, is it not? Mamma loved it. I can almost hear her reading it out aloud to me . . . It was in Moscow, one evening, just before she went out to dinner, in her jewels, rubies I think, in such a beautiful dress . . . How solemn and pale you look, Miss Daisy! Think happily of Mamma, you said!"

Varya laughed suddenly. Her face showed scarcely a trace of tears. She flew from Daisy, running down the stairs and out into the hot afternoon, casting as she went a farewell glance at Daisy, a look that gleamed with a kind of triumphant mockery, of fleeting knowledgeable amusement, as if she had suddenly got the better of her, had guessed the secret of a love that Daisy herself had not yet realised; seeing, with a certain tough realism, that her governess was a bit of a softy. Varya had lived long enough in the world of her parents to imbibe some of its glittering many-faceted hardness, not long enough to acquire its easygoing tolerance and kindness, its worldly give and take.

Her voice could be heard ringing out from below. "Time for the sea!" she urged her brothers. "Come on, sleepy Ella! Time for the sea!"

In a flash of self-knowledge, instantly dismissed from her mind, Daisy saw herself as she felt she had become—a shadow, a sucker, a sitting target for exploitation, a helpless giver to the world's many takers. And this was not goodness, it was simply weakness: no glory, but a shame. This was she who had longed for the challenge of travel, for adventure and danger; had hoped deeply to pit her strength against the world's enormous ills. All had added up to a monotonous and ineffective routine beside an alien sea. Briefly, she knew what Varya had maybe as briefly divined—that there was nothing noble and unselfish about Daisy's faithfulness to her charge, that she stayed on because she had loved one brother, and because she now, with agonised reluctance, was coming to love his wayward elder.

Deflated and thoughful, she sat on the windowsill, while shouts, splashings and laughter sounded from the rocks and the sea below. The moment passed. Varya was only an innocent; guessing nothing, swinging childishly from passionate grief into the relief of merriment. Slowly at first, and then with increasing briskness, she began to tidy Varya's bedroom, as Varya had known that she would.

Normality was regained; the martyr image faded. Daisy was able to laugh again at herself as she folded Varya's possessions and put them back in their places. Firmness is the kindest way with children, she told herself, but sometimes one cannot be bothered. All that remained was a small hidden nugget of knowledge, of recognition of her own nature and of its needs.

Another bitter winter passed. The dusty storms of autumn were succeeded by the sudden thunders and lightnings of the Euxine, crashing over the mountains, leaping in brilliance across a troubled sea. January mists rolled off the waters, were followed by icy winds howling down from the Caucasus. Food supplies became ever more limited. A spate of letters from her parents besought Daisy to return. An armistice had, it seemed, been signed in November, the German submarines had ceased to menace peaceful shipping. "Don't spend your life in Russia," Mrs. Pelham mourned. "Things there sound horribly dangerous, even if they are quiet near you. The whole country must be uneasy and unsettled. I'm sure your father has told you we would welcome all the children here." Why do I stay? Daisy wondered, and invented for herself a number of plausible reasons. She wrote back, "You say the minefields are still not cleared, and I've heard that ships are still being sunk in them. Dare I bring someone else's children through anything so risky? I promise you that we are well out of the trouble zone here." Yet ill rumours came from Novorossisk, and Gleb and Anna's daughter seemed to look at the children with an increasingly hostile gaze. She was betrothed to a young man who worked on the railways; from time to time Gleb would shake his head over his future son-in-law's political views. His daughter was growing sadly independent, and all because Anna had not let him chastise her often enough when she was young and there was still time. The two of them, with their sharp Turkish eyes, had ganged up against him.

Spring came suddenly and the sun grew hotter and hotter, the smells of honeysuckle and of climbing roses crept into the air, cypresses stood still as minarets in the noontide heat. In the afternoons, the dust blew in little whorls along the road by the sea. "Where is Misha?" Ella demanded. "Why doesn't he come back again?"

"Perhaps he hasn't got any money either," Arkady surmised gloomily.

"Misha always has money; why ever not?" Varya demanded. "He does not come because he is fighting too hard. Many Russian generals of the Imperial forces are now fighting the Bolsheviks. Soon they will win and we shall return home and all will be as it was." She spoke by rote, as if repeating a self-taught lesson.

"Not soon," Nikolai insisted. "The war must last long enough for Arkady and me to fight in it. Actually, we could be perfectly well fighting in it now. For instance, we could look after Misha's horses, and whoever is doing that now could be in the front line."

"Perhaps he fires a rifle as well as grooming and watering?"

"And why should not we? Soon we shall be ten. Boys as young fought in the Tartar wars. If Misha would only come back this summer we could make him take us to the war."

"I'm so hot," Ella sighed. "Can't we go up *really* into the mountains?"

"Gleb can drive. We could hire a horse and cart," Arkady pleaded. "Or Yuri Andreivitch has a wagon. He could come too. We could go for a whole day!"

"You've never even seen the Scythian dol— dol— what is it, Arkady?"

"Dolmens. Scythian tombs made of great huge stones. Papa used to take us to find them in the forest."

"Scythian?"

"They were some of the first Russians," Varya told her importantly. "Pagans, of course. But they made the most beautiful things, out of pure gold: ornaments and rings and everything. Wreaths of laurel leaves, made of beaten gold."

Why not? Daisy thought. It couldn't cost much, and the children had so little fun. She herself longed for a break in the sameness of their days beside the glittering sea, by the harsh glare of the rocks. The thought of the forest and its streams was enticing. "Are you sure it's quite safe up there?"

"With Gleb, and Yuri? Whyever not?" Varya asked scornfully.

Two days later, in the mist of very early morning, the children piled into the uncomfortable cart. Gleb, accompanying them, pointed out gloomily that there were wild boars in the high hills. "Many," Yuri Andreivitch echoed, flicking the reins unenthusiastically. The horses plodded interminably up winding roads, until the blueness of the Black Sea lay far below, unflecked by a single cloud, and the sun, long above the mountains, grew ever hotter, scorching their backs. Flies teased, a hot wind sprang up, dust rose in clouds from the track. Daisy's face was a study in doubt—could this really be a pleasure trip for anyone? She remembered suddenly what it felt like to be ten, bent on a daylong picnic, and her face cleared.

"Boars," Gleb volunteered, "do not attack unless they are cornered and provoked past measure." And that, thought Daisy, is just what they will be, if the twins find one and run true to form. "A hole scraped in the ground," Yuri said, still more gloomily. "If you see an oval hole scraped in the ground, you should move on quickly. Wild boars scoop out such a hole in the ground to sleep."

"But do they sleep in daylight?"

"Don't you *have* wild boars in England?" Varya wondered.

"Not any longer," Daisy told her firmly.

"Poor things! You've killed them all."

Slowly the clouds of flies thinned out as the wagon toiled upwards into cooler air. The cypress, arbutus and bay began to be replaced by oak, birch and beech. The hills became thick with trees, dense woods broken only by an occasional spur of tawny rock. In the far distance a shadowy mountain sketched itself against the eastern sky. Mountain, or cloud? Beside a clear running stream the wagon was brought to a halt, the hobbled horses set to graze, the children's hot little bodies cooled by a bathe. They picnicked meagrely enough, but Anna's strange vegetable pasties went down better here in the cool of the trees. Birds sang in the woods and the noise of distant waterfalls could be heard. It's like Scotland, Daisy thought, contentedly dangling her feet in the stream, only hotter and more exotic and with a blissful smell of wild azalea. *Azalea ponticum*, she thought; of course, pontic azalea, azalea from the Black Sea! She half remembered a tale of her father's of the Greeks making themselves ill on a march by eating azalea honey; but that surely was on the other side of the Black Sea? I wish I wasn't always the eldest, having to teach all the time and never to learn.

"Is that really all the food there is?" Arkady demanded.

"If we had brought bows and arrows we could have shot a deer and had roast venison," sighed Nikolai.

"Or shot a boar and had roast pork."

"Why don't we make some? That creeper there looks strong enough for bowstrings."

"The dolmens," Varya called after them, "are the other way!"

"We've *seen* them," Arkady shouted from over his shoulder.

"Don't go far if you aren't coming with us," Daisy warned them. Scrambling over boulders, clutching at hazel bushes and beech branches and caught by creepers, she and the two girls made their way upstream. There were mare's tails, growing head-high, wood anemones, wild paeonies and a host of other flowers unknown to Daisy, and a delicious refreshing coolness of leafy air and damp moss that made the hot journey into the hills but a short trial to have endured. "Can you manage, Ella? Hold my hand over this part." The twins, breathing heavily, had raced to overtake them.

Suddenly, amongst brambles and boulders, they came on a number of primitive houses, each made of four great hewn stones, with a fifth acting as roof. Their little slit of an entrace was halfway up the walls; such huge stones must have been erected with gigantic labour—to what end?

"Tombs," Arkady pointed out pleasurably.

"But how did the Scythians get the bodies in?"

"Cut them up small and pushed them through that hole," Nikolai volunteered.

"Nonsense," Varya told him. "They built the dolmens *round* the bodies, of course."

The thickly wooded hillside was a strange haunted place, the tombs backed by a dark thicket of buckthorn. The sound of the stream came but faintly, and no birds sang. Daisy gave an involuntary shiver, but pulling herself up sharply, thought, I must read about the Scythians. "Tell me all you know about them," she asked Varya, who was delighted to oblige.

"They came long ago from Persia . . ." The twins, bored, disappeared into the buckthorn thicket where they could be heard breaking branches and discussing the relative merits of beech and hazel as material for bows and arrows.

"Do you think, Miss Daisy," Ella wanted to know, "that there could be any gold inside? I think if you helped me up, I could just squeeze in."

"But if you fell, darling, we should never get you out again."

"I wouldn't fall."

"But if you did? I'll lift you up, anyway, to have a look in."

Varya was nettled. Her lecture had been interrupted. Ella, by being so good, and not saying much, seemed always to command attention when she did speak. "When Scythians died," Varya went on, loudly and clearly, "their wives and horses and servants were all killed and buried with them." Startled, Ella descended rapidly from her search at the tombs' opening. "And then a year later, the Scythians brought fifty young men and fifty horses and sacrificed them all too."

"They can't have done that for *everybody*," Daisy pointed out, "or there wouldn't have been any Scythians left. For kings, perhaps?"

"For everyone," Varya insisted. "And there aren't any Scythians left." She had begun to look nervously over her shoulder all the same, having succeeded in frightening herself with her Scythian tales. "They buried them round the tombs," she went on bravely. "That was before the time of our Saviour, you understand." Suddenly, her nerve went. "Let's come away," she urged Daisy, tugging at her sleeve. "I don't really like it here, without Papa to make jokes. Come away, Ella—it's a heathen place."

Both children crossed themselves. Daisy felt another shiver down the spine. How catching fear was! The woods seemed suddenly quite still. No breeze blew, no leaf stirred, even the voices of the twins were silent.

"Arkady! Nikolai! Where are you? We're going back to the picnic place, you can bathe now in the stream again, it's an hour since luncheon. Nikolai! Come on, boys!"

Silence. No rebellious voices argued from the thicket. Not a twig snapped.

"Nikolai! Arkady!" Varya's voice had a wild note in it. She was echoed by Ella's little pipe, entreating her brothers by every possible affectionate variation upon their names to return to her at once.

"We should never have come here," Varya's voice wailed in panic, when they had called in vain for five minutes. "The Scythians have got them! They've been spirited away! The evil spirits of the Scythians have come for them! They'll sacrifice them!"

Don't panic, Daisy told herself. Keep calm. But the stillness of the woods unnerved her. Could there really be watching eyes? Aloud she said, "They're just hiding, little wretches. And I'll skin them alive when I find them." Her heart was racing all the same. The boys' disappearance had been so horribly swift and sudden. One moment they had been there, and in the next they had vanished.

Gleb, attracted by the calls, came lumbering up through the wood. He too crossed himself when he saw the dolmens. "Ah, those boys," he mourned. "They should be at school. They should have a man in charge of them. They should have a father." After this helpful contribution to the problem he sank into gloomy silence, as if the total disappearance of the two small boys were a matter ordained by fate.

"Nikolai! Arkady! Come back at once!" Daisy called again, struggling to keep the panic from her voice.

The woods gave back the echo, but otherwise the silence was entire.

"I shall pray," Ella said firmly. "I shall pray and they will be found."

"You do that, darling. That's the first practical suggestion I've heard. But pray back at the picnic place, because I want to find Yuri Andreivitch to help us to search, and we mustn't lose you too."

"Are they indeed lost?" Varya quavered.

"No, of course not, Varenka, just mislaid." But fear was mounting in Daisy. Should they have searched the buckthorn thicket? Had one of them fallen? But then, surely the other would shout? They could not both be lying unconscious. Yet this abrupt, mysterious vanishing? A thorough search, she thought, of all the hillside, spread out . . .

"Aie! Aie!" cried Yuri, slowly descending from his nap in the wagon. "There are bears here sometimes. They have stumbled on a lair."

"Wild boars! Wolves!"

"Serpents!"

"They are torn in pieces!"

"Wild men of the hills have taken them!"

"The Tartars have grown wild again in such times as we know now!" The two old men and the two little girls set up an antiphon of grief and fear.

"*No*," Daisy insisted. But why do I say no? I know less than any of them.

Varya began crying uncontrollably. Ella prayed steadfastly through her pouring tears. "Mighty protectress of the sorrowful, chaste Mother of God . . ."

"I'll look downstream. You look upstream again, Yuri. Can you go a little way up the hillside, Gleb? Call and listen, all the time. Varya, you stay by the wagon and look after Ella."

"No! No! Don't leave us! We must come with you!"

"Is there anywhere, Gleb, where we could get help?"

"No one lives in these mountains. No one."

"People must sometimes *come*. These streams are full of trout. I've seen some."

"Few come. Few come now, in the war, in these troubled times . . . Few indeed . . ."

"Help of the afflicted," Ella prayed, "shelter of the universe . . ."

"Then we must search alone. Go, Gleb. If the Prince was here you'd have been halfway up that hill by now. Go, Yuri."

Yuri obeyed, grumblingly, his moans increasing as he went slowly upstream. "Few come to these lonely places. Why should the children leave their home to be brought here? For idle pleasure alone!"

"Alack the Prince!" mourned Gleb. "Alack the Princess! To lose three sons!"

"Most probably one of them has hurt himself and the other has stayed with him. We must just go on calling and searching." But, oh God! If anything bad has really happened to them! Why did I bring them to this wild place, however beautiful? I must have been mad. Daisy felt a sickening clutch at her heart.

Suddenly, checking to help Ella over a rock, Daisy looked up to see, away down the valley, a parting of the azalea bushes, and two small figures running purposefully up a track away from the direction of the sea.

"Stay here now, Ella, Varya—don't leave the wagon. Pray now that we may catch them. Look after her, Varya, and call Yuri back if you can, but don't *stir* from this spot. Gleb! Come with me. Run if you can. We must bring them in earshot and your voice will carry further. Thank God they are safe!" Daisy sped down the hill, her knees shaking with rage, fright and the steepness of the descent. Fury and speed made her breathless; she ran on, careless of stumbles, hoarse with shouting, so that when, halfway up the opposing hillside, she came upon the twins, who had paused to refresh themselves at a small stream, she was incapable of communication and could only seize them, in a vicelike grip, by the wrists. Revealing a surprising turn of speed, Gleb lumbered up close on her heels. The twins, cornered, faced her defiantly.

"Nikolai!" panted Daisy. "Arkady! How *could* you? What do you mean by running away from us?"

"Oh damn!" Arkady said, unruffled. He sat down on a fallen tree. "I never thought you could run so fast. We so nearly got away."

"But what on earth were you running away from?"

"From?" Nikolai asked, baffled by this notion. "We were not running *from* anything. We were running *to* the war, to Misha—"

"To the war!"

"We are twelve now, you know. Old enough to be of use in a war. And strong enough."

"But the war isn't in the Caucasus," Daisy pointed out, slowly regaining her breath.

"We planned," Arkady said with dignity, "to come down beyond the pass and steal horses from one of the Tartar farms. We should have

brought them back after the war, naturally, or paid for them, as soon as
we met Papa or Misha. We can load rifles. We can shoot, even. We could
help Misha, look after his horses."

"We understand horses," Nikolai pointed out. "We know how to cook
on campfires."

"Do you realise how you terrified us? Varya and Ella were heartbroken
thinking something bad had happened to you."

"That's silly. We are men now, I tell you; all men are needed to fight
the Reds."

"Oh no! You are still children!"

"The Reds kill children, do they not, Gleb? You told me so yourself. So
why should not children kill them?" Arkady asked with calm logic.

"You do not understand, Miss Daisy." Nikolai's bright eyes flashed.
"We have had enough of singing songs and eating vegetables."

"And of arithmetic," Arkady added sombrely. "And of stories. Even
your children in the New Forest did *something*, caught wild cattle. They
did not just sit quietly, learning lessons, while *your* Reds broke up the
images of the saints and threw the bones of your kings through the
stained glass windows of the cathedrals."

"How did you know about that, Arkady?" his twin asked, interested.

"I read it."

Both boys had lost the look of childhood, the infant softness and the
roundness of their faces. Their high cheekbones stood out more strongly
than ever. The blue eyes of Nikolai held a dangerous glint; he looked as if
at any moment he might again break away.

"Once Papa took us," Arkady volunteered suddenly, "to see the battle-
field of Kulíkovo. It was a huge enormous battle against the Mongols, and
two hundred *thousand* Russians fought in it, and nine out of every ten of
them were killed."

It must, thought Daisy, have been a very badly organised fight. Like
Borodino. She repressed this heresy and asked, "When was it fought?"

Arkady's look was solemn. "On September the 8th, 1380. Between the
Nepriavda and the Don rivers."

"At sunrise," said Nikolai, "Prince Peresvet fought in single combat
with the Mongol chief Telebei. The Mongols were Moslems. And then
their cavalry came on with spears and arrows, and nine out of every ten
Russians were left dead on the field. Nine out of ten. But the Russians
won the battle. And the candle of Russia, of being Russian, was not put
out."

"Nine hundred out of every thousand men," Arkady echoed proudly.
"Papa told us it was the biggest battle of the Middle Ages."

"So did that finish off the Mongols?" Daisy wondered.

Arkady's thoughtful eyes were fixed on some enormous and remote
horizon. "No," he said bleakly. "They came back next year and kept on
coming for hundreds of years more . . . I think they will always
come."

Ah don't, Daisy thought, dedicate yourself to being one of the nine out of ten! Are there not other ways of life? Unbidden, a memory of an old letter she had once seen at her uncle Ian's came to Daisy's mind, written by a Victorian colonel, Anthony Sterling, from the Crimean war—"I cannot believe that any amount of calamity would break up Russia." Like it or not, the colonel had added, "it is a great nationality; such is the *fact.*"

How *can* I cope? felt Daisy, plodding down the hill with a twin's hand firmly grasped in either of hers. They are getting too big for me. Even physically they are strong enough to get away. They may try it again. I must get them away.

Varya had stopped crying and was trying to restore her hair to its normal state of elegance. Ella was all ecstatic smiles—"the Mother of God has heard our prayers and sent them back to us." Yuri Andreivitch left the cart and joined Gleb in an admiring paean of delight. "They are bold! How like their father! They wish to make war! How like Prince Mihail! They are brave boys! How boldly they went up the hill, fearing nothing!" No, thought Daisy, I cannot cope singlehanded. Misha must come back soon. I must take them to England, even if it turns out to be barratry, or whatever you call forcibly taking people away in ships. What if we got to the Crimea and found the Bolsheviks were there already?

As if in answer to her fears, the sound of great guns, fired far away to the northwest, came booming over the hills, a widespread shudder in the summer air.

Chapter 19

The guns, half-heard and immensely distant, came in fact from their ultimate rescuer. A squadron of the Royal Navy was now active in the Black Sea, attempting to help the divided Whites—so difficult, factious and noble—in their desperate struggle to contain, and ultimately to defeat, the Red armies. It was a desultory business, compounded of the uncertainties in the high command of the White Russians, and a limited mandate from home, where, after five years of a bloody and expensive war, weariness was very much in evidence.

Anchored in Kaffa Bay, the British admiral in command of the Black Sea Squadron, whose name was Michael Culme-Seymour, was writing to his brother-in-law, another admiral, serving as Commander in Chief in Bermuda. The bright hot sunlight of early May danced on the waters, the flagship *Emperor of India* swung in the tide. "This forenoon peaceful," the Admiral recorded, "after six days gunfiring at the Bolshevists. They have made three big attacks in four days, in two of which they drove back the right of the Volunteers, but the latter eventually restored their line, or rather we did for them . . . . Our fire drove the Bolshevists out of the

Volunteer trenches they had taken, but one cannot go on for long using 15.5, 9.2, and 6" guns instead of field batteries." The business of helping the White Volunteer Army from the sea with no land forces of one's own was awkward.

"The Volunteer Army are holding a line between Arabat Bay on the north and Kaffa Bay on the south, 11 miles across and the narrowest point of the Keitel peninsular. They have only some 2,500 against 8,000 to 10,000 Bolshevists, and no-one will send them any reinforcements, so I expect they will lose Keitel sooner or later, as we cannot stop a really determined attack in a mist or at night—or by day for that matter.

"Last night they began firing at us with a couple of what looked like 6", but we could not make out where from. A long way off, and they were over a mile short, but I suppose they will move them up soon. . . . I fancy it may be an armoured train and if so it cannot get any closer as we got a 13.5 salvo right into the junction of the Theodosia and Keitel lines and blew the line up for some 200 yards, and the train is the wrong side of that. We give them one or two rounds a day to delay the repairs."

We had, he explained, three wars going on. War weariness was much in evidence amongst some of the Allies, as it was in the Russian troops. The first war was at Sevastopol, "Where the heavy guns put the fear of God into the Bolshevists on the only occasion they were fired, and the French took advantage of this to make an armistice. We could have held the town for any time but the French as usual were not for it. And the result has been this unnecessary and deplorable evacuation. They—the French here—disgraced themselves both at Sevastopol and Odessa and are universally loathed. The culminating point was the mutiny in the French Fleet, which was really serious. Their demands were to leave for France at once and in company, and various other things. They were out of hand for three days and had a procession ashore with the local Bolshevists which was fired on by the French soldiers with some forty casualties. Eventually *La France* sailed alone and it died down.

"I offered to take over the defence of the town, with the French Army, and leave the French Fleet free to sail, but they were only too glad of the excuse to clear out. So now they have cleared out of the whole of their zone, we have taken over the Sea of Azof and they are supposed to be watching the entrances to Nicolaieff to prevent the Bolshevist submarines and destroyers coming out from there. Of course they ought to have destroyed them before they evacuated that place, but didn't. A most disgraceful business, their whole conduct.

"The 2nd war is here in full swing. The Bolshevists went back about 3 miles yesterday, I expect to wait for reinforcements and artillery, but they have also been fighting among themselves; the infantry in some cases are driven to the attack by cavalry with whips and by Chinese with machine guns! So at present there is not much goodwill in their attack. But the Volunteer Army on the right go back for the least thing, and are played out. This side they are better.

"The 3rd war is in the Caspian, two actions with Bolshevist destroyers fromAstrakhan since the ice melted. They have a good many there and some submarines, besides armed merchant ships. We have at last got some aeroplanes out and have bombed Astrakhan, but no detailed report yet.

"I want to get up to see Denikin, but cannot leave at present." The Admiral was longing to stretch his legs ashore— "My only visit to the shore since we passed the Dardanelles is one of two hours for golf on the opening day of the Constantinople course, otherwise my shore visits have been confined to Embassy and G.H.Q. in a motor! and voyages in trains to Baku and Ekaterinodar. . . ." He had at least the distinction of being the only British admiral ever to fly his flag on the Caspian Sea.

Possibly the worst part of the business was that the people in authority at home were either ignorant or else wilfully misreading the situation for purposes of their own. As if anyone, after five years spent fighting the Germans to a standstill, were seriously thinking of invading Russia! "Lloyd George is all wrong. It *would* take a gigantic force to conquer Russia, but we don't want to do that: we want to defeat Bolshevism, and a comparatively small force would help Denikin and Kolchak to do that." But would such a force be forthcoming, with Lloyd George in the saddle, half in love with Bolshevism himself, without having the smallest idea of what it meant in practice? Sadly, the Admiral feared not.

By the last week of July he was feeling a little more hopeful. "I spent most of yesterday with Denikin at Ekaterinodar," he informed his brother-in-law, Admiral Sir Trevylyan Napier, from off Novorossisk in the *Emperor of India*, "about various subjects—our new war to force entrance to Khersin and Nicolaieff, the return of Russian interned ships, the repatriation of Russian prisoners from France (there are 60,000 of them, all Bolshevists or nearly all), the transfer of our Caspian fleet to Denikin, etc. Daresay you know, or perhaps you don't, that we are transferring Caspian to the Volunteer Army and abandoning Caucasus. As we sank about ⅓ of the Bolshevist fleet at Alexandrosk and ½ the remainder have gone above Tsaritsin where they are stuck, I don't think the fleet part matters; but to abandon Caucasus is to leave Denikin's rear unprotected and open to attack by Georgians who are all semi-Bolshevists and longing for the chance. An act of treachery, as I have told the Admiralty.

"Otherwise, Denikin is getting on well. He will have to come back from his advanced position I expect, but the people in the country he had occupied are sick of Bolshevism and welcome him with open arms."

Mike himself was feeling a certain weariness of war. "If I start on the situation I shall go on for ever. Like you, the 'peace' leaves me cold. I have had and am still having far more war here than at any time during the four years. The situation at home seems most unpleasant." And yet, "I envy you very much. A summer at home is what I have longed for for years." In the last seven and a half years he had spent only twenty-seven nights at his home near the New Forest—"We earn our extra pay!" His wife was not well, and he was very glad that his sister and brother-in-law had gone to Liebe's confirmation and sent him an account of it and of her— "do go and see Michael at West Downs next term."

Thinking of his children, the Admiral was suddenly more cheerful. Trev had sent him the latest volume of Pepys to be printed, and "Pepys is always splendid." And he might be promoted and sent home— "or more likely turned out." Something unexpected was always happening in and around the Black Sea. "In fact my stay here is like the state of the fore-yard of the *Sanglier Frigate*—or was it the *Diomede*—that Mr. Charles reported as 'precarious and not at all permanent!'" If anything at all could still be done to save Russia he seemed willing enough to stay on and do it.

Much as he wanted his nephew to join her, he must point out that the *Emperor of India* "was *not* and never would be a smart ship," though her gunnery was good and she was in good order. "The Captain and Commander are both gentlemen and personally delightful, but they are modern and think that gunnery efficiency and 'brightwork' cannot be combined. They don't see rope-yarn lying about, don't mind if the side is painted in patches and seem quite astonished when I call their attention to these things. And the Captain told me the other day, when I said the men were to fall in at noon when the peace salute was fired, that he didn't think the order would be popular with the men!! . . . Time I left the Navy."

Could it be that the laziness and indiscipline, and its supine acceptance by authority, were blowing offshore on the land breeze? To her midshipmen at any rate she seemed as fine a ship as any in the Mediterranean Fleet.

A similar sense of lost causes afflicted Admiral Michael Culme-Seymour as August wore on. "We are clearing out of the Caspian now and finish this week," he informed his sister May, whose son was now serving as a midshipman on board his ship. "Then our troops leave the Caucasus and that is the worst mistake of the two. Denikin can, I think, look after the Caspian now that we have sunk or cleared off most of the Bolshevist ships, but Georgia, etc. in his rear will be a great danger to him." Their father, Sir Michael Culme-Seymour, was now a widower living in Northamptonshire. "I don't wonder the Admiral is depressed about the state of England. Our government are far too alarmed at taking any responsibility." At Batum, and across the mountains at Baku on the Caspian, he had found people entreating us to take over, to make them part of the British Empire and thus save them from the Bolshevism they so deeply feared. The talk of "our taking the mandate from Constantinople to Batum, Baku, across the Caspian and on to Samarkand, and all to the south of it may sound ridiculous, but it is what *all* the inhabitants want, and the only way of keeping order or peace." But what a hope! "*Our* Bolshevists won't let the government do anything and they submit to be dictated to. . . .

"So Kolchak is done, and the White Sea is to be abandoned and we now rely on Denikin only to fight the Bolshevists, and I daresay we shall chuck him as soon as our spare stores and ammunition are expended. If he don't beat the Bolshevists in Russia, no-one will, and they will spread all over the world.

"But I have hopes. The country is so dead against them."

There was not much cheer in the prospects of the Black Sea Squadron either. Round the Black Sea, the dismal tale of retreat, defeat, and divided counsels continued and there was nothing much for the Navy to do except watch the process, with little power to do more than mitigate disaster.

The *Emperor of India* was in a fog, and proceeding slowly from Sevastopol to Constantinople. It was April 5th, and seemed a good moment for the Admiral to put his old father, who was also an admiral, into the Black Sea picture, which seemed to him to be one of increasing gloom.

"The present situation is this," the admiral wrote. "The Volunteer Army were driven back on Novorossisk, or rather retreated in more or less disorder and we evacuated what we could to the Crimea. . . . The Crimea is over-crowded, some 40,000 troops in it, all squabbling among themselves and with no morale, and it is difficult to find enough to hold the front. It must fall directly the Bolshevists attack in force—if not before—and the only thing to be done is to abandon the struggle and for the Allies to get as good terms for them from the Soviet as they can. That, or declare war on the Soviet—which they won't do—through they will have to sooner or later.

"Denikin resigned yesterday and refused to nominate a successor; he said the Council of Notables must choose, and they chose Wrangel. I arrived at Sevastopol yesterday morning from Constant with him, Wrangel, on board to attend the Council. He expected to be asked to succeed Denikin, but on the way weakened on it and eventually wanted to be taken back to Constant; (he has not, I fear, much guts) but they induced him to stay.

"Our government has sent out to say that the struggle must cease and that they can no longer support Denikin, and will endeavour to make terms with him, etc. When we got to Sevastopol yesterday we found to our astonishment that Denikin was not there, nor had he any intention of coming. He remained at Theodosia and directly he heard the decision of the council, left for Constant in one of our destroyers and is now somewhere close to me in the fog. I knew he was leaving and left Sevastopol last night to bring him down myself in *E. of I.*—I wanted to do honour to him! But he wouldn't wait, so I turned round and came on direct. Have seen a lot of Denikin at N'sk and Theodosia. . . . We shall no doubt evacuate Batum, the result of delay in making peace and in not taking a strong line with the Bolshevists from the first."

At least, the evacuation of Novorossisk hadn't been a failure. "We had more success in getting the people away from Novorossisk than we hoped for. The Volunteer Army put up no fight, utterly played out. We, and the Russians assisted by us, took away some 40,000 troops, there were I daresay another 20,000 left to disperse. I doubt if there were ever more than 5,000 to 10,000 Bolshevists attacking, if that. The work of our destroyers on the last night was first class, taking people off. Mercifully, the weather was perfect." The Admiral himself had not been in bed for 48 hours and his barge had never stopped plying.

And yet, what a shoddy affair! "It was not pleasant to see the Allied Fleet flying before one field gun in the morning, but it was on an armoured train in the middle of the town and we should only have killed a lot of women and children if we had fired back . . . Besides the upper deck was full with 2,000 Russian troops and even field gun shrapnel would have given them a bad time. I daren't put them below because of risk of typhus which was bad enough as it was. . . . We did fire a bit on the day before the evacuation—it delayed the Bolshevists but the Russians never spotted for us, or took much interest in it—all they thought of was getting clear. With good troops and our fleet Novorossisk could have been held for ages. Except for food; there were only 7 days' supply there."

This debacle had come about for three reasons: "Lloyd George's speeches, our half-hearted support, bad behaviour of the Volunteer Army, especially the Cossacks (they were as bad as the Bolshevists as regards loot, etc. during their advance), incompetence of the Volunteer Army Generals and officers both in a military and political sense, and *chiefly* their utter failure to make any sort of civil organisation and system of civil administration behind their advance. We ought to have done this for them."

The term Volunteer Army was confusing, because the White Force was made up of three parts, "the Volunteer Army proper, the Don Cossack Army, the Kuban Cossack Army. Latterly the Dons have refused to fight at all. The Kubans in places turned on the Volunteer Army and on one occasion after a desperate fight wiped out a whole regiment. The Vol. Army are the only reliable people and even most of them were against Denikin lately; only a week ago two of the most trusted units went over to the Bolshevists from the Perekof Front—the Cadet Corps or a part of it—who had almost alone held the front for a long time, and a battery of artillery complete—they said they weren't going to do any more fighting while the remainder are doing nothing. So the disorganisation is complete and it is no use hoping for them to go on. The Red Army are also in a bad way, but are well-led, partly I think by Germans. . . . It is a sad end to it all."

There was the particular exhausting shame in seeing a country that one had served all one's life behaving with so much shabby indecision; helping and then not helping and never helping enough. "A sad three months in the Black Sea," he wrote his sister at the end of April, "and the end of Denikin; but they are hanging on in the Crimea under Wrangel. I fear the Bolshevists will get in there if they attack seriously and there will be a dreadful catastrophe if they do. However, our govt. have started negotiations with the Reds. Thanks to one admirable Russian, a naval engineer called a General, who was captain of the port, and thanks to perfect weather, we got them clear of Novorossisk without disaster."

It was to remain the one consoling thought. By the end of June the *Emperor of India* was at Batum "to superintend the evacuation of our troops and the transfer to the Georgians," the Admiral wrote his sister, now in Bermuda, where her husband was Commander in Chief on the North American and West Indies Station. "It also means the evacuation of a great many Russians who would get their throats cut if they stayed." He hoped it could all be done without opposition, "but an attack is possible from either the Turkish Nationalists, the Bolshevists, or a tribe nearby known as the Adjerians. A nice complication. I am sick of evacuations!" (It was his seventh.) "Thank goodness there is nothing more in the Black Sea to evacuate, except the Crimea, and that is too big a job to attempt. . . . Wrangel is doing well and has reorganised his army and the country, brought down food prices, etc. and is very popular—wherefore we have now ceased to support him."

Wrangel was even carrying the war into the enemy's camp, and this bravery had been too much for Lloyd George. By July 22nd, the Admiral was so sickened that he could hardly write. "Our behaviour to Wrangel has been too disgraceful," he wrote his sister, "and I cannot write all about it. We withdrew our mission at a most critical time for him, and also all our support from him in every way, *because he advanced*. If he had stayed in Crimea he would have starved. And now our Govt. have the impertinence to propose to the Soviet that Wrangel shall retire again to Crimea—what's it got to do with them? As I said, he can't possibly do so without starving.

"And we also try to force an agreement on the Poles which will release the Soviet troops to attack Wrangel, so the latter seems bound to be done either way. It almost looks as if our government were going to use force to make him come back. I should refuse to take action against him if I was ordered to."

Fortunately, the Admiral was not so ordered, and the Black Sea Squadron steamed into the Mediterranean once more. The capable, and in the event daring, Wrangel was left alone. When the winter ice formed, a Bolshevik force crossed the Strait of Perekop and compelled the final White Russian withdrawal from Russian soil on November 15th, 1920. Aided by the miseries of war, a handful of determined and pitiless men had seized a great empire and imposed their absolute rule in the teeth of some ninety percent of its inhabitants. The Western Powers, exhausted by their desperate battle against Germany and Austria, had supinely allowed it to happen, a piece of lassitude for which they were to pay dearly.

The late summer weather was pleasant enough at the Villa Rosa, but it was on a sultry day of southeast winds that George Bennett proposed marriage. He had determined to ask Daisy to be his wife that day, and ask he did, in spite of the sticky heat and the gusts of blowing dust. Daisy was moved in spite of herself by the vigour and straightforwardness of his freckled face. Here, she suddenly perceived, was one who would never sulk, never turn tail from difficulties, never let down the people he loved. Or anyone else for that matter. He was strength and safety, and in her loneliness she very nearly said yes. With real regret and sadness she saw him drive away down the dusty road, the high red wheels of his dogcart creaking over the stones.

George's heart felt sick with disappointment. He was heavily sad at his refusal, frowning crossly at his horse's ears as the dogcart rattled along the coast and turned up the hill. Flies teased him and dust powdered his eyebrows and parched his nostrils. He was not permanently discouraged, and far from able to believe that such refusal was final. He had been foolish, he told himself, to expect Daisy, at so unsettled and distracting a time, to take such a great decision. And in any case, with the mounting danger from the north, he himself was in no happy position for marriage. He must stay on the coast until every last stray and reluctant British subject had been taken off and shipped for home, his only reassurance the continuing presence of the British Squadron.

But he loved Daisy deeply, feared for her, longed to be in a position to take charge, to organise a safe departure. Drat the children. Damn in fact, all Russians, *pro tem*—particularly Mihail Dubelsky.

She had been so sweet to him, and indeed affectionate, in her refusal that he would be an idiot to give up hope. Time might even be on his side. And Daisy's removal from Russia most certainly would.

Whipping up the little pony along the dusty road, he began to regain cheerfulness. It was sadly lowering to be refused, in this the most vital question one ever asked, but as the Bay of Novorossisk opened up before him he felt sturdily that while there was life there was hope. She had looked so far from horrified or put off at the idea, simply surprised and very very kind.

George found himself wishing that Amelia were still in Russia. She had been able without apparent difficulty to instill some of her crisp common sense into Daisy. And she had thought most Russians unreliable and the rest rather silly. For her, they sang and danced and gloomed and rejoiced in vain. But Amelia had, he had heard, married an Irishman in

the war, and must now be further away than ever. The problem was all
his own.

The loneliness of Daisy's situation seemed to deepen every day, and
now she had perhaps lost her one reliable friend. She longed above all for
a holiday from responsibility and decision, for restfulness, for adult conversation. When I see Daddy and Mummy I shall talk to them for about
six hours, without ever stopping. To sit in our own drawing room at home
and hear Mummy and the children playing and singing! To see a green
English lawn, wet with dew, and fat thrushes hopping on it! To laugh
and talk with one's own people, to giggle at family jokes, even to listen to
old Martin Broadbent complaining in the garden! Above all to go to one's
own church, in one's own village, and hear one's own father uttering
those beautiful and intelligible words, in one's own tongue, with one's
own ways of thought, feeling and worship, one's own quiet and humble
holy communion. I never, ever, ever, want to go abroad again! Supposing
one were caught like this another time!
Her father wrote, beseeching her to return with haste.

> I'm assured by all the friends who know that it is now real-
> ly safe for you to come back by sea. Admiral de Robeck at
> Constantinople will look out for you. I know what you must
> feel about waiting in case the children's parents should come
> to Novorossisk and find them gone, but I fear one can count on
> nothing with Russia in her present state. One must face the
> dreadful possibility that they may not have survived.

Daisy recognised the voice that would not, far from the scene, actually
command, but was in fact relying upon her obedience. Next week, she
thought, next week I really will start talking to George about it. If only
he hadn't asked me to marry him, which makes asking him to do things
so awkward . . . Next week, next month anyway . . .
The children played happily enough on the beach, sunburned and
healthy. Summer had again brought fresh eggs, vegetables, fruit from the
garden. There was fish from the fishermen, flour and occasional butter
from inland; there was the local wine, though tea and coffee had ceased to
exist. Daisy's father managed again, through the consulate, to get some
money to her. The sun rose in a cloudless sky, sank over a calm blue sea.
The crystal clear water fell gently on the sandy shore. It's all beautiful,
Daisy thought, but nothing is beautiful when one is anxious and frightened and undecided. An air of menace seemed to brood over the high
bleak mountains, even as they glowed in the setting sun. Varya was fifteen now; if the Reds came what would they do to her if they knew she
was a princess, one of the race of the hated oppressors? They must *not*

know. But if that malicious, envying daughter of Anna's were to tell them?

What had those distant heavy guns meant? The approach of the Red Army?

Tomorrow, Daisy decided, or next week, anyway, before the weather breaks for winter, I will walk over the hills to the fishing village and ask about a boat to the Crimea. But it's still only September. And what if Misha were to come? Or to write? And how, in the chaos that is Russia now, should we ever all find each other again? Danger and death, she still felt in her bones, were things that came to other people. Not to those who stayed innocently in their own houses and asked for no trouble. Her English confidence and sense of security lulled her. Sufficient unto the day was the evil of whatever went on over the hill. Only in the looks of Gleb and Anna could be read the age-old melancholy and apprehension that a history of savage invasion had taught them.

George Bennett had persuaded the others into a walk along the shore, but Varya had stayed behind. She sat out on the terrace, staring moodily at the bright sea, from whose wide expanse no brave vessel with gallant helmsman arrived, to make an admiring rescue of an exiled princess. A few distant fishing boats decorated a pencil-thin horizon, on which the smoke of a still more distant ship could faintly and uninterestingly be seen.

Varya was growing fast, becoming, as she could hardly help knowing, more beautiful with every passing week. She had bypassed adolescent plumpness and awkwardness, arriving directly by this route at a supple adult gracefulness. Most of the time she forgot about all this and raced up and down with the others. Today it sat heavily upon her. She was not going to walk in the company of a young man who had no eyes but for Daisy. Who *was* there, she demanded of herself, to praise, flatter and love her; to gaze at her and to court her in the way that was her due? Hearing the crunch of gravel, she turned with interest to see half a dozen young men walking up the short drive towards the house.

On a closer look she stood up, her eyes widening with apprehension. These were peasant boys, or boys from Novorossisk; yet there was something menacing and determined about their approach. Workmen they certainly were, but resolute workmen with heads held high. There was nothing of the apologetic shuffle usual in such men when approaching the dwellings of the great. They disappeared round the corner of the house, and a minute later, from Anna at the back door came a furious high-pitched screaming. Varya, whatever else, was no coward. She ran boldly into the house towards the sound of Anna's distress.

* * *

Busy by the shore, Nikolai was not too preoccupied to see that George had taken Daisy's hand, and that she had failed to withdraw it. Nikolai was a romantic, he followed the progress of the affair with interest. He drew the attention of Arkady. Daisy was looking down, but was not, as she sometimes was, looking away.

Arkady had no time for such matters. He liked George and pitied his inability to get himself accepted as a combatant. He was still hoping that the rules would be relaxed and that George might find a worthier purpose in life than the pursuit of Daisy. What, he wondered, could a sensible man like George be saying so persistently, ignoring the sea and the rocks and the possible presence of shrimps, simply in order to gaze into Daisy's blue eyes and go on and on talking to her? What magic in so ordinary a sight could cause a man to abstract himself from the larger splendours of life?

The afternoon was proving a disappointment, had slumped into nothing much. Luncheon had been the usual unsatisfactory meal, but since then George had arrived, and had brought out some tins of meat. It was sad stuff, as Arkady knew from experience; yet he felt hungry at the thought of it. Should they not now go back, and have supper, or at least tea? The sea was too cold to enter, icy as it was with melted Caucasian snow, and Ella kept getting stones in her shoes and calling upon Arkady to stop doing whatever he was doing and hold her hand while she took them out. He was pleased suddenly to see Varya running in the distance, running full tilt. She was joining them after all, had come out of her would-be-grown-up sulk. She ran well, Arkady reflected; it was a pity she had given it up of late.

She was flying now towards George Bennett, and towards Daisy, upon whom she flung herself. Not, Arkady hoped unsympathetically, more tears, more fuss, more delays!

Varya's face was distraught; her dark locks wild and dishevelled. "While you were out," she gasped, her voice rising in a crescendo of fury and reproach, "while you were out some men came, some men from Novorossisk, and they came in the house, and Gleb couldn't stop them, and they took, they took—"Her voice died away in a gasping shudder.

"They took! What did they take? Wait a moment, darling, and get your breath back."

"All the silver, all the dishes, all our spoons and forks and knives, and all the food and wine they could find . . . and I think they were friends of Anna and Gleb's daughter, and Anna scolded and scolded but they took everything. The tins of meat you brought us—everything. Nothing of Gleb and Anna's, only of ours.

"And they were horrible men, horrible. If Anna hadn't scolded them, they would have, they would have— There was such a noise, and it all happened so quickly. Gleb was calling on the saints to help us, but Anna wasn't. She was cursing, and kicking, and spitting. If Anna hadn't stopped them, if Anna hadn't put me behind her . . . if, if Gleb hadn't stood behind me . . . only because they wouldn't hurt Gleb or Anna they would have raped me, killed me—"

"Don't tremble so. You're safe now. There, Varya, you're safe, you're with friends. George is here. We are all here."

"For how long! For how long! They looked horribly at me! They will be back again." Her eyes rolled in terror. "They have killed the pigeons. They have killed even *them*. They will return to kill us!"

Daisy could scarcely believe her. They had lived securely for so long. She soothed Varya, as George collected the other children from the rocks. There was no need to frighten them, and Varya was now sufficiently collected to have ceased crying. "The thing is," Daisy told the twins and Ella, "we've been robbed. A great bore, but I expect we can eat with kitchen spoons and forks." The walk home was a trudge; Varya's trembling hand dragged on her arm.

They found Gleb crestfallen, shamed and trembling, but the sound of Anna's outrage filled the Villa Rosa, seeming to bounce from wall to wall. She was beyond consolation, praise or soothing. "No daughter of mine!" she was shouting. "No more to me a child! No more! No more!"

She paused for breath. "Don't mind the stolen things," Daisy reassured Gleb. "You were very brave—you saved Varya. You were splendid. When the Prince hears of this, he—" Anna's renewed cries drowned her voice: "No more! Never anymore! Those were her friends who came to rob!"

Gleb retreated to the garden, sniffing vigorously. "She will recover," he told the boys, when safely out of earshot. "Tomorrow Anna will love our daughter as much and as blindly. Ah, wicked girl!"

Arkady, moved, gave the old man a kiss. "You are a brave hero," Nikolai added gravely. "We salute you." Slowly, Anna's screams died down. Slowly, the old man took heart again. But his life seemed a weariness to him. Tenderly, he felt the cheek that Arkady had kissed. He knew well where his allegiance lay, but would he have the strength to hold to it?

Later, George drew Daisy aside. "Surely now," he said gently but very gravely, "you see the absolute necessity of leaving? Things like this will be commonplace. Wrong won't seem wrong to boys like those. Law and order will go, have gone, and with it kindness, compassion, respect for women, everything."

Again he saw the veiled obstinate look draw down over Daisy's face. "How could you protect them or save them?" he went on. "They could even be safer without you, with Gleb and Anna, just a Russian pair with grandchildren. The presence of an English governess is the surest possible giveaway."

"They are given away already by that horrible daughter of Gleb's and Anna's."

"An extra reason for going."

He is right, Daisy reasoned to herself. I can't protect Varya, I can't control the twins; what *am* I doing here?

"So about passages to Constant—" George continued. But as if on cue, Ella rushed suddenly into the room. Leaping on the sofa in order to get to grips with Daisy's standing figure, she cast her arms round her neck. Something of Varya's terror had communicated itself. "Never, never leave us Miss Daisy! We love you! We love you absolutely. You will look after us like you did with those wicked men in the train."

The facts of their journey across Russia had become a little blurred in Ella's memory. She knew only that Daisy was her last available haven in a storm-tossed sea, and that she loved her, and trusted her, in a way that cast out every ounce of her nine-year-old independence and dignity. "You won't ever go," she repeated with moving certainty. "You won't ever go, I *know*. I *know* you won't. We love you, entirely, forever. All of us, we all do. Nikolai does and Arkasha does. Varya doesn't say, because she is proud, but she does, too!"

George could see that Daisy herself was near tears. He knew when he was defeated and turned to go. He had confidence in her essential reasonableness, once this storm of emotion was past. He would go ahead with the booking of passages for them *all*. With her hand thus forced, she would probably leave Russia.

Daisy, making sure of the locks at night, testing the bars of the shutters, felt a deepening apprehension. Soon, *soon*, Misha, tell me what to do! Come soon!

Chapter 20

Misha lay stretched out in the shade of his horse. He and his cavalry troop were posted near the top of a ridge between two villages. Below ran one of the many little rivers of the Don basin. It was August of 1919, and he had been fighting all summer, a war of movement to and fro across the steppe. Since there was nothing to be gained by occupying the empty plains, both White and Red armies concentrated upon gaining and keeping such vital points as river crossings and railway bridges, hoping thus to isolate their enemies and bring their forces to battle. Misha had been leading his cavalry scouts for six months without rest; he was burned dark brown by the sun and wind of the steppe, his fair hair a corn-coloured thatch. His men, mostly Cossacks, were old soldiers and had become expert scroungers—they had supped the previous night on a sumptuous diet of wild goose and honey, and had eaten, drunk and been merry. On every tomorrow they might die.

Far out from the main forces, they lived under continual risk of capture, and even on these tough men the strain was beginning to tell. The troopers might, indeed, recant and escape by changing sides—many Cossacks were fighting for the Reds—but for an officer capture meant torture, mutilation and eventually certain death under the supervision of the Red Army's commissars. In recaptured villages, Misha had seen many bodies so treated, and he had resolved never to be captured. Since one would be a dead man anyway, better to fight it out and take as many as possible of the bastards with one.

There was a peculiar bitterness between the Cossacks on both sides. They had in general followed their leaders, who acted according to their individual politics. A third army, known as the Green, and made up of partisans and guerilla fighters, attacked both sides impartially, tortured the peasants for food and seemed in the main nonpolitical and merely out to raise hell while the opportunity lasted.

Misha cast a gloomy eye round his troop and their mounts. The White forces in general suffered from a lack of good horses, since the Reds had driven off the best of them in 1918, before the Whites had driven Bolshevik forces away from the Don and the Kuban steppes. But Misha regarded his chestnut stallion with affection; he had captured it from a Red horseman killed in a surprise raid on his camp: he was a marvellous, tireless animal, but like all stallions, had to be muffled before a surprise attack because of his tiresome way of betraying his owners by neighing wildly to the horses in the enemy camp. All the same he was a beauty, with just that touch of devilment that Misha enjoyed.

The Red forces were a mixture, and in many ways Misha hated fighting them. To be at war with Russians! They held a hard core of Bolsheviks, fighting passionately for a cause in which they wholeheartedly believed; but there were also a great many pressed men liable to desert to Denikin, the White general, when they saw a chance. Over these doubtful members the commissars brooded with fanatical vigilance. Then there were the Chinese, who had been in the Labour Corps during the war against Germany. Misha had found them brave and resolute enough as opponents, though he was aware that they were hampered in attack by being unable to understand a word that was said to them. They fought for the Reds for food and clothing rather than from any revolutionary zeal, could as easily be made to fight for Denikin if he had had any money with which to persuade them.

The Whites fought with real passion too, for Holy Russia and for the murdered Czar, the troops retaining their curious mixture of gentleness and ruthlessness. Their officers commanded them in a friendly and communicative way, addressing them collectively as "My children." "Health to you, Plastunis," the commander would call to the brigade of infantry on parade. "Welcome to you, our commander," the parade would shout back with equal warmth. Officers of the British Military Mission who were training them in the use of Lewis and Vickers guns and indeed fighting with them, were alternately delighted by their enthusiasm and gentleness, their straightforward simplicity, and exasperated by their laziness. After a very brief time of great interest in their instruction with the guns, they would announce with a beaming smile, "I know it all now," and immediately lie down and fall fast asleep. And yet, seeing them march out from Novorcherkask, their enthusiasm and devotion never failed to touch Misha's heart, the leading men starting a song and the following columns taking it up in their deep resonant voices. Hour after hour of a long gruelling march would go by, and they still sang on, inspiring each other, cheering and sustaining each other. At their night halt, now, only thin soup and badly baked black bread were produced. Without blankets or overcoats, they lay drenched by the cold dews of the high steppes. Not more than half of them still had boots; they wore sacking tunics which barely met across their chests, small caps which gave no protection from the sun, and no underclothes. Thus clad, they had already fought through one Russian winter, and in summer typhus and cholera had taken their toll.

All three armies, for all their stalwart courage, committed atrocities with equal ferocity, Misha had to admit.

No less dogged were the peasants, though fighting on neither side. Riding through the Don country this summer, Misha had watched them cutting the corn, indifferent to the passing of armed men, binding it into sheaves, humping their creaking wooden carts with it. They rose as the day was dawning, at three in the morning, leaving their village after a meal made up only of sour milk and watermelons, and worked until the stars came out and dusk veiled their fields. All the while they knew full well that when the frosts and blizzards of winter came, marauding armies might rob them of all their hard-won grain and leave them to starve.

Misha was beginning to see what Kolya had been driving at, all those years ago, in the peace and plenty of Moscow or Jevrenskaia. Such men as these, peasant and soldier alike, rated high, deserved more from life than they ever had had. They deserved freedom, and the right to farm their own land and enjoy the modest fruit of their labours. But they also, Misha thought, needed the guidance of such a man as his father had been, and the knowledge and authority of better educated men, until such time as they got learning and experience for themselves. Above all, they needed a helping hand when things went wrong, when beasts died or crops failed. And impatiently he remembered the Russian artillerymen, asleep beside their vital guns in the middle of the half-learned lesson of how to use them.

Information as to how very differently the Red Army lived had come from its numerous deserters. There, the sleeping men would simply have been shot on the principle that there were plenty more where they came from—the inexhaustible womb of Russia. Lenin and Trotsky seemed to have no feeling for Russians as such, or even for Russia as a country. They looked on the Fatherland, Misha reflected, simply as a base from which to convert the rest of the industrial world to communism, shaken as it was by the disruptions and miseries of war.

And yet, thought Misha, with what vigour and enthusiasm the Red Army fought! They were lions—and he hated them and was proud of them in the same breath. They were full of hope, even the prisoners, drunk with the fantasy of their imagined new world, happy as kings to be free of the weakness and indecisions of the Czar, the muddle, the short-ages, the divided counsels; free also of the corruptions and the lassitude that the absolute power of Rasputin had wrought in the government of the Orthodox Church. With a fierce release of long pent up emotion they fought for an imagined world of happiness, prosperity and freedom.

They were entirely unaware of all that was going on behind their backs—savagely triumphant in victory, never guessing that success would only further enslave them and leave them victims of a tyranny far more searching and repressive than the worst achieved by the Czars. They knew only that factories had been handed over to the workers: they did not know that pay was now handed out irrespective of skill or the volume of work done, so that production had already dropped to one sixth of what it had been, and that disappointed workers looted both products and plant. They understood few of communism's implications. How should they? They knew that all private trade had been abolished early in 1918 and all shops closed; they did not know that this had led directly to starvation in the towns. They knew and rejoiced in the fact that all private houses were confiscated and used for the housing needs of the people, but were unaware that such seizure barely touched the fringe of the problem of homelessness, while in a land teeming with forests, in the commandeered houses a priceless heritage of furniture, carved doors and pictures was being broken up and used for firewood.

Not only the food and fuel supplies, but all the accepted and ordinary framework of life had been disrupted in the interests of the brave new order. With fierce delight, banks were demolished, but this had led not so much to the demise of capitalism as to the loss of many humble private savings. All land was declared to be national property, which meant in practice that it came under the absolute control of a few remote and ruthless men who had no knowledge of its needs nor interest in its prosperity—were no husbandmen but savage rapists. Many priests were killed and church property was included in the grab, so that no succour for the starving was any longer to be found in monasteries bereft of their monks, in sisterhood hospitals where the ailing poor had long been cherished.

How many of those who fought with such fanatical fierceness, Misha wondered, understood what was being done in their name? And yet, in the enormous empty spaces where the civil war was being fought out, fantasy held sway, and the beautiful dream of freedom and equality turned men into demons.

Where Misha lay the grass was long and deep. Across the valley in the distance the steppe rose in an abrupt cliff that did indeed seem like a gigantic step hewn in the earth's surface. Below this the small houses of a village clustered round their church—and here lay their objective. But who lurked in the thick belt of forest that lay stretched between village and ridge? For the moment, Misha had been forbidden to probe and find out. Cavalry losses had been too great of late, and small parties too often cut off by the enemy.

The stallion munched contentedly, apparently unaffected by the blaze of the noonday sun. Fodder was short, let him graze where and when he could, poor beast—this was no war for strict cavalry discipline. The breeze had sunk at noon, and the flies were tormenting. To the left of Misha's troop, a company of Plastunis lay waiting in the grass, murmuring to each other and occasionally rolling over in the lush grass to cool themselves. The redheaded Scot, James Kennedy, who was in charge of the Vickers and Lewis guns, came along to chat. He spoke no Russian and sought out Misha whenever possible in order to elucidate problems or simply to have a talk. Urged by Winston Churchill, the British Government, since her war with Germany was over, had dispatched to the aid of Denikin's army surplus guns and stores to help the Whites win back their country. The accompanying officers had strict orders only to instruct in the use of guns and not to take part in the fighting, but Kennedy and many another had decided that instruction could with advantage be carried into the field of action. The Vickers and Lewis guns were admirable, but none of the thousands of fine woollen British uniforms, warm and new, had found their way either to Misha's Cossacks or to the Plastunis. There was a rumour that one of General X's staff had sold them all off to the Jews of Rostov. The British officers were helpful and well-liked, Misha reflected, and generous with their supplies of whiskey. But there was a strange unseriousness about them: they had a tendency to leave the slow-moving troop trains and spend a day walking up partridges or hare, or an evening flighting duck; catching up unconcernedly a day later as the train wandered round the steppes, sometimes almost back on its previous day's track. They seemed to regard the war simply as an unusually dangerous shooting expedition.

Kennedy hopefully asked him for a cigarette, but Misha, who of course had no such thing, looked on this as the normal British Army way of opening a conversation. Kennedy was a townsman, with no knowledge of horses, he sat down suddenly rather too near the chestnut's heels; it lashed out viciously, narrowly missing him, and Misha advised him to move nearer himself. He liked the cheerful, reliable Kennedy, with his abrupt but pointed tales of Glasgow life.

"I'm getting the hang of some of your Cossack songs," Kennedy told him companionably. "I like fine to hear the way your chaps sing on the march. Never heard such voices. What's in store for us today? A couple of squadrons of Red Horse in that bit of forest?"

"Lucky if it's only a couple," Misha said. There was a kind of tension in the hot air, a smell of danger. They had been waiting where they were for too long. From a clump of birch to the left where the second Lewis gun's crew were hidden came a burst of laughter, but there was a hectic quality in it.

"In this high grass," Kennedy continued imperturbably, "we'll have to fire the Lewises from a man's shoulder. It's the only effective way. Not much fun for him; the gun soon gets very hot. We have to pad his shoulder with old bits of canvas—and in the rush of the moment the boys forget. Or they put the gun on their left shoulder, and that makes a balls of it too, because the gun ejects from the right, so the fellow gets a mouthful of empty cases. But we'll manage, we'll manage. The lads'll remember this time. Maybe."

Kennedy could hardly have been less like Kolya, except in his friendliness, but his presence suddenly took Misha back to just such a wait with Kolya, on a hillside in Galicia, years back. Ruined villages that had stood since long before the Time of Troubles in the seventeenth century had lain in their path, smoking quietly in the dust and rubble of their broken houses, and then on a hillside covered in gorse there had been just such another tense wait to hold the mouth of a Carpathian valley through the hot noontide. There had been the same sweating soldiers in dusty tunics, laughing halfheartedly. There had been a different smell, of cooking cabbage, and an overpowering waft from all that flowering gorse in the sun, but there had also been the same strong sense of danger, of imminent death. They had held the valley, but after it was over Misha had thought that the wounds that war inflicted upon men were more terrible than the most lively imagination could have pictured.

He was relieved when a young soldier on a sweating horse rode up with a message. For him at least the wait was over. He was to take half his squadron and scout towards Filonov, reinforcing the men who were attacking the railway from the north. He was to leave his second in command with a troop to cope with the problematic Red cavalry in the forest. Ulanov, his lieutenant, was a superb horseman, adept at all the Cossack skills, standing in the saddle at full gallop or leaning almost to ground level at speed to snatch at a cup of wine, but he was also young enough to be impetuous, to charge hell for leather before the moment was ripe.

"Don't chance your arm too far," Misha told him, mounting the chestnut horse. He turned to Kennedy. "I am sorry to leave you, not knowing what you are up against. We'll be back."

The red face of Kennedy creased in a smile. "We will manage. The lads will certainly manage. But I am sorry too." Returning to his gun, he raised a hand in salute, walking with a kind of slow unconcern, as if this were Brighton Beach. "*Au revoir*," he called, pleased to have achieved even one French expression in his long sojourn in foreign parts.

The chestnut horse, moving proudly for all his privations, bore Misha away down the ridge. There was a track here, but keeping to the grass, the troops avoided raising the telltale cloud of dust from its powdery surface. Twenty minutes later, as Misha's men jingled away past recall into the dusty bed of the valley, the Bolshevik commander decided to attack. Kennedy and the Plastunis had scarcely time to deploy before three squadrons of Red cavalry came galloping out of the forest, advancing with drawn sabres upon the thin line of the Whites, and seeming to have begun their charge even before they left the shelter of the trees. They shouted as they came, and the thunder of hooves and the flashing of sabres in the sunlight made their impetus appear irresistible.

From the right, Kennedy blazed away with his Lewis as the charge drew near. It did appalling harm: horse and rider rolled over and loosened sabres flew through the air. Ulanov and his remnant of horsemen were attacking on the flank and appeared to be carrying all before them. But to his horror James Kennedy saw out of the corner of his eye that Ulanov was riding through the rear ranks of the Red cavalry, apparently with the object of reaching and taking the village in their rear, leaving the Plastunis to deal with the unbroken Red squadrons and then to follow up his charge. It seemed to Kennedy a fatal miscalculation; with the Plastunis and his own guns Ulanov could hope to hold the village for at most half an hour. And it was clear enough that he was soon going to find himself without them.

Halfway down the line no further firing came from the clump of birch where the second Lewis gun crew were sited. The poor devils had got in a muddle, Kennedy concluded, and he could not leave his own gun and get to them to disentangle them. More seasoned men than these youngsters, he reflected, had lost their heads when faced with a cavalry charge. One stoppage at so short a range was fatal. Kennedy worked on with his gun, cursing to himself. More horses reared and fell, but the determined rush of the waves of Red Cossacks never faltered. Flashing sabres rose and fell round the place where the second Lewis gun had been.

No orders came, no reinforcements, nor was there anywhere on this great grassy plain to which to retreat and make a further stand. Nightfall was their only hope, and night was far away. Kennedy blazed on, but even the brave Plastunis were breaking now, and flying; hiding in the long grass, in the scrub, anywhere to be away from those gleaming hacking sabres. Ulanov, Kennedy could see, had now reached the village; tiny, far-away horses and men stood triumphant in the village street. If they had their wits about them, and could see what was happening on the hillside, as they surely could, they would now gallop off the scene and go like scalded cats till they rejoined the main force. But they were doing no such thing, and now two Red troops had been detached in a pincer movement to cut them off.

This is the finish, thought Kennedy, his eyes and hands still busy with the gun. This whole country is plain boiling mad and that's the size of it. A survivor from the second Lewis battery was running towards them, had all but reached them, disappearing briefly in a hollow in the ground, when a single sweep from the sword of a charging Red Cossack sent his head clean from his shoulders and rolling down the slope. Kennedy had heard this feat boasted of, but had never quite believed in it before; he felt a moment of admiration for so complete a professional skill.

His own fate was closing in on him. Holy smoke, what a country, Kennedy thought again, as the Cossack charges swept ever nearer. An unaccountable echo reached his heart, a long ago cry from a countryman dying, as he himself was to die, in a far country; one episode from a history lesson half-listened to at school on a Glasgow hillside, with the sun pouring down outside and the distant hooting of great steamers on passage down the Clyde. Die hard, Colonel Inglis had shouted, fighting against Napoleonic France at Albuera in Spain. Die hard, 57th, die hard! And die hard he would himself.

For the last time, his eyes took in the enormous noble sweep of the steppe. Yes, yon's a mad country, thought Kennedy, but they're bonny fighters, and I love them. This forgiveness of Russian sins was his last conscious thought; from thenceforward every skill and energy was concentrated into killing and being killed. No sense of futility assailed him. There was even, somewhere within his being, a kind of fierce happiness.

Two hours of hard riding brought Misha and his men to the appointed railway crossing. This had already been taken, and the line north lay broken in two places: repairs would not be rapid. On the embankment two White Army colonels appeared to be arguing the toss. When Misha reported to them they told him exultantly that Denikin's advance guard had reached Orel, only two hundred miles from Moscow. Nothing could stop his triumph, they assured Misha: the Reds were doomed. Across the line another troop of horse, summoned from who knew where, were to be seen on the further side of a field of enormous ripe sunflowers, the horses flicking their tails against the flies that beset them in the warm afternoon sunshine. The men's long lances stood up amongst the sunflowers like stems that had failed to flower, or so many headless blooms. Why had Misha's men been sent for, when these had seemingly not even been engaged? Wounded men from the infantry unit lay groaning in the two ambulance carts; others sat bandaged and shocked on the embankment. Misha asked and received permission to return to Ulanov and the rest of his men. He felt by no means sure that the Reds had yet been driven from the village upstream. Had any order yet been sent to the Whites to attack?

The evening light, golden, but with a kind of greenish glow in it, was flooding the steppe as the weary horses retraced their ride. Their purple shadows stretched long beside them; the harsh sound of frogs came up from the river marshes. Approaching it with caution, Misha found the village deserted. It had been taken, and retaken, and finally abandoned by both sides. But scattered about its small houses lay the bodies of thirty of his men, shot or sabred. Sprawled in midstreet was Ulanov, the brave and mocking companion of the last long bitter winter, and of this summer of ceaseless gruelling campaigning. The men had at least been killed outright; but Ulanov, as an officer, had been less lucky. He had been mutilated and tortured to death in a manner that made even the hardened Misha avert his gaze.

He sought for wounded along the ridge and found none; all were dead or had managed by some miracle to escape. Sabred in a score of places, and stripped of his scant possessions, James Kennedy lay dead beside his Lewis gun, his stubborn sandy head bent backwards against the brilliant green of the deep grass. Through five long years he had fought his own war to a standstill, to a bitter and bloody victory. And now he had come to Russia of his own will, to die in a pointless skirmish for a village abandoned as soon as won. He had fought, against orders from home, and entirely because he liked the threadbare singing Plastunis and their officers, enduring the hopeless lack of organisation and the short commons for no other reason, no hope of gain, promotion, or success. He would never return to Scotland to teach his friends in the local pub the songs he had learned in this strange land. With reverence, Misha straightened his body and closed his eyes.

Denikin is near Orel, Misha told himself. Denikin is near Orel, and the Reds are done for. Kolya was dead. His parents might be. Ulanov and Kennedy and scores of other brave men were dead, but Denikin was near Orel. In the light of that, all the quarrels, the futility, the fantastic jealousies and pettiness of the higher command could be forgiven.

Chapter 21

For all Misha's hopefulness, it was as if every effort of the White armies had long been cursed. The tragedy, confusion, misdirected effort and heroic sacrifice were not confined to the small pocket of futility within Misha's horizon. Yet the cause had held so much promise. General Kornilov, escaping from Bolshevik imprisonment, had joined General Alexeyev to establish a centre of resistance in the south, and many escaped officers from central Russia had made their way to him. Thousands of peasants had joined him. The Social Revolutionaries, who had been the biggest party in the Constituent Assembly, set up in Siberia an autonomous government hostile to the Bolsheviks. Another of the same complexion held power in Vladivostok, while Colonel Semenov, a monarchist, held Trans-Baikalia, and a like-minded General Horvat, who had been a Czarist high official, held power in Manchuria. All these disconnected and conflicting forces loathed the Reds and were prepared to fight them to the death, and their efforts were assisted by the Czech armies under General Masaryk who continued, alone, to fight the German armies, and after peace was made, won permission from Trotsky to make their way, through Siberia, to the Western Front. Attacked en route, they had reacted vigorously, and during the summer months of 1918 had made themselves masters of the Trans-Siberian Railway.

England, failing in her negotiations with the Bolshevist government for joint action against Germany, had seized Murmansk and Archangel and set up another Social Revolutionary government there, which came into being just too late to help an all-but-successful rising led by Russian officers at Yaroslavl in the first few weeks in July. Too late also had been the Czech entry into Ekaterinburg in the same month. The Czar and his family, whom Kerensky had sent to Tobolsk for safety, had been brought back by the Bolsheviks to the Urals, and had there met their fate a week previously.

But hope had not vanished. In September of 1918 Admiral Kolchak in alliance with the Western Powers, confidently formed an Eastern Front in Siberia; a Directory was chosen from various parties and set up at Ufa to coordinate the struggle against the Bolsheviks. All too soon Czarist leaders and Social Revolutionary generals were at loggerheads. By November 18, Kolchak had been obliged to set up a military dictatorship, if the war was to be prosecuted at all. Assisted by the gold reserves of Imperial Russia, which the Czechs had captured at Kazan and brought with them to Siberia, Kolchak had pushed ahead, driving the Red forces before him. In the early months of 1919 he took the great city of Perm and advanced nearly to the Volga, battling through the enormous wastés of snow and over the frozen ground. In the north, his forces were within reach of Kotlas, from where he could have joined forces with the British at Archangel and been able to draw upon western supplies.

But in the south the great Kornilov was killed in action, Alexeyev died, and the forces in south Russia had had to pause for regrouping under Denikin. Somehow all these giant efforts had come to nothing. In central Russia the sense of being threatened on every side brought about the acceptance of Bolshevik dictatorship and made possible their sharp centralisation of all power. Isolation and opposition stimulated and strengthened the central government—they relived the days when Ivan the Terrible had been threatened by the Tartar hordes. Though they were often near ruin, an immense system of propaganda fortified the whole, becoming a substitute for education.

The summer of 1918 had been very hot. No news from the outer world came to a breathless Moscow, now the capital city once again. Rumours of the Czar's murder went the rounds; many disbelieved, a few rejoiced, all felt the tremors. Since an early decree of the Bolshevik government had said that no peasant was entitled to the exclusive use of his own cattle or sheep, the peasants accordingly slaughtered all their beasts, salted them and buried them for future use, thus causing appalling food shortages in the towns. Those few nobles who were still not imprisoned exchanged clothes and furniture for food, and the poor, always the first victims of revolutions made on their behalf, starved in great numbers.

There had already been a holocaust of grand dukes, their wives and children; all killed secretly and by night. Great batches of aristocrats, intelligentsia, small shopkeepers and peasants were murdered. *The children of the aristocracy are dogs. They have no right as citizens, for they are not human beings,* ran the decree. All went on in secrecy, in silence, underground. There were no rolling tumbrils and public executions as in revolutionary France, to excite the pity and admiration of the beholders. But no great sympathy was aroused by the disappearance of the Czarist secret police, and it was not yet apparent that a far more sinister secret force was now in being. In the towns the survivors collected and sawed up wood, pumped the water and filled their cellars as winter drew on, with the ice without which no food would keep in summer. But would they live to see another summer? Life was conducted against a constant background of terror, hunger and anxiety. Such had always existed in Russia, but now they were universal.

After August 30, 1918, when Uritsky, Director of the Bolshevik police, was assassinated, and a Socialist Revolutionary called Dora Kaplan lodged a bullet in Lenin himself, the screw had been tightened, since only by an intensified terror could a small group of fanatics impose its will on a whole people. There had been immediate and wholesale massacres in all the prisons. In Gatchina eighty victims were told to dig their graves and then shot by a woman; she was not very effective and most of the victims were only wounded, then buried alive. But all this ruthlessness let loose an astonishing burst of energy. Red soldiers fought with a kind of desperate yet triumphant vigour, a reckless, Napoleonic outpouring of courage and force. Peasant risings were crushed as ruthlessly as any other. Since many people were starving, food was now given in preference to manual workers and to those serving the government.

November also brought the armistice in the West; the Allies, aware of the division and failure of the anti-Bolshevik efforts, now all but lost interest. Britain and France were exhausted, ravaged by a lethal influenza epidemic, and bled half to death by their losses on the Western Front. Since they were no longer required to fight the Germans, the Russians, it was felt by all but a few, could be left to stew in their own juice, especially since they were stoking up the fire so spectacularly themselves. Slowly the Allies withdrew their military missions, abandoning in turn Semenov in Trans-Baikal, Kolchak in Siberia, Miller in Archangel, Yudenitch in Esthonia, Denikin and Wrangel in the south. Of these, Kolchak and Denikin in particular were disinterested patriots; but in all the White forces there had been too many reactionary officers who allowed or even committed atrocities as bad as the Reds', and behind these there was only the wavering support of ineffective politicians with diverse opinions and no real authority. Among the troops, once the Czar was dead, there was an absence of any powerful and binding cause. All sections, ill-fed, ill-clothed, exhausted by continuous fighting, had found their nervous energies frayed, their morale crumbled to pieces. The generals had but small forces fighting in huge voids; their most decisive actions annulled by outflanking movements. The vast scale of Russia defeated all their puny efforts; no help came from outside; in time their hearts were broken.

In the summer of 1919 they had rallied for a great effort and though after a close examination during May and June of Kolchak's intentions, the Allied governments had failed to recognise him, he had fought on.

But his first reverse encouraged the quarrels among his generals and complicated the political dissensions. His armies were driven back in increasing disorder, first to the Urals and then to Irkutsk. Here he was disgracefully surrendered to his enemies, and met his death with great gallantry on February 7, 1920. The failure of his armies meant that the British evacuated Archangel in the same month.

Yudenitch in the west was no luckier. From Esthonia he fought his way into the very suburbs of St. Petersburg, only to be defeated there by a vigorous concentration of Red troops, organised by Trotsky. It was as if the stars in their courses were fighting on the Bolshevik side.

Of these events and struggles, past and to come, Misha, leading his depleted troop over the steppe and away from the river, had but a sketchy notion, and no sad prescience, only an abiding confidence. Though all were filled with fatigue, and present sorrow, the hope of victory and the return to home seemed to be just over the horizon. They rode on, in the failing summer light, to camp at last in comparative safety in a birch grove near the fringe of a great wood. They would have to be reinforced, regrouped perhaps, maybe sent elsewhere, possibly even given a flying leave, a glimpse of the golden domes and the fleshpots of Novocherkask. A huge harvest moon shone over a camp unusually silent; the fires burned low. Tomorrow might bring forth better things, and all, in any case, was with God.

Denikin might have passed Tambov, might be near Orel, and the line north of Filonov might be cut, but the great retreat of the Don Army had in fact begun and would continue. The river line and the railway junction at Filonov was lost, was recaptured, was lost again. Rumours came that Denikin was ill, that he was badly wounded, that he had been killed in the moment of triumph, like the great Kornilov—he who had started with a bare eighty followers and had raised an army of two hundred thousand men, fought through a winter of terrible hardship in Kuban and all but conquered every province of south Russia from the Reds. Could all this be in vain?

Misha, employed all autumn with his brigade in defending bridges or in holding attacks that enabled the brigade to disengage and withdraw, was unable to believe that it could. Was not General Yudenitch operating actively from Esthonia? And General Miller, supplied by the British from the sea and pressing the Reds in the north from Murmansk and Archangel? In Siberia Admiral Kolchak was known to be advancing and driving the Reds before him. All these must soon converge, and then the number of those murderers in Moscow and St. Petersburg would soon be up.

Rumours of all kinds flowed from headquarters at Ekaterinodar, but between this town and the front line the brigand Green Army was in operation, disrupting communications, cutting off supplies, murdering stragglers. And of what use was it for Denikin to probe so far to the north and west, when he was dependent upon bullock carts, creaking and winding across the interminable steppes, to bring him food and ammunition? Striving to hold his conquests and to establish organised government, Denikin had no men to spare for his widely stretched brigades.

Hard-pressed by roving bands of Red Cossacks, ill-nourished and worn out, decimated by typhus and cholera, the Don Army was driven slowly southwards. The Reds at length were able to cut Denikin's one link with his southern base by taking Tzaritsin; and in the Reds' brilliant and successful defence from his subsequent attack two tough young men called Stalin and Voroshilov particularly distinguished themselves. Denikin, with his forces fatally dependent on the slow trek of oxcarts across hundreds of miles, was obliged to withdraw them from their once hopeful positions around Orel. There was a pause, while the Reds consolidated their hold on Tzaritsin as a base for further operations.

Autumn was well advanced at the Villa Rosa, the flocks of sheep were down from the hills with their half-wild dogs howling after them, and the chestnut braziers once more glowing in the marketplaces, before Misha came briefly to the Villa Rosa—to make sure, as he said, that they were all still alive. He was muddy, tired, very thin; all the youth had gone from his face. His straw hair was ill-cut, his overcoat in a pitiable state and his boots not much better. But his blue eyes still blazed in his face; his white teeth flashed at the children in the same confident smile. "Soon," he assured them, "our armies will join up with each other. All the peasants are with us; the Reds are hateful to them, their armies commit dreadful deeds. It may be that his Imperial Majesty still lives; no one knows for certain that he is dead in captivity, though it would be like the Reds to lay violent hands on him. Maybe he can still be rescued. If not, there are others of the Imperial Family—" His eyes, scanning the sea, seemed to see again the huge splendours of St. Petersburg, the wide streets of Moscow in the starlight, under snow; the jewels and the brightly coloured uniforms, the laughter and the dancing under the chandeliers; the holy splendours of the gold-robed priests. Sounds of music, secular or sacred, entranced his ears. For him the candles still gleamed through the dark churches, the censers swung, gold saints looked out from their sombre backgrounds in timeless reassurance; his wild spirit melted in worship.

To Daisy, glad to see him as if in answer to her prayers, he had never been more welcome.

He came suddenly down to earth. "If the line no longer holds, you must all go to the Crimea. The Reds can never cross the isthmus, if indeed they ever come so far. Go to Sevastopol, and from there—"

"But how shall we get there—"

"There are still fishermen in the bay, I imagine. Command a vessel; seize a time of fine weather." He was still the same lordly Misha, for all his gaunt looks; his young brothers and sisters gazed at him with delight. He lifted them out of the dog days, made them feel once more grand, important, beloved of many. "When you are fifteen," he told the twins, "*when* and not before, I shall come for you and add you to my squadron. Perhaps more than a squadron by then. You must practise sword drill, revolver shooting, controlling a horse at speed."

"But how, Misha, how? Arkady and I haven't been on a horse for months. Years, even."

"That can be amended in time. But mathematics also are important, and geography. Study the map of Russia very closely, all her rivers, valleys, plains, mountains—you will need to know them like the back of your hand."

Inspired, the twins scrambled for the atlas, wrestling amiably with it, and after a while, less amiably. Ella simply leant, silently, on Misha, but Varya demanded to know what the ladies of Novocherkask were now wearing. "Their skirts? Are they still as long?"

Misha noted by common consent, none of the children referred to their parents, or to Kolya, as if they wanted to keep the few hours of his leave as cheerful as possible. Daisy had told them about Kolya's death.

"Come, Mishoska, are you too tired to dance?" Varya cried. "Play, please, Miss Daisy!"

Of course, he wasn't.

Late at night, when the children were all finally in bed, his mood changed with alarming swiftness. His broad shoulders drooped in an immense weariness. Yet now that sleep in a bed was available he seemed not to want it. "Where are my father and my stepmother?" he demanded of Daisy. "If I could know for certain that they were dead, I could reconcile myself to it. Are they in prison? Starving? Wandering from place to place without shelter? Did Kolchak rescue them from Perm? I think too often of Kolya. Did he sacrifice his life for nothing? For a dream of Russia that can never be?" His fair head dropped in his hands.

"The Reds have lost everything, have given away everything for which we fought. That cowardly treaty that they made at Brest Litovsk!" His mood had shifted into indignation. "All was lost, given away, all that Russian arms had gained during the war, all the Allies' promises, Constantinople, the Dardanelles. All was given away, even that which Peter the Great had won! Independence for the Lithuanians, for Latvians, for Esthonians! Independence for these countries is but another name for German exploitation."

He was in full flow, needing no answer, waiting for none. Which was as well, Daisy reflected, listening in silence, as she had not the smallest idea where Lithuania, Latvia or Esthonia were, let alone whether they had or had not been exploited by Germany.

Misha stood up and started to pace the room. His slight limp had become more noticeable. "And Finland!" he demanded. "And the Ukraine! Separated from Russia, Ukraine is ruined! And upon Roumania, our best ally in our frontier, they have imposed the most ruthless of terms. It is said that in Germany it is to be read openly in the newspapers that the Reds have given Germany a free hand in the economic exploitation of Russia. But what does Lenin, what does Trotsky, or any of them care for Russia? They value her only as a base for their designs upon other countries. Your turn will be next, your turn and the turn of France, to be taken over by these monsters who neither fear God nor cherish man!"

His mood turned again to sorrow with the swiftness of a Caucasian storm. "We were friends," he protested passionately. "We were friends, Kolya and I, with every peasant boy at Jevrenskaia. Why have the peasants turned against such as Kolya? He was their friend." The sense of lost friendship continued to gall Misha. "We served together as altar boys. We always called each other by our Christian names. I was not a prince to them, nor was Kolya. I tell you, there was no difference between us. There was more difference in Austria, in France, in Germany, more distance even in England, I think. Was there any distinction when we crowded together standing shoulder to shoulder in church at the holy festivals? There was none, none." He looked at Daisy a little defiantly, as if she were about to challenge this statement. But challenge came there none.

"All night we would watch the herds with the country boys," Misha went on, "sleeping sometimes, as they did, on sacks on the edge of the woods. We would lie and look at the stars, and hear the cattle quietly grazing on the open land. There was always a great fire going; and in the early mornings we would eat together, the hot roast potatoes from the ashes of the fire. We were together in all things, and now those same boys are turned into savage beasts to tear us, and we in our turn repay their savagery . . .

"We would play together down by the river, swimming naked with the village boys. What difference was there then, what standing away, what offending pride? We played soldiers together, cooked meals out of doors together. When the peasant fathers brought the horses in from the field, we would help their sons to feed and groom them and take them down to the river and to the pasture, riding bareback with the other horses haltered and led.

"The horses, the horses . . ." As he thought of all those magnificent grey Percherons, arching their proud stallion necks at pasture or straining across the great acres of black plough, his voice faltered and fell. Where were they now? Killed, no doubt, and chopped up for food by peasants who would, he believed, always eat their seed corn if given half a chance. But the peasants, too, for all their fecklessness, he had liked, understood, protected from mischance and folly.

Daisy continued to listen to him with wide sympathetic eyes. How much Russia has lost, she thought.

Her argumentative strain seemed in abeyance; her silence persuaded Misha to continue.

"And the boys, the peasant boys . . . we worked with them as hard as any, and all these boys were friendly, amiable, ungrudging. They were religious, simple-hearted. There was no enmity anywhere between us, except such as boys have wrestling on the river bank, running races, testing our strength in pummelling matches. And at nightfall, when the huge moon came up, we would sit round the fire together and listen with just the same attention to the old men's tales. Do you think there was then any shadow of enmity between us, between Kolya and me and any other boy at Jevrenskaia?

"And how rich it was, our black black earth, with no fences breaking the distances, and those huge ribbons of dark earth unfolding under the plough! And now! Who directs the farming of it, who cares for and helps the people who work it? How was such a bond broken, the bond of hundreds of years?"

Misha was in tears, or as near as made no difference. Daisy watched him with her eyes glowing with compassion. Wisely, she continued to keep silent, feeling that there was nothing she could say that did not sound as if it came straight off an embroidered doily offered for sale in Leicester Market on a Saturday. Misha talked on far into the night; his tales broken only by an occasional assent from her, until he had talked himself into a kind of peace and fell asleep at last in the middle of a sentence.

She was powerless to awake him and could only cover him with a rug and leave him.

Next morning the wind blew cold and steady from the north, waves flecked a dark and heaving sea whose grey horizon faded into greyer sky. The waves pounded mournfully on the seashore as the children were blown along it or forced their way back in a mist of flying spray. The wild wind, and the presence of Misha, incited the twins to a fever of daring activity; it was a relief to Daisy to feel that when, inevitably, they fell into the waves or slipped headlong off the wet rocks, Misha would be there to do the rescuing. He was like a boy himself, laughing, climbing, leaping from rock to rock. "We used to go, Kolya and I—" Then, suddenly remembering that Kolya was now dead, his face would turn to stone, he would climb down from the rock with tiredness and sorrow in every line of his body.

Varya had grown gentler since her fright and narrow escape from assault. Taking Misha's arm with great tenderness, she looked up into his face with her melting dark eyes. "He is with the saints, he is with God. Let us never cease praying for him, and for . . . for our parents." Daisy surprised in herself a strong pang of jealousy. Misha responded to the

caress with touching affection. He had been shaken by the tale of her
fright.

In the afternoon they stayed indoors while the waves mounted and the
Tauric pines creaked and tossed in the gale. Inside, the porcelain stove
crackled and glowed, shutting out the groaning cypresses bent double and
the few sad leaves left on the climbing roses that flicked against the
windowpanes. Misha was reading aloud to Ella, old creepy Russian fairy
tales that he had loved himself as a boy. He talked Russian more than of
old, Daisy noted, and French and English less. Cosmopolitanism was a
thing of long ago; Russianism was the thing to be clung to.

Presently they found the heart to sing, to learn a ridiculous new tune
that Daisy's sisters had sent to her. In a minute they were dancing, Misha
was whirling Varya round, teaching her a new dance he had somehow
managed to acquire at Novocherkask.

"It's me," cried Ella, "me now, my turn!"

"No," Misha told her firmly. "You are the smallest and you come last.
It's Miss Daisy's turn to learn it now!" His eyes shone with irresistible
enjoyment. It was as if war, death, grief, exile never existed, never came
near the human race at all. Anna, out of nothing much, concocted a splendid dinner, completed by peaches in brandy and by the nutty, sticky
sweetmeats of which she was a past master. There was Caucasian wine,
there were healths, Gleb had even unearthed some port, a drink that
Misha particularly disliked; he drank it with a right goodwill. Towards
the end of this repast even Misha's lips trembled some of the time, as
though this glimpse of home had finally unmanned him.

The wind had died, a pale half-moon shone on a sea now only gently
stirred, its roar reduced to a melancholy sighing. Misha was to leave next
morning at first light.

"Unless you sleep now," he announced as the clock struck ten, "you
will never wake up to see me off in the morning, for which I would be
sad." Ella was half asleep already; he was able to prevail on Varya and
the boys to follow her up the stairs.

To Daisy, although he had behaved kindly enough, he had never
seemed more remote, more wholly centred on the children and their lives
and happiness. She had watched him through the two days with something that was almost pain; beneath his bravado he displayed a chasten-
ing of the spirit that seemed almost too complete. As she clattered down
the stairs after the children's goodnights, he begged her to come and sit
with him. He appeared to be wrestling with some kind of pronouncement;
his English speech, always formal, became more formal still. It isn't possible, thought Daisy, that he's alarmed? Of me?

But possible it was. "I can never say," he began rather primly, "how
much we owe to you for your goodness and care of these children."

"There's no need. Really, there's none."

Misha appeared disconcerted by this reply, as if he had learnt a set

speech—"Unaccustomed as I am to thanking anyone for anything—"
Daisy had interrupted him in the middle. "Why do you say *we?*"

"Kolya and I. And my parents, wherever they may be, in this world or
another. Tell me, do you not feel frightened after the rape that so nearly
happened to Varya? Or lonely here? All these months and years? And
frustrated from what you would rather be doing?"

"Lonely, yes," Daisy admitted slowly. "But not frustrated. At least, not
all of the time. I used to long to do more in the war, our war, I mean. And
now I do long to go home, to see my family again. If that's frustration,
then I am."

Misha, who had had in mind another sort of frustration and loneliness,
began again. He had a great desire to tell Daisy at least part of the horrors
he had suffered, warring with a feeling of concern for her that surprised
him. She was thin and shabby, but no less pretty than of old. The round
little face had gone, the lines of its fine bones were more apparent. She
was beautiful. She had lost that priggish folding of the mouth, her
gaucheness, her aggressive little tilt of the head, some of her schoolgirl
bounce. It flashed through Misha's mind that he might even have lost
some of his own.

His old ideas of what would or wouldn't do had long deserted him, his
notions of who or what would be suitable for grand Misha. Never very
strong at the most prosperous of times, they had been washed clean out of
him by the naked realities of war, defeat and poverty. His own life was
now worth so little, his span might be so short, that he had ceased to think
about the future. They were all—Daisy, the children, himself—in a desperate position, where danger stalked behind the mountains and might at
any moment launch a tiger spring over them. The emotion he had gener-
ated on behalf of Russia now needed a more immediate target.

Caution fled from him; an affection he had long suppressed took over.
Whatever he felt, this passionate desire for closeness, for forgetfulness,
for the loss of himself in another—he could not yet name it, even to
himself, as love. It seemed to have no name, to be simply the next inevitable move in some mysterious game in which he was now no more than a
pawn.

Whether pawn, knight, or king, he remained aware of the need for a
careful approach to Daisy. Her innocence was appalling. She must now be
twenty-four, twenty-five? The folly of attempting verbal communication
with such a being struck him suddenly and forcibly; they would reach no
understanding this way. He took Daisy's hand, and finding it responsive
was moved to further measures. Misha felt unsure whether he was mildly
drunk, too tired to know what he was doing, or behaving in a natural and
sensible manner. Either way he ceased to care. Soon he ceased to think,
and was happy, the tears of his fatigue running down his face and onto
Daisy's cheek, to which it was closely pressed. She did not draw away.
Even, she seemed to be weeping a little too, and now at last he did what he

had often desired to do, holding her close in a long and enjoyable kiss.

Daisy's surprise was complete, and yet their behaviour seemed the most natural thing in the world. After a while, it seemed the most intoxicating thing in the world. Still later, as she slowly woke from her long abstinence, it seemed altogether outside the world. In brief moments of conscious thought she was able to reflect on the strangeness of loving so wildly someone she had never really liked, as she had always and instinctively liked Kolya. And then Kolya returned to his secure and heavenly cloud, and Daisy was a drowning being with no more straws to clutch. They sat, in total silence, closely embraced. All the patience of her long lonely vigil dissolved into a soaring impatience that met and matched the impatience of Misha.

There was a resounding knock, and Gleb stood in the doorway. "The Prince is summoned," he announced, like the third gentleman in a Shakespeare play, and wearing the same doomful expression. Behind him the figure of another man was discernible in the hall. Both regarded the scene with unabashed and lively curiosity. "He brings a message," Gleb sighed. "They told him of it in the village. You are to return at once, Mihail Andreivitch, not waiting for the morning . . . He has horses . . . He says there is haste . . . the enemy . . ." Neither Gleb nor the village messenger made the least attempt to go away. If drama was afoot they were not prepared to miss one gesture of it. Their large pale faces hung silently together like twin moons.

Misha rose slowly, as from a dream. His face expressed what seemed a mortal sadness. "In happier times," he said, taking no notice whatever of Gleb or the messenger, who were listening keenly to every word. "In happier times we could have had a life together . . . Fetch my things down, Gleb." Misha was dragging on his patched overcoat, reaching for his tattered cap. "In happier times we could perhaps have been happy." He seemed already far away, hardly conscious of what he was saying. Still disregarding Gleb and the soldier in the hall, he took a last hurried embrace and was gone. He seemed not even to have opened the letter that the soldier had brought. The horses clattered up the drive to the road, the iron gates shut with a clang. Misha had not even left a message for the children. Gleb, with melancholy emphasis, was relocking the door and shooting all the bolts.

Daisy stood for some while, still and stupefied, like one too dead asleep for sudden waking.

The moon had now set, the cypresses waved gently and the waves fell scarcely perceptibly on the shore. Daisy lay a long while on her bed, incapable of thought or action, capable only, and too greatly, of tumultuous feeling. She woke in the morning to a world entirely different. He was drunk, she told herself, unable to believe in the reality of this new world; he had no notion of what he was doing or saying. Just the same, the world continued to feel wholly different.

"Without these sad times," Ella said at breakfast, "these sad times of Misha going away, our happy times would be less happy," and for once, no one mocked the exquisite priggishness of this observation.

Love had been briskly dismissed from Misha's mind. The Whites, he noted, lying out on nights already icy cold, were going down with all flags flying. Within the sound of the firing those behind the lines made the night ring with song and dance. There was vodka in torrents, Caucasian wine and zakouska, and wild sword dances with the blades flashing in the firelight and the Kubans firing off pistols into the night. In Novocherkask the golden domes of the cathedral still gleamed in the winter sunlight, pretty girls appeared as if from nowhere; every saint's day was celebrated in full gala style, with caviare, and roast goose, the calling of toasts and the flow of still more Caucasian wine.

It was as if they could not allow the long glorious party to be over—the chaos, the beauty, the fantasy of Imperial Russia, that seemed to have sprung from the very nature of her climate and her huge spaces—the extremes of heat and cold, of rich and poor, of intimacy and vastness, of melancholy and merriment, of cruelty and warmth, of holiness and degradation; as if in nothing was Russia capable of half measures, of the compromise and common sense by which the rest of the world rubbed along. No one in the army of forlorn hope at Novocherkask could accept the reality of her death—holy and Imperial Russia, jewelled and dirty, full of songs and alive with lice, bursting with love and empty of justice, locked in a long winter of indifference to human suffering in general and overflowing with the warm summer rivers of concern with the particular woe. All night long the singing and the dancing went on, almost within sound of the enemy machine guns, and the wineglasses came sailing through the open windows into the mild midnight air and crashing down onto the cobbled streets. Chaos had come again, chaos and primeval night, and refuge could be found only in fantasy.

Chapter 22

In the consulate at Novorossisk, George Bennett ran his hand across a furrowed brow. The task of British consul was never an easy one, and in the current circumstance, impossible. Especially if one were only the deputy, and without the authority of the actual consul, who had all but died in the influenza epidemic and was now having a long convalescence in Cyprus. The Reds, this March of 1920, were nearing Novorossisk, and tales of the horrors they were perpetrating on the civil population of towns on the route, regardless of age or sex, news of the devastation of the countryside, came from sources whose authenticity he could not doubt.

Yet he remained an unheeded Cassandra, uttering tales of doom to which the doomed declined to listen. The British community, the merchants and their wives and the retired expatriates left in his charge, were unanimously refusing to move to the safety of home.

There was the problem of Esmeralda Moss, who had run away from her employers to set up house with a Turkish fish-merchant and was living the life of Riley away down the coast and declining to answer any communications. There was old Colonel Ombersley, married to a Russian wife and living in a villa some miles to the east; he was deaf and lame and rather ill and entirely refusing to budge. There were the businessmen's wives, who would go on playing bridge with each other up till the last five minutes, and would then demand to be evacuated instantly, complete with their Russian servants, their dogs and cats and canaries, their silver and their linen and their cabin trunks, and as like as not with the drawing room furniture as well. Ships of the Mediterranean Fleet were in the Black Sea and would be prompt in just such a contingency as George Bennett dreaded, but they were not, as he patiently pointed out, Messrs. Pickfords' removal service. If anyone wanted to be sure of leaving with all their goods and chattels they must leave now on the next ship. It was only a twenty-four-hour voyage to Constantinople.

"Don't panic, George, dear," they urged him as if he were engaging in an un-British activity. The fatal shade of Sir Francis Drake playing his game of bowls as the Spanish Armada swayed up-Channel hung about their resolutely chintzy drawing rooms. Under every copy of that picture, reflected George, there should be a caption saying, DRAKE HAD MADE READY IN EVERY DETAIL; HE ONLY PLAYED BOWLS BECAUSE THE STATE OF THE TIDE DIDN'T ENABLE HIM TO WORK HIS SHIPS OUT OF PLYMOUTH SOUND.

And their gardens! the ladies pointed out to him. Their roses were already budding: were they to miss them in full flower? "What about dinner on Friday week? I know you don't play bridge, George, dear, but—" The ships, they felt convinced, could snatch them and all they owned from any threat of danger, and without appreciable difficulty. Was the Royal Navy not operating on the landlocked Caspian Sea, slap in the middle of Asia? British citizens everywhere were as safe as houses. "Do sit down, George, and have a cup of tea."

In the intervals between these persuasion sessions, George was besieged by offers of marriage from beautiful White Russian women, not so much desiring him as a share in his passport. Some were slant-eyed, calculating, pressing home upon every flicker of sympathy; others were so tearful and beautiful in their grief that George was sometimes all but melted. After all, they needed him only as a stepping-stone; in England they could always be divorced. With some difficulty he hardened a naturally generous heart. There simply were too many other things to see to. And a Russian wife, as he well knew, involved a Russian mother, father, grandparents, nieces, nephews and probably a couple of great-aunts as well.

And now there was Daisy Pelham, the worst of the lot, the most remote and vulnerable. With great difficulty George had come to see what personal persuasion could do; she had politely, but with a kind of dreamy firmness, declined to take the slightest notice of his urgent pleading that she should leave now, at once, without delaying another day. She was unusually silent, and seemed to be in some kind of trance. Tired out, poor little thing, he thought. An essentially sweet nature, exploited by these charming and exacting Russian aristocrats who would take it all for granted and never give her a second thought. If she would only have married me—I could have had her out of all this long ago. But at least she was now talking.

"When the weather is finer, we'll go to the Crimea. In a fisherman's boat. It's too cold and rough really now, George, to take the children. It wouldn't even be safe if a storm blew up."

"Well, of course. But why not in a proper ship, from the port at Novorossisk, and to Constantinople?"

"We've been told, the children's brother said, we were to go to the Crimea. He says it's safe there. And it's still Russia."

George's normally cheerful face looked lined and tired. He regarded her with exasperation. "Safe! But for how long? We have to face the fact that Imperial Russia has lost this civil war."

"Oh no! He didn't think so, and he'd been right in the middle of it. What about Admiral Kolchak? And Yudenitch? And the British in Archangel?"

"The British Mission is evacuating Archangel."

"Oh, how feeble! Don't they *know* what's at stake? But anyway, what about the masses of White Russians still here and in Siberia?"

"I don't know enough to estimate their chances. What I do know is that the war in the south is lost."

Daisy went pale and turned away her head as if George had struck her.

"Listen. I cannot get the petrol to bring this car out here again. I do seriously beg you to collect the children, and what things you can't really do without, and come back with me to the consulate. You'd all be safe there, at any rate until I could get you all onto the first ship for Constantinople."

"I . . . we . . . he said . . . it was better not to take the children into Novorossisk. I know the consulate is safe, but would they be safe getting there?"

"Who would betray them? Certainly not old Gleb or Anna."

"No, I'm sure not. But that horrible daughter of theirs would."

"How should she know?"

"She's in the house now, talking to Gleb and Anna. I heard her voice being angry with them. Truly, George, I mustn't take the children into Novorossisk."

George sighed. The time had come, he perceived, when he must really frighten Daisy, as his last hope of getting her to move. He spoke slowly, as to a child, and with all the emphasis he could command, unaware that his very reliability and his continuing presence in the port were some of the reasons inducing Daisy to stay.

"Whatever happens in other parts of Russia, the Whites here, the whole Don Army of them, are really on the run. It's March already, the Reds will be over the mountains any day now. And then there'll be a real panic. Not only the British and other foreigners rushing to escape, but every Russian in the entire area who owns anything, or who has ever owned anything, knowing full well they'll get short shrift. And the wives and children of all the White Russian soldiers, flying ahead of them, over the hills. I tell you, all hell's going to break loose."

"I still think we should stay till the weather gets warmer and then go to the Crimea. I promise I will really start asking about a boat, if you like. Surely no one is really going to hurt the children? And I'm English— nothing to do with it all."

George took a deep breath. He must somehow break that trance-like gaze. He had never heard of a death wish, but there was something decidedly odd about Daisy's looks and behaviour.

"I can't and won't describe to you what the Reds have been known to do to the children of the Whites. Lenin has laid it down that the Whites are *not human beings*. They wouldn't just kill these children, they would slowly torture them to death, probably forcing you to watch it before they started on you. You simply don't know what passions this civil war has unleashed, the awful accumulated rage of people who feel they've been oppressed and exploited for hundreds of years. And as for being British, we know for a certainty, from eyewitnesses, that the British Transport officer at Rostov was crucified by the Reds. And had a fire lit under him, for good measure."

George had been right in supposing that this would bring Daisy out of her trance, but had not anticipated that her reactions would not be of fear, but of extreme rage. She went crimson with anger, breathing deeply and having to fight for her words.

"How dared they! How could they! Even the Romans didn't do that to Jesus! A fire, as well! How can they call themselves Christians?"

"These were Reds."

"But brought up Christians like everyone else in this country that isn't a Moslem. Brought up with priests and religion and constant going to church. How could human beings do such things? In the twentieth century!"

"I don't know. I am only telling you," George said soberly and firmly, "that that is what they do . . . That is how safe it is to be British. Anyone and anything that stands in their way has to be blotted out. As cruelly as possible."

"What's the good of all this worship and inner holiness if it isn't even skin deep and ends in crucifying prisoners of war? What's the good of it?" Daisy continued furiously.

George had never seen Daisy so passionately angry, or even angry at all. He put out a hand and took hers. The hand vibrated with feeling; her whole being was shaking with an intensity of anger whose cause he felt unable to fathom. Feeling, himself, a certain detachment as to how Russian people felt and thought—which in any case was apt to change with amazing rapidity—he could not understand Daisy's overwhelming concern. He looked steadily and calmly at her, but she refused to be mollified. Unable to keep still in her anger, she broke from him, pacing to and fro from the fireplace to the window, restless as any tigress in an intolerable cage.

Why, George wondered, had she mounted this sudden high horse over the Russians, whom she had always previously liked? He failed to realise that the extent of her previous affection was the measure of her disappointment and rage, mingled with a contradictory and painful passion for Misha.

Arkady, passing the window in company with his twin, caught sight of Daisy's expression and pulled a long face at his brother. Nikolai nodded agreement. "Poor Mr. Bennett," he said, "is catching it." They sped past. Daisy enraged was a new and uncomfortable phenomenon.

"It's a temporary madness," George suggested. But Daisy would have none of this. In the rush of shock and anger that were shaking her heart, her feelings poured from her without concealment.

"Temporary madness! They think we are hardly Christians at all, yet you'd never, not in a million years, get English people to crucify anyone! How utterly, utterly horrible! And the fire, too—how *could* they? I don't want to go away, George. Oh, how I would like to fight them myself! I want less than ever to go! *I want to stay and fight them!*"

George perceived that he had lost the battle, or at least the first round. "And the children? Are they to fight too? Seriously, Daisy—this country is now no place for any of you."

"Why should we not join the Whites? Some must have their families with them."

"Daisy, are you mad? What good could *that* do? Don't you understand? The Devil himself has been let loose here."

"Not among the Whites. They are fighting for their country, for their freedom, for a noble cause!"

George's essential fairness, his factual mind, was not prepared to let this go. "Even among the Whites. Terrible tales come to us of what is going on in the Urals, in Siberia. Not just the requisitioning of supplies without payment, but torture, rape, even cannibalism. Oh, I don't say that your friends are responsible for it. I don't suppose it was ordered by Kolchak when he was in power, nor perhaps by his generals. But it exists in the subordinates—"

"No. *No.*"

"I do assure you. There is nothing, not a hair's breadth to choose between the cruelty of the Reds and the savage cruelty of the White armies. Only the Green Army, of bandits, are worse, because they fight for no cause, only for their own greed and cruelty." I am telling her the truth, thought George, and without exaggeration, but am I being fair or simply jealous of that White officer whom I fear she loves? But it is necessary to make it all clear, so that she knows there is no hope for any of them in Russia now. "There is not just the killing of prisoners," he went on. "There is mutilation. There are things I can't describe. Particularly the things done to women, and to children as small and helpless as Ella."

Daisy turned pale; her eyes burned with bitterness. Love and trust confounded were turned to contempt and hatred. "How can they call themselves Holy Russia? I mean, the proof of the pudding is in the eating, and by their fruits one can know things! How can they invoke the Mother of God, as they do all the time, and then savagely kill women? Why keep kissing ikons of the Christ child if it doesn't stop you from mutilating children? Is it possible to imagine . . . could we ever come to such things in England?"

George considered this with his usual deliberation. "Not, I should think, while we stay Christians, or have a sort of basic ethic of Christianity. But if it ends in England, what after that? How long can a tradition live on its capital? A rainy climate isn't enough by itself to keep people sane." A thought, unconcerned with jealousy or any other petty passion, rose from somewhere within his being, drawn out by the necessity of making Daisy realise the seriousness of her predicament. "Being under the control of holy men is dangerous. To worship very intensely, as these people do, is to play with fire. It lays you wide open to influence from both sides."

"You mean, the Devil as well as God?"

"Forces of evil," George corrected her, hoping to sound more modern. "Yes, I do mean that."

"But *why*, George? Why should it?"

"I don't know," George said, as slowly as ever. "But if you look about in the history of humanity, it just does. Why else should *Russia* let loose this flood of horror and evil upon the world?"

There was a long pause. Daisy, shuddering slightly, considered all she had just heard. George sat very still. To get them all to the consulate at Novorossisk and hence to England might not at once be possible, but at least he might have precipitated them towards the Crimea. With great caution, he glanced at his watch. In another five minutes he would have to go. As it was, all hell was probably breaking loose in the office.

"I do see the children must go. I do see that now. And be brought up in a civilised country. Our country." She heaved a long doleful sigh. "A country that is still Christian—still sane."

"Yes."

Daisy besought him for reassurance. "But I still don't understand. Although they hate outsiders, Russians are so charming . . . so loving . . . so spontaneous."

"You can understand their suspicions of strangers," George admitted. "Right up to Tudor times, they had Tartars dominating great stretches of their country, burning their homes, enslaving them, threatening them with forcible Islam, and great other stretches held by Poles and Lithuanians, threatening them with forced Catholicism. Moscow was regularly sacked and burned. Poles, Swedes, Lithuanians, Tartars, even other Russians were always at them. You can easily see how Church and country became welded together, with all outsiders seen as evil."

"Yes. Yes. Oh yes!"

"It's as if we'd had, up to the seventeenth century, the Spaniards dominating Scotland, the French Ireland, and the Turks the southern counties. Makes you a bit on the suspicious side. But what you can't understand," George went on, deliberately and seriously, "is the abominable mixture of religion and cruelty. Ivan IV had a monastery built where he used to pray for hours, beating his forehead on the floor in prostration until the blood ran, in between bouts of appalling torture inflicted on the innocent, in the next room, by his own hand. Two of the Czars murdered their own sons, praying like billy-oh for their souls. Ivan the Terrible even helped to pile the fuel that burnt alive, for no reason, his bravest, most successful general, Prince Michael Vorotinski. But he stayed immensely popular. No one thought the worse of him for his wholesale massacres, his boilings alive of old friends. And he didn't fail to go to church on the right days. All of this horror is nothing surprising, nothing new."

"But one hoped grown out of, grown *out* of," Daisy implored, with tear-filled eyes, as if Misha himself had been personally involved in boiling his best friends alive just for the hell of it.

"There's scarcely been a ruler of Russia whose hands haven't been dyed in blood—even poor Nicholas, by proxy of course—and I doubt there will be now."

"But why does nobody stand up to them and stop it?" George noted that her eyes were desperately searching his face, as if for hope. He decided to give her a little, but not much. If she calmed, even slightly, she might see sense and realise her predicament—and the children's.

"Some," he began, "like the Old Believers, were very ready to die for the version of Orthodoxy they thought the true one. It may be that some brave priests that we don't hear about did defy the Czarist horrors, and died for their pains."

"Yes! Oh yes! I'm sure they did!"

"But the Church too could be cruel. It murdered not a few on its own account. And it was and is so deeply involved in Czarist autocracy that it *must* take the blame for some revolutions, certainly for this one."

"But the saints? Weren't some of them very rare and special?"

"Undoubtedly. There are saints all over the place if you look closely enough. Some advertised and some not. But in general, all that great fear and reverence of priests puts too heavy a burden on priesthood; it's too much to ask of human beings. Of course they get arrogant and self-righteous."

"Not with the help of God. Surely there must be holy men?"

"Up to a point. The difficulty is to pull up sharp." George took a deep breath. "Once these ultrareligious chaps get the bit between their teeth, away goes humanity and decency and all the other virtues. They take religion like drink, like hashish. You've seen these sleepwalking addicts in the Turkish markets, with those bloodshot eyes, not knowing where they are going or what they are doing? Look at the countless martyrs to religion there have been: the French wiping out the Albigensian heretics, Catholic Spain and its Inquisition. Look at Cromwell's Puritans in Ireland. Look at American Puritans drowning their witches; and ours doing the same, come to that. Think of all those mad Moslem mullahs inciting their followers to frenzies of cruelty and violence. Or Hindus, chopping up their untouchables, Sikhs, burning widows, butchering Moslems, Buddhists—" George halted in full flow, unable to think what wrong was done by Buddhists.

"But . . . but surely—"

"Even Buddhists, callously indifferent to human suffering, letting it go on all round them, unhelped." He took Daisy by both hands. "Please try and see what I am telling you."

"The indifference is because they are so holy, and above such things."

"Nonsense," George said crisply. He experienced a powerful desire to take his loved one by the shoulders and give her a slight shaking. "What I am saying is that when a fanatical religion takes over—and communism is a religion, a black religion, believing it's delivering the human race and killing all who don't agree—the thing to do is to run for cover, to go like a scalded cat until the fury is spent. That is, if you are a young woman, in charge of four children."

"But apart from our situation, mine and the children's, isn't holiness the highest thing, aren't we supposed to be holy?"

"Holy smoke! We aren't apart from your situation," George replied furiously. "No religion, *nothing* is holy that has to live by cruelty or indifference to human suffering!" He had by now indeed lost patience, and a cold voice at the back of his mind was asking him whether it was really possible to spend one's lifetime with someone so silly as Daisy was now proving herself able to be. *"Holiness!"* he shouted, so that even the twins, up an arbutus tree at the end of the garden, could hear his furious tones, and caught each other's eye in amazement. "If you want to look at holiness itself, who was Christ angriest at? Not ordinary sinners, not Roman colonizers, not soldiers, not prostitutes, not Caesars, not thieves, not adulterers, but *professional holy men!* Eaten up with spiritual pride, certain that they knew it all, frightening simple people for purposes of their own power and prestige, grinding down the poor, inciting hatred and scorn of all outsiders! Fussing round with their piddling little rules of diet and observance and dead to justice and mercy!"

In the kitchen, Gleb and Anna stood transfixed with interest. "You think that English people are without passion, Gleb. Listen now!"

"He has laid violent hands on her, you think?" Gleb asked hopefully.

"No. Or she would scream and cry out. She does not love him. She too is angry."

"It is of no concern, since she is not too angry with the children," Gleb pointed out. Anna stopped rattling the saucepans and listened for more. But the loud voice, though no less urgent, had gone quiet.

"And who was it who in the end killed Christ?" George asked. "Tell me that! Professional holy men, aided by a nervous governor whom their passion alarmed and overbore . . . They get to think they are superhuman, above humanity, but when they get fanatical they end in being subhuman."

George's voice had moderated and there was now an exhausted silence. Gleb and Anna, waiting hopefully for the matter to culminate in shrieks of wrath and the hurling of handy objects, went disappointedly back to their tasks. George had had his say, and found himself instantly forgiving Daisy for her daftness. To his relief she seemed a little calmer, but intensely pathetic also, as if she might burst into tears the minute he left. She gave a heart-breaking sigh. No sooner stir a girl out of her calm, thought George with resigned tolerance, than you have to calm her out of her stir, at least to the point where she would make a rational plan, or listen to one. But anything, he supposed, even tears, was better than that dreamy optimism, that hapless waiting upon events.

Possibly the moment had now come for a little sympathy, for reassurance, for at least a halting attempt to explain the inexplicable. She looked at him helplessly, as if she no longer had the will to do anything.

"But why, George, why? Surely there was no need for all this cruelty and horror?"

"I can only guess at why. But it seems that Russians are locked, their Church is locked—that influences them so deeply—in a dream of complete unquestioned rightness, like the Pope, only a different kind of rightness, as if they and only they held the key to holiness and truth. They lost Byzantium because they wouldn't be told. Now, for the same reason, they are losing Russia. That's an oversimplification. But perhaps only in exile, only in the bitterness of persecution, can they get to realise that none of us is infallible . . . that we are all, spiritually, in a sort of kindergarten."

Now well out of her dreaminess, Daisy regarded him with astonishment. Ordinarily he was more inclined to talk about the insides of motorcars, to point out a hawk in flight or a promising stand of timber. Now he was eloquent, and full of passion. Was it only in moments of danger that people, Englishmen anyway, could dig into themselves and reveal their deepest conclusions?

"You won't stick to the plan of the Crimea?" George went on.

Again Daisy slid away from agreement, from clearly committing herself to departure. But at least she was calmer, capable of a rational observation, had fought off whatever knife was digging into her vitals. Her tear-stained face had a hopeful gleam in it. If he were just to take her in his arms?

But Daisy, as if she had anticipated this, had moved away from him and was speaking from the windowseat. "George, I know you don't go to the Opera, or not often, but there's a bit in *Khovanschina* where Golitsyn sings, 'O Holy Russia, the cruelty of the Tartars is still a part of you!' "

She'll feel better now, thought George, now she's put it all onto the Tartars. Aloud he persisted, "The plan for the Crimea?"

"For now, yes, the Crimea. I did promise. But later, perhaps, England. And I will, truly, go tomorrow and make a plan with the fishermen. I still have the money that my father sent."

At least she was out of her strong fatalistic trance. At least she was now listening to him. George's face lightened a little. He ventured on a smile of reassurance. "If things heat up suddenly in Novorossisk you might be taken off by a destroyer from one of these coves along the coast. If they do, I'll send you a message, saying where and when. It will be brought, probably, by a very dirty small boy. Write something back—just 'very well' or 'all right,' with your initials. Or just"—here George's imagination got the better of him—"write, St. George. St. George for England; St. George and the Dragon."

At last she was smiling, had returned to the land of the alert, had turned her face towards him, however pale after its angry flush. "A dirty little boy! How lovely. Like Kim." She held out a hand. "St. George and the Dragon; I know you weren't thinking about that as yourself, but I do."

"Promise you'll get ready? And act?"

"I promise." She felt a strong wave of compatriot affection for George and his square-jawed face and brown steadfast eyes. It was good of him to come out all this way again just to warn her and the children. "The Great Game!" she told him, suddenly flashing a smile. "The wicked Russians over the mountains!"

George had an uncomfortable feeling that she was laughing at him. After all that grief! There were moments when the resilience and incurable optimism of his countrymen oppressed him. But he looked at Daisy affectionately all the same, and parted from her with a warm and brotherly kiss for which she appeared grateful.

George had failed, but he went away happier than he had felt for some weeks. Her farewell had been warm, almost loving. Had he, he wondered, taken an unfair advantage, with his resolute Englishness, with his truths about Russian history? Was it needful to alarm her so much? Was all fair in love and war? No, not by a long shot. And there had been cruelty at home, he recollected. But at least when Richard III had the little princes smothered he had to do it, even at that date, on the quiet. He didn't personally torture them or stand by watching their torture being inflicted, with people all round abjectly admiring him, convinced that whatever he did he was God's minister on earth.

Chapter 23

For the next four days high winds blew persistently and heavy waves rode in from the southwest to pound on the shore, their sombre repetitive thunder stretching still further Daisy's already stretched nerves. Every day dawned to the lash of rain on the windows, to scurrying grey clouds low over the sea and the unceasing noise of the waves. Salt spray drenched the steps up from the beach and stung the arbutus bushes of the cliffside. The cypresses flung their branches and bent double as if they must soon snap under the continuous tempest of wind. The shutters of the villa rattled dismally, and even Anna exhibited signs of a certain tension and came near to burning the cabbage soup.

It was no moment for haggling over open boats. Every evening Daisy hopefully searched the stormy sunsets for signs of a break in the weather; and the sky showed a hectic greenish light, foreboding further storm. The children, guessing her anxiety, chose this season to be unusually quarrelsome, and Nikolai resorted to open defiance.

The fifth day dawned fair; the mountains had come back out of their mist and shone with an after-storm brilliance, the shadows of small high clouds chasing one another across their stony slopes. Leaving Gleb and Anna in charge, Daisy set forth on the considerable walk to the fishing village on the further side of the point. Thirsty and footsore, for it was past noon by the time she came down the hill to find the whole place lying peacefully under the spring sun, she walked round the harbour to where the stream, full now from the rain, swept into the sea from under a small stone bridge. The whitewashed boxes of village houses were clustered close together, some between high walls that enclosed tiny gardens with their shading pine and fig trees. The glittering waters of the harbour, still heaving gently, were set with the usual brightly painted boats bobbing at anchor. A donkey brayed in the distance, and was answered by another.

But where was Pavel Mihailovitch, from whom they were wont to buy fish, or his brother Grigor? Or Tomas, who sometimes used to take the little boys out fishing with him? Of course, it was noon, Daisy reflected;

but wasn't the quayside strangely deserted, even for noontide? Hardly so much as a cat was stirring. No lean and hopeful dog snuffled and grubbed among the harbour rubbish.

Realisation came slowly, chillingly. The harbour, generally holding a score or so of the big fishing boats, was empty even of a single one. No nets hung out to dry. All the remaining boats, and there were few enough of them, were little rowing skiffs. No one drowsed under the plane tree in the square or sat drinking in the café by the fountain—its door was shut, its windows shuttered. Daisy made her way to the church; it was closed and silent; there was no bearded priest to be found. It was a village of the dead; the noon silence brooded over it.

Yet it was not wholly deserted. On the steps at the back of the priest's house, in a patch of shade, a very old man sat very still; he was saying, "Let them go. Let them go where they will. Let them all go." He raised a rheumy eye and contemplated Daisy with hostility, as if her coming had interrupted some pleasing fantasy in which he would rather have stayed.

"You," he suggested. "You go also. Go with them. Pursue them over the sea and go with them. Go where you will."

England's child was not going to depart without knowing why. In her halting Russian, Daisy extracted from him the information that the fishermen, with their families, goats, sheep, dogs and cats, had all put to sea as soon as the tempest dropped. "At sea they stay," the old man went on, "until the Red Army passes. Until the Red Army has come and gone. They stay at sea. Out of reach, till the armies have clashed, and departed, going down the coast to the oil regions, to Batum, to Baku, and beyond . . ."

"And you?"

"I am old. I would not go. They pressed me to go. But I would not listen to them. Better to die here, in a place I know. When they come back, they will bury me. Go, you, quickly! Better for you to face the sea, in some small boat, than to wait, a young girl such as you, for the Red Army. They call themselves deliverers. Faugh! A curse on such deliverance! Listen, and go now. They have all gone. They remember the *Potemkin*, the Red terror of the *Potemkin*. They came for our food. Many many fishermen were killed."

A cat slunk along the wall in the sunlight, and from the other side of the harbour the donkey brayed again, left perhaps without water in the haste of departure. Otherwise the silence was absolute. Until, for the first time, from amongst the northern mountains, came a sinister booming reverberation, the distant sound of heavy guns.

The old man fixed upon Daisy a level dying gaze, a look from somewhere infinitely remote, as if his spirit had been left on this shore long ago by the ancient Greeks or shared the fated resignation of the more recent Turks. He and Daisy seemed to be holding their breaths together.

"You stand still to listen," he told her hollowly. "But go now. You, as well as I, heard that sound of thunder from the mountain. You, as well as I, know what it means."

Half-running, half-walking, exhausted and hungry, parched with thirst, Daisy struggled back along the stony miles. Spring had brought a brief rash of little flowers among the rocks. There were tiny irises, toy tulips, red anemones in great drifts; a gentle breeze rustled the olive trees—things, at other moments, to delight the heart. But Misha, Misha, where was he now? *Cavalry cannot operate in mountains* she remembered his telling the boys. But perhaps their horses were all now abandoned and they were fighting on foot amongst the chestnut forests and the red rocks of the mountains, firing and retreating, and firing and still retreating. At what point did one give up and run? Oh God! Keep him, keep him safe.

She ran on, gasping and stumbling, and then pausing for a moment to draw breath and fight the fear that made her less surefooted. It was an enormous relief to see the little boys still busy among the rocks by the beach—no matter that they were evidently practising warfare on each other, running from rock to rock to take cover or rushing into sudden attack with a handful of sand. But on the terrace of the villa stood Varya, looking pallid, and Ella, wild-eyed and tearstained.

"They have gone! Gleb and Anna have gone! We came up for tea and they weren't there!"

"Haven't they just gone to the shop? To the village for something? Perhaps their daughter is ill."

"No, no," Varya insisted. "She was here, before luncheon, with her husband. Gleb was angry, I heard him shouting No, no, no."

"But Anna? Was she shouting no, too?"

"More quietly," Varya considered. "Just grumbling, more. It is a strange thing for parents, but I think they are frightened of their daughter. And more frightened of the husband. I also am frightened of him. Miss Daisy, what will happen?"

"Maybe they have only gone for this evening. Perhaps the daughter brought the message that one of Anna's brothers was ill." But why, Daisy thought, in that case, hadn't they left a message? How absurd I am—neither of them can read or write. Though the son-in-law surely could; he is quite high up in the Railways.

"Oh no," Varya insisted. "They cannot be coming back. We looked for them in their room and it is quite empty. Anna has taken all their things, their ikon, everything."

Suddenly, for the first time, Daisy felt very frightened. Nothing except the most dire and terrible danger would have induced Gleb and Anna to leave the children. What terrors were now approaching them from behind the distant hills? And how, alone with the children, could she cope with them? More than she realised, she had come to rely on Gleb's kindly melancholy bulk, on Anna's sharp capabilities. There had even been a kind of plan in her mind that they could all move into the servants' quarters and that the children could pose as Gleb and Anna's grandchildren. All hope of this subterfuge was now gone. Ella clung to her with frightened eyes and down-drawn mouth. With a shudder Daisy recollected the deserted village, whose entire inhabitants had put to sea in the wake of such a storm as there had just been, rather than stay and face the terrors that came hourly nearer from the already stricken north.

"Are you certain, absolutely certain, that Gleb and Anna have gone? Have they truly taken everything?"

"All. Even the Turkish mat by their bed," Varya added. "They cannot mean to come back."

It did indeed seem final. And where was George, his message, his help? A moment of pure panic again seized Daisy. Mad, mad that I was not to go when he told me, not to go at once. And now by my stupid delay I have left all these children in fearful danger. Should we take the little boat and row out to sea? Anything seems better than to sit here waiting for certain death. Even if the Red soldiers by any lucky chance fail to pass this way, you may be sure that that odious daughter of Anna's will tell someone where the children are, and worse still, who they are. This panic comes from my hunger, she told herself. And faintness from that long walk in the sun without food or drink. Sustained by bread and tea, she felt better able to think and plan.

Faced with actual danger, Daisy believed, Gleb would indeed have defended the children to the death, if need be. He feared not the Red soldiers, but Anna's nagging tongue, the threats of his sullen daughter, the future power of his son-in-law to menace and dominate his life. He had taken, under protest, the line of least resistance; who could blame him?

The departure was final enough. At least, Daisy thought, it absolves us from leaving Gleb and Anna alone in the house. Perhaps it's the best thing, but after all these years, couldn't they have *told* us? From the mountains once again came the boom and reverberation of heavy guns. Daisy strove to sound calm. "We too," she said, "will collect our things."

"Misha will come. Misha will tell us what to do," Ella pleaded.

"Meanwhile we must be ready. Fetch the boys, Varya, please. We will eat first and then we must choose what to take. It must be only what we can carry. No more. A change of clothes and very little else."

"A change of clothes is *not* what I would choose," Ella said petulantly.

"You could wrap Marie-Celestine up in them, Ella darling. We may go by night and she would feel the cold."

"And the jewels?"

"We will wait till it's truly dusk. Then we will dig up the jewels.

Before we need to use a light. Lights can be seen from far off." As if in answer, a light winked suddenly from far away out at sea, and Daisy drew from it what reassurance she could. Were the British ships near?

Nikolai, wet from the sea, was running across the terrace. "Warships," he cried. "Will they bombard Novorossisk, do you think?"

Arkady said nothing. He hurried to the kitchen, where he proceeded to sharpen the kitchen knife on Gleb's whetstone and to fasten it with tightly bound string to an old broom handle. If he tied a hairribbon of Ella's to it, he reflected, it would be exactly like the lances he had once seen borne by a lancer regiment at a review in Moscow. This was life as it should be. No more games of war. Here was a real enemy, as real as the Tartars had been. The sounds of the guns had awoken in his eyes a savage, distant gleam, had carried him back unknowingly three hundred years to the old desperate struggle to possess the land of Russia, with its black rich steppe, and its fish and furs in the north: an atavistic, uncomprehended determination to survive and inherit the earth that was his homeland.

"Arkady, are you packing up? Are you finding what you want?"

"I want only this lance," Arkady said between clenched teeth.

Meditatively, he felt the edge of the blade, whistling, and then returned to work with the whetstone.

In the dawn hours the guns grew louder; their flashes could clearly be seen in the hills. All were up early. "Miss Daisy, there's a very dirty boy knocking on the door," Varya reported distastefully. "I have told him to go away."

"A Red spy, probably!" Nikolai cried. "Arkady! Do you have my bow?"

"No! No!" Daisy cried. "He has a message, probably. A message from George Bennett."

Daisy brushed past them with excited hope. A tattered and grubby urchin stood determinedly by the front door. But his eyes were very lively, and he clutched a scrap of paper which bore the appearance of having been rolled in the dust. "For Miss," he said. Daisy read: *Seven o'clock tonight, Friday, the cove to the east of Kam Point.*

"Nobody," the urchin assured her, "has read it." Daisy could believe him; she could barely read it herself.

"Write, miss, or I shall receive no money . . . no," he added patiently, when she started to apply her pen to the paper, "not on this paper, which you are to tear and burn."

Nikolai and Arkady looked at him with increasing respect.

Daisy tore a sheet from an exercise book that lay on the table.

"Actually," Ella said with dignity, "that was one of the things I had chosen to take."

St. George, wrote Daisy, with trembling fingers. It all now felt less like a Kipling tale and more like a nightmare. *St. George*, she wrote, five times, underlining the words. George, or whoever received the message, would know that there were five of them. *St. George, St. George, St. George.*

The grubby boy departed without haste, by the seashore.

The noise of the guns grew louder, and now, among it, she could distinguish the crackle of small-arms fire.

"Should we start *now?*" Ella asked. "I think, Miss Daisy, that we should start *now.*"

Chapter 24

The morning seemed intolerably long. Waves of panic kept rolling at Daisy, who had to quell them, only to experience other and more sickeningly powerful flows. She felt a wild desire to gather the children and make a dash for Novorossisk, to find the consulate and batter on the door, to seize on George and cry "Help, help! Help us now, however idiotic I have been!"

New and unaccountable noises continued to swell from over the hill. All the children grew white and restless as the morning wore on. But it was raining now, with a soft persistence that would have wetted them all to the skin long before the evening. To wait in shelter seemed the wisest course.

At noon the sky cleared. Daisy took a last look round the house. The jewels were now concealed in her clothes; there was to be no more risking the children. She said goodbye to the Villa Rosa with a pang of regret that almost drowned her gnawing fear. Who now would tend the roses, smell the honeysuckle, rejoice in the bright splotch of the oleander flowers? Shuttered, the house already wore the melancholy look of all deserted dwellings. Even the cypresses looked gloomy and bereft, dark sentinels whom no changing of the guard would relieve.

The morning of waiting had been the worst part. Now, after a scrappy luncheon of beetroot and potatoes, eaten at noon, and with bread and hard-boiled eggs to sustain them during their wait on the shore, they were at least on the move. Varya carried her best dress, an old satin evening dress of her mother's, found lurking in a cupboard and lovingly seized upon, her silver-backed hairbrushes and a small Swiss wooden bear. Ella bore the ikons, clasped to her breast, and Marie-Celestine, repaired after the search in the train, wrapped in clean underwear and her nightdress. Nikolai carried his bow and a quiverful of arrows, his change of clothing wrapped round the copy of *David Copperfield*, to which he had taken a fancy. Arkady bore only his lance, with the bundle of clothing insisted upon by Daisy grudgingly clamped under his left arm.

From the top of the cliff which led to the cove under Kam Point they were suddenly able to catch a distant glimpse of the road which led down from the hills to Novorossisk. They halted in amazement. It was as if the whole population of Russia were on the move, a multicoloured stream of running figures, riding figures, trudging figures, figures leading horses that drew carts piled high with indistinguishable objects. None seemed to make for the sea or divert into the comparative safety of the hills and the surrounding countryside. All poured closely together, as if they were indeed a river confined within its banks, towards Novorossisk, where the only certainty was that they would be trapped. How merciful that she had checked the impulse to join that lemming throng!

Ella drew towards Daisy. "Suppose, suppose Misha is one of those people? He's going the other way from us."

"Misha is with the soldiers, fighting of course," Nikolai pointed out scornfully. "Those are just peasants, Ella, running from the battle. Not *soldiers.* Anyone can see there are no soldiers." But of this, Daisy felt less certain.

They trudged on, under the warm afternoon sun. "Do you think, just for a while, you would please carry Marie-Celestine and all these hot clothes?" Ella asked Daisy, who kindly complied.

When at length they arrived at the cove, it was still only three o'clock. There were four more hours to wait.

Even the boys felt the tension. They hung about, for once unwilling to explore these novel rocks and caves. Ella sat very close and from time to time Varya shuddered slightly. Half an hour crawled by.

"Can't we have tea yet? What's the time, Miss Daisy?"

"It can't be still only twenty to four! Surely your watch must have stopped?"

The guns, echoing from the hills, now sounded very near. The children, taking heart after some food, engaged in a little desultory paddling. The sea, which in happier times they would have insistently described as boiling hot, was now pronounced to be too cold; they soon returned to sit by Daisy. With infinite slowness, the sun began to slope towards the west.

"What's the time now? Surely more than twenty past five?"

"I'm hungry again. Very hungry."

"There's a little more bread, Nikolai."

"Oh, *bread.*"

"How do we know this ship will come?"

"How do we know they'll take us when they do come?"

"I think," Daisy told them, "it would be better to speak only in English. No French, no Russian." Daisy's calm voice belied the tension she felt.

"Won't they take us if they know we are Russian? Why won't they take us if we are Russian?"

"Of course they will take us all. It would just be more polite to speak English. You know very well it is not good manners to speak together in a language other people do not understand. It's as bad as whispering."

Now that safety was so near, Daisy felt her fear mounting.

It was immediately caught by Varya, who burst suddenly into wild uncontrollable tears. "They are near!" she cried. "They are just coming! I don't want to die! Don't let them kill us! Why do we sit here waiting for death? Why don't we run, run, anywhere away from here?"

"Where to, for heaven's sake?" Arkady demanded. "You don't want to swim out into this ice-cold sea, do you?" Nikolai, straddle-legged, gazed at a picture of a gun he had traced in the sand. His hands trembled slightly. Ella was crying, quietly but despairingly.

Their misery, their dependence, gave Daisy a sudden fresh injection of courage. Smiling determinedly, she assured them that all would soon be well.

Ten minutes to six . . . ten past. Had ever any afternoon dragged by more slowly? But the light was beginning to fade; under the evening chill a thin mist was creeping from off the sun-warmed land.

"Shall Arkady and I go out to the point to see if we can see the ship coming?"

"Better stay here together. The ship might come early."

"Or the Reds might come first."

"What use to frighten your sisters, Nikolai? Wait a little while longer. The ship might come from the other direction."

"If it was coming from the other direction and was going to be here by seven we could see it already."

"I suppose that's true, Arkady. All the same, better to keep together. It won't be long now." Try as she might to exude a cheerful confidence, her voice came forth high and agitatedly.

"But will they come for us? Will they *come?*"

"They have said that they will come. And they will come."

They gazed doubtfully at her. Certainty had long since departed from their lives. What could distract their attention, pass the time? A new sound had crept into the noise of gunfire, the chattering sharpness of small arms.

"When you go on board the ship, it is good manners to salute. For boys, I mean. English boys would."

"Salute what?"

"The captain, I suppose. Actually, I believe the quarterdeck, because the image of a patron saint was once carried there."

For a brief moment the twins looked pleased and important. "Have a practice. Pretend you have arrived at the top of the ladder."

"If the boys salute the saint, I will salute too," Ella declared.

Varya, rising to the demands of a social occasion, announced, "I shall make a small bow, thus." She sketched a formal graceful obeisance.

This ploy was soon over. It was still only twenty past six.

Ella sat silently on a rock, her small shoulders hunched, her teeth chattering audibly. Varya wavered on the verge of hysteria. Nikolai was trembling, but seemingly more with rage and anticipation than with fear.

Even the stalwart Arkady gazed at Daisy with a wide-eyed, fixed stare, as a drowning man might gaze at a distant shore. "Should we pray, do you think?"

"In our hearts, yes. But be ready to move in a moment. We are here so that the boat's crew can see us. We may have to run further in under the cliff."

"We had better go further in under the cliff *now*. The Reds could see us from the top of the cliff."

"After seven we will go there."

"But by seven you said they will certainly come. The *ship* will come?"

"There might be a small delay. But I don't think so." Daisy searched her mind for anything that passed the time, allayed panic as the longed-for hour approached.

"Shall we play 'I Spy,' now, while we can still see things?"

"Yes, yes, I'll begin," Ella cried. Her gaze searched the horizon, the shore, the cliff-top. "Something beginning with 'S.' "

"Sea?"

"Shore?"

"Sand?"

"Ship?"

"No. No. No. And there isn't any ship."

"I am not playing anything," Arkady declared. "I am keeping watch. I am on guard."

"Doesn't that sort of chattering gun sound very near now?" Varya's voice trembled.

"Shoes?" Daisy persisted.

"Socks?"

"Shells?"

"No. Not any of those things. You aren't looking properly. Do you give up? I'll tell you," Ella triumphed. "There—at the top of the cliff! A soldier!"

And there, indeed, long-coated, silhouetted against the evening sky, was a Russian soldier.

A feeling of near despair seized Daisy. They had been so nearly safe, within minutes of security on board a British ship. "Hide! Keep down, Ella! Here, behind the rocks. Quickly, Arkady, or he'll see the red pennant on your spear! Keep its head low."

They ran, dodging between rocks. What is the good, thought Daisy. It is only postponing what must be faced. She ran fast, all the same, nearly whirling Ella off her feet.

"Marie-Celestine! You made me drop her! Wait! Wait!"

But the sharp-eyed Nikolai, crouching low and peering between two rocks suddenly shouted, "No, don't run! It's all right. I'm sure it's him. I know him by the way he walks. It's Misha. *Misha! Misha!* We're here! We're all here!"

He tore across the sands to the figure now descending the cliffs. The man was limping, more than slightly, and wore a bloodstained sling from his left shoulder. Reaching the level, he seemed to stagger, but came on. Daisy's despair turned into a radiant joy. Beyond question, it was Misha, dishevelled, haggard, unshaven, but smiling from ear to ear.

"Misha! Mishoska! Mishoska!" Nikolai was caught up in the sound arm, whirled round, embraced.

The joy of the reunion was entire, and drove away the hideous panic of the last few moments. Misha's troop, he told them, had been all but wiped out. There were not more than a score of them left. Under the merciless pounding of the machine guns their horses had been destroyed. Command counsels, as ever, were divided. Some were for making a stand at Novorossisk. His own general, realising the hopelessness of this, had told his men to disperse to the hills and get themselves as best they might to Ghelenyik, or failing that to go on to Tengenskoe. Here, perhaps, a defensive line could be formed, or shipment to the Crimea, still firmly in White Russian hands, could be achieved. Novorossisk was already all but surrounded; Yekaterinodar had already fallen to the Reds.

He looked at Daisy eagerly, but addressed her with a shyness that was new to him. Her heart was racing.

Telling them of the long, gradual defeat, Misha felt a renewed sickness at heart. Yet he was immeasurably rejoiced to find them all, and still more to hear of their impending rescue.

Daisy noted that he cast an apprehensive glance up to the clifftop, as if he expected the Reds to appear there at any minute.

He had made for the coast, he said, as the safest route to the villa, and had been on his way along it when he had caught sight of Arkady's pennant, appearing over the rocks, and a whisk of little girls' frocks, and had come down to investigate. He had meant, if they were still there, to take them to sea in the Villa Rosa dinghy—risky enough, but safer than awaiting the coming of the Red soldiers. "Do you feel sure that this ship will come?"

"Yes. Yes. I feel sure." If one ceased to believe that what the Royal Navy promised to do, it would do, there was nothing, in terrestrial terms, worth believing in. "They'll come for us. In about ten minutes from now."

Misha sat down on a rock, with Ella still clamped like a tight hot fur collar round his neck. He looked very pale, and as if he had lost a great deal of blood. "The army is broken," he told Daisy miserably. "For the moment the game here is over."

"Only for the moment, perhaps."

"You did not go to the Crimea. Are there no boats anymore on this coast, no fishermen?"

"They have all fled in front of the Reds." An inspired notion entered her head. "Come too, Misha, come with us!"

"I think not," Misha said with flat finality.

Daisy's deepest impulses urged her to fling her arms round him, to insist, beg, beseech him to come with them, but her reason told her that she would be doing no good. And such feelings were mingled painfully with the long-felt primary purpose of somehow bringing the children to safety. Should she, when the boat came in, let them all go without her, to where they would be perfectly safe, and stay ashore with Misha? But of what use could she be? None, simply an added burden. Burden or no, every instinct shouted to her to stay. I can be brave when I *have* to, she thought. I managed in the train, and I feel less afraid now, since I faced that. Courage is practice, or no one could go on fighting a war for five minutes. Oh, Misha, come!

It was now truly dusk. Suddenly, and silently as a ghost, the bows of a destroyer appeared round the point, moving slowly, as if her engines were stopped. She quickly brought to and lowered a boat. Seeing the British seamen rowing ashore, so smartly and imperturbably, Daisy could have wept for joy. Arkady and Nikolai ran to the shore, dancing excitedly in the shallows, their abandoned shoes tied round their necks.

"You must come too." Daisy, made bold by fear for him, seized upon Misha's ragged coatsleeve. "You *must* come with us. Don't leave us again. Don't leave the children."

"I think not," Misha reiterated. "There could still be a fight for it at Novorossisk."

"But you said yourself it was hopeless! And what good could you do, with that bad limp, and your right arm injured? And your men scattered?"

"They are more dead than scattered. With my left hand I could at least help to load a machine gun. I could fire a revolver. I wait here only to see you safe in that ship."

"But are there any machine guns left? Or ammunition? Or will to fight? I saw some of them this morning—they were a rabble, running for their lives."

"Marvellous things can be done with a rabble," Misha persisted stubbornly. "And not all are rabble. Many fight on."

"But not cavalry, surely, defending a town? You said yourself—Oh, Misha, this is not the time for death or glory!"

The boat was nearing the shore, the splash of the oars sounding clearly in the stillness of the evening. Glancing at her watch, Daisy could almost have laughed for pleasure and affection. It was exactly one minute to seven. Delighted whoops came from Nikolai and Arkady as the boat grounded in the pebbly beach. "Come—*come*, Misha," she urged him desperately.

Varya and Ella were running to the boat, skipping across the sand as if they did not know what fear or fatigue were.

"Even if I would go," Misha said, gazing after them, "would the captain take me? A White Russian soldier on the run? The British have withdrawn support from General Denikin," he added bitterly. "Perhaps Wrangel now fights here. Alone."

The children's voices sounded faintly from the water's edge. "Misha! Come, Miss Daisy, the boat is here! It is here!"

"Could you swim as far as that ship? Give me a few minutes to talk to the captain, and then come. He won't send you back."

"War makes people different."

"Not *that* different. Could you swim so far, in the cold sea, with your bad leg and only one arm?"

"Easily, unless the current is very strong. And as the ship has not moved, I think that it cannot be strong."

"Well then? Please decide, Misha, quickly, since the boat is now in."

"I cannot leave Russia. Not now. Not in this hour of despair. Not while I still stand."

"Oh, Misha!" The boat had now grounded. She longed to give her adored one a slight shake. "They might put you ashore in the Crimea! Or you could fight in Siberia if you came. The Whites are fighting there, still, George Bennett says. Wouldn't you be of more value there?"

"I stay," Misha said sombrely, then paused. "Will your father receive my brothers and sisters?"

"Of course!" Daisy cried impatiently. "He's a Christian and we have seven bedrooms."

"I believe you," Misha said with sadness. "And may God's blessing be on you all. Go quickly now, Daisy."

"And you'll swim? In ten minutes. Swim, or I'll never forgive you."

He shook his head, eyeing the ice cold sea.

She was running now over the sand. "Never say die," she shouted over her shoulder. "Swim and stay alive!"

But Misha, stubborn as a rock, stood quite still on the sand.

The rescue boat's commander was a fair-haired boy who appeared to be about sixteen. "Miss Daisy Pelham?" he enquired politely. "Midshipman Tarrant, H.M.S. *Goshawk*. I've come to take you off, and we'll go sharpish if you don't mind."

"Mind! You don't know how glorious English voices sound. Here are the children."

"Children?" Tarrant asked doubtfully. "I've no orders about any children. I was told to pick up Miss Pelham, and Colonel and Mrs. Ombersley and Miss Esmeralda Moss. Not any children."

"These are my brothers and sisters," Daisy told him with a voice of surprising assurance, hoping that the gathering darkness hid her flushed face. "Climb in, Varya, Ella. Come, boys."

"But look," began Tarrant. "Are you *sure* there's no one else?" Not naturally a serious character, recent experiences had sobered him up; he took his duties keenly. Somewhile back he and a teammate from the *Emperor of India* had gone ashore at Sevastopol, and, repairing to their favourite tree-lined avenue in the heart of the town had been brought up short to see it transformed into a scaffold. From every spreading tree a communist spy was hanging, like some huge and terrible withered fruit. Man's inhumanity to man, seen at such close quarters, had for the moment sunk even the spirits of midshipmen. Seen in retrospect, it made him feel more mature and responsible. He eyed Daisy sternly. "Where are the Colonel and his wife? And Miss Moss?"

"There's been nobody here. And we've been here almost all day. At least—"

"Better take off this lot, sir," the coxswain advised, "and come back if the other parties show up." The gunfire was indeed sounding very near, almost as if there were men firing just over the brow of the cliff. "Someone's still fighting," a seaman pointed out. There were stray rifle shots, the staccato stammer of machine guns. "Poor bloody locals trying to save their stock, I fancy," the midshipman said. "All right, coxswain, give way there."

Willing sailors had bundled the two little boys into the bow, where they sat with their eyes fixed on the destroyer, unaware that Misha was left behind.

"But where—" Varya began.

"Ssh—later. Sing something, darling," she added in a low voice, hiding her great misery at leaving Misha. "Some nursery rhyme to show them how English you are. But quietly. This is still a secret escape."

Obediently, Varya piped up, joined by Ella and intermittently by the little boys from the bow of the boat.

> Upon Paul's steeple stands a tree
> As full of apples as may be,
> The little boys of London Town
> They run with hooks to pull them down,
> And then they run from hedge to hedge
> Until they come to London Bridge.

To these murmured strains they approached the ship's side, the oars dipping steadily. With every stroke Daisy felt a lift of the heart. If only Misha would see sense! Looking back through the failing light to the shore, she thought that she could see figures along the top of the cliff. Was it only a trick of the light? More refugees? Or had Misha been seen and pursued?

"Go Shawk," Arkady read out. "Why is the ship called that? What's a Go Shawk?" The ladder was already down, willing hands waited to help the children from the boat. Once on board, thought Daisy, once on board. No power on earth, no prime minister, would make a captain and crew of British sailors land four children by themselves at nightfall on a hostile shore. Not unless the world were truly turned upside down. Smoothing her tattered skirts, she went up the ladder with what grace she could muster. What sort of captain would be waiting at the top?

Commander Browning was small, wiry, determined. His sandy eyebrows met in the middle, which, Daisy recollected, was supposed to be the sure sign of a bad temper. It was difficult to read the expression in his eyes, but the thick freckles on his face were visible by any light.

"Miss Pelham," he began, "I'm delighted to welcome you on board." Varya, he thought, was perhaps Miss Moss, though she looked too young to be on her own, earning her living so far from home. But who was the little girl with the doll? The twins finally stumped him. His tone changed abruptly. "But what's all this?"

"They are . . . they are—"

"Her brothers and sisters, she says," put in Tarrant.

"I think not," Browning said. "Who are they? The truth, please."

We are back, Daisy thought, in the land of the truth. In the country where it is safe to tell the truth, and rather unsafe not to. Tell the truth and shame the Devil. "I am responsible for them," she said boldly. "They are Russian children, and their parents have disappeared, and I am in charge of them." From the rocks in the cove now came the sound of shooting.

"It's Gos Hawk," Nikolai said. "A kind of bird."

"Misha!" Arkady broke in. "Where's Misha?"

"It's all right," Daisy soothed him. "It's too dark for them to see him. He will be all right."

"You left him behind! You let them leave him behind! The Reds will get him!"

"Who exactly are these children? We have orders to take off four British subjects. And where is Miss Moss and old Colonel Ombersley? And his wife?"

"Make this captain send his boat back again for Misha!" Nikolai demanded imperiously. "They don't understand! He'll be killed."

"Colonel Ombersley died, I heard, just last week, and his wife went to the Crimea. And Miss Moss has gone far away down the coast to be safe. To Bakum, I think. And the children won't eat any more than they would have eaten, or take up any more room," Daisy pleaded, wishing Nikolai would keep quiet. "Their name is Dubelsky. This is Varvara, and Ella, and the twins are Nikolai and Arkady. We don't know where their parents are, and if they are to be put ashore I will go with them."

"That's all right, Miss Pelham, no one is thinking of putting them ashore. I just needed to know who they are, and why they are here."

"She *said* they were her brothers and sisters," Tarrant repeated.

"Quite right. No time for explanations, with the Reds just over the hill. Her brothers and sisters they are forthwith. Come below, Miss Pelham. You must have been through quite a lot."

"It's only that the children are so hungry."

"We'll soon put that right," Browning assured her briskly. "This way, Miss Pelham. I'm in my sea cabin, so you and the children—what *is* it, Riggs?—can have mine. I see you've not much baggage. Never mind; we can rig up the children and have you in Constantinople in no time. Yes, Riggs?"

"Sir, there's a swimmer off the port quarter."

"Very well. Are they keeping him covered? He could be a Bolshevik soldier. Is he alone?"

"For all we could see, sir. The first lieutenant has him covered. But then, sir, he seemed in distress; he had his arm up, waving, like, so the first lieutenant has got the boat away again, to pick him up."

Could this be Misha? Daisy wondered. *Let it be Misha!*

"Captain Browning, I think he may be—"

"Don't stand there, Riggs! Keep him covered and watch out to see if there are any more. Miss Pelham, better come back on the upper deck with me. Quartermaster!"

"Captain Browning, I think he may possibly be the children's brother—"

"What? How came you to leave one of them behind? Ah, they've got him. He's not exactly a *small* brother, is he? See he's not armed, Tarrant. And help him up the side. Can't you see the fellow's nearly dropping? How the devil could he swim all this way with one arm?" Why the drama? the Captain wondered. Why had he not come off in the boat? There seemed to be something fishy here.

Misha, spent and dripping, with fresh blood oozing from his injured shoulder, was hauled before the captain. Shot at by what appeared to be a platoon of Russian soldiers, and unable to escape from the cove, he had been forced to make a rapid change of mind. The swim in a sea icy from Caucasian snow had taken most of his remaining strength. He stood silent, concentrated on remaining upright at least until his breath should return. His delighted siblings gathered about him, pressing themselves to his cold wet back and legs.

"Take these children below," the captain ordered Riggs, "and dry them off and give them something to eat. And stow them, two on my sofa and two on the bunk. Make them as comfortable as you can. And, now, young man, who exactly are you? And don't try to pull any wool over my eyes as your friend here endeavoured to do."

"I pull no wool," Misha said, slowly and breathily. Still dripping copiously and rather bloodily all over *Goshawk*'s fine clean deck, he drew himself up and sketched a left-handed salute. His blue eyes blazed in a manner that struck Daisy as incautious. "Major Prince Michael Andreivitch Dubelsky," he announced himself firmly; "Third Imperial Cavalry, latterly fighting under General Denikin, in the Volunteer Army, the army of his Imperial Majesty the Czar."

"A White Russian officer, by God," the captain said. "Of all things." The fellow must surely be aware by now, he thought, that the Czar is dead. He called to mind that to aid and abet such a one had recently been strictly forbidden him. The bloody politicians! Only a few years back, the same Imperial Russians had been staunch and valued allies. He regarded Misha a while in silence, with a level considering gaze.

Misha was principally wondering how much longer he could stand.

"Lloyd George be damned," Midshipman Tarrant was heard to mutter in the background.

"Keeping you is against all orders," the captain pointed out sternly.

Daisy lost control. "Oh no!" she cried. "You're *not* going to put him ashore! He's wounded, and the cove is full of Red soldiers. They'd butcher him, they'd kill him at once. They don't make prisoners of Czarist officers. They'd kill him."

"So be it," Misha said, looking suddenly very doomed and Russian. "I have no wish to put you in trouble, Captain."

Commander Browning was irritated by these dramatics. "Don't be upset, my dear Miss Pelham," he advised crisply. "No one will be put ashore tonight. Or into the sea." Why must the far-away government in London confront one with this sort of problem, visiting the sins of the Czarist regime upon all its adherents, young or old, and this spent and agreeable-looking fellow among them? He could, of course, be a spy . . . But had everyone forgotten what sort of hard-fighting allies the Russians had been a few years back, before the Reds got at them and forced them to make that shameful peace? He had privately no intention of landing young Dubelsky anywhere in Russia, unless it were the Crimea, but for form's sake he would go through the movements enjoined by his orders. He accordingly confronted Misha with a heavy frown.

"I can't help you. Since a few months ago, we have other orders. Later on, at my convenience, you will be rowed ashore. Or you may be landed in the Crimea. Now, Riggs, take him below and give him some dry clothes and some brandy and a square meal. And ask the doctor to look at him."

But Daisy, overwrought by hunger, suspense, relief and fear, could stand no more. "Don't put him ashore," she wailed. "I love him. We are engaged to be married. Don't let him go!" Impervious to his dampness, she clasped Misha's wet and weary form in her raggedly clad arms.

The first lieutenant, who was a devoted operagoer, thought they looked like something from the finale of a well-staged second act.

"Don't let him go! Please, Captain Browning. I beg and implore you!"

"Is this true, Major?"

"Entirely true," Misha said, and from the tone of his voice it was impossible to tell if he was glad or sorry. Which was not surprising, as this was his last utterance before passing out. Briefly, Daisy held him up, before he was saved from a dramatic collapse by the intervention of two stalwart sailors, who, aided by a third very small one, presently carted him below.

The captain put an arm round Daisy's weary and disconsolate shoulders and patted her kindly on the back. "You're a brave girl," he told her, "sticking by that bunch of children. Don't fret. They'll look after him. By a lucky oversight we have still got our hostilities-only doctor, who is first class. He'll see to that wound."

"You won't be putting him ashore?"

"Orders, Miss Pelham, are made for the instruction of the simple and the interpretation of the wise."

Daisy was immensely grateful to this sensible man.

In the spacious accommodation that was still a captain's privilege, Daisy found the children eating corned beef and baked potatoes as if they had never eaten before. Gathering speed, the destroyer was proceeding steadily towards the southwest. The captain presently joined her, holding out to her a large glass of brandy. "Dinner in half an hour," he said cheerfully. "Would you care to wear this jersey of mine? It still gets cold in the evenings. The jersey's not exactly new, or chic, but it's clean.

"Listen, Miss Pelham, I don't exactly know what the relationship between you all is, nor do I much care, and I'm not totally convinced that that young man is not a spy, but he is very badly in need of medical attention, and if he were Lenin and Trotsky rolled into one, on board my ship he is going to get it. So put your mind at rest. I am not handing him over to anyone, and tomorrow evening we shall be in Constantinople, where he can go straight into hospital."

"And then?"

"After that it's up to him. But if he's survived the war so far, he appears to me very well able to take care of himself."

Gorged and exhausted, the children were soon asleep. Cleaned, warmed, rebandaged and doped, Misha lay in the sickbay, sleeping like the dead, unconscious as he had not been able to be unconscious for many months.

Rest was not yet for Daisy. Ella, as good as she had been all day, had nightmares: time and again she woke screaming. Varya, out of patience, removed herself from the captain's bunk and lay rolled in a rug on the floor of his day cabin. Replacing her, Daisy held Ella tight, but at regular intervals Ella made the cabin flat ring with her yells.

"They'll get us! They'll get us! The Reds are coming to get us!"

"No, darling, it's all right. We are safe. We are all here. We are safe in a ship, going fast in the direction of England."

"How do you know," Ella sobbed, "that the Reds won't get us *there?*" A fresh misery struck her. "And I forgot and ate meat. It's Holy Week, and we all ate meat for supper." Her tears fell anew.

"You are children."

Ella's brow cleared. "You won't get up out of this bed and leave me? Promise?" But, having extracted the promises, she went on crying quietly all the same, and Daisy's soothings seemed powerless to stop her.

There was a knock on the door, and Riggs appeared with two steaming mugs of cocoa. "Perhaps you'd fancy this, and the little girl?" he suggested. "Funny how they go on like that, isn't it? My youngest kid was just the same. Nothing the matter, and yet she'd wake up night after night, screaming. My Lucy, every night, round midnight, regular as clockwork, off she'd go, screaming blue murder. No pain, no nothing. You wouldn't credit it, the fancies kids get in their minds. Leopards, it was with her. She would have it they were under her bed. Wouldn't listen to the Missus, wouldn't harken to me. Kittle-cattle, that's what they are. You drink this up, there's a little duck. Now, my eldest—" Having a pretty girl on board and a bunch of children and a nice chat in the evening made a welcome break in the routine. Certain of sympathy from Daisy's wide-open blue eyes, Riggs embarked on a long saga of his domestic woes and blisses. Ella, unable to understand an English different from any she had previously heard, yet soothed by the sound of Riggs's comfortable voice, fell gradually asleep, and Daisy, sipping the hot brew, felt no less soothed in listening; Gladys and her measles' complications, Derek's difficulties in teething, Bobby's exceptional promise at school, the holiday on Hayling Island when Lucy had been lost on the sands—all flowed over her mind like balm.

An enormous sense of homecoming filled her heart. She was back in the land of beings who listened to reason (most of the time), were not drowned in political passion, did not murder and laugh in the same breath. She would have liked to get out of the bunk and embrace Riggs warmly on either cheek, but that, alas, was a thing that Russians might do but not the English. Not, at least, without misinterpretation. If only the English could learn from the Russians how freely to express the warmth of their hearts, and the Russians glean from the English some of their refusal to be cruel, their practical common sense!

Ella, finally reassured of safety by the voice of Able Seaman Riggs, lay deep asleep.

Daisy lay long awake, filled with relief, with excitement and joy. Somewhere in the same ship lay Misha, his wounds dressed, his enemies distanced. He was safe, the children were safe; she herself was alive to see the day. The thought of George, still in threatened Novorossisk, yet the author of all this safety, crossed her mind very occasionally with a feeling of unease.

Rejoicing returned, and drowned all other thoughts. Very slowly, as she lay listening to the quiet thrumming of the engines, the tension eased out of her.

Early in the morning, before dawn, the vessel heeled over in a sharp alteration of direction. Had Daisy been awake to look out of the porthole at the dark water, she would have seen the ship's wake lying like a great white U on the calm sea. In response to a signal, H.M.S. *Goshawk* had reversed course and was now headed towards Russia.

Chapter 25

"May I ask you about something, Captain Browning? Have you a safe on board and may I put something in it?"

"By all means. If it's not too bulky." Opening her little chamois leather bags, Daisy poured forth the jewellery over the captain's polished table. It lay winking and glittering in the bright morning sunshine.

"Holy smoke! Some spoils! How on earth did you get them away safely?"

"Arkady wore them round his waist and the twins changed places and were clever about them. I had just a few sewn in my petticoat and Misha had a few sewn in his clothing."

"It beats me," the captain said. "I'll put them in the safe right away. These ought to keep the family going for some while. Pay your passages home anyway."

"My father said he would foot the bill for that. He sent some money to the consulate at Constantinople some while ago. But how do I prove that I am me?"

"Your passport. That survived, I hope?"

"Yes. Captain Browning, these jewels belonged to the children's parents, but whether alive or dead, I feel absolutely certain that they would like you to have one, perhaps one of these uncut emeralds, for rescuing the children. Do, please, take one. Only I suppose they might belong to Misha, now. But I know he would agree."

"Get thee behind me, my dear Miss Pelham. Rescuing stranded British nationals is part of the job, and the children are your . . . adjuncts, and as such are very welcome. I'll get these splendid spoils tucked up, and then—Ah, Number One, just put these in the safe for Miss Pelham. And hark. We get to Novorossisk this evening and anchor offshore. We go alongside tomorrow morning at first light. It will be Easter Day. There is a special drill for any Russian officer coming on board, which please learn, and instruct the rest of the ship's company. The Russians will bow and say to you, *Christos voskresye*, which is to say, Christ is risen. You bow back to him and reply, *Vo istinu voskresye*, which is to say, He is risen indeed. Drill over. Understood?"

"Aye aye, sir."

"Well, just take that loot and put it under lock and key. Better get the Pay to make a little list of what there is, or how many leather bags there are anyway." He turned back to Daisy. "Miss Pelham—about young Dubelsky. The doctor had a good look at him last night when he tied up his shoulder. His leg has been broken and very badly set, and unless something is done about it, and the sooner the better, he'll apparently limp for life. Which would be a pity. His shoulder also is full of bits and pieces which need to come out. He's lost some blood and is dead tired, so the doctor wants him to rest today and be operated on first thing tomorrow. What do you think?"

"I don't know. Should we ask him? Could he stand it after losing so much blood? He seems exhausted this morning."

"We could wait for the hospital at Constant, but the situation seems so fluid that God knows now when we'll get there. Campbell's a clever doctor, a surgeon in shoregoing life. He knows what he's at."

Lost in the problem of whether or not to operate, Daisy had been unable to get a word in to express her horror and fear, her incredulous astonishment that they were not yet safely clear of Russia. "You didn't say, you didn't mean we were headed back for Novorossisk?"

The captain was equally astonished. The denseness of landsmen, and particularly of landswomen, never ceased to amaze him. Last night the ship had been headed towards the sunset, with the land on the starboard quarter. This morning it was headed towards the sunrise, with the same land on the port bow. And yet, until told, those who were not sailors seemed unable to take in that they were therefore necessarily on a reverse course. He began patiently to explain, only to be interrupted at the first pause by an agitated Miss Pelham.

"The thing is that he mustn't, Misha *mustn't*, go ashore at Novorossisk. Are we *really* going back there? Do we have to?"

"A signal came early this morning. It seems that the authorities greatly overestimated the number of British nationals along the coast. We were told we'd have to pick up three or four hundred British subjects, Cypriots and Maltese, and so on, of course included, but they've all vamoosed already, none of them telling the consul, of course, and it's turned out more like three or four dozen. Novorossisk is holding out for the moment—they got themselves dug in—and we're ordered to go in there and help the *Emperor of India*, the battleship which is the Black Sea flagship, and pick up women and children Russian refugees—women and children only, it's emphasised. No soldiers. The *Emperor of India* will take as many of those as they can."

"Does Misha know we are going to Novorossisk?"

"He didn't seem to be conscious of anything much when I saw him this morning. Just about played out, poor fellow. And he's on the starboard side of the ship. Can't see anything but sea."

"He mustn't know! He simply *mustn't*. And if he hears that they are still fighting at Novorossisk, he'll simply swim ashore."

"I can't exactly put him in irons."

"There'll be no other hope of stopping him."

"What there won't be a hope of," Captain Browning said, "is of a single White soldier, let alone an officer, surviving in Novorossisk once the Reds take it, as take it they must."

"Oh, what are we to do? He'll get ashore! I know he'll get ashore!"

"How fond is this young man of you? No, don't answer that. I had no business to ask."

"I ask it myself," Daisy admitted honestly. "But one thing I do know. He's fonder of Russia."

"Good for him. But you must stop worrying, Miss Pelham."

"This is all such an odd and unconventional way of meeting that couldn't you call me Daisy? So long as you don't ask me to call you anything except Captain Browning. The captain of a ship *is* different from a refugee."

The captain laughed. "Very well, Daisy. I'll tell you my plan for Dubelsky. It's quite straightforward, really. The doctor can go right ahead on that operation early tomorrow morning. The sooner it's over the better; he may be busy later with the refugees coming on board and possibly needing medical attention. We'll be at anchor, but the sickbay has no porthole, so Dubelsky won't know where. Before we go alongside we'll shift him out of the sickbay and into Number One's cabin, and lock him in. He'll only just be coming round from the anaesthetic and won't know a thing till we are at sea again. We can only hold a limited number of refugees, so embarcation can't last long. Rely on me, we'll keep him on board."

"Oh, Captain Browning, I do. I do."

The quay at Novorossisk alongside which *Goshawk* was secured stretched inland for a couple of hundred yards to a line of warehouses. It presented a spectacle of appalling turmoil. The young and the old, stout peasant women and smartly dressed citizenesses, children of all sizes and bent old men were mingled inextricably with a motley of harbourside characters. There were fruit-sellers, long-coated Caucasians, Tartars in their fezzes, Cossacks; and at the rear, by the warehouses a line of interested spectators hoping somehow to cash in on the event. There were soldiers in every degree of exhaustion, wearing every variety of uniform, white with disease, decrepit with age or privation, running the whole gamut of demoralisation. All were desperately thronging to the quayside, mad to escape from the approaching terror and in imminent danger of being propelled into the water by the ever-mounting pressure from behind.

Half a mile from the wharf the battleship *Emperor of India* was anchored in the bay. Earlier in the week she had landed parties of seamen to organise and assist in the digging of trenches from which the approaches to Novorossisk could be defended; there had been a march through the town in order to steady the local nerve by the unruffled confidence of the sailors' bearing. But it is not possible to defend people who have not the heart and will to defend themselves. The Russian nerve was now past steadying. Tales of Red atrocities whistled through the small town like the shriek of wind in the trees before a full-force gale.

The battleship was berthed well clear of the shore and buildings, which enabled her to fire her 13.5 inch guns to delay the advance of the Reds and allow more of the White soldiers to reach the entrenchments outside the town. A very few halted bravely and died there. In the main they poured in a disorderly mass into the town and through the town to the port, where they could be ferried to the waiting ships. The bay was full of the comings and goings of ships' boats, and the smaller ships, one French ship among them, lay alongside, slowly filling up. Armed parties, needing all their strength to hold back the crowds, were guarding the gangways that led on board, up which a steady stream of panic-stricken refugee women were pouring, amidst heartrending scenes of farewell between themselves and their menfolk on the quay.

Wails and lamentations filled the air. Some of the women were refusing to leave alone and were being forcibly pushed by their husbands and fathers. The soldiers, with weary fatalism, waited on the stone steps for their turn to be borne off by the relays of small boats. Some of the young soldiers were mere boys, no older than the midshipmen who succoured the refugees—must all such be left behind to be butchered? Civilians, equally fearful of the Red vengeance, fought and drove their way to the safety of the ships. There was an animal wildness in the sound of the cries, in the massed cacophony of grief and fear, a terrifying infection in the universal emotion. Guns on the outskirts of the town fired with monotonous regularity, and panic raced over the concourse like a visible presence.

Through a megaphone a naval officer who was a Russian interpreter was telling the crowd of men to seek escape along the coast while yet they might. The *Emperor of India* had embarked General Denikin and his wife, and could take two thousand soldiers but no more. Ten thousand at least were seeking refuge and a transfer to the Crimea. Nobody listened, few of his words were heard. The crowds continued to press relentlessly on, deaf to reason, deaf to thought. *Goshawk*, with her increasing load, was already appreciably lower in the water; already *Montrose* was packed, *Emperor of India* looked crowded beyond measure, her forecastle was solid with massed soldiers, her boats were ferrying further loads to ships further out in the offing. Where would they draw the line, and what would happen when they did?

Daisy had a terrified feeling that this huge mass of panic-stricken people would presently break bounds and swarm into the sea. Would the ships then fire into the crowds to keep them back? At that thought she hid her face in her hands. It was a scene of unforgettable horror, where all that made man a civilised being had deserted him, all law and custom had broken down, everyone had become a wild beast with no thought but his own desperate desire to survive.

Not all had thus disintegrated. As ever, in any scene of human degradation and horror, there were the saints, heroes and redeemers. By the warehouses a stalwart Russian officer was doing his utmost to slow the stream of men pouring dangerously into the ever more crowded space between him and the edge of the quay. At the top of the steps stood a tall, pale, almost willowy Russian officer in charge of the port, greeting all who came, making a way down the steps to the boats, translating the orders of the British officers running the boats. Knowing that he must in the end be left ashore to certain death, he stood there, hour after hour, unwearyingly reassuring in his explanations and greetings, insisting that they would meet again to continue the fight at Theodosia, and giving a last comradely touch of the old Russia to those bound for exile, perhaps forever. *Christos voskresye! Vo istinu voskresye!* This way, Matrushka, be of good cheer, friend. Christ is risen; he is risen indeed. And in the crowd were a few bearded veterans, who knew that their hour had come, but who faced it with the stubborn fatalism of their race, never ceasing to raise up trampled children, to force a way through the crowd for terrified women; bearing up the faint-hearted, plucking virtue out of this scene of terrible fear and evil. *Christos voskresye!* This way, pass this way, mother. *Vo istinu voskresye!* Now, through here, quickly my son, quickly my child.

And at the gangway were the helping hands of British sailors, men who had fought through five years of bitter war, who had endured the winter Atlantic, the black nights of creeping fog, the cold, the exhaustion, the unceasing danger, who had faced the worst that the enemy could do to them. Some of them had not yet been back to the homes they had longed for for many years. Incurably cheerful and gentle, they manhandled the streams of frightened women and children on board with tireless patience. "Here, Ma, gie' us your hand, I'll carry that bit of a bundle for ye . . . Come on then, son, step up and never fear. Christ is risen. He is risen indeed. Lay hold, my darlin', you're right enough now . . . Wait now, ma love, till I find you a nice snug corner . . . There now, ducks, lay hold of me."

The shouting and the pressure seemed always to increase. A very old man had somehow crawled and wriggled his way to the front of the crowd, where he knelt, holding up a crucifix, as if this symbol could melt the heart of the captain on his special behalf, could make the ships larger, could do the miracle that would save them all and himself in particular. Christ is risen! he shouted despairingly. Would another day's risen sun no longer shine on him? The crowd pressed forward, knocking him over; he disappeared below the trampling feet. Women screamed as the pressure of the crowd crushed them almost to death; already several wretches had fallen off the end of the quay and were struggling in the water with no one to know or care.

Why do I stay? Daisy wondered yet again, but the horror somehow held her. *Goshawk* had now taken more people than she could safely, or unsafely, hold. At the very last moment a little group of children, orphans, perhaps, as they were in charge of a nun, had been thrust on board. The order to cast off was given, but men were clinging to her cables, attempting to swarm up them as *Goshawk*'s engines began to swing her away from the quay. Daisy could see Browning giving the order to cut the cables. In a final mad gesture, she saw the driver of a military truck somehow plough his way through the crowd, regardless of who stood in his way, to the very edge of the quay, as if by some inconceivable method he could save himself and his vehicle by driving it on board the departing destroyer. With a sickening sense of nightmare Daisy saw driver and vehicle pause too late, hang on to the edge of the quay and plunge finally into the harbour water, slowly sinking between shore and ship. No one attempted to rescue him: he would be dead in any case by nightfall. An old woman clutched Daisy's arm, crossing herself, muttering something. He is risen indeed, Daisy replied, automatically—but to look at all this you wouldn't think so.

The lost driver had somehow missed his way to the further wharf, barred off from the crowds, where a confused mass of military stores, trucks and field guns were being hoisted onto two Russian merchant ships, in great haste and in any order. Here also, trucks and field guns were pushed over into the sea in the confusion and lost. On the deck of each ship a leggy midshipman with a party of sailors could be discerned, directing the loading of the holds by gestures, their youthful voices raised in an effort to stow the precious vehicles safely, to reduce the chaos to some sort of order. Without these, the remnant of the Russian Army would be unable to fight on.

"Turns you up, don't it, to have to leave all those poor bug— all those there behind? " a sympathetic sailor confided to Daisy, seeing her stricken face.

Sobbing now, as the gap between *Goshawk* and the quay widened, Daisy was barely able to tell him that if it had not been for him and his mates she and the children would have been a part of that milling crowd, perhaps crushed and hopeless beneath it. And where and how was George Bennett? From the quay, as they drew away, an enormous hopeless groan went up from the abandoned crowd.

On board *Goshawk* there seemed to be a sea of distraught women and crying children everywhere, wringing their hands as the ship drew out to sea and they felt the throb of the engines under them. Fighting their way through the mêlée, sailors were handing out cups of tea and ginger biscuits. The ship was well clear of the harbour now, and even the battleship could not for much longer absorb the huge flow of soldiers, nor the refugees, coming not only from Novorossisk but from all along the coast— regal, aged aristocrats from cypress-girdled villas, who had never believed that this could happen to *them*, or to their pale and beautiful daughters; the terrified wives and sisters of lawyers and doctors from Yekaterinodar; prosperous-looking tradesmen's assistants from up the Volga, Jews from Rostov and Novocherkask, veiled Tartar women from the hill villages. After the supreme effort of escape, *Goshawk*'s quota of such women lay exhaustedly wherever they could find space, staring into nothing, hardly aware of where they were or of how they came there, waving aside the proffered tea, conscious only of a common and bewildered misery. Kicking babies were having their diapers changed on top of coils of cable, and from every corner of the upper deck, in this ship, so light and spear-shaped, and so little adapted to carrying passengers, came the persistent baffled wailing of small children. The pressure of people was terrific; there were legs sprawled and huddled bodies wherever one stepped. Treading her way carefully through them, Daisy was aware of the first lieutenant, patiently sorting out the turmoil and barely able to make himself heard amidst the hubbub. He was accompanied by Varya, translating with lordly curtness, and occasionally tossing back her long black locks to emphasise her detachment from the sordid scene. With the first lieutenant she was less detached, fixing him whenever possible with a dark limpid gaze.

The ship was now well into the open Black Sea, still calm and clear as a summer lake. The twins, who now regarded themselves as sea dogs of long standing, had been allowed on the bridge by the captain, and Ella had attached herself firmly to Riggs.

"Number One," Browning shouted down. "Better bring the lot onto the forecastle. The sea's a millpond and we can sort them out more easily—those that must go to the refugee camp at Salonica and those that have friends at Constant. It's going on noon: better feed them some corned beef sandwiches."

Slowly, as if fearful that they were to be dumped in the sea, the women started to climb down the ladders, to spread out on the deck under the bridge, to move along from the quarterdeck. Like alarmed cattle brought into a strange market, they stared and hesitated, backed nervously the way they had come, glanced nervously sideways, started at the sight of the sea rushing past them. The simple among them, and those who had never left Russia before, far outnumbered the sophisticates, the tall proud nobles wearing their nobility about them like a costly robe, since it was all that remained to them of their ancient splendour, and as such, was to be hoarded and guarded. But all wore a dazed look, not yet able to believe in safety, nor to realise exile.

Out in the bay the *Emperor of India* was decanting some of the thronged Russian soldiers into a surviving Russian destroyer. On the battleship's upper deck the British bluejackets were handing out great chunks of bully beef to the famished Russian soldiers. Many of their fellows lay stretched on the deck in rows, in their fur hats and long overcoats, too exhausted even to eat, sleeping like the dead in the sunlight.

The Admiral stood in conversation with Madame Denikin, welcoming her to his squadron; the General, nearby, sombrely regarding the remnant of the fine army that had come almost within distance of Moscow, only to fail for want of communications. The admiral was an able and much-loved character, known to the sailors, owing to his considerable beard, as Rasputin, or, alternatively, with cheerful blasphemy, as Jesus Christ in Number Ones (Best Uniform). He admired Denikin's brave efforts and felt sorry for him. Denikin, for his part, with an air of medieval courtliness, presented the admiral with a beautiful carved sword in an elaborately decorated scabbard. Invariably polite, Denikin longed perhaps for the onset of a good square meal.

On board *Goshawk*, the first lieutenant had paused on the bridge and was gazing forward with a sad and soulful look on his face. His concern was such that Daisy felt moved to ask him what the matter was. Varya, who thought him wonderfully romantic, drew near to hear, she hoped, a tale of hopeless passion.

"A first lieutenant," he told Daisy sombrely, "is a head housemaid. I'm brooding on what will happen to my fine clean ship if any sort of a sea gets up with this party on board: 'There's not a sea the passenger e'er pukes in/Turns up more dangerous breakers than the Euxine.'—Byron."

Varya could not believe her ears.

"Did he say that?" Daisy asked.

"Who else? Strange how he haunts this part of the world, and the seas round Greece, larger than life, making bad jokes and worse rhymes and being excellent company. I suppose he was a proper nuisance at times. But we could do with more like him."

"Do you write yourself, perhaps?"

"In moments of weakness, yes."

That is more like it, Varya thought.

"I can't tell you how odd it feels to be talking to somebody English!"

"Odd?"

"Very odd, and very nice."

Astern, the smoke of burning Novorossisk rose in the still cold air, a giant black column. Daisy shuddered involuntarily.

The first lieutenant turned to her kindly. "Ever heard of the Sicilian Briton?" he asked. She shook her head. "No, why should you have? He's someone known only to history as that. When Rome fell to the Goths and was sacked, A.D. 410 or some time like that, and everybody was weeping and wailing and St. Jerome in Jerusalem was keening away fit to bust, the Sicilian Briton went on record as saying, 'It isn't the end of the world.' And Britons have been saying it ever since."

"You don't think," Daisy quavered, "that we'll say it once too often?"

"No," the first lieutenant said stoutly.

From a gun in the town shrapnel was now falling ineffectually into the still sea. *Emperor of India* was getting under way for Theodosia. From the crowded wharf the remaining soldiers, convinced at last that there was now no hope of escape by sea, hastened from the town and along the coast in the general direction of Batum or the safety of the Caucasus mountains. They were overtaken next day by the Red Army and slaughtered to a man.

* * *

The simpler folk among the Russian women had had no thought but of escape from the Reds, whose atrocities appeared to take no account of standing, high or low. They were sickened by the tales of horror, and had bolted in a blind precipitate flight. Now freed from these abominable fears, which had filled their minds to the exclusion of all else, they were suddenly made aware of exile, of separation, of the irrevocable departure from the known and loved shape of their lives. With a pang they realised that they were bound for strange countries where no one knew them or would understand their simplest speech. Many of them were still clutching candles, or hard-boiled eggs with brightly decorated shells, and little almond cakes. They looked like children interrupted in the middle of a party and pushed out into the cold dark night.

They gazed landward; suddenly the sight of the vanishing hills of Russia was too much for their overstrained emotions. A dreadful broken-hearted wailing set up. Infecting each other with their grief, women rushed to the ship's side, beat their breasts, held out their arms in wild longing for the shores of home.

"There's logic for you," Able Seaman Burton commented to Daisy. "No sooner snatched from the jaws of death, but what they want to jump back in them. There's no suiting some people."

The wailing rose to a frantic pitch. More women surged to the landward side of the ship, fighting through each other for a last sight of home. "This will never do," Browning shouted above the melancholy din. "They'll be throwing themselves over the side before you know. Can you sing?" he bawled suddenly at Daisy. "Here, you, Thompson—fetch your concertina. Shake up Mr. Tarrant and send him up with his guitar. Riggs, get your fiddle into action. Here, boy, what's your name, Nikolai, sing out to those women in Russian. Tell them for God's sake to keep back from the side. Tell them the ship will sink if they don't."

Nikolai looked blank. "He doesn't mean *sing*, he means *shout!*" Daisy called.

Nikolai, delighted to take command, complied, in the language and tone he had heard his father's steward employ on peasants who were getting things wrong. But his shrill imperious pipe was drowned in the banshee wailing from the forecastle. Amidships, more women were pouring towards the side. *Goshawk* heeled over alarmingly.

"What was that you said in Russian, boy? Repeat it. Repeat the words to me." The captain's voice, in mispronounced Russian, came out with the full ring of authority. "Ah, Tarrant. Now, Miss Pelham, *sing!*"

"Sing what?" Daisy bawled back.

"Sing anything. Anything cheerful, nothing weepy, no perishing laments—anything to divert attention—anything that comes into your head. But for God's sake nothing emotional! Here, Number One, you are up to this sort of thing, you conduct. Keep your eye on him, Riggs. You too, Thompson."

Daisy's mind, hitherto a blank, suddenly cleared. Supported almost at once by the children, she launched into *The Twelve Days of Christmas*. Their thin sound was inaudible against the sorrowful din of wailing women. Then the accordion took up the tune, and the violin; Tarrant's guitar thrummed out; half a dozen sailors who were on the quarterdeck and attempting to stem the rush to the side joined in with a good heart. The wailing voices began to falter in midstream; astonished, their owners gazed incredulously up at the bridge. Slowly the crying dwindled into gulps and sniffs. Some began even, tentatively, to join into a chorus now swelled by the rich bass of Captain Browning, by all those sailors who could sing and by quite a lot who couldn't, even by some of the watch below.

On the fourth day of Christmas my true love sent to me
Four colley birds
Three French hens
Two turtle doves
And a partridge in a pear tree.

"But, Miss Daisy," Ella objected indignantly, "it's *not* Christmas, it's Easter."
"I'm sorry, darling, but I don't know any Easter carols."
"But it's quite, quite wrong, to sing Christmas carols on Easter day!"

On the eighth day of Christmas my true love sent to me
Eight maids a-milking
Seven swans a-swimming
Six geese a-laying
Five go–old rings

"I'm *not* going to sing this on Easter Day!"
"It's not as if we were in church. Think of it as just a song. Look how cheered up all those people are looking."

Four colley birds
Three French hens
Two turtle doves
And a partridge in a pear tree.

Goshawk steamed on through the translucent dark seas, her bow wave, smooth as glass, curving upwards, her white ensign streaming over her straight wake, her decks ringing with a strange but not inharmonious medley of voices, defiantly singing the strange medley of song. She speared her way steadily on towards Constantinople, freedom and exile. To Misha, still swimming to the surface through the clouds of chloroform, still in pain and only dimly aware of the sickbay steward bending over him, the sounds seemed a part of some extraordinary dream.

Some of the irrespressible Russian children were now dancing and clapping their hands.

> . . . . Six geese a-laying
> Five go—old rings

Caught by the singing, distracted for just long enough to halt them from mass hysteria, the refugee women began to settle into little groups about the upper deck, as they were borne on irresistibly into their unknown and desolate future

> Four colley birds
> Three French hens
> Two turtle doves
> And a *PARTRIDGE IN A PEAR TREE*!

Presently they allowed themselves to be comforted by bully-beef sandwiches, slices of cake and mugs of sweet, milky tea. The babies, sustained, fell asleep. The afternoon sun veered round, lay ahead. Children munched their almond cakes, their coloured eggs, their Easter *pashka* and *kulichi*, their round dark heads bent over sticky fingers. The capricious winds of the Euxine mercifully slept.

Chapter 26

Constantinople in the pearly dawn rose out of its mists like a dream city, and the world of freedom, as the Bosphorus narrowed, seemed to Daisy to open like the gateway to a dream life. The water slid gently past as the ship drew to the anchorage, and the refugees, stumbling out on to the upper deck, gazed around them in silent wonder at the domes and the minarets of this fabled city that must now be, at least for a while, their home.

"They'll all be taken ashore, by degrees, during the forenoon," Captain Browning said thankfully, descending from the bridge as his ship was finally secured. "Poor devils—one wonders what their future is. Salonika, and then what? The doctor says the young man has had a good night and you can look in on him after breakfast. But only for a few minutes. In about half an hour. After we've had breakfast."

Misha, propped on pillows, looked very much better, though still in pain. He lay at ease, like a rumpled Caesar, the kind of Caesar who would always fall on his feet, always be hauled on board, always find someone else to shave him. Daisy, on the other hand, felt suddenly shy.

"How do you feel?" she asked him in conventional tones.

"Happy." He flashed Daisy a brilliant mocking smile. "Happy as should a man newly betrothed." With the astonishing resilience of his uncomplicated nature, he seemed fully recovered, and fully affectionate, not to say fully passionate.

"Oh, darling Misha, no! You'll only put your temperature up."

"It is up already."

"The doctor said—"

Reflected sunlight danced on the ceiling, the sound of the children's running feet thudded overhead, through the open porthole a composite smell floated in, made up of harbour water, Turkish coffee, inadequate drains and powerful wafts of Turkish cigarette smoke. Voices shouted from the surrounding brightly painted small boats. In confident tones Misha declared that as soon as he had been to Vladivostok, defeated the Reds and reestablished the new Czar, he would retrieve Daisy and his brethren, rebuild Jevrenskaia, train as an engineer—he had always wanted to be an engineer—and live happily ever afterward.

Could he still be lightheaded, Daisy wondered? But he seemed perfectly serious, and as though this programme presented no insuperable difficulties. His eyes shone, his face glowed. It seemed to Daisy that she loved him with all her heart. But then, she reflected sadly, I have felt this way before. But surely not *quite* this way?

The voice of authority made itself heard amongst the now cheerful hubbub of the refugees in the corridor, and the doctor, entering the cabin, cast one look at Misha's face and bustled Daisy gently but firmly out of the cabin. "The more he can sleep the better, and the captain wants you, about going ashore for a visit to the consulate." Refugees, in their various parties, were being led ashore, and the sailors fell to, clearing up after them.

"Who pays for all this?" Daisy wondered aloud. "Feeding them and everything?"

"We do," the first lieutenant told her cheerfully. "And if we are very lucky, eighteen months later, we all get back three and sixpence from a grateful country. You and your children are the captain's guests. He insisted on it."

"Best not take the children ashore with you yet," Captain Browning advised. "Constant is full of every sort of plague. Use your scarf as a *yashmak* if the smells get too bad. Tarrant will go with you to find the consulate and send a wire home and try and fix your passages. My guess is that your parents will be mightily relieved to know you are here. Dubelsky's report is good; he seems much better. I've put a reliable sailor in charge of the children while you are ashore."

"Oh *thank* you . . . You don't think, perhaps, *two* reliable sailors? The twins have a way of going off in opposite directions."

"Two reliable sailors it shall be." With a marvellous sense of relief and freedom, of being at last able to relax from responsibility, Daisy stepped ashore on the quay.

Constantinople, which no one except its inhabitants had yet thought of calling Istanbul, when seen close to seemed less romantic than it had looked in the dawn light, but equally interesting. Daisy felt a great longing to explore mosques, to drift up narrow alleys, to take a little steamer and go chugging away down the Golden Horn, to wander through palaces and courtyarded houses. But the down-to-earth James Tarrant led her unswervingly to the British consulate, where harassed officials were striving vainly to resist the blandishments of alluring White Russians in haste for Paris, Rome or London, and all claiming, probably accurately, to be close relations of King George or Queen Mary. Yes, Daisy was told, the consul had her father's money, and, yes, there was a French ship sailing late that night for Marseilles, where they could pick up the home-going P. & O. due in there shortly from India, that is if she and the children didn't mind roughing it, and a bit of a squash.

Mind! Goodness no, it's so gorgeous to be going home! And, since both she and Tarrant baulked at the difficulty of getting off a telegram through a Turkish-only-speaking post office clerk, would the consul be enormously kind and send one off to her parents?

He would, and he handed the message and the money to a Turkish messenger who hurried out into the sunlight. Here the messenger reflected that he had had a bad night of sleeplessness and abuse from his wife, and that what he really needed was a cup of coffee and a prolonged moan with his brother-in-law; accordingly he handed the message and the money to his nephew, a scapegrace youth who had recently fallen into bad company and who pocketed the cash, sank the message in the Bosphorus and lit off into the country until the anticipated storm should blow over.

Well satisfied, Tarrant and Daisy came out into the bright hot sunshine, the smells, the cries, the narrow streets. It was too long since Daisy had been footloose in a dazzling foreign city—couldn't they, she urged Tarrant, go for a little stroll? "Since they won't let me even sit with Misha, and the children are in such good hands?"

Nothing had been said, Tarrant admitted, about immediate return; their business had been completed in far less time than he'd thought possible. He was sure that Captain Browning, who was a good enough old sort, would like Daisy to see something of the city; it was a shame to be in Constant for the first time and not have a brief look round. Daisy's eyes shone; Tarrant's gleamed in response. One little stroll led to a further little stroll; at the end of the street was a high cool mosque that must be explored, a square with shady trees, a fountain. After which they were hungry and thirsty, and sat down to consume yoghurt, which led on to kebabs, savoury rice, and thick black Turkish coffee. We really must go . . . Oh, do you think that street leads back? Well, this will be quite as quick a way . . . We aren't actually *lost*, are we? Of course not, just up this street and we'll come on—well, the next street anyway . . . Do you remember that café, and all the pigeons? Yes, but weren't we walking the same way then?

It was nearly four o'clock before a flushed and happy Daisy climbed back on board *Goshawk*.

The two reliable sailors, exhausted, had been allowed ashore. "What have you been doing since then?" "Drinking and playing cards in the wardroom." "Drinking?" "Yes, a lovely kind of fizzy lemonade. Look what I've won! I've won sixpence! And Arkady's won what they call a shilling, which is even more!" Ella said nothing, she was too deeply involved with that forgotten delight, a large piece of toffee. Varya, Daisy noticed, had set up a mild dalliance with the doctor. All seemed to regard H.M.S. *Goshawk* as their happy home.

Warm with the sun, with excitement, with anticipation, Daisy made a dash for the cabin which held Misha. Asleep he might be, but he must wake up soon and be given a mug of tea drowned in revolting condensed milk, and be told all about the city, and her success with the passages. His, too, was booked for a week or two later.

The sun still poured in through the open porthole, since the ship had swung with the tide. The unrelaxed features of the second lieutenant's parents still gazed from the photographs on the chest. A few flies zizzed. The bunk had been neatly made up again, and there was no Misha. She felt, at first, no alarm. He's been moved, he's back in the sickbay, they've moved him into the fresh air, on deck. He was stuffy down here.

A folded paper on the chest caught her eye, the sort of piece of paper that one might either consign to the wastepaper basket or, perhaps, in a moment of idleness, glance at. Daisy snatched it up, having caught sight of a scrawled name: MISS PELHAM. She skimmed the endearments, came to the nub.

> There is a Swedish ship alongside, bound for Shanghai. There may not be another for many weeks. They can take me. There is a doctor to dress my shoulder and my leg, the sailors will shift me, the captain is kind and has lent me the passage money and some more. The ship sails *now*.
>
> When we have defeated the Bolsheviks I will come back. Wait for me. Wait until you are certain without doubt that I am dead. Wait for me, Daisy. I must go, I told you how it is. I love you. I love you very much, more than any girl—
> MISHA.

Under his signature and as if feeling that his last sentence was inadequate, Misha had written in a small crabby writing, "I love you indeed truly."

Daisy was stunned, unbelieving. She sped up the ladder like lightning, as if by arriving on the upper deck she could somehow halt Misha's departure. Defeated, she sped down again, searching dementedly in the captain's day cabin for the large fair form that she knew would not be there. Calling his name, she ran to the sickbay, where a few sailors with mild fever regarded her more feverish face. She ran back to the cabin he had occupied and stood there sobbing and reading his scrawled letter over and over again. Finally, she became very angry.

No, really, she told herself, this is too much! This is too wild, too Russian, too incalculable. How can he leave like this, without any words together, any chance for me to plead, even any proper goodbye? I have never even told him how much I love him. And now it's too late, and what's more, I can't and won't go on loving him. How can one love such a man? He's impossible. Really impossible. I shall stop now, from this minute, ever thinking of him again. As well be in love with the wind. Furiously, she crumpled up his untidy half sheet of paper and threw it out of the porthole, and then, instantly repenting, leant out to see where it had gone.

It bobbed briefly on a dark blue and oily sea. To the west, the sun was in decline, and she could see an ungainly looking cargo vessel making its way down the Bosphorus and into the sea of Marmora. Planks were lashed to the decks—was that the Swedish flag? Against the sun it was impossible to tell. But it seemed likely. And on board, no doubt, was Misha in the saloon, utterly disregarding the doctor's orders to go to bed, failing to keep his leg up, drinking vodka and swapping stories and laughing with his new friends, one might be sure. He would be lounging there at ease, no doubt, impervious to her sorrows, her loneliness, her despair.

The dashing of such hope, such brilliant happiness only three days old, filled Daisy with choking desperation. For a long and desolate moment she doubted his ever having loved her at all. This was succeeded by a fury with herself for having thrown away the only letter she had ever had from him, the only hard piece of evidence that she possessed and one to be lovingly cherished and read and reread in dark times. Her first appalled violence of feeling slowly subsided, but a dull continuous pain filled her heart. She stared unseeingly at the fabled shore, the pencil-fine minarets soaring above the clustered houses, at the glittering sea. All its history, all its heartbreak, all the weariness of the thousands of women immured for life in its harems, seemed summed up in her own.

I thought of all the disasters, she told herself, of everything fearful that could happen, but of this utter desolation of being deserted by Misha I never did think.

The life of the ship—brisk, happy, grumbling, tolerant, intensely purposeful—floated through to her. Men living for years on end and at unbearably close quarters, with great discomfort, no privacy, none of the joys of home. How did they endure it? Remain cheerful through it all? And how was she, now, to endure her life?

Oh Misha, Misha! To the detriment of the second lieutenant's neat white regulation bedspread, Daisy cast herself down on his bunk in a storm of hysterical tears.

From their cardboard frames, reposing upon an imitation leopard-skin cloth that had been the gift of the second lieutenant's servant, and intensely disliked by him, the second lieutenant's parents regarded her stonily, as if she had been guilty of some monstrous impropriety.

Privately, Captain Browning considered that Daisy had much better forget her wayward Misha and turn her mind to the idea of settling with a good reliable countryman. What future had these Russian exiles, poor devils? They would hang around, he supposed, giving music lessons, like those poor blighters of French émigré nobles after *their* revolution. It seemed difficult to picture Misha patiently bent over the keyboard. Well, the world was now wide; he'd find something, settle in Kenya or Rhodesia perhaps. He doubted whether Daisy would soon forget him. These very pretty girls were always wilful, wouldn't be told, were a law unto themselves, went their own way; they always had done and always would do. The captain addressed himself to a mild reprimand for Midshipman Tarrant, who had been expressing himself too freely and publicly as to his dislike and scorn for Lloyd George.

Daisy's stricken white face touched Captain Browning when she came to say goodbye. She told him her sad story. He tried to console her. "Yes, it must have been a shock to you. But go he would. And he was right, you know, my dear girl. I meant to see you first myself, and tell you what had come up, but signals kept arriving, and I got involved. This chance came up and he was right to take it; he had to do a pierhead jump, take a quick decision. Dr. Orme had a word with the Swedish ship's doctor; he knows the form, he'll see to him. No worry there. From Shanghai he can get himself to the fighting, and the Whites aren't doing at all badly in Siberia. There's a rumour that Kolchak has been taken, but if he has, someone else will take charge and fight on. That young man would hate to be out of it. Having lost one round, he's understandably anxious to have another smack at the Reds."

"Oh no! How I hope the fighting is done!"

The captain looked at her with pity. "I've lent him a little money and he's got an old suit of the doctor's, fortunately also a lanky chap. He'll manage. He'll be all right. He's a good manager, I fancy. Must be a born survivor or he'd never have come through that Denikin business. There, I'm sorry—"

Daisy broke into tears. "I was ashore, enjoying myself . . . I never knew . . . I never thought . . . I never dreamed he'd go away like that without even seeing me again."

"Give him his due; he hadn't a chance, and in his present state of health a painful farewell would not have done him much good."

No, thought Daisy, but it would have given me a chance to tell him, to tell him to take care, to tell him how dearly I love him. The futility of telling Misha to take care struck her, and she was silent.

"Look at it this way," the captain went on, in his kind slow tones. "He'd have been in trouble here in Constant. No papers, no legal status, in fact. No nationality, now, and the Turks are naturally edgy about the Russian revolutionaries; who's to say they'll stop in their own country? Revolutionaries don't: they like to spread the gospel. The Turks, they say, are brooding a revolution of their own as well."

"But if I could have *seen* him—"

"He'd have been in trouble with the Turks, and trouble in Turkey is the most long-winded business on earth. They might even, under pressure, or as part of a bargain, have handed him over to the Reds—and you know what his chances would have been then. God knows what has happened to the Czar's family. Dubelsky's done much better to ship himself off to Shanghai. Plenty of White Russians there, I gather, and I've given him a chit to our consul. He'll be all right."

Daisy's pallid face continued to stare blankly past him. She had forgotten the children, forgotten that they were all shortly due on board the French ship. Too much had happened too quickly; she seemed to have gone into a kind of melancholy coma.

Browning shook her very gently by the shoulders, switching with naval briskness from Misha to the practical business in hand. "I'm delighted," he said, handing her a strong whiskey, "to hear you've been so successful over passages, sorry though we'll be to lose you all, as we're off again to the Crimea as soon as we've revictualled and all the rest. And you got your telegram off? I fancy your parents will be mighty relieved to get it; I expect it's some while since any letters got through. And you look as if you could do with some feeding up. Not that England's exactly flowing with milk and honey at the moment, but everything's comparative and at least there are regular rations."

Seeing Daisy incapable of speech, Browning continued to talk. "Mind you get in touch with my wife in Essex if there's any hitch when you arrive. Got her address put away safely? Don't forget to stow all your sparklers away in the ship's safe, will you? There now, dear girl, allow yourself a small weep. Dubelsky's going off must have been a shock, coming on top of everything else. Drink this up—do you good. He'll be all right. A capable fellow, I don't doubt. You might all still be milling about on that quay at Novorossisk. Think of that."

They must be well into the Sea of Marmora by now, Daisy thought. *Shanghai!* It's the other side of the world. He couldn't, if he'd tried, have gone further away. He's gone off to Shanghai as if none of us existed. He was playing me along.

And yet he wasn't. Or *was* he? I'm much too much a run-of-the-mill person for him. And yet I believe he was telling the truth. But Daddy said I was far too ready to believe people, to take things at their face value. I still haven't got deeper than the face of things. I went away lovelorn, to be cured, and now I'm trailing home lovelorn. Not to be cured.

She managed a handshake and warm thanks to Captain Browning and to other *Goshawk* friends, but as the ship's boat sped her across the harbour with the children to board their French liner, she knew, with a kind of stony sadness, that she had lost Misha. In Shanghai there were plenty of White Russians, plenty of his own sort of people, instinctively understanding him, easily loving him. Not hardly and slowly, as I did, not being bewildered and hurt by what he does and doesn't do. Accepting it as natural.

Either he'll settle there or die in horrible Siberia, with all that snow, and ice, and wolves, and Reds. In a flash of recollection, she saw Misha laughing at her for these sentiments, and felt better. She, too, would soon be amongst her own sort of people, understanding her, loving her as she was, not separated by an alien inexplicable way of going about things, a remoteness of thought and feeling.

"I am sad that Misha has gone," Ella said, being put to bed a night or two later. "But he saved us all, didn't he, Miss Daisy?" The sequence of events had become slightly confused in her mind. "He came back just in time to save us all."

Daisy had not the heart to tell her that their salvation had been accomplished rather by *Goshawk* and her ship's company, and by the contrivance and forethought of George Bennett of the unfashionable bathing suit.

Chapter 27

Tilbury, the rainy dockland, the policemen in their domed helmets, the merchandise sheds and the flat green fields beyond presented themselves to Daisy as endearing and welcome, to the Dubelsky children as something considerably less. But where were her parents, their message, their telegram?

Kind Commander Browning had alerted his wife, crop-haired and jolly; she appeared in a small rattling car and drove them all off to her small rattling cottage in Essex. Here the wind blew the latched doors open, swept the curtains onto the dressing tables in the tiny bedrooms and carried Ella's precious ikons off them and onto the floor. To Daisy the bright fields and green lanes were delectable and fresh even under their driving rain, but the children were restless and disappointed. Rain streamed down the windowpanes and the telephone lines to Leicestershire remained continuously busy.

The children missed the company and challenge of shipboard life. "What is there to *do* in England?" Arkady asked Daisy in tones not quite low enough.

Mrs. Browning, unquenchably kind and hospitable, offered the twins free range over the railway system of her absent prep-school sons, and presently summoned them all warmly to supper—which consisted of baked beans and scrambled eggs. There was no wine, and margarine where there should have been butter. "You'll soon get your ration books," their hostess said comfortably, "and then it will be easier. Have some more, Tanya; is it Tanya?" She pronounced the name as if saying "tanyard."

Varya regarded her sombrely, and her refusal, though politely worded, came out with an ungracious effect. "I don't like this pretend butter," Ella said suddenly and loudly; while Daisy became uneasily aware that they were all wolfing the supplies which probably constituted the week's rations for Mrs. Browning and her cook-housekeeper. Their hostess's unstinted kindness, her readiness to share the little that she had, made Daisy blush for her unthinking brood with their incurably lavish notions. Their months of near starvation seemed to have dropped out of their consciousness as if they had never been.

By half past seven the lines were at last free, and Daisy waited with trembling joy to hear her father's or her mother's voice. Over the line came nothing but a flat heavy Leicestershire voice unknown to her—not Mrs. Wilson, not Nelly, not Ethel. The voice, which clearly looked upon the telephone as a dangerous newfangled invention liable to explode at any moment, spoke and listened at a distance from the instrument. It declared that there was no Mrs. Pelham there, nor Mr. neither, and this was Mr. Bulstrode's house, and she couldn't say where Mr. Pelham was nor Mrs. neither.

"You're not Nelly?" Daisy queried with diminishing hope. What was going on?

"No, miss, there's no Nelly here nor has been this long while." After which the nerve of the unknown voice broke and it hurriedly hung up and retired to the kitchen to make itself a cup of tea.

There seemed nothing to do but try the Kettles. Daisy imagined the ringing in the anteroom under the antlers and the Sartorius, and the measured tread of Collins coming to answer it. His at least would be a familiar voice, a voice whose owner would know where her parents had got to.

But to Daisy's surprise Lady Kettle herself answered. Times must indeed have changed.

"My dear Daisy! You are actually back quite safe! How wonderful, my dear!" The voice sounded as full, rounded and comfortable as ever; maybe times were not all that changed. The voice had the grace to sound warmly delighted. "How pleased your dear father and mother will be! Did you see any Bolsheviks? Isn't it *dreadful* what's going on in Russia now? Worse than the French Revolution! How *relieved* your parents will be!"

"Lady Kettle, it is *very* nice to hear your voice. But my parents—I don't know where they are! I tried ringing up, but—"

"Oh, my dear—they left here almost a year ago. Well, actually, I think it was September. Your father was offered another living. Herefordshire, I think. No—it was Warwickshire. Wait a moment while I think. No, I'm almost certain it was Herefordshire. Your mother wanted a milder cli-

mate, but I can't myself *believe* it is so very different. We miss them all
dreadfully—I still can't think why they went. Reggie doesn't care much
for Mr. Bulstrode, between ourselves. I told him how it would be, but he
never listens. It was all because it was the Bishop's turn, but Reggie could
have held out and argued with him. As it is . . . , yes, I mean the Bishop's turn to appoint to the living here. I feel sure that with a *little* patience
he would have seen the force of Reggie's point of view. Their address? I
know I've got it somewhere, but unhappily my address book is being
rebound. Reggie might know, but he's at this meeting. You'd find a great
many changes here, you know. Collins has had to give up and we haven't
replaced him. A parlourmaid only, and she gets in such a muddle with
the wine. You must come and see us, Daisy dear, I am longing to hear all
about the Bolsheviks and everything—If you'll hold on, dear, I'll see if I
can lay my hands on their address. It's so unfortunate—Here's Richard.
It's *Daisy,* darling, you know, Daisy Pelham, back safely from the Bolsheviks, and I'm sure she's longing to tell—No, just a minute, Richard
darling, I must just let her know. You heard, Daisy, that Richard lost his
arm, dear, didn't you? His *left* arm. We must be thankful for small mer-
cies." Poor, poor Richard, thought Daisy. "I'll see if I can lay my hand on
it, but I'm almost positive it was *somewhere* in Warwickshire. The other end
of the county from ours. We had such a pretty Christmas card from them.
We miss them all very much. Here's Richard. He lost it at the Somme. The
second day—"

Richard's voice was assured and happy. "Daisy, my dear old girl! I
can't tell you how pleased I am to hear your voice! How are you? How did
you get out? Did you have a ghastly time?" The welcome might be lacking in romance, but certainly not in warmth.

"No. We were very lucky, but it's marvellous to be back. You sound
exactly the same." Strange to think how one once trembled to hear that
slow, lazy voice.

"I am, pretty well. And you? I'm the same minus an arm and plus a
wife and two children. I wish you were all still here! Crikey, you should
meet Mr. Bulstrode! He wears buckle shoes and waves incense about the
place and his wife gives piano recitals and won't go near the Women's
Institute. I mean, they'd be fine in Birmingham or somewhere, but imagine sending them here! Heart of a good hunting country! I mean, it's
absurd!"

His voice went on—light, unselfconscious, unconcerned. Either he has
totally forgotten that I once loved him very much, or else, more probably,
he never knew. How daft girls are! How daft *I* was anyway! Such a song
and dance and six years' exile about something that meant nothing, lit-
erally nothing, to the other half of this *grande passion.* I was simply a good
companion, someone he liked being with and kissed whenever he felt
particularly randy and wanted a cuddle.

"Poor old Dad has apoplexy every Sunday service and Mother moans
your parents' departure every month when it's W.I. night, and lots of

other times as well. And guess what? We've no horses, and poor old Barrett's learning to drive. He never will; he's an absolute menace. Thirty miles an hour, always on the crest of the road and shies whenever he sees another car coming. Oh, I'm all right. Soldiering on. Learning a bit about farming. Jill's all right. You remember her? Jill Mount? Two boys. Yes, they're all right. Amusing little beggars. Tom, the eldest one—But what about you, Daisy? You didn't marry a Russky after all? Your father was scared stiff you'd marry a Russky. A beastly Muscovite and all that."

"No, I never married a Russky." Although I wanted to marry two, she sighed inwardly.

"There must be something wrong with the Russkys, then. Well there is, isn't there? Plenty wrong, poor blighters. After all those years—four, five was it? You'll see some changes all round here. Nothing is the same, but we soldier on."

The same old "Let's Pretend," thought Daisy—the same old stiff upper lip. We soldier on, with one arm and no butler, and no horses and an unsatisfactory parson. The same old never say die, the same old not knowing what has hit us, and ignorance of a world in convulsions and of Christian people cutting up women and children into small pieces like in *Macbeth* nine hundred years ago. They are good and brave, and soon I shall think again exactly as they think, and forget the ravening outside world—but is it good enough? At any rate, he and I are friends, and it's all easy again, and that at any rate is a comfort.

She was back to being dear little Daisy, and Richard was back to teasing her again, with a pleased edge in his voice all the same. "So you actually never married a Russky, Daisy, after all. Were they all Bolsheviks? Your father, bless him, will be so pleased that you never did."

"No," Daisy said, suddenly recovering her spirits. She spoke in level tones. "I never married a Russky, but I've come back with four Russian children. Four, in six years."

"*What?* What did you say, Daisy? Here, hold on, Mother, we're talking."

But his mother ruthlessly removed the instrument from his astonished grasp. "I've been lucky enough to find the address, Daisy dear. It was on the back of their Christmas card. I generally send them away to the orphanage in Brinkstone, they love to have them, you know, for the children to stick into scrapbooks, but this one was so particularly pretty that I kept it. No, it wasn't Warwickshire. Nor Hereford. I don't know why I thought of Hereford. I used to stay there a lot, as a girl, and it was such a pretty county. Funnily enough, it was *Worcestershire.* I knew it was somewhere in the west. Oh dear, now I've dropped the card. Richard darling, where are you? Would you very kindly pick it up for me? Ah yes, Werrington Rectory, near Worcester, Worcestershire. That's pretty country too, I believe, though I've never stayed in Worcestershire, only driven through on the way to Ireland. My dear, have you *heard* about Ireland? Poor Reggie has been told not to go to his fishing on the Blackwater this year; he's been told it's inadvisable—the troubles—so he's missing it for the first time in seventeen years, can you imagine it? Yes, that is it, Worcestershire. Of course you must ring them up straight away. Come and see us soon. It's been delightful hearing all about Russia, and we're all *delighted* you are back safe. I shall tell Reggie as soon as he gets back from his meeting and I know how pleased he will be . . . Yes, of course you must. Oh, and just one more thing—can you imagine it, the Bulstrodes have painted those handsome iron gates of the Rectory *rust* red. Tell your parents; they will be horrified. Your father and mother always had such good taste. It's the last colour they would have chosen; they wouldn't have *dreamed*—goodbye then, dear—" Lady Kettle was disappointed to hear the click of the telephone; Daisy had hung up before she had had time to recount to her even half of the local disasters, changes and chances.

"No, I'm sorry, Richard darling, she's rung off. Where from? I've no idea. I hope she hasn't lost her looks, away all that while; she must be getting on. She had such a pretty complexion. I wonder she didn't marry some Russian or other."

"Well, I don't know—" Richard began, and stopped, overcome briefly by discretion. He was less open, his mother reflected, than the Richard who had gone off so gaily to war in 1914, in the days when they were all so certain that it would be over by Christmas. Perhaps it was as well that such a very pretty girl as Daisy, for whom he had always had a *tendresse,* was no longer domiciled right under his nose. The war had been so unsettling in that sort of way. And indeed in others. Lady Kettle brooded a moment, sadly, over the scarcity of kitchen maids and the marked deterioration in their manners, and in another moment had forgotten Daisy. There were no genuine dramas, no true events, except those occurring within her own family or her own immediate neighbourhood. The rest of the world led a phantom life, and would not, unless its activities impinged directly upon her, ever achieve reality. How otherwise should one stay sane? She had known Daisy from infancy and liked her well enough, but would have been quite as content had she stayed permanently in Russia.

Richard, on the other hand, continued to feel worried about her at least until breakfast next morning when some agricultural news in the local paper drove her comfortably out of mind.

Replacing the receiver, Daisy sat down with a sigh.

The rain had now ceased beating on the panes of Mrs. Browning's mock-Elizabethan windows, and outside in the dank dripping evening a few blackbirds were indomitably singing. The loss of her longed-for home was a sharp blow to Daisy. So that had been the news in all those letters that failed to arrive at the Villa Rosa! The thought that she would never again sleep in her old bedroom, with the rosebud wallpaper that she had been wont to condemn as soppy, and the piece of sloping roof over the washstand, would never again swing round that particular landing or dash down those particular stairs, struck with unexpected heaviness on her heart. No more swoops on the swing hanging from the copper beech at the end of the garden, no more familiar walks and rides, no stable yard with Mouse looking out over her half-door, no ripe apricots all warm from the kitchen garden wall, no complaining Broadbent lumbering home to his cottage in the dusk.

And none of those pleasant neighbours whom she had known from infancy, welcoming her into their houses, telling her their news, listening to her own—a countryside of customary friendliness had been whisked away overnight. There would be even a different church, with a different smell of old stone and unknown memorials on its walls, unfamiliar stained glass windows and church bells that sounded an unfamiliar chime. Countless times she had pictured going into her father's study and taking out his books and blowing the dust off them and putting them back again, all the while muttering remarks at him over her shoulder that would be instantly understood. The whole framework of a world of acceptance and love had been, after six years of longing for it, proved insubstantial as a dream.

Now she was a stranger everywhere—not Russian, not loved by the man she loved, not from Leicestershire, with its rolling hills and green pastures—English still, but displaced and uprooted. She had lost, seemingly forever, a local habitation and a name. Her mind fed itself on gloom. What have they done, she asked herself passionately, about Spot's grave, and Tiger's? Who now would cut the grass on them and push those dog-sized tombstones straight? Her mind fastened itself with peculiar intensity upon this comparatively slight grievance. Outside, gently but persistently, the rain had started to fall again, and even the blackbirds were muted.

The kind voice of her hostess was heard suggesting a cup of Ovaltine. Daisy turned her back on the disconsolate evening. England might drip rain, but at least she didn't drip blood. There was, after all, infinite reassurance in being home.

The rain fell quietly and steadily all night. At three in the morning Daisy woke to find Arkady, in a very long nightshirt that he had somehow gleaned on his way to England, standing in the doorway with a stricken face. "Where is *our* mother now?" he demanded miserably. "Who can tell me that?" His eyes, stern and piercing, searched Daisy's face. Momentarily, all the childhood had gone from him; he was a man, with a man's grief. Not even the absurdly large nightshirt, clinging to his stringy boy-legs, could take away from the massive dignity of his sorrow. Daisy could find him no answer; the facile consolation died on her lips. As if bleakly aware that this was something he must come to terms with on his own, Arkady departed as silently as he had come, leaving Daisy to lie awake till dawn brought the singing of the blackbirds and thrushes she had so much longed to hear.

London looked essentially the same, but sadder and shabbier, the front doors and iron railings of her handsome squares no longer glossy with new paint. And during the long taxi ride from Liverpool Street Station to Paddington, the cockney taxi-driver failed to volunteer a single joke or make a solitary wry comment upon life and times. The very stations wore the same weary look, of scruffy rolling-stock and carriage seats with worn-out upholstery. Rain dripped intermittently from leaking panes in their glass roofs. Even at wayside country stations the people on the platforms looked worn and dispirited. To Daisy's dismal fancy the very horses waiting between the shafts of carts in station yards seemed to hang their heads. Where was that spick and span look she remembered so well and so affectionately and whose continuance she had always taken for granted?

No longer were there small flowerbeds on the little stations, carefully built up against their white-painted wooden palings and crammed with wallflowers, polyanthus and daffodils, and surrounded with tenderly arranged whitewashed flints. Sadly she realized that the men who would have seen to such matters were lying dead in Flanders. The absence of the flowerbeds struck her keenly, bringing home forcibly the reason for such lack.

Will we ever recover? Daisy wondered, as the changeless green of the west countryside flashed past her. There was not a family in the British Isles, Mrs. Browning had told her, that had not lost a son, a father, a brother, a nephew or an uncle. Whole villages were bereft of their menfolk, whole streets of the cities held only widows or orphans or old grieving parents. And for those lucky ones at long last come home, there was no work to be found, no money to pay for the work.

Britain had poured out her blood like water in the common cause, Mrs. Browning had said with cheerful realism; it was small wonder that her people looked wan and debilitated. And not only her blood. All the accumulated wealth of centuries had been spent, much on her own war expenses, and a far greater sum on shoring up her crumbling allies on the Continent. With the sad realism born of long experience in lending money to allies, she had forgiven her debtors; but had not been forgiven the much smaller debt she owed America, who had lent in goods and services and now was insisting on being repaid in gold. And of gold there was now virtually none.

In her overpopulated islands Britain must live by trade, and her trade was in ruins. During the three years between the war's outbreak and America's entry into it, U.S. traders had quietly and not surprisingly taken over the markets of the Western World which Britain could no longer supply. In the East, Japan had done the same. Not only wealth, but the means of regaining it were gone. An exhausted people, their natural leaders skimmed off by war, were left with what felt like an insoluable problem.

The green hills were rising more steeply now into the contours of the west. Daisy reminded herself sharply of the need for those who had borne the burden and heat of the day not to be disagreeable about those who had not. Of the victors, France had suffered worse than England, and as for poor Russia!

"Why does England have such tiny, *tiny* fields?" Nikolai demanded a trifle loftily. A signal box with one of its windows cracked slid past as the train slowed down. Had all been washed away in the tide of loss? Daisy wondered—London pride, and the smart and competent efficiency of such honoured institutions as the Great Western Railway?

At the junction, where they changed trains for Werrington, Daisy looked eagerly out for her parents. But the delivery of a telegram in deep country was, as she knew, a chancy matter, dependent as often as not on whether the postmistress's ten-year-old nephew had or had not gone fishing that morning. On the platform instead was an elderly lady making an enormous bustle about the disposal of her luggage on the porter's cart. He was a young man of eighteen or nineteen, too young to have been in the war, Daisy thought, or to have had more than a few months of it. His manner, patiently redistributing the baggage, according to the old woman's agitated directions, held everything of tolerance and nothing of servility, and as he turned to face Daisy to take her suitcases from her and add them to the cart, his grave young face creased at the temple with an almost imperceptible wink. The old woman, in whom a lifetime of preoccupation with her possessions had bred an extremely sharp glance, turned a suspicious gaze on Daisy, as if someone else's luggage must infallibly carry the germs of leprosy.

"I thought *I* had engaged your services," she told the porter with such vicious energy that Daisy made a movement to retrieve her offending baggage.

"That's all right, miss," the porter said, unmoved by his client's sharpness of tone, well acquainted with the vagaries and bitterness of old age, and fully accepting them. He led the way along and across the platform, explaining to the old lady in kindly terms that the express had been late and the local train would be off in five minutes. "Plenty of time," he added soothingly. Exuding an untroubled amiability, he accepted a small, mean tip from the old lady and a lavish one from Daisy with equal good grace, but a splendid broad grin creased his face from side to side as he touched his cap to Daisy and departed, whistling, down the platform.

Daisy forgave the station its down-at-heel look, the dripping roofs, the peeling paint. While there are still people like that porter, like Florence Farmborough, patiently and devotedly nursing the wounded and stricken Russians in their bitter retreats, while there were people like the officers and men of the *Goshawk,* we would recover. It might take a hundred years—but we would recover.

A fine and gentle rain was now falling over the undulating fields, the small wandering streams, the banks of primroses, the trees just struggling into leaf. This, to Daisy, was unknown country. Nonetheless, the overwhelming joy of return mounted in her. Even Misha and his desertion were forgotten as the train puffed steadily up the green inclines towards her waiting family.

The homecoming itself proved uproariously heartwarming and successful. Mrs. Pelham was all happiness and welcome, and the plight of the exiled and perhaps orphaned Dubelskys completely engaged her sympathies. Any jealousy that she had felt at Daisy's prolonged stay with them in Russia melted at the first sight of these unusual and handsome children, with their courtly manners and their wan faces. Long may this last, thought Daisy, hoping fervently that her mother's heart would become inextricably engaged before the other aspect of these travel-worn darlings made itself too evident. Mrs. Pelham bustled about in a state of pleasurable fuss, at once engaging and silly, as if it enormously mattered that Varya should have a bedspread to match the blankets on her bed, that Ella's room should face east and get the morning sun, that the twins should have enough cream on their breakfast porridge. Virginia and Jenny, caught up in the general euphoria and excitement, hauled out the old doll's baby carriage for Ella, showed her the doll's house, lent Varya their dresses and taught her the latest way to do her hair. Mrs. Wilson and Nelly, who had come with the Pelhams to Werringham, cooked and cleaned for the extra children with enthusiastic sympathy, confronting them daily at every teatime with bigger and better layer cakes—since Mrs. Wilson's brother was a grocer and knew where to lay his hands on an extra pound or two of sugar and butter, and had no hesitation in doing so, now that the war was over and rationing no more, in his view, than a tiresome government fad.

With her father's look of beaming relief Daisy could find no fault. Here at last was one who would truly listen—absorbed, horrified, fascinated—to her traveller's tales. He welcomed the children with open arms, read stories to Ella, encouraged Varya to talk French to him and set out at once to build a tree house for Nikolai and Arkady in the garden beech tree. He seemed in no hurry to discuss their future, their finances, their education. He seemed simply brimming with delight to have them all there, and his daughter safe at home under his own roof. How dreadfully I have missed talking to him all these years, Daisy thought. We shall never catch up with all there is to tell, and hear. And one couldn't help, she reflected, but bask a little in the feeling of being once again a hugely important and valued part of a family, instead of a useful adjunct hovering on its fringes.

"Prices have risen horribly," her mother told her. "You can't get a good pair of shoes for less than a pound! And that little doll I bought Ella for a shilling would have been threepence halfpenny before the war! We are so fortunate that Cousin Blanche quite unexpectedly left your father her money, so that we are just about the same as we were before the war."

"Which was? In those days I never used to think about such things, except that I knew that theatres, and taking too many taxis, were extravagances. And leaving the lights on all night in the hall."

"You remember how it was, darling—not rich but comfortable."

To Daisy everything about England seemed comfortable. Hearing the chink of milk bottles delivered every morning, seeing the slow-speeched, kindly policeman strolling so unthreateningly down the village street, being greeted by shopkeepers only too willing to sell her food and clothes, even postwar England with its railway strikes and unemployed returned soldiers seemed to Daisy a haven of unbelievable peace, order and prosperity. "You don't know the bliss of feeling safe again, and with enough to eat," she told her parents.

They noted with pleasure that she was putting on weight, losing her drawn expression, recovering her looks. She even began to accept invitations to tennis and dances from the neighbours. Perhaps after all, they reflected, the Russian experience would fade from her mind, had not proved the shipwreck of her matrimonial chances. Almost automatically, Mrs. Pelham began to cast about in her mind for suitable young men. Alas, if only so many of the right sort hadn't been killed in the war! Mr. Pelham simply hoped that Daisy's laugh would gradually grow less hectic and that she would think of something that she really wanted to do. At least she had grown into a woman—responsible and serious.

At nightfall Daisy's thoughts would turn with longing to Misha. Why had he not sent one word, one whisper, from Shanghai? It must surely be a place where pen and paper and stamps were to be had by anybody who really wanted to lay hands on them. If one wanted to enough, one could write, send a telegram, a message through the consulate. China wasn't a desert island. Oh Misha, Misha! His long figure still moved triumphantly through the landscape of her mind, strode through her heart, but each week, gradually, imperceptibly, the sound of the footfalls grew less loud, the tread fell more lightly.

Chapter 28

For a cavalryman, Misha reflected, he had spent a great deal of the war on foot. Once more he trailed over the stony hillsides in retreat. His foundered horse had had to be shot, some time since, but now he and his companion had at least acquired a small, tough Mongolian pony on which they were proceeding in turns. Misha almost preferred to walk, since his

feet all but touched the ground when he rode; they also wished to spare
the poor beast as much as possible in order to sell it for enough food to take
them through to Manchuria. He and his surviving companion, Vassily
Ivanof, said very little as they tramped on. There was very little to
say.

Before Misha ever set sail from Constantinople, Admiral Kolchak's
cause had failed; he had been shamefully betrayed to his enemies and was
now dead. His allies had failed to help him, his supplies had dried up, and
now the White Russian state of Eastern Siberia had collapsed. The last
struggles fought by the remnants of the White Army, retreating ever
eastward, had petered out in a series of pointless skirmishes. Desperate
strongholds up inhospitable valleys held out for a few weeks; there were
sorties doomed only to prolong the agonies of the war, despairing ambushes in precipitous valleys, after which the dying as well as the dead
had to be left lying for the beasts and the birds. There was every horror of
a lost cause—the rains sweeping down at night on fallen friends, the
voices crying out of the darkness: "Finish me off, Misha, don't leave me to
the Reds! Shoot me, Prince, shoot me, I beg of you, Prince! Mihail
Andreivitch, in the name of the Mother of God!" And then the horrible
work of mercy and the leaving of the bodies for the vultures and the
wolves, the tearing maws of crow and fox. Finally, the end of the ammunition. By then even Misha had had enough.

The cause of Holy Russia, he firmly believed, could not fail forever, but
must now bide its time. Europe was not a ship of fools, despite plenty of
evidence to make one think so. She would understand in due course the
folly and wickedness of Marxism, based as it was on ignorance of history
and on false science, and apt as it was to seize and exploit for its own vile
ends the diverse miseries of man. So Misha consoled himself, trampling
the shingly borders of a river in the cold gathering of dusk.

Vassily Ivanof, son of an exiled Russian lawyer, had persuaded him to
take refuge in Kanto, in the southeast corner of Manchuria, in what he
admitted was a poor little Korean homestead, his parents' home since his
father had fallen into disgrace under the Czardom for the propagation of
some mildly liberal ideas. It was a bitter country, Vassily told him,
scoured by dry bitter winters, swept by summer rain, and having a growing season of only 150 days, though there was grassland and rich brown
soil. To the east, where he lived and worked as a woodman in more normal
times, there were high mountains and forests. Sometime, perhaps during
Kanto's hot short summer next year, it should be possible to cross these
mountains and escape through Korea by sea to Europe. His own parents
were aging, and Vassily himself had given up all notion of escape during
their lifetime: "Without me they would undoubtedly perish."

Any port in a storm, thought Misha. The thought of a roof of any kind,
and of a hot meal cooked on a stove, was infinitely enticing. The edges of
his greatcoat were frayed away, his elbows protruded. Tufts of yellow
hair sprouted through his worn and battered fur hat. Hard riding and

short commons, and latterly hard walking, had sharpened the lines of his face, and incidentally enhanced his good looks. The rough roundness of youth had fallen from him. He looked gaunt and grim.

They wound their way through cold hills and splashed across the shallows of wide rivers where great sheets of ice were borne past them headlong to the sea. The Mongolian pony had to be sold a fortnight before they came at last by rough cartroads to the far southeast of Manchuria, where Vassily's parents were living out their exile in a small wooden house at the end of a Korean village. They welcomed Vassily with wild cries of delight, and Misha with warmth and kindness. Only for a day was he Prince, only for another two days was he Mihail Andreivitch. Within half a week he was Misha, and had gone to work with Vassily at the felling on the hillside a mile or so from the village.

Terenty Sergeivitch Ivanof, Vassily's father, had a thin clever face, a gentle voice, and a lame leg; his wife, Serafima, was plump and silver-haired. Both thirsted for every detail of news from Russia, and sighed and wept over what there was of it to be had. Exile had made them sad but not bitter: Terenty beguiled his days by learning all the local dialects; his gentleness and intelligence had made him friends in the neighbourhood. How came the Czarist government, Misha wondered, to exile such as Terenty and leave so many real firebrands at large? In return for shelter and succour, Vassily's parents asked only of Misha that he should avoid any action liable to make them conspicuous, that he should lie low.

"Everywhere now," Terenty told Misha, sitting over the stove in the evening of his fourth day, "we White Russians live on sufferance. We carry only the passports of a dead power. We have no political standing, no official representation. We have no one to whom to appeal in persecution or difficulty. We are sitting targets. The Japanese police who dominate Kanto are very suspicious of Russians. Since the Treaty of Portsmouth in 1905, following our disastrous war, the Japanese in Manchuria are what Imperial Russia once was—the paramount power. It is therefore very very necessary not to offend them." Terenty gazed seriously at Misha, who endeavoured to transform his bold defiant face into a submissive shape.

"The Manchus, the people of this country, are all but gone, dispersed," Terenty continued sadly. "The Chinese pour into Manchuria, their two warlords Chen and Li Lien-Ching contend for power. Chen has taken my other son, Pavel, to fight in his army. There was no argument—they took him away. Four years ago, and now his mother and I do not know whether he is alive or dead. The Chinese too, as well as the Japanese, call us filthy Russians, homeless nobodies. Anyone—Chinese, Koreans, Japanese—have the right to do what they will to us now." The old man's voice sank to a sad whisper. "We are exiled. We are despoiled. We are a reproach to all the nations of the earth."

By no effort of the imagination could Misha transmogrify himself into a filthy Russian or a homeless nobody. Nor did he see the need. But his heart, not yet high after his privations and the long trek to this inhospitable land, sank into his boots. There must be no waiting for the short hot summer, this or the next. He must get away to the sea at the very first possible chance.

In a corner of the room Serafima was praying steadily, her voice full of yearning. Ending, she sat down heavily. "Ah, to worship in a house of God once more!" she cried.

"Peace, peace, Sima," the old man answered her. "Do not trouble your heart with vain wishes. Even were we at home in Russia now, the house of God no longer stands." Vassily sat silent at the table, working a piece of wood with his knife.

For now, thought Misha, rolling himself up in his rug to sleep, I must live this peasant life and be thankful. Through his drowsiness he could hear Serafima insisting to her husband that no matter what the Bolsheviks did, the house of God stood forever. To make sure that Misha was comfortable, she padded across the earthen floor towards him in her Chinese cloth shoes. Her kind head bent over him; she patted his rug very lightly, and slippered away again. The *kang*, the raised platform, was hard lying, but Misha slept.

He woke early, in the still greyness of cockcrow. He felt a sense of refuge, kindness, and safety in which his thoughts turned to Daisy tenderly and sadly. The cocks crowed louder and more lustily; there was a bleat of goats, the noise of Korean voices engaged in a mild wrangle. With hazy melancholy, Misha's thoughts dwelt upon Daisy, upon her infinite remoteness and the unlikelihood of his ever seeing her again. She is my love, he thought. I don't know how this came about, or why—but so it is.

In Worchestershire the lush and peaceful valleys were bright green under a summer sky, but in Werringham Rectory the situation had undergone a gradual deterioration. Jenny, deprived in Varya's interests of a cherry-colored velvet dress that she had hardly worn and was still fond of, had reacted unfavourably when Varya had decided, three weeks later, that the colour was unsuitable and unbecoming and dumped it in a crumpled heap back on her bed. An over-enthusiastic Arkady had broken one of the blades of the mowing machine—obsolete and so irreplaceable—on the same morning that Nikolai was discovered to have left the field gate open, thus allowing the entry of a dozen trampling bullocks into the newly planted shrubbery. Ella had decided that Marie-Celestine was too old for a doll's carriage and had left it in the coalshed, but had managed to break most of a doll's tea-set still dear to the heart of the adult Virginia. Even Nelly, despite extra wages, complained at the amount of extra

washing, and Barton, the new parlourmaid, could be heard muttering in
the pantry about the regular baptism of jam endured by her tablecloths.

Daisy had handed her father one of the large uncut emeralds. Feeling
self-conscious, he had taken it to his London banker, who had told him
where best to dispose of it. The firm in question named a sum so staggering that Mr. Pelham was bereft of comment. "Or you might do better if
we were to put the gem in our next auction?" they suggested, mistaking
his stunned silence for dissatisfaction with their offer. Mr. Pelham hurriedly placed the emerald in his bank's safe and went to see his lawyer,
who told him that he must form a trust fund for the Dubelsky children,
and appoint trustees to administer it. Had he not better stay up another
night at his club and consider the matter? How very complicated, thought
Mr. Pelham, a simple thing like taking in children becomes! Even to a
heart that was sensible, kindly and not bothered by legal niceties, it
seemed an awkward situation: he was not the children's guardian, legal
or otherwise, and neither was Daisy. He foresaw a train of complications
of a legal nature, as well as a series of unauthorised decisions as to their
education, careers, even their marriages; he prayed to get it all right.

For some undefined reason, some irrational hope that she declined to
put into words, Daisy had not disclosed, even to her father, the extent of
the Dubelsky hoard. He would have made her bank the jewels. The Russian Revolution and their flights from it had left Daisy with a deep
feeling that no institution was really safe. Lawyers could abscond; banks
could be rifled by wild soldiery or their funds be claimed by sudden
changes of government. She kept the jewels in a shoebox at the back of her
underclothes drawer, innocently supposing that no burglar would search
there. The secret troubled her—she felt dishonest and guilty of disloyalty
to parents who deserved no such treatment.

During the night Mr. Pelham had a bright idea. He had heard at his
club that some of the public schools were offering places to penniless
Russian refugee boys, but Nikolai and Arkady were too young, and in
any case, not, it seemed, penniless. He hated to send them away, two years
too late, to a tough English prep-school, and he had let them run wild all
summer with only an hour of Latin and mathematics which he taught
them himself every morning. They had objected to Latin, on the grounds
that it would be of no use in the forthcoming struggle to retrieve Russia,
but on being assured that mathematics certainly would be needed, they
had consented out of good manners to learn Latin at their host's whim.
But now the autumn term was approaching and something must clearly
be done. Ella was to share a governess with a family in the village, and
Varya, more to her own delight than Jenny's, was to accompany Jenny
back to her school in Wiltshire.

After breakfast, Mr. Pelham rang up a friend in Worcester, and subse-
quently departed there with both the twins, returning late for lunch.
There were pleased expressions on all three faces.

"They passed the voice test with flying colours," he announced delightedly, "and they can both be taken next term, by the greatest good luck. It won't mean leaving home; Barlow can drive them in in the trap every morning and one of us can fetch them in the car in the evenings, and of course there'll be games, and the education is quite excellent, I believe." He beamed proudly at Daisy.

To Mr. Pelham's amazement he found Daisy in opposition to this plan for the boys: it was their first argument since her return, and it shook both of them. How could she object to the famous Cathedral choir school?

"Would they have to sing in the cathedral?"

"Yes, they would. That's the point. They get a wonderful musical training, pleasant to them for the rest of their lives, whatever they grow up to do, and an excellent education into the bargain. Let's just hope their voices don't break too early."

"I am very sorry, Father, but I don't think it will do. I don't believe their parents would like it."

"But whyever not? They'd come home here every night, and they would have each other as support against bullying, if that's what you fear."

"Oh no! It's because of singing in the services every day. They are Orthodox, you see. Their church is, I mean."

"Orthodox are Christians, aren't they? If the boys were still in Russia they wouldn't be allowed any religion at all," Mr. Pelham objected.

"The thing is, that they mind very much. The Orthodox, I mean. We think of them as other Christians, and not very impressive ones, with all that assassination and torture going on in Russia, but they think of us as hardly Christians at all—heretics and quite beyond the pale. They think Roman Catholics are almost as bad, just a rather more archaic and slightly more respectable kind of Protestant. And, so, I think they would hate to have their children every day in a Protestant service. Or a Roman Catholic one, come to that."

"But you . . .?" Had she gone this far from him?

"Oh no! Many Russians I really loved—but not their Church. It was too self-worshipping, too far away from justice and mercy. There must be priests who are good and saintly, but I never came across any. They seemed to be sly and proud. And I just don't care for the fancy-dress-party way of approaching God—"

"Isn't it supposed to be a celebration?"

"Oh, Papa, you know what I mean! Spanish churches with Madonnas dolled up in dusty net dresses and covered in real jewelry, and children dying of want in the street outside! If I could ever change, which I never would, it would be in the opposite direction—more simplicity."

"The whitewashed chapel on the windswept shore?"

"Exactly that. It's in those little, rough-hewn, plain old stone places that you can really feel the Holy Spirit moving, almost breathing. In remote places in Scotland, Austria, never mind where."

"Yes."

"Perhaps we are the same, really. In Russian churches I hated the men and women being separate, like Jews or Moslems, as if family life were something grubby, to be left behind at the church door. The only part I liked was all the warm candles, and the children milling about all over the place, which seems more natural than trying to make them sit still and quiet. The sameness is that *part* of what the Russians love in their Church, is its total involvement with Russia. And part of what I love about the Church of England is its being made of the fabric of this country, woven into its history and all its deepest feelings of freedom and kindness and people being allowed to be themselves. Most of that you only notice when you go to places where there isn't any of it."

"Those poor fellows in Russia," Mr. Pelham mused. "They will suffer so much. And we can do so little for them . . . not that persecution isn't the greatest help to a church. Torment one Christian here on a Wednesday for his faith, and on the Sunday after every church in the three kingdoms would be full of ardent worshippers. Laughing at religion, or belittling its beauty and grandeur, is a far more potent weapon against it. But keep in mind, Daisy, that what unites us all, all Christians, is infinitely greater than what divides."

"But for practical purposes?"

"Sometimes—oh, a fig for practical purposes! Leave it to the Holy Spirit. But if we must have them—some sort of federation. Real unity only when we have been brought to think alike. Meanwhile, a truce to enmity. You are certain of what the Dubelskys would have wanted?"

"Yes. At least I think I am."

They sat in silence, facing each other but not looking at each other. How can I go against his good plan? thought Daisy miserably. But then, Prince Andrei! Dead, perhaps, but these are his sons. What would Misha think? Or do?

Mr. Pelham's forehead had become slightly less puckered. "Surely they could come to nothing but good, singing to the glory of God in that beautiful cathedral? First-rate music, too. Are you sure you know best?"

I am sure of nothing, Daisy thought, except that I love Misha and wish to God he would come back. What a *muddle!* I do an ordinary kind thing, like sticking with the children. Papa does an ordinary kind thing, like taking us all in. It only ends in our being stubbornly at odds with each other. Looking at her father's disappointed face, his greying temples and his lines of tiredness, her heart smote her. The power that full-grown children have to wound their parents, thus suddenly discovered, seemed terrible to her. Its very force made it more of a temptation; its strange surprising cruelty gave one a horrid compulsion to go on. Are we enemies of our parents, that their very vulnerability should give us a kind of evil delight? With a revulsion of feeling, Daisy saw herself as one of those gorged clumsy nestlings, flapping off the edge of the nest without one look back, away from the thin parent birds who had fed them from morning till night throughout every day of their lives, leaving them because that is the law of nature. The relationship has fulfilled its purpose, is at an end, can only be broken. How much of what I feel is part of my own determination to be free, and how much is loyalty and love for Misha, and how much is considered judgement?

Mr. Pelham got up and walked away across the room. No, Daisy steeled herself, don't be influenced by his bowed shoulders and his slowing walk. He wouldn't want you to be; he would want this decided on its merits. I am a clumsy nestling that will come back to you, she vowed silently. Just for the moment, let me fly!

At the window, he turned round to look penetratingly at her. "Are you sure you are right about this? No one is going to take advantage of their helpless position and proselytize them. If their religion is bred deep enough into them it will stick; and as adults, with free movement, they can return to their own Church. Where in Worcestershire they could find Orthodoxy, God knows. If you feel all this so strongly, should they not, maybe, be found a home in some Russian émigré household elsewhere?"

Daisy looked at him aghast. "You *can't* mean that you are tired of having them?"

"I can't mean it and I don't mean it. They are welcome here so long as there is a roof over any of our heads. All I am saying is, is it logic to demand strict Orthodoxy and yet to let them grow up so far from anyone who shares their form of faith?"

"Russians don't go in for logic. I am just trying to stick to what their parents would have wanted."

Mr. Pelham subdued impatience and went off on a different tack. "We in this country have possibly concentrated too much on loving our neighbour and too little on worshipping God purely as an end in itself, and letting what will flow from that. Though you should have seen and known the piety of my father and his generation; faith was their be-all and their end-all, and their way of life. But there's no future in this hurling of anathemas at each other."

"But if they hurl them at us?"

"Exile!" Mr. Pelham wondered. "How would *we* all stand up to that, I wonder?"

"Well enough, I should think," Daisy reassured him. "People turn tough when they have to be strong. *You* certainly would."

"Maybe, in the sorrow of exile and powerlessness, the Russians will learn to know other Christians and no longer shut themselves up in suspicion and enmity. They will learn from us. And we will learn from them."

"Daddy, you are wandering from the point. The children—" Mr. Pelham went on, not listening to her. "To leave our comfortable rectories, our much-loved churches, our dear respectful villagers. To operate in dim cellars, at risk of our lives, in furtive, hurried services." To his daughter he sounded almost regretful. "It would certainly do us good, as a church—but no! The cost is too great in terms of misery for countless thousands of innocent people. Yet we need some harsher trials, even, than this war."

He was right, and Daisy, having also suffered, knew it. But meanwhile . . .

"The *children*, Daddy."

Her father returned to the problem.

"Are you sure, Daisy, that you are not being a little too faithful to what you imagine their parents would demand in all this? Didn't Prince Andrei at one time contemplate sending his older sons to Eton? They would have had Church of England services there. I'll abide by your decision—but be sure of it."

"Perhaps that was why he didn't, in the end, send them to Eton."

She could never remember having been seriously at odds with her father before. Had she become, in that long six years, subtly Russianised? Demanding the impossible, changing her mind, too illogical to live with? She longed for someone from outside her immediate world, of her own generation, someone who also knew Russia, with whom to talk it over. She was divided and confused. Sometimes she felt immeasurably older than her parents and her neighbours. More often she felt remote, and still too immature and passionate in her judgements. Was she daft to go against her father? Was his plan right? Was she being silly, and too emotional, and all those things that people complained women were?

At heart she agreed with him. From her soul she hated the part that enmity and exclusion played in religion, that terrible heritage of self-righteousness, of the arrogant sweeping aside by men in priestly robes as if in fear of contamination, that, along with much good, Christianity drew from Jewry. Russian standoffishness was a sign of fear and weakness rather than of strength. But if the Dubelskys were dead, and she in charge of their children? She seemed unable to think, able only to go on feeling, strongly and cloudily.

In the hall, unannounced but as if in answer to her prayers, stood George Bennett, exactly as ever, the same brown face and hazel eyes, the same reassuring smile. As soon as the introductions to her parents were over, and the exuberant greetings of the children had abated, she confronted him with her dilemma.

"But of course," he said, once apprised of the situation. "Of course they must go to the choir school. Lucky to get there. Don't be absurd, Daisy. Talk about overconscientiousness! It's an excellent plan. The Dubelskys are fortunate that their children should fall on their feet like this—kind people, a happy home—look out of the window at them now! Happy as kings."

"But, George—it's my responsibility. Surely I should be the one to decide?"

"Of course. But before you turn down the plan your father has made, think first what they escaped. Take your mind back to Novorossisk, to all those lost bewildered Russians going ashore at Constantinople with no money and no future. The children have a fine future life here. And you've got a decision. Either let them adapt to that, with all that it offers in the way of security and a happy family life, or ship them off to some Russian émigré family who are strangers to them, and probably living in some grim street in a dreary part of London. Of course it's entirely up to you."

With relief, Daisy fell in with her father's plan. George, with his certainties and his clear and definite ideas, was a solace to her troubled spirit. Something at least was settled, and everybody, not least the twins, was happy. All the same, Daisy continued to feel something of a misfit, a little way distanced from her parents without being planted anywhere else.

Misha lay drowsily stretched out on the *kang*, half asleep in the late summer night. Rolled in his rug a foot away, Vassily was very gently snoring. Behind a partition at the other end of the one-room house, Terenty and Serafima were already deep asleep in their box bed. From outside came the distant sound of rushing water, and the crow of a cock that had started up too early.

Misha's contentment surprised him. It had deepened over the summer months. The Japanese firm that employed him and Vassily in deforesting the local mountainside demanded very hard work and paid negligible wages, and the Japanese overseer treated the woodmen with such malignant scorn that Misha had wondered for the first few weeks whether it was possible to endure it. But he treated the Chinese and Korean workers with exactly the same inhuman contempt, and even paid the two Russians the doubtful compliment of allotting them the harder tasks possible to their superior strength. Vassily's patience and calm had been a sustenance to Misha, and he had grown very fond of him. A deliberate pleasing wit lay under Vassily's precisely worded sentences and his careful, lawyer-like weighing of the pros and cons of his actions. He would wait a long while before he said anything, or even answered a request—the quick-witted Misha had at first found this irritating. Now he knew Vassily better. Under that dark curly thatch was a deeply thoughtful mind. Whatever else Misha was going to lack in this cold comfort province it would not be mental stimulation.

"You are my lost brother," Vassily had told him, walking home from work one summer evening, with the kingfishers darting from the river bank and great azure dragonflies hovering among the reeds. "We do not speak of my brother at home because my mother weeps always at his name."

"Can he ever come back?"

"I think not. General Chen is no fool. Pavel is strong, as you are, as I am. He is not like these poor Chinese, with their bodies like scarecrows and their thin legs like two crutches. No Russian ever returns from a Chinese army. For years he fought the Germans, he fought the Reds, and now he fights for nothing—dies, perhaps, for nothing."

"Is it impossible to buy him out?"

"For a fortune, maybe, who knows? Chen, like his rival, is forever short of cash. But the question is academic."

Here in these forests, working side by side with Vassily in his silence and devotion, Misha had unwound himself, he now realised, from the hatred that had beset and enchained him during his long struggle with the Bolsheviks. He felt suddenly free and light-hearted.

"You have been my medicine," he told Vassily, putting an arm round his shoulders. "I was far gone in the disease of loathing and rage. Now I shall fight, but not hate. You've been my purge."

Vassily looked away, uninterested. Aloof by nature, and free of self-consciousness, he was unable to see it that way himself.

When Daisy and the children had been in danger, Misha had thought often of them. Now that they were safe, there were times when they almost vanished from his mind. Sometimes indeed, Daisy's light figure walked before him down the forest paths, or her fingers seemed to tweak his ear in remonstrance as he ran a discerning eye over the pretty Korean girls who pattered down the village streets or rode with their fathers to market in the high-yoked Russian carts. Physically tired out, he would return with an untroubled mind to the little wooden house of an evening, from whence wafted out the enticing smells of the Russian food that he knew and liked. Serafima would welcome him back, fussing amiably over him, piling his plate, regarding him with the kind of uncritical adoration to which his childhood had accustomed him. Terenty would argue with him and listen to him, sometimes displaying a sharp sardonic wit that was the very opposite of his son's slow railleries. Vassily would laugh at Misha's jokes, complain to him of his parents' old-fashioned ways, listen with sympathetic grunts to his occasional grumbles, accept with cheerfulness his melancholy moods. Daisy lived, insistently, but at the back of his mind.

Tonight she moved firmly into the foreground, stood for a moment before him, loved and vivid, disturbing his rest, haunting his heart. Outside, a waning moon shone over the harsh and dusty hills. A far country, indeed. Was he himself a prodigal son, coming back repentant not to his own father but to Terenty, father of others? Misha turned himself over, kicking Vassily lightly as a suggestion that he moderate his snores.

A mood of gentle, mild resignation invaded him. He must stay here always, he felt. This was Russia, whatever its flag, or constitution, or form of government. He was exiled from Russia, and yet back in Russia's heartland—here on this high bleak Manchurian plain. Nothing was missing, or nothing essential—the warmth, the inconsequence, a certain quality of humble self-derision, the smell of incense, the hissing of the battered samovar. On a small triangular shelf in one corner of the wooden room a tiny lamp burned before the ikon of the Mother of God; leaning on the windowsill was a broken-backed copy of Pushkin's poetry. Russia was a spiritual realm: she knew no earthly frontiers, no little lines drawn on maps. In touching loyalty, Terenty had pinned up a photograph of Czar Nicholas II, by whose order he had been consigned to exile. All was as it was at home—the charm, the fecklessness, the hospitality used without grudging; here was the hope, the zest, the melancholy, the echoing despair, the joyful refusal to believe that the party would ever be over. Evenings, friends would be summoned in for singing and dancing on the rough earth floor; at other times, leaning into the tent of light cast by the table lamp, old Terenty would sit expatiating upon his liberal politics, and Serafima, half listening, would respond softly, affirmatively, in an almost ecclesiastical antiphon, so closely did her thought, at such times, chime with his.

Restless on the *kang*, Misha's mood swung from resignation to aspiration. With a pang of sorrow, he dismissed Daisy from his heart. There was to be no sparkling happiness for him; fate had ruled otherwise. Misha would stay here forever, enduring the long, sub-zero winters, the short, baking summers, lying hard at night on a *kang*, his only bed this brick and plaster oven of the small and smelly Korean house. A sensible marriage arrangement would have to be made; for now he would take to himself a pretty Korean girl, travel in due course to Harbin to find a Russian wife, some sensible girl who would cook and clean and help Serafima as she grew older. He would suffer the hardships as Terenty and his wife suffered, as Vassily suffered.

Here, Misha thought, he would lay his demons to rest. He would work hard, share his scant wage with this adopted family, patiently abiding, as they did, the will of God. He would await with them the redemption of Russia from the Reds that would surely come, not in his day, maybe not even in his children's day, or his grandchildren's. But come it would, and he would have great-grandchildren who would somehow also be the descendants of Kolya, sharing his ideals and his goodness of heart, to rejoice in this restored Russia and build it anew, to walk in it without fear.

He would be to Vassily the brother Pavel whom the Chinese warlord had swept from him; he would love the serious deliberate goodness of Vassily as he had once loved the brilliant zestful goodness of Kolya. He would revere the gentleness of Terenty, the humble patience of Serafima; he would comfort their old age as he would have comforted the old age of his own very different parents. For the moment, the whole Ivanof family seemed to Misha angelic, and in his heart he became a part of such angelicness.

A grand exaltation possessed him. Turning over once again, he submitted without rancour to a further thunderous outbreak of Vassily's snoring.

Chapter 29

The day on the hillside was almost done. The late-summer sun still blazed fiercely over Manchuria, but chill came swiftly with evening. Misha's powerful limbs ached with fatigue. Vassily was lingering on the hill, very slowly searching for a lost knife. The Chinese and the Koreans looked unusually exhausted as they laboured at their final task. Their halloo of warning sounded faintly, as from parched lips. The phrase "hard bondage" recurred to Misha's mind. Since they had both finished their task, he wished that Vassily would hurry. If it was not his god, Misha's belly was at least high up in his hierarchy. It was Vassily's saint's day, and there had been talk of ducklings for supper.

Misha turned to remind Vassily of this pleasing hope. The sun was off all but the highest peaks of the eastern mountains and the valley was flooded in shadowy blue light. With a final effort, the huge tree on which the Chinese had been working swung in the air, toppled and fell with a kind of bouncing crash.

With paralysing horror Misha realised that Vassily had failed to hear the warning cry. Bent double in his search for his precious clasp-knife, he had been directly in the path of the falling tree. Its second bounce had caught him amongst the scrub oak that concealed him from the Chinese.

It seemed to Misha that he had cried out too late, or perhaps soundlessly. In any case, the bent figure of Vassily would have had no time to move. The falling tree had crashed fairly upon him, and then, rolling and bouncing ever further, had seized his body in the turning of a great branch and flung it far, as a well-fed terrier might fling a dead rat that it had killed for sport. Vassily lay spread-eagled, crushed, his neck and back broken, a look of surprise on his careful sensible face, untouched by the accident.

Speechless, Misha bent over him, lifted him, gazed unbelievingly into his friend's wide-open grey eyes. The Chinese woodmen crowded round giggling nervously, a reaction to death that was not unusual to them. The Koreans uttered dismayed cries. Moments passed; Misha knelt still, as if paralysed. The Japanese overseer bustled to the scene.

"Leave him," he said with a rapid, hissing indrawing of his breath. "Leave him be." Misha, robbed of initiative by the shock, stood up obediently. Vassily's body had fallen across the pathway, and the overseer, as if fearing to dirty his hands, delicately turned it over with his boot. Shocked by this, the Koreans increased their cries of dismay. Vassily had been liked by them all. Misha bent over him again, but the overseer pushed him aside, insisting fussily that the body must be left, that the police must be informed, that there must be an enquiry, an inquest, an apportioning of blame. He was seriously annoyed to lose so good a worker, and emphasised this by giving Vassily's body a contemptuous kick.

With sudden silent ferocity Misha dealt the Japanese a ringing blow, and he fell with his head on a tree stump and lay stunned. Terrified, the woodmen fled away down the hillside. Misha gathered up his friend in his arms, slung his body over his shoulder and strode away down the hill.

All the way across the fields, with Vassily's heavy body growing cold across his shoulder, Misha murmured the prayers of his childhood in stunned repetition. His thought was only of Vassily and of his parents. First Kolya—now this second brother. Dead. How? Why? The implications of what had happened and the possible consequences to himself had not yet entered his consciousness. At the door Serafima stood, noting only that Vassily must be late and that Misha was carrying a heavy burden. She was beaming at the thought of the ducklings and of the appetites of two hungry young men. They were done to a turn, and the stuffing—then realisation came in a dull rush.

"I knew it, I knew it! Both my sons! Aie, aie, Vassily, Vassily! Ah God, he was too good, too good . . . ah my son, Vassily, my son, *my son!*" Her wailing filled the air. Terenty, receiving his dead son in his arms, bowed his head in a speechless, agonised acceptance. Misha told them what had happened, tears welling in his eyes.

Through the twilight and into the darkness an interested crowd of villagers stood outside in the dusty road. This, at least, was an event. Such a fine young man, the only son left to his mother! Not for many hours did the little wooden house cease to echo to Serafima's heartbroken cries. "Sima, Sima," the old man implored, rocking her in his arms. "Listen—cleanse him, light the candles and I will read the psalms." Misha helped. The power of ritual asserted itself; Terenty's voice rose and fell. The candles burned steadily, a full moon rose over the hills. As the hours passed, an exhausted calm fell.

"Lord," asked Terenty, his old body rocking as he chanted, "who shall dwell in thy tabernacle: or who shall rest upon thy holy hill?

"Even he that leadeth an uncorrupt life: and doeth the thing which is right, and speaketh the truth from his heart.

"He that hath used no deceit in his tongue, nor done evil to his neighbour: and hath not slandered his neighbour.

"He that setteth not by himself, but is lowly in his own eyes . . ." Terenty's voice trembled a little, gathered strength again.

He's not got far, Misha thought. Psalm 15, and there are 150. To Serafima he whispered, "Could you not rest a little now? To be strong, to chant the psalter when Terenty Sergeivitch tires?"

"No rest, no rest, ever again," Serafima mourned. "And besides, at midnight, Grigor comes to chant. Rest, you; tomorrow may be an evil day, more evil, it may be, than today. They may come demanding Vassily's body. All days are evil now. Our lives are done. Our sons are lost to us."

"Matrushka, listen—"

The old brave voice of Terenty arose in triumphant affirmation; transcending exile, night and death.

"The Lord himself is the portion of mine inheritance, and of my cup: thou shalt maintain my lot.

"The lot is fallen unto me in a fair ground: yea, I have a goodly heritage."

A few late-returning Chinese, attracted by the sound of chanting, stood outside the house, thin shadows in the moonlight.

"I will thank the Lord for giving me warning: my reins also chasten me in the night season.

"I have set God always before me: for he is on my right hand, therefore I shall not fall.

"Wherefore my heart was glad, and my hope rejoiced; my flesh also shall rest in hope.

"For why? thou shalt not leave my soul in hell . . ."

"Rest now, Matrushka, I beg of you," Misha's whisper pleaded again. "I will watch by Vassily. I will tend the candles."

"Thou shalt shew me the path of life," Terenty insisted, "in thy presence is fullness of joy: and at thy right hand there is pleasure for evermore."

Serafima's hand suddenly clutched the arm of Misha, so strongly that he almost cried out. She had turned to the surviving strong young man. "You now," she cried, "must be our son! You, the friend of Vassily, you, his brother, who loved him, you will stay with us, to comfort our age, to close our eyes, to say the psalms for us, to pray for us in the hard passage of death. Promise me! Promise me! You will stay with us to be our son! To be for us Pashenka, to be Vassily!"

Terenty had paused for breath before embarking upon his next psalm. A glance at his face told Misha of his longing for any comfort for his wife, for strength for himself, for help in their increasing physical helplessness. The candles were now burning low; in their flickering light Vassily's body seemed to be speaking the same message—stay with them, cherish them.

Trembling with shock and grief, Misha promised, as if compelled by some ulterior force.

The old woman's grip relaxed. "Rest you, also, now," she advised. "Rest you, my son."

Misha lay down on the *kang*. I am caught now, he thought. Trapped for ten years, twenty, without Vassily, without hope, in this little house, in this strange land. To stay of free will was one thing; to stay perforce was another. Terenty's voice grew fainter; Misha was dimly aware of Serafima renewing the candles. He fell into a sad restless sleep.

In the small hours Misha awoke with a shudder. Terenty was shaking his shoulder urgently. Around Vassily's body the candles had again burnt low; Serafima was bending to renew them, the tears again pouring down her face as from some inexhaustible spring. Grigor, an elderly man with an extraordinarily deep, harsh voice, continued the singing of the psalms, in a scolding manner, as if he were indeed the jealous God of the Old Testament. Terenty went on shaking Misha gently as if to be certain that he was really awake. "You must leave, now, quickly!" he said. "A friend has sent secretly to tell me that they have found the Japanese foreman and he is very ill, perhaps dying. The police will come in the morning to take you away. As soon as the Chinese report for work in the morning they will tell them who struck the overseer."

The danger to Misha had cleared the sorrow from Terenty's once clear head. "You must go, but not by the stations and railways where there are always Japanese police. Even if the overseer recovers, they will seek you. You have broken the law in bringing us back Vassily's body—may God forever bless you for it. Go southeast, to the frontier into Korea. On the frontier, across the Tumen river, go into the high mountains. Make south from there always, coming in perhaps a month to Seoul, where you can take ship."

Sleep, relief and sorrow struggled for mastery of Misha's mind.

"Take with you your good Russian boots for this rough road," Terenty advised.

"Aie, aie, no! The bandits would kill him only for those boots," Serafima protested, deflected momentarily from her mourning.

"And your greatcoat. When you come down from the hills, wear Chinese clothes again—"

"With that yellow hair? Aie, aie, of what use?"

"If questioned, you must be a Swede or a Norwegian."

"How could he speak such languages?"

"Who in Korea will know what language he speaks?"

The voice of Grigor sounded very loudly, as if reproof for their whispering voices. "They imagine wickedness, and practise it: that they keep secret among themselves, every man in the deep of his heart."

"He could alternatively go over the mountains to Seishin and take the German ship to Shanghai."

"But God shall suddenly shoot at them with a swift arrow," Grigor chanted indignantly, "that they shall be wounded. Yea, their own tongues shall make them fail." He cast a severe glance at Misha, who was pulling on his boots.

"In Seishin," Serafima objected, "the Japanese police are everywhere. He is too tall, they will see him standing up above the crowd. It is a great sadness that he is too tall. At the port of Seishin they will cast him into prison."

Terenty was enchanted to hear her indulging in rational speech. "You are right, Sima my dearest. He must go to Seoul, keeping to the hills, avoiding the towns."

"Thou that hearest the prayer: unto thee shall all flesh come," Grigor pointed out sonorously. "My misdeeds prevail against me: O be thou merciful unto our sins."

"Teryoshka, the hills are full of bandits!"

"Better to risk the bandits than to wait here for the Japanese police. At Seoul there are many, many foreign seamen—the police will not notice you. At Chemulpo, which is the port of Seoul, there will be many ships: French ships, or English ships, or American ships."

"And both of you?" Misha asked. "Come with me. I will help you over the mountains. Do not stay here in trouble."

"I, with my lame leg? And Serafima, who walks hardly at all? Pavel, too, might return and find us gone. There may be no trouble, or brief trouble, once you are gone. I have friends."

"What can they do to us? We have lost all, all, all. Our two beloved sons."

"To walk will take three weeks, a month, six weeks," Terenty went on.

"How can he carry enough food for that?" But already she was stuffing cooked rice and dried meat into little bags of cloth.

"Keep from the main roads; keep always to the hills, to the small tracks, the mountain ways and little villages. The Koreans will shelter you at night, they do not love the Japanese who took their country ten years ago."

"There are tigers in the hills! Great Siberian tigers! There are snow leopards!"

"Have you a compass, Mihail Andreivitch?"

"There are bears also, and wolves."

"I have my rifle," Misha pointed out. He had retrieved it from its hiding place in the thatch.

But Serafima was suddenly desperate with fear and sorrow, for themselves, for their empty lives, for Misha's safety. "Take no rifle, Misha, I beg you. Cast it away. There has been too much of shooting and of killing. Cast it from you. Cast yourself upon the mercy of the Mother of God!" Misha, for all her tears, could not bring himself to follow this advice.

They stood for some moments, the Russian pause for recollection before starting a journey.

Grigor's voice, which had sunk a little from its extreme angry pitch, gathered itself as if for a valediction. "Thou shalt shew us wonderful things in thy righteousness, O God of our salvation: thou that art the hope of all the ends of the earth, and of them that remain in the broad sea. Who in his strength setteth fast the mountains: and is girded about with power. Who stilleth the raging of the sea: and the noise of his waves, and the madness of the people. They also that dwell in the uttermost parts of the earth shall be afraid at thy tokens: thou that makest the outgoings of the morning and evening to praise thee."

"I hear the sound of men tramping," Terenty cried out in terror.

"Quick, Misha, quick!" But when after a hurried tearful farewell to Serafima, they came out into the street, there was nothing there but the light of the sinking moon, veiled now under scurrying clouds.

Terenty went with him through the village. "I will take the road that leads to Harbin, returning at first light, so that watchers in the village will think I set you upon that road, to join the many White Russians who are there, and the Japanese police on that route will be alert for you."

"And Serafima Nikolevna?"

"She will be busy enough preparing the food for those who come to pray with us. And food for those saints who we do not see but who also come." Terenty blessed Misha and stood for a moment, leaning his weight on Misha's shoulder, a sad, heavy embrace. "You have been a son to us."

"If ever," Misha whispered, "if ever I can—" Terenty shook his head and with a final kiss turned westward, never looking back.

Misha doubled back swiftly through the outskirts of the sleeping village, across the creaking wooden bridge. He was soon in the foothills. Dark streams rushed past him, pine trees rustled in the dawn wind. Striding out strongly, for all his rifle and pack, he climbed higher and higher, scarcely pausing to look back at the last of his Manchurian valley or at the river path where he and Vassily had walked happily not a day ago. For all his shock and anger, his bitterness and sorrow, he felt refreshment simply in being on the move. His spirits rose uncontrollably with the rising sun, with the sharpened appetite for life that the very newness of this desperate adventure brought.

But when, sitting down on a boulder in midstream for breakfast, he saw that Serafima had included in his provisions the two ducks that had been cooked for Vassily's feast day, the tears suddenly rolled down his cheeks and mingled in the mountain waters. If ever he came safe to civilisation he would send them the money to buy their first son out of the Chinese army. Money, he surmised, could do as much in China as elsewhere. His mind had in no way adapted itself to the fact that he was no longer a very rich man, able to obtain the cooperation of smiling cashiers in any bank in the world.

The death of Vassily and the heartbroken grief of Vassily's parents lay heavy on him, a leaden burden he must carry up the mountainside. With Vassily he thought of Kolya, of a hundred lost friends, of his vanished parents. The sound of Serafima's weeping, the noble broken voice of Terenty reading the psalms above his dead son, echoed unceasingly in Misha's heart. Do I doom all whom I love? he asked himself in a fresh access of misery. His own survival seemed a mockery, almost an indecency. He had not understood how deeply he had come to love Vassily, to rely on his taciturn, rocklike good nature, his ready responses, his sudden slowly delivered jokes. His presence had made the gruelling work bearable. The poor but freely offered comforts of his parents' home had sweetened every bitterness of exile. Without him, thought Misha, I would undoubtedly have died in this far country, and now he lies dead and because of my rash act his parents weep alone.

For too long he stayed by the stream, mourning Vassily in his heart. Only the immense difficulties of the long journey, and the imminence of pursuit and capture at length spurred him on to shoulder pack and rifle and press ahead.

He proceeded by guesswork and instinct, steering only by the sun, hoping that each valley he pursued would not end abruptly in impassable precipice. The autumn sun rose high and heat struck back at him off the sheer dry mountain walls. Each ridge, at length topped, was succeeded by another; they appeared to stretch on interminably. Maybe in such solitude there was safety, but the harsh rocks that echoed nothing, the huge stillness and silence of these high valleys, the inhuman emptiness of every horizon struck cold on his heart. Here, twelve hundred years before Christ, the Chinese leader Ki Tze had invaded Korea and found nothing but savage cave-dwellers. It was as if the spirit of these long dead men lurked still in their forbidding fastnesses.

On the twelfth day Misha came down out of the mountains. Already the air felt milder, moister, gave a hint that across the coastal hills the ocean lay. The frontier had offered a stiff climb and the sketchiest of tracks, but no other difficulties. When Korea had been a province of Imperial China, this frontier had been but vaguely defined in the gap between the Tumen and the Yalu rivers; it was scantly guarded now. Misha had swum and walked through the immense pale river Tumen, low now after the summer heat, with his rifle and pack held over his head, brushing his way through the thick fringe of osiers and scrunching through the pebbly shallows. Then had come the long increasingly hungry climb, through high bare rocks when even the scrub oak and thin pines had faded out and purposeful eagles wheeled overhead. There had been hunger pangs and bitter chill in the high mountains, but no encounter with either tiger or snow leopard, though he had heard them sometimes, distantly, by night, a hungry call shuddering across a valley. No wolf had howled under the diminished moon, and no angry disturbed bear had come lumbering towards him on the lower slopes where the pines grew thickly and where great crags loomed out of the morning mists and rapid rivers roared and steamed in the valleys below.

Misha had not seen, even in the distance, the campfires of bandits, and a day or two earlier, desperate with hunger, he had stalked and shot a deer. The noise of his rifle shot echoing round the cliffy mountains and sounding from crag to crag made him afraid for the first time. Every Japanese patrol in Korea would come running to such a sound, to so long and repeated an echo—or some bandit, desperate for his rifle, would stalk him from ridge to ridge. Not daring to light a fire and cook his kill, for fear of the betraying smoke, he had slashed off a few raw pieces and hurried from the place. To kill a deer for so little reward in food! Behind him he was aware of the ever watchful eagles gathering: their soaring vigilance added to his apprehensions.

But when, next day, he rounded a high rock and saw a wide valley opening before him, where scrub oak and birch gave way to ash and chestnut and a spread of small fields round the brown roofs of a Korean village, he felt a wave of confidence and hope. Already he must be halfway to Seoul. The village looked small and not unfriendly, and his year working amongst Koreans had given him a smattering of their tongue. Sitting under a tree in the still warm sun, he chewed with enthusiasm at a piece of his venison.

Following the stream, he was well down the valley and coming through thickening vegetation before he became aware of unusual activity in the village below him. As its significance struck him, he halted abruptly. Fanned out across the valley were fifty or so Japanese soldiers, their line thickened by a sprinkling of coerced Korean villagers, all advancing methodically towards him up the steep valley, beating every shrub and scrap of scrub oak as they came. Beyond the belt of trees behind him was the bare hillside with no scrap of cover on it. He was too hungry to sustain a long uphill run. Up each side of the river a Japanese officer walked, methodically searching each fall and rocky pool, shaking every birch and aspen tree. Japanese soldiers followed, prodding with their bayonets each clump of azalea overhanging the river.

Misha's shot had indeed been heard. Sharp brown eyes had spied him from behind the rocks as he came downstream. They had been waiting for him, and he had walked into a trap as carelessly as the rawest of recruits.

Chapter 30

Life at home in England, so much longed for, had become to Daisy increasingly dissatisfying. People were kind, and everywhere was safe, and food, however rationed, was always forthcoming. She found herself shirking disagreeable jobs, growing idle, complaining of pointlessness when persuaded to do things.

There was no sign or sound of the Dubelskys, and Misha continued to make no communication. Even a return visit to Leicestershire had proved disappointing. One expected people to mark time while one was away, and felt put out when of course they did nothing of the kind. Serena Doughty had married Toby—unimpeachably suitable—and they had had four children, all of them handsome and one of them reported to be a genius. The race, it appeared, was not always to the swift nor the battle to the strong. Sam Orme, no longer freckled, had a business in Nottingham and had become stout. Rupert waltzed no more, but he at least was delighted to see her, and rang her up repeatedly if a little boringly from London. The Wilson twins—those detrimental boys— had been killed in the war—they would never again delight and torment their indignant old father. Even Cousin Imogen had died, leaving as it were a five-shilling tip to all her cousins and the bulk of her fortune to a home for tired war horses. All those infant sessions at Tattersalls had left their mark.

What might have been an amusing visit to Serena in all the glory of her family importance turned out flat and unrewarding. The waters of family life seemed to have closed over Serena's head; it was impossible to hold her attention for more than five seconds. By Sunday evening Daisy felt provoked into telling Serena that her letter of 1914 had been the cause of her own staying on in Russia, and thus being caught by the war— "And you never really came to St. Petersburg in the end."

"No. How awful! I didn't, did I? Mummy got in a complete panic, and Daddy gave in and let me off it. I was so relieved not to have to come. And *I* might have been stuck there too, and never have married Toby! Wasn't it *wonderfully* lucky? But did I really persuade you to stay on? How *awful* of me!" Serena's voice held more of pleasure than of any other emotion. "What is it, Martin darling? Well, tell Jeremy I'm coming up to say goodnight in a minute . . . What extraordinary socks you have got on, darling! Whatever possessed Nanny to put on you such things?"

"Nanny's sister gave them to me. She knitted them."

"Oh. Well. They're very interesting and original and it was *wonderfully* good of Nanny's sister. But perhaps—well, never mind."

"But you said—"

"I mustn't keep poor little Jeremy waiting. I'm sure Miss Pelham will read you a story while I'm away."

"But she said, Mummy said . . ."

"What were we talking about?" Serena enquired, returning half an hour later. "Oh yes, Russia. But surely, Daisy, it was all *wonderfully* interesting?"

"Well, of course it was, but—"

"Yes, Peter, I know I promised, and I'm really just coming. Oh, these boys! No peace! *Do* forgive me, Daisy."

One is crazy, thought Daisy, to expect gratitude, but five minutes of attention wouldn't come amiss.

Even after the boys were all in bed, Serena was constantly at the telephone with plans about their schools, their holidays, their parties, their health, and an immensely long and elaborate ruse to change Nanny's day off without hurting her feelings. Toby, away on business in Paris, was never glimpsed, and Daisy had a strong feeling that she had been summoned to stay simply in order to read stories to the boys at the times when Toby normally did. Mother love was a wonderful thing, but was mother *obsession?* How about a little wholesome neglect and telling the boys to get on with it? Daisy departed with warm expressions of congratulation—the boys really were a very good bunch—and feelings of heartfelt relief.

To be the bullied and dominated child of selfish parents, as Serena had been, seemed to have a bad effect either way. One grew up either to bully and dominate one's own children or else to love them to the point of suffocation and neglect all else. Clearly the latter course was the lesser evil. And anyway, Daisy reflected, as the train rattled her home, they are all happy; even the dearly loved and sensibly brought up children don't always grow up so very perfect. There's a great element of luck. We are all a long way away from getting it right, she thought sadly.

Toby was always the best of good sorts, and I am glad he survived the war and found himself a happy home. Yet running through all her thoughts was always the feeling that Misha had gone from her forever—a kind of persistent refrain which ran, *And what about me?*

After a while she ceased listening to it. Remembering Serena's parting remarks, she could hardly help laughing; they had been so completely in character. "What a pity," her hostess had said, "that Doughty was away with Toby's mother, and so you missed meeting him. *So* disappointing for you. Though I say it who shouldn't, Doughty really is brilliant. There's no other word for him. Simply *brilliant.*"

At Smetherton Sir Reggie was very old and vague and forgetful; Daisy was left with the feeling that half the time he didn't really remember who she was. Claire was a war widow and Irene divorced and bitter, and Richard—alas—unmistakably pompous. Even Lady Kettle was less handsome and exhilarating: she pretended more and seemed to have become excessively patronising. She gave Daisy a watercolour sketch of the Rectory that she had painted long ago, and said she hoped she would soon settle down. "Your parents would be so pleased if you would marry one of your many admirers," she had sighed. One should not go away for so long, Daisy brooded sadly; people alter out of recognition, and so one does oneself. If I had stayed here all the while, I would hardly have noticed it happening, and I would like them just as much as ever. As it was, she was neither Russian, nor, any longer, wholly English. Looking round at mourning, depleted, storm-washed England, she continued to love her country dearly, but reflected that there was only one worse thing than defeat after a long war, and that was victory. The battering received either way was numbing, paralysing, induced a kind of discouraged bewilderment—yet victory took away from such chastisement all the humbling of the spirit that might otherwise be gained. From defeat we learn with horrible and violent force: in victory there is only a kind of disillusioned amazement that things are not better. From the harsh facts of loss and impoverishment people were seeking to escape into a hectic fantasy of excitement and pleasure. Where, in all this, was a niche for a displaced governess?

The sudden appearance of Amelia, only very shortly after the receipt of her telegram, was as welcome as it was unexpected. She arrived on a soft summer evening, wearing a smart feather hat and a skirt of exactly the right length.

"Hm, pretty," she said approvingly, standing back to gaze at the Rectory's handsome Georgian front with its screen of wisteria just past their prime and of great glossy magnolia leaves. She was quieter, less pert and cocksure. At dinner the Pelham parents surprised themselves by beginning to like her. Walking next day on the hill behind the village, she began abruptly to tell Daisy of the husband who had been killed on the Western Front a year after their marriage.

"What a waste," she said detachedly. "He was the most divine dancer you ever met. Waltzing with him was like a dream. Oh, what a waste . . . But one can't dance forever," she added realistically. "We would never have lasted. On his last leave, even after only about ten months of marriage we were cat and dog. He was Irish—Ferrall O'Leary. He insisted O'Leary was a fine old Irish name, but to me it sounded like a cross between a music hall act and a dirty old man in his cups. I can't wait to be called something else."

"Like something in particular?"

"Like nothing in particular."

"I wish I had known him."

"So do I. We had fun together while it lasted. Poor Ferry! He wasn't cut out for matrimony. The war and the general misery of it made him drink like a fish. We would never have made it, but I loved him all the same. Some of it was bliss, but in between we fought like tigers. Long past fun. Claws really out. And his as long and sharp as mine, God keep him . . . And you, Daisy, anchored here for always, minding those thankless Russian brats?"

Daisy was up in arms, just as of old. "They are *not* thankless. Truly they are not."

"Possibly the younger ones aren't. Ella is clearly very much *en rapport* with your mother, who will simply take her on as a fourth daughter. And the boys will learn cricket from your father and fall on their feet and turn English. But nothing will persuade me that Varya is not a spoilt brat, all set to make some good man happy for a fortnight and miserable for the rest of his days."

"If you'd seen her in Russia, in the bad times—"

But Amelia refused to retract. "Guess who I saw in London, at a party the other night?" she asked. "George Bennett, exactly as ever, unruffled, unrushed . . . He asked me out to lunch last week; not dinner, mark you, a safe cautious noncommittal luncheon. Mainly to talk about you, I imagined. But actually we talked more about Russia—and about trees, of course. I don't, myself, know a tree from a telegraph pole, but he manages to make it interesting."

"Yes."

Amelia ignored the brevity of this reply.

"He's a pleasing contrast to the general hecticness of London now, which is full of people madly trying to make up for the trenches. As if one could."

"Well, he wasn't in the trenches."

"Do you blame him for that?"

"Of course not," Daisy said sharply. "The army wouldn't have him."

"He's the only noncombatant I've met yet who doesn't feel the need to go round explaining and apologising about it," Amelia said.

"*I* feel the need to apologise for sitting in a villa on the Black Sea while everyone else was right in the war," Daisy told her. She felt a strong unaccountable desire to switch off the subject of George. "I find now that I like things to be difficult and if possible dangerous, and certainly demanding. I would *love* now to go to India and work with the Untouchables, or in a Glasgow slum . . . and anyway I'm not trained for anything."

"For teaching, perhaps?"

"Experience, yes, but no training. Did you hear about Florence Farmborough? She became a real heroine at the Russian Front, nursing, and she escaped through Siberia and—"

"Oh, if you aren't ever going to switch off Russia!" Heroism, for Amelia, had a boring quality about it. "I'll tell you something. My father's made a fortune. He's what they call a war profiteer. Disgusting, isn't it? Bless him. And since he was rich, once, before the war, he knows how to spend gracefully. And he's spent a handsome sum endowing me."

"Oh, how lucky! Where will you live?"

"Not with them. They are a party in themselves. And settling at Cap d'Antibes. We were never exactly a family, more of a loose confederation of states. And they've never quite forgiven me for being still alive when my brother was killed at Hill Sixty. And furthermore, I bet there are as many surplus women in France as there are in England."

"But where will you go?"

"The world is wide. Canada, for a start. I have some cousins in Vancouver. Then the States. Perhaps." Amelia slanted at Daisy a peculiar oblique look. "I'll bet you feel disoriented and all no-how?" she questioned.

It was wonderful to be able to tell someone how she felt. "Going away to Russia," Daisy began, "was in a way like the first time of going away to boarding school. When you come back for the first holidays you think how glorious and warm and accepting home is. All the same, you've been part of another world, where it's tougher and where you have to survive on your own. And it has a fascination. And you've seen other parents, against whom you begin to balance your own. Oh, it's not that they aren't still the King and Queen of Hearts—they are, but—"

"But?"

"You've seen there are other suits in the pack. And you *know* there are Knaves. And you even begin to suspect, half excitedly, that there are Aces."

"Ace being high?"

"Yes."

"And now?" Amelia persisted as they strolled down the hill. "Now you're home for the second holidays?"

"Now I feel older even than the King and Queen of Hearts. They've become the ones to be protected and loved. And goodness—it's disconcerting to come back to it."

"But not for always? Not a life sentence?"

"No. I've developed an appetite for the whole pack. To be truthful, I long to be back among them, dodging the Knaves, and—"

"Looking out for the Aces?"

"Just now there *is* no Ace," Daisy said bleakly.

Amelia was off again in a couple of days, embracing Varya coolly and all the others warmly. "She smells scrumptous," Jenny said, dazzled by Amelia's clothes and sophistication. "I hope she comes soon again."

"Keep shuffling the pack," Amelia advised Daisy, "and it can't help turning up trumps in the end. Or an Ace."

"It is strange," Mr. Pelham said at dinner, apropos of nothing much, "how something as inhuman as war seems to humanise people. Those it leaves alive."

Daisy was helping herself with pleasure to lamb and new green peas, and nobody saw her hand falter or her face suddenly blanch with pain. Where now, dead, alive, wounded, cast away, was Misha?

The months rolled slowly by without sight or sound of him. She had stopped getting up early to go through the letters, though at the sight of an odd-looking envelope her heart would still leap in an indefatigable hope.

Autumn was mellow and golden as ever. The church bells rang softly in the still evening air. Sun pierced the mists of morning, the bright leaves sailed gently down onto the dewy lawns. "You wouldn't care to start hunting again, you used to enjoy it so much?" Mrs. Pelham asked tentatively, for in the hunting fields of her youth many a *beau mariage* had been made.

"Oh no—I must get a local job," Daisy countered, "now the children are away at lessons all day."

"Not yet, darling," her mother pleaded. "Stay at home a little longer and rest and fatten up a little more!"

Fatten up! It sounded to Daisy ominously like a sacrifice.

The winter passed slowly, and with never a word from Misha.

"Are you still up, Dad?"

"As you see. Rounding off a sermon."

"The thing is—do you mind if I stay for a bit?"

Mr. Pelham repressed a sigh. Whatever great thought he had been about to formulate had escaped him. He had had a hard day. His colleague in the next village was away in hospital and one of the man's parishioners, a farmhand previously unknown to Mr. Pelham and hitherto considered perfectly sane, had suddenly gone berserk and killed his wife and two children. Mr. Pelham had spent a harrowing four hours with him in his prison cell, clutched by the arm and dazed by his unceasing singsong cry of "I didn't do it, vicar, I didden do it—I loved 'en." The man was utterly bewildered by his own action, desperately staving off the horror of self-recognition. Don't be too sane, you poor devil, Mr. Pelham had thought, or you'll swing for it. Yet, perhaps, wasn't that better than living his life out in full recollection of it? The man was only thirty-four. "Don't ye leave me, vicar, you make 'em see. I didden do ut, I loved 'en." "I know that you did," he had told him. "I believe that you did." "Then whoy?" the man had demanded.

"I think," Mr. Pelham said to Daisy, "I'm going to have a glass of port. Would you like one? Barton will have gone to bed. I'll get it."

"Yes, no. Well, yes, perhaps." Daisy's face was flushed and excited. "George," she began as soon as her father had returned with the decanter and glasses, "has given me an ultimatum."

"Good for him."

"He's being sent to America, to Oregon, by his timber firm, and then on to Vancouver, and he says I must marry him and go too or it's goodbye for good."

"Sensible fellow. You've been living in each other's pockets these last few months. Time you decided."

"Yes . . . but what?"

Mr. Pelham felt the port moving warmly and pleasurably down inside him. "Who can decide that but yourself? You are grown up. You have probably decided already for yourself. Nothing I say will make the faintest difference. Nor should it."

"Maybe. But I like to talk to you. And it clears my mind. Saying things out makes them sound silly, or not."

"You know pretty well whether they are silly or not."

"Oh, darling Daddy! Do be more help."

"How long have you known each other? Months? Years?"

"Ages. About six years. Ever since I went to Russia."

"Then I imagine it's not the first time he has asked you?"

"No."

"Sip it slowly," Mr. Pelham advised. "Don't gulp port as if it were ginger beer. Tell me about him. He seems a good fellow from what I've seen of him."

"Oh, he is! Kind, and unselfish; and good-tempered, really; except he gets a bit fed up sometimes—but who doesn't? And reliable. And truly very nice. And we get on pretty well together. Only—"

"Only what?"

"Only I don't find him irresistible," Daisy said slowly. "Don't laugh, Daddy—*please do not laugh.*"

"You don't find him attractive?"

"Well. In a kind of way. Like one does a beautiful horse, or a very charming dog, or a little fat baby."

"Not as one does a man, or a woman?"

"No. But I am always, *always* pleased to see him."

"Many a happy marriage has been made without irresistibility on either side."

With a massive effort, Daisy refrained from asking him the obvious question. "But if," she said, "one afterwards meets someone who one *does* find irresistible?"

"That is the risk. But you'd be surprised, with two people of good feeling, what a strong bond custom and living together and shared children does form. Quite apart from solemn promises."

"I know that I am lucky to have a father I can talk to. Lots of people don't . . . but I believe you *want* me to marry him."

The night was cold, and Mr. Pelham poked up the somnolent fire. One should never, he thought, through ambition, or a feeling that the proposed partner was a bit dull, *discourage* a child from marrying anyone so transparently a good fellow as George was; because one never knew what the alternative might be—marriage to a rogue, bitterness, a long dull loneliness, shipwreck of all kinds.

"What I want or don't want hardly enters in," he told Daisy. "If you seriously wanted to marry George you wouldn't have come and asked me what to do. Or even discussed it. Are you certain you are not just trying to shift the blame for refusing him?"

"I'm not sure of *anything.*"

"There must be a strong element of wanting to give to, as well as to get from. But really, it's just a question of whether two people *suit.* And you must know that by now."

"We do, in a sort of way, suit. I like him really enormously . . . and after all that long waiting time in Russia, and the fears and feelings involved, he is peaceful. But would I go on liking him, day in, day out?"

"Yes, would you? That's the crux."

"I'm twenty-six. I love it here, I love being with you and Mama. But, failing a job, I want a home of my own, and choosing the chintzes and everything, and making it nice, and making somebody actively happy."

"Naturally."

"And I haven't a career, so I need it still more."

"Understood."

"And then Virginia getting engaged—"

"That really *is* nothing to do with it."

"I know it isn't really. But having a much younger sister being married next June does rather underline one's spinster state."

"Time enough to talk about spinster states in ten or twelve years. If there is ever a time. Those gentle patient unmarried women are far less a prey to nerves than many a wife, and about as near sainthood as one is likely to meet."

"But, Daddy, I do *not* want to be a saint!"

"I don't imagine you are in any considerable danger of it."

Seriousness departed, briefly, from the conversation. Mr. Pelham cast a longing sideways look at what he had been writing, and then reflected that one's children were not always prepared to have a serious consultation with one, and were famous for choosing the least convenient moment.

"I expect soon to get fond of a cat," Daisy said dreamily. "And terribly fussy about everything being just so, in the house."

They sat in silence, the remains of the fire flickering and slowly fading. "You don't think liking is enough?" she asked finally.

"No, Daisy. Neither do you."

She sighed deeply. It's not as if I'd heard, she thought, it's not as if it wasn't an eternity since Misha went. But whether I'd heard or not, I don't really love George enough. Aloud, she argued, "I seriously have moments of thinking that I *do* love him enough."

Exasperation with his loved one set in in Mr. Pelham. "From all that you've been saying I am pretty certain that you *don't*. Anything *like* enough. I have not once heard his point of view advanced, for one minute, throughout this conversation. Men should never be married as husbands. Or providers. Or exits from boring situations. Or functionaries of any kind. Only as people. Women too, come to that, shouldn't be married as the only way of getting them to bed."

"But half the people in the world wouldn't marry if there wasn't something in it for *them!*"

"No. But even looked at selfishly, the best thing there could be in it for them, the most lasting, the most blest, is their own unselfish love. Of course there are other things. There must be at least a good deal of physical attraction. But unselfish love happens to be the one that bears the biggest dividends. Or goes on bearing them the longest"

"Daddy, you are an impractical idealist."

"I hope so. It's my job. But there is more pure love around than you think. Often of a rough and ready kind, but pure. Unselfish. So much in love with the other that it isn't even aware of being unselfish."

"You set impossibly high standards."

"Good. What isn't my job is to pronounce doom on people who will fall short of them."

"I would *prefer* not to fall short of them. But what if life organises things another way?" Daisy asked a little piteously. "No Mr. Right and all that stuff?"

"If you know at all what real love is, and I suspect that you do—"

"Mm. Mm." She got up from the fireside and stood with her back to her father, gazing at his well-loved Impressionist, a rainy street scene in Paris.

"If I read that noncommital grunt aright, it should put you past playing around with the other kind, the kind that is just vanity and wilfulness and a love of being admired and desired."

"But how are you going to find out if you do love people unless you go around with them for some while?"

"Fair enough. The key question is the length of the while."

Cornered, Daisy took refuge in pettishness. "You are not going to tell me to thank heaven fasting for a good man's love!"

"Not exactly. More, not to keep a good man, for six years, hovering between hope and fear."

Daisy's head was bowed. For the moment she looked stricken, returned into the world of childhood, where a scolding bit deep.

The words of the murderer rang in Mr. Pelham's mind: "I loved 'en, I loved 'en truly. I didden do ut, I didden hurt no kids of mine. I loved 'en. Summon else must a done it." How many of us love our children truly and kill them without meaning to? But if, he guessed, she's sad, she's sad for another reason, not for anything I say to her. He pressed on. Truth must be told.

"If you have decided, for goodness sake tell him so quickly. And gently. Go easy on the devastating indictments. Take the blame on yourself, where it belongs. Leave him every ounce of self-esteem that you can. There's a theory that only girls have hearts to break. It's false. Young men may not suffer so long, but they suffer just as deeply at the time. More deeply, very likely."

"I shall miss him very much. I shall be sad and lonely without him."

"That's a small price to pay for years of fun and companionship," Mr. Pelham said crisply. "My sympathies are with the young man." He took the stopper out of the decanter, thought briefly about it and replaced it. An owl hooted from the garden and they both looked rather solemn.

"Perhaps," Daisy said, in a hangdog voice, "I don't deserve a good husband." The humbug of this remark, once delivered, caused them both to giggle.

Perhaps, thought Mr. Pelham, after that long responsibility and growing up on her own, she needs the occasional luxury of pretending to be a child again.

Daisy gave a gulp and recovered. "I shall start looking about for a really sympathetic kitten . . . Daddy, I will have ditched your sermon."

"Not permanently." They kissed goodnight. Upstairs in his bedroom he prayed long for the man who had murdered what he most loved. Later, he prayed for George Bennett, and that his dear daughter should find a way of life. Only a good demanding job would do, he thought. Or better still, a good demanding marriage.

Next morning they faced each other alone across the breakfast table. Ella, who rose early, could be heard in the drawing room practising Chopin with energy and precision. Pro tem, her spiritual yearnings were centred upon music. The twins, who still sang like birds, were already in Worcester, where they even occasionally applied themselves to their long-neglected Latin and mathematics. Away at school, Varya was enjoying a continued success. As a run-of-the-mill princess, she might have been disregarded or even ganged up against and taken down a peg; as a foreign princess, and one who had had her house burned down, and been rushed into exile, had seen Czars, wolves, bears and even Bolsheviks, she was on firm ground. Jenny, a little piqued, had had to fall back on her presidency of the Science Club and her superior skill at lacrosse.

Daisy, her father noted, was facing him across the white tablecloth, the highly polished silver, and the honey and marmalade, with a wicked grin. "I might just," she said, "have a change of heart between now and seven this evening, when George is coming."

Mr. Pelham looked at his daughter over his glasses and declined to rise. He swam firmly away from her into the waters of *The Times*.

In the kitchen Mrs. Pelham was engaged with her cook in an amiable discussion on the pros and cons of raspberry or apricot jam in Queen of Puddings, a subject that interested them both greatly. Mrs. Pelham's orderly and uneventful life flowed on, affording her only very occasional qualms or difficult situations in which she felt cause to become plaintive. One of her daughters was already engaged to be married, and another one might quite easily be so by nightfall.

Chapter 31

Immediately below Misha was a cleft in the river bank where a small stream flowed into it. A crack in the low cliff wall was partly covered by a birch tree clinging to the rock with gnarled precarious roots. There was an exceedingly faint chance that here he might escape detection. It was slim indeed, but his only chance. And, he told himself, they cannot be entirely certain that I came down by this particular valley and not another. They will be in haste to search this one and move on to the next.

From the top of either bank of the river the Japanese officers were directing operations. Downstream a Japanese soldier was wading along the further bank. On Misha's side of the river a small scraggy Korean who could have been any age from thirty-five to sixty was scrambling from rock to rock and wading through the pools. On him Misha's hopes were based, for the Korean could hardly fail to see him: the riverside bushes were not thick, although the overhang protected him a little from above.

The searchers took a long time to come up the stream. They had a great deal of thick vegetation to search. To his relief, Misha could hear no dogs. Possibly, as the slope grew steeper and the vegetation thinner and less likely to conceal a hunted man, their search would grow less assiduous. Now that he was out of bandit country it would be as well in any case to jettison his rifle, as Serafima had urged him to do. To resist was useless; there was little point in taking with him several poor Koreans or even some lousy Japanese. There was a slim chance that if they found him unarmed the Japanese might take him alive to be interrogated in Siensin, where perhaps fellow Russians or the British consul might be persuaded to take an interest in his fate. A poor chance. But to fight it out gave him none at all. And now, away from his own war, and so near safety, he felt an urgent desire to survive.

It seemed improbable that he would, as the noise of the beating sticks and the shouts of his pursuers grew louder. The Japanese were a trigger-happy race who did not believe in surrender. As a Russian he was odious and dangerous to them. To the Koreans he was almost as bad, since Imperial Russia was known to have cast covetous eyes upon their strategic peninsula, with its numerous safe and ice-free harbours and its proximity to Vladivostok. The notion of being shot helplessly where he stood was hateful to him. Should he shoot it out, keep them at bay perhaps till dark, escape in the night? But it was barely noon, and his supply of ammunition was small.

A beautiful place, thought Misha, in which to die. His body would lie between the round boulders, and the splashing waters would fall on him. Here ends wonderful, important, unique Misha. Suddenly he became perfectly certain that here he would not lie. Kolya had died, and Vassily, and Ulanov, and Kennedy, and hundreds of others whom he had known and admired or loved—because of them, he must use every wit and nerve to go on living. All of them seemed to gather within him. With a pang of compassion and hope, he thought also of Daisy, forgiving her for all those ways that used to rile him and turn him from her.

On the bank overhead a Japanese officer appeared, shouting instructions across the river, then disappeared again. The small Korean in the river bed climbed nearer, halted in midstream, and approached Misha's cleft, where he stopped, quite still, and looked straight into Misha's eyes. Unmoving, Misha awaited his shout of discovery. The Korean came a step nearer. Sweating himself from fear, Misha could see every line of his sweating face, of his thin garments soaked by the river and clinging to a body which appeared to have been turned out of its mould by a niggardly hand. Upon this wisp, this shadow of a man, Misha's life now hung, since nothing was more certain than that the Korean had seen him. Was he simply savouring his triumph, enjoying this moment of power over this huge and foreign man?

Casting a nervous glance over his shoulder, the skinny form approached a cautious step nearer. Moving with intense and calm deliberation, Misha now chanced his arm, very slowly raising it to point to the neighbouring bush where his discarded rifle lay, open to so close a gaze. "For you," he said, under the noise of the stream, pointing significantly to the rifle and then to the Korean.

The man hesitated for so long that Misha meditated throwing his boots into the bargain. But without them how traverse more stony mountains? He and the Korean gazed steadily into each other's eyes. This thin little man with a masklike face was slowly and carefully calculating whether or not to deliver Misha up to death. His eyes narrowed; he made no movement. The life or death of another man meant nothing to him; he was simply weighing up the pros and cons, perhaps deciding whether to deliver over Misha now or wait for some more fell but profitable purpose later. Misha in his turn made no move; to plead for pity would have been useless and probably nothing but an incitement to cruelty. Expressionless, they stood gazing at one another for a full, long minute.

The voice of a Japanese officer called, harsh, bullying, insistent, as if accusing the Korean of lagging behind or slackening in his duty. The Korean had all the while kept his distance, far enough away to cry out for help should Misha attempt to pounce on him and silence him. Now, turning his head in the direction whence the Japanese officer had shouted, the Korean contorted his face into a mask of hatred, of bitter scorn and anger. Motioning to Misha with an imperious gesture of his thin wrinkled hand to stay exactly where he was, the Korean continued upstream, splashing the water loudly and beating the rocks and scrub as he went, shouting occasionally as if to flush out hunted game.

Tightly within his niche, Misha stayed still. His heart continued to race, waiting, with an ache of suspense, dreading the return of angry excited voices, and motionless as a hare crouched in its hollow, under the shadow of a wheeling hawk.

Very slowly, the time passed. There could well be more Koreans following the chase up the valley and hoping to see the fun of the kill. Misha stayed so motionless that a couple of frogs leapt out of the reeds and landed almost on his foot. With faculties sharpened by danger, he noticed that Korean frogs had vermillion stomachs. Did that, he wondered ravenously, make them poisonous to eat? As the day cooled, more of them hopped from the water, regarding him with their bulging supercilious eyes.

As never before, Misha now feared death. When the Korean returned, would he come with many other men, armed, wanting only to keep this killing to themselves and not share it with the hated Japanese? Could he invoke any power, any threat, any promise that would make them set him free? In Manchuria they had seemed to him neither a cruel nor a vicious people, but then, they had not had him within their power. That did things to men, and especially to the oppressed, anxious as they were to take their miseries out on someone.

More than ever, Misha wanted to live. For the first time his life seemed to him precious and valuable, as it might seem to some near and loving kin. Other lives, other spirits, were now involved in his survival: Kolya's life, Vassily's, Ulanov's, a hundred others. He knew, too, exactly what he wanted to do with it. His mood of resignation had wholly passed. He knew now, when maybe it was too late, that he loved Daisy very dearly and had no other wish but to return to Europe and spend the rest of his life with her. The redemption of Russia must wait: for now, this came first. The thought of Daisy came to him with piercing clarity, as the hours of daylight, and perhaps the last hours of his life, dragged slowly by.

The light left the stream, a chill mist crept up at him off the water. Its sound, and the noise of its many small waterfalls, worried him, drowning as they did all trace of approaching footsteps. At least, he reflected, he had his back to the wall; no sudden knife could strike between his shoulder blades.

It was dusk before the Korean returned, scrambling warily down the river bank. With enormous relief Misha saw that he was alone, and brought with him no band of armed and excited followers. His face, wizened and exhausted, was almost friendly.

Misha uttered his few words of Korean greeting, and together they gathered brushwood and concealed the rifle within the bundle. In the gathering darkness the Korean led Misha to his small wooden house, steep-roofed and clinging to the hillside. He can't now betray me without betraying himself, Misha thought—the look of intense hatred for the conquering Japanese that he had glimpsed on the man's face was a further guarantee. Saved by hate, he thought, but the hatred wouldn't have been enough without the rifle, and the rifle wouldn't have been enough without the hatred. Together they had tipped the scale. If you are one of an oppressed race, the possession of a rifle is a pledge of manhood, he supposed, a private recognition that you are not enslaved, a promise for the future.

As if reading Misha's thoughts, the Korean embarked on a passionate tirade against the occupying power, encouraged by Misha's few words to suppose that he understood all. Who were the Japanese to dare to plant their feet here? Was not this *Korea*, the very word meaning "high and beautiful?" To him and to his fellow countrymen it was also the ancient and famous *Choson*, the Land of Morning Calm. It was true that the Japanese had built roads, had made railways, but only the better to extract and export the riches of Korea's rocks, her iron and tungsten. They had oppressed and murdered countless Koreans and driven thousands more into exile in China and Manchuria. They exported for themselves great quantities of rice, leaving the Koreans to starve. Nearby, almost within sight of his house, they were ransacking the hills for copper.

Misha sat wearily by the stove. His hunger oppressed him like a living presence. He was about to press this point, when the Korean's three enchanting little daughters appeared, dressed as for a festival in bright pink, lime green, and white. They were small-boned and delicate as birds, and the colour of their garments a welcome change from the universal dull blue of the Chinese. Their father, taut with parental pride, ceased dwelling on his country's wrongs. Bending and swaying, the little Korean girls danced solemnly before Misha in their bright dresses and Korean shoes with toes upturned like the prows of little boats, graceful as flowers in a mountain meadow. He smiled and clapped. Exotic odours floated from the back of the house. Misha cared nothing; he would have eaten horse, dog or cat. In the event, the meal was of barley meal and beans, strongly flavoured with radishes.

Mindful of Terenty's words, Misha insisted that he was a sailor who had come ashore at Siensin, where he had fallen foul of the Japanese police, had given them the slip and was in haste to cross the country in secrecy and pick up his ship at Seoul. Seoul, Seoul, he repeated. The word for a ship eluded him; with his knife he scratched a rough picture on a piece of wood. The Korean looked blank. The children, fascinated, drew near to observe Misha's artistic efforts; it was the eldest of them who divined his meaning.

After the meal the Korean left the house and returned half an hour later with a wiry young man whom he introduced as his sister's son, by the name of Ree. Straining to catch the words, Misha heard the Korean instructing the boy to conduct him, by the remotest routes, over the mountains to Seoul, starting just before dawn next day. Ree was regarding him through narrowed eyes. Would he, Misha wondered, once at a safe distance from his uncle and the rifle, betray him for a good round sum to the Japanese? Reflecting that beggars couldn't be choosers, Misha at length fell asleep, still hungry, even now half expecting to be aroused by a babel of excited Japanese voices.

Ree was ready before dawn; Misha could only hope that the Koreans had as powerful a family feeling as had the Chinese, and that uncles in Korea were faithfully obeyed. Ahead of them, the mountains tossed like an ocean in storm, and Misha was thankful enough to be shown the pathway through them. It was a heavily forested country; even above the timberline were dwarf pines and creeping juniper. The higher valleys were incredibly rich with rhododendrons and azaleas, some of which retained their last crimson blooms. Lower down were birch, oak and chestnut. They tramped on through valleys thick with ash, hornbeam and maple, over streams fringed with willow. Sometimes, on the hillside, a great red pine towered up. It was a glorious landscape. It was also a good country for concealment. They travelled over the mountains, took hillside paths, avoiding roads, and when obliged to cross a valley, moved only at dusk and in the very early morning, when they would arise stiff with cold and drenched in dew, to be refreshed only by a handful of rice and drink from the mountain stream. Outside the huts of their villages, the slight Korean women would be reactivating their clay ovens.

Twice, a small Japanese patrol met them on the hillside and Misha lay hidden while Ree, who seemed to be a natural clown, distracted attention by inventing imaginary errands which he illustrated by a wealth of pantomime. Once they came suddenly round the bend of a mountain road straight into two Japanese policemen. Fortunately they were in the company of a dozen Korean peasants on the way to market. Misha slouched in their rear, bending to conceal his size. His height and fairness made him horribly conspicuous; his too-short coolie trousers inadequately covered his battered Russian boots, and an ancient Korean coolie hat was crammed down over his blond locks and shaded, rather than concealed, his glaringly blue eyes. Each time they passed through a Korean mountain village, Ree made some explanation of Misha's presence that appeared to convulse the inhabitants with amusement. Misha suspected that Ree had described him as his dancing bear.

Fear was constant, the cold at nights was beginning to be intense, and they subsisted entirely on a diet of rice and dried fish, supplemented on lucky days by chestnuts and berries. Starting late on the third morning, they topped a rise and were confronted by an astonishing range of mountains, pink in the rays of the early sun. Their lines were fantastic, a series of incredible peaks, like some gigantic graveyard whose tombstones were battered or worn by the sea. "Kum-gang," Ree said. "The Diamond Mountain." The peaks soared like towers, a futuristic vision of a skyscraper town. Misha stood amazed and spellbound. The uttermost parts of the earth, he thought. There was something unbelievable in the sight—magnificent, remote, uncanny, unlike any mountains he had ever seen or dreamed of. He did not know that early Western travellers had likened the land of Korea to a sea in a heavy gale.

For a long while the fantastic mountains stayed on their horizon, somehow adding to the lightheadedness that Misha's increasing hunger made him feel. On the fifteenth day after his near-capture they began to come down, into flowering meadows with the shadows of clouds flying across them. Here were many more people, and low stony hills crowned with pines and temples. There were clay huts with their roofs thatched with rice straw, and an occasional pavilion whose curved tiled roof, outstretched like the wings of a bird, gave it a look as if about to take off in flight, soaring into the intensely clear blue of the Korean sky. Syrian hibiscus, the biblical Rose of Sharon, grew everywhere, sometimes a late bloom flamed red against their thick shrubby green. Small treeless hills were silhouetted in the bright air of the autumn mornings, houses nestled closely together in the narrow valleys.

As they drew further south there were more Buddhist temples with curved tiled roofs, the village houses had raised floors with heating furnaces and hot-air flues underneath them and paper windows framed by wooden lattices. Outside, smoking their long thin bamboo pipes in the last of the summer's warmth, were white-coated grandpapas, their heads crowned with high black horsehair hats. The tracks became more full, there were carts now, drawn by oxen or patient bearers of huge loads in wooden frames strapped to their backs, talkative pedlars with wheeled stalls. The women, graceful and swaying as the willows that fringed their river banks, trod the ways with babies strapped to their backs by gaily coloured quilts, or knelt outside their houses, pounding red peppers with a pestle in a heavy stone mortar.

At all this, in happier times, Misha would have stared with keen interest and an exchange of greetings. Now he shuffled along, his head bowed, never meeting the sharp and interested glances, fearfully leaving all conversation to Ree. As they neared Seoul their danger greatly increased.

One more day's march, Ree conveyed to him, as the sun rose redly over the low hills. Mist shrouded a valley of apple orchards; a sad bell sounded from a Buddhist temple. Misha strode on in hope, when the turning of a bend revealed to them both in the road not a quarter of a mile away a group of ten or twelve Japanese soldiers pressing purposefully on in the early-morning light. Clutching Misha's arm, Ree halted dead in his tracks, his thin hand trembling.

There was no cover anywhere, not a tree, a shrub, a rock. Like a giant stairway climbing up the hill, the terraced rice-paddies swept up to their right. Not a ditch presented itself to their sight, not a hollow. Enormously conspicuous in their solitude and their ludicrous difference in height, they stood still in the middle of the road, hope and inspiration deserting them.

Quite suddenly, and as if in answer to prayer, a sound of distant chanting struck their ears. Winding slowly towards them from a village on the plain was a funeral procession. As they drew near, Misha could see the band of mourners, dressed in sackcloth, their heads and waists bound by cords of twisted straw. Close family feeling had drawn many to the procession, and behind it followed the usual motley procession of followers—children, old men, beggars, and all the ragtag and bobtail of the village, trailing out behind in dusty sympathy or curiosity. Quickly Ree pulled Misha into a sitting position at the roadside. The Japanese were for the moment out of sight. All now depended on whether they or the funeral procession reached them first.

Minutes dragged by. At any one of them the brisk Japanese must surely appear. Had they, improbably, paused for a smoke? The funeral procession, slow, sad, and dignified, moved imperceptibly nearer. The still air brought an ever-louder sound of chanting. Encouraged by the increasing warmth of the sun, some huge Korean butterflies floated gaudily past Misha's ear.

Suddenly, the dusty feet were shuffling by them. Not daring to move until the mourners themselves had passed, Ree and Misha inserted themselves into the tail end of the procession. Misha had picked up a stick. He leant heavily upon it, bent nearly double.

The Japanese patrol, bored by such ceremonies, passed indifferently by, without interest or reverence for the occasion. From the shade of the coolie hat, Misha dared to shoot a sideways glance at them, striding arrogantly by as if the Koreans were so many grasshoppers. For the rest of today, Ree said, we find a hiding place and stay hid.

With relief next day, Ree brought him at dusk over a hill to where they could look down on a modern city blazing with streetlights, secure in its cup of hills. Below them spread Seoul, with its royal palaces and the Secret Garden of the last kings of the dynasty of Ti, Seoul with its grandeur and prosperity and its ubiquitous officials of the paramount power, and their civil army—the teeming Japanese police. A thin line of lights led away down a dark ribbon of river to where, twenty-five miles to the west, Chemulco harboured the trading ships. "Seoul," Ree said thankfully. "Seoul. Now I go."

Misha had long since parted with his gold watch, but round his neck beneath his coolie tunic he still wore a gold chain with a small cross. He tore off the cross and put it in his pocket and handed Ree the chain. Without a word, with scarcely a look back, the young Korean faded into the darkness up the hillside and Misha was left alone.

For the first time, within sight of safety, he felt a kind of frenzy, a wild desire simply to run for Chemulco and cast himself into the nearest ship. He must if possible avoid entering Seoul and make his way, if necessary by starlight, across those intervening miles of countryside, approaching Chemulco in darkness, lying low by daylight to spy out the land. He could not now return to Russia, where certain death awaited. In England lay hope of reunion with his family and with his love.

Five or six cargo vessels lay alongside the quay. Almost at the furthest end of the line was the smallest and most battered of the lot, flying the red ensign. Her shoregoing crew, Misha imagined, would be sure to make for the bright lights of Seoul and to return to Chemulco as late as possible. He lay low until dark, then made for a small square which he had recognised to be the streetcar terminal.

There, sure enough, seated at a table outside a scruffy eating house, were a group of obvious seamen, enjoying a last glass of beer. The blessed sound of a cockney oath reached Misha's listening ears. He shambled very slowly across the square, and passing the table, said over his shoulder and in a low voice, "Do you mind if I sit with you?"

The four men gazed at him, startled by the height, the fairness, and the educated voice of this coolie-clad figure. One was small, pale-faced and determined looking, another had a thatch of red hair and an aggressive expression, a third was large and red-faced, with huge gorilla hands from which the grease could never altogether be removed. A crop of dampish curls crowned the round cheerful face of the fourth. All looked at Misha with a slow, rather suspicious, but deeply considering look. They would clearly have no truck with a tall tale. He must from the start present himself as what he really was—a refugee Russian—and tell them the truth. The small man made the faintest gesture of assent and Misha quickly sat down.

When he finished his tale the faces of his listeners wore a wary blankness, as if they hadn't quite heard what he was saying or, if they had, were unwilling to understand it. Presently the small man spoke to the very large one. "What you think then, Jacko?"

Jacko's face remained a study of nonreceptivity. "Take a bit of managing, getting him on board," he ventured at last. "We don't want no trouble. Same time, I'm not one for helping the Jap police. I'm not one for doing their job for 'em."

The others brooded on this sentiment. "Me neither," the redhead said at length. "What you make of it then, Curly?"

"How do you reckon the old man would take it? And Johnson?"

"You hungry then?" Jacko asked unexpectedly. "You look a bit tucked up. He looks a bit tucked up, don't he?"

There was a long pause, while they sat quite still, considering Misha's case. He must, he realised, be both patient and humble to stand a chance. Last time, he thought, I was tried for my life by a Korean judge; this time it's an English jury, less eight. Four good men and true. The verdict would be correspondingly slow in coming.

"The Nip on account of what they's after him, was the one what kicked his mate, lying dead that minute," Curly pointed out, in case anyone had missed this part of Misha's narration.

"He done right to do what he done. He done right."

Their very deliberate considering of his case would conceal, up to the last possible moment, their growing readiness to help.

"Seeing as how we are short-handed, any road—"

"Taking into account that he ain't done no crime, not in this country . . . and us sailing on the morning tide—"

A trio of Japanese police were crossing the square. They bustled up to the table, enquiring officiously, "This man molesting you? This man pestering you? You like us send him packing?"

There was a further silence. Finally the enormous Jacko spoke with slow and heavy emphasis. "He's not molesting us any."

"Thanks just the same," the diplomatic Curly added. The Japanese, mollified, drifted away.

Their intervention had applied a certain spur to the discussion. The seamen would effect his rescue in their own way, at their own pace, but they would effect it. Misha suppressed a wild desire to dash ahead of them, crash through the dockyard gate and hurl himself into their ship.

There was another considerable pause. Then their voices went on.

"Mean you'd have to lend him your coat, Jacko. He's not going to get past in them coolie togs."

"Don't do no good to go looking over your shoulder that way, mate. You want to sit tight. Here, drink up."

"Seeing as how Dai Griffiths was lost overboard, and Todd sick at Singapore . . . Can you cook, mate?"

"'E don't need to cook fancy. Being as how anyone can peel spuds."

"The old man thought as his papers went overboard with him. But he was wearing oilskins, and his papers was still in his jacket, hanging up. I took 'em out. See here, mate, your name is Griffiths, David Griffiths, if the Jap police was to arst you. You taken that in? David Griffiths. Left your papers on board. And if they's trouble, one of us, one of your mates, will fetch them."

Misha breathed again. The verdict, seemingly, was in his favour.

"There'll be another lot of chaps along on the last tram. Late at night the Japs don't count so careful, not wanting trouble, not when there's a big bunch coming in at the gates."

"You better put on them Russky boots of his, Jacko. No one's going to take *you* for a bleeding Russky. He can wear yours."

Having decided to take Misha, they were now prepared to defend him with their lives. They proceeded at once to deprecate the whole thing.

"It won't be no fancy trip."

"Not like one of them whore's-boudoir liners."

"We're no express train. Bound for Kobe, with tungsten—you better lie low there, not get going ashore—then load up and sail for Singapore, Sydney, Perth in west Australia, the Cape, the lot. Matter of months before we get home."

"March. April maybe."

"The cook's not got what you'd call a pretty temper, neither."

"Another thing," Curly said seriously. "I reckon the captain will be agreeable, seeing as how he is two hands short. After he's hummed and hawed like, for a while. But he trades regular with the Nips. He's got to come back here. Keeps coming, he does. He won't want any trouble. Same time he don't like them any."

"Look, if we was to help you on board and there was trouble, real trouble, not just them talking themselves big, but real trouble—"

"I would give myself up," Misha said, speaking for the first time since the discussion opened. "That is understood." Mastering distaste, he finished tying up Jacko's boots. They fitted him well enough.

A streetcar clanged to a halt. A dozen men descended from it. "Come on then, mate," the redhead urged him. "And keep your trap shut. Act simple; Dusty here will do the talking for you."

* * *

A shake of the shoulder aroused Misha. Still terrified of Japanese arrest, he sprang up. But it was only the hand of Dusty. "Made it all right with the old man," he said. "Bit of an argy-bargy, but he come round." The China Sea heaved beneath Misha. From the galley came the smell of bacon being cooked in thrice-used fat. He was in the country of the free.

Chapter 32

"You see," Daisy continued lamely, "we are too like each other. We agree on almost everything."

George's voice had turned dry, clipped, unfeeling. "Isn't that believed to be an essential?"

"Believed! Not by me. Nor by you either, really. There should be a sort of tension, surely; a kind of quarrelling feeling to keep one alive and kicking?"

George had moved away from his seat on the sofa beside her and was now pacing up and down.

"We would be dull together. No sparks struck, ever. My fault, more than yours." Her voice came out wrong, sounding tight and discouraging. George's long sigh, Daisy noted, was one more of bewilderment than of despair. He will recover, she thought, the sense of her guilt lessening—sooner than he thinks. Already his look of misery was lightening into thoughtfulness. He continued to pace, until Daisy, following him with her earnest gaze, began to feel like a Wimbledon spectator.

"I haven't explained anything properly. I haven't made you understand . . . how fond I am of you, admiring, appreciating. But not a possible wife." Her voice, high and nervous, rang with a sincerity that only made it sound more false.

Now that all persuasion had failed, George wanted very much to get right away and endure his pain in solitude. But Daisy, perversely, would not now let him go without some kind of friendly farewell.

"You haven't told me which part of Canada you are going to after the month in Oregon. Is it the far end, where all the forests are? Won't it be beautiful?"

George turned on her a look of bafflement. The attempt at polite conversation really wore him down. His words came out with difficulty.

"British Columbia. Vancouver."

It was on the tip of Daisy's tongue to blurt out, "Oh then you'll meet Amelia!" but discretion for once held her. Of late, George had made one or two very friendly references to Amelia. If two people, or if only one of two people far from home, really wanted to get together, and the other was at least acquiescent, they would succeed. And had better succeed unaided. So this had been the meaning of Amelia's quizzical sidelong glance!

Her friend, Daisy reflected, had not come down in the last fall of snow. Amelia had every wit about her and would have contrived, however casually, to let George know her address in Vancouver. And people arriving lovelorn in a new country, Daisy remembered ruefully, were sitting ducks. He'll be like I was. And that's that.

All the same there was a sadness mixed with the relief with which she heard the scrunch of George's tyres moving away over the new gravel. She had swapped the continuing presence of the Rock of Gibraltar for a card every Christmas. *With love from George and Amelia*—and the contrary thing is I shall have to try quite hard not to feel jealous . . .

But when this brief pang was over, and the shock of surprise had disappeared, it was succeeded by a flow of generous pleasure. George and Amelia! How settled, friendly and familiar it sounded already, as if their coming together had been inevitable, right from the beginning.

At Werringham, by mid-April, the Easter holidays were in full swing. Within the first week Jenny had fallen off Mouse and broken her ankle; she swung about the house on crutches, complaining that there was nothing to do. Virginia too, was a little broody; her future mother-in-law was making difficulties about the wedding arrangements, and she suspected that she herself had made several serious and irretrievable mistakes over her trousseau. Varya was insisting that she must at once, now that she was sixteen, have a long black evening dress, to be worn with a dark red fringed shawl. No white, nothing pale; nothing at all *jeune fille* would possibly suit her. Surely Mrs. Pelham *must* see that!

Coming back from the village for tea, Daisy entered the house to the sound of a prolonged and resounding crash, followed by cries of protest, cries of denial, a yell of plaintive apology. Daisy hurried in their direction. In the dining room her mother, with her thin face for once pink with justifiable annoyance, was contemplating the wreckage of the newly laid tea-table. Sponge cake, scones, jam, honey, squashed-fly biscuits and tomato sandwiches were spread in inextricable confusion amongst broken china and glass, and a stained white tablecloth lay crumpled on the floor. Off the edge of the carpet a large pool of hot tea was in the process of removing the polish from the parquet floor. Arkady, chasing Nikolai, had tripped over a chair and caught at the tablecloth to save himself from falling. Far from realising their enormity, both twins were doubled up beside the sideboard, in wild uncontrollable mirth.

It was dreadful that Mrs. Pelham's cherished tea-set should thus be destroyed, but Daisy, sternly rebuking the boys and compelling them to stir their stumps and help clear up the mess, found, with a pang at her own disloyalty, that she was more in tune with them and their laughter than she was with her mother in her distress. In England do we not all mind too much about such things? She put an arm round her mother's shoulders, but this only served to precipitate her tears. "Too absurd of me, I know; but that was my mother's tea-set; so many happy memories of home involved with it—"

Varya appeared in the doorway, in her cool, calm and collected mood, looking remarkably pretty. She surveyed the scene with disdain and without concern. Clearing up is a matter for serfs, her face conveyed more clearly than any words. "Ella's fallen out of the treehouse," she announced, "and I think she has broken her wrist. It is doubtful if she will ever be able to play the piano again. Certainly her hopes of a professional career must be ended." A distant melancholy wailing seemed to confirm this diagnosis. Wiping honey and tomato off her hand with the wrecked tablecloth, Daisy rose from her knees to go to Ella. From the hall came the persistent ringing of an unanswered telephone; at length, her father's footsteps crossed the hall from his study to answer it. They seemed heavier than of old, almost reproachful, the steps of an old man feeling that one of the girls or one of the maids might have seen to this.

Ella, retrieved, seemed bruised rather than broken; but she had shocked herself, and insisted upon an elaborate process of medication from the bathroom cupboard, followed by a prolonged session of cuddling. "El, you're too big for all this, really you are. Now do *stop* crying."

"For you, Daisy," her father called up from the hall.

"What is?"

"The telephone. I'll tell them to hang on. Some name I couldn't make out. Oh. They've rung off. Or been cut off. No doubt they'll come back again."

But they didn't. Which was as well, Daisy reflected, helping Nelly to scrape raspberry jam from the carpet. "Mind the broken china. *Mind*, Arkady, you'll cut yourself, and between Jenny and Ella we have finished up all the bandages in the house." Tea was late and scrappy and the atmosphere was rain-washed. Even Nikolai for once was silent, Jenny aggrieved, Ella still gently heaving and gulping. Varya guarded her look of aloof unconcern.

"I think I'll just take a cup along to your father," Mrs. Pelham said. "He's writing."

Somehow, she did not return to drink her own, and Daisy could not in honesty blame her. Half an hour later her parents' voices were still to be heard, in sustained and gentle argument, from behind the study door. To Daisy the underlying note seemed to be one of sadness.

Next morning her parents were themselves again: a bluebell picnic was mooted; comfort and order seemed restored to the framework. But nothing is really settled, Daisy thought. They've accepted this whole situation, and nothing would make them go back on that. But ought they to go on having to accept it? They are not so terribly young or strong. I suppose one must now face the fact that the Dubelsky parents are dead, or they would surely have shown up by now or made some effort through White

Russian organizations, if there are any, to get in touch with the children. Poor people! And poor children! They never seem to talk of their parents now. It's as if the thought is too bitter, as if they *want* to forget. Varya is shaping up to be a real problem, and with a child that is not one's own, how can my parents cope? Once away at school, the twins will be all right, and Ella is little enough to adapt, but Varya never will. She is Russian to the core and ought to be allowed to be.

Ought! Ought! Ought! Too many irreconcilable oughts. I don't seem to concentrate, or make a plan, or do anything but dream impossible things. Misha has gone forever, and now, so has good and sensible George. If I could go away and work! But not much good came of that last time. The trouble is that one doesn't get away from oneself, which goes on besieging and nagging and pushing itself to the fore. I suppose I was so wound up, all that long time in Russia, and now I'm like a clock that's run down. Or whose spring is broken, more likely . . .

What is happening at the other side of the world, in Siberia? The fighting was over long ago. So he *must* be dead. There's no possible alternative. Knowing Misha, there probably is, but the most likely thing is that he is dead. And lying out unburied in some horrible wilderness. Oh, *Misha* . . .

"There's the telephone again, Edward," Mrs. Pelham called. "I won't answer it; it'll be for you. The Dean—he said he was going to ring you up again to settle details."

The call turned out to be for Daisy.

The voice unbelievably, was that of Prince Andrei Dubelsky! They were alive! In England! Daisy's heart raced when she recognized that well-remembered voice. Yes, they were both safe. And the children? Yes, yes, yes, yes. For a while Daisy couldn't get her breath, but the Prince continued as if they had all parted last Tuesday. Yes, yes, yes. Quite near, a house in a village called Lodminster. Could they get over? The Dubelskys had as yet no car. Yes, they had at last escaped from prison at Perm and somehow crossed Siberia, been imprisoned again at Vladivostok, waited many weary months and been at length extracted through the influence of some French friends. The children had been reported as having escaped to America. The Dubelskys had been there for two years, searching desperately. Then a letter from London had spoken of four children of the right age having been rescued with the writer, on board the destroyer *Goshawk*. The Dubelskys had crossed to England in the next ship and arrived excitedly in London, and then had great difficulty in tracing the Pelhams, since all the Kettles were away from home and no one else seemed to know their whereabouts.

"I can't believe it. I can't. I can't." This was like a dream come true.

"Can you be over at once? In time for luncheon?" the Prince asked.

Yes, they could, at least directly after, because the twins had now gone fishing and had to be fetched up from the river. "And here is Varya, and

can you hear Ella jumping up and down? Yes, yes, yes! . . . Varya, let
Ella speak, you have had long enough . . . and now, come quick; we
must wash both your hair . . . I can't *believe* it! They are safe. They are
here. Not twelve miles away. Oh, thank God!"

Turning on the tap, Daisy sank down on the bathroom chair in an
enormous shudder of relief.

"Russian, is it?" repeated the village postmistress at Lodminster.
"Well, no, I couldn't say. I couldn't rightly say. I'm not one for foreign
names, never have been, never will be. If it's Russians you are wanting
you would do better to ask them up at the big house. Polish or something
of that, they are up there, just arrived and the house all no-how, Mrs.
Potts told me. She was really put about; no beds aired, no nothing. Not a
bite of food in the place, it's been empty for months, and never a word nor
a line to say they were coming. Best thing you could do is you could ask
up at the big house—big iron gates a quarter of a mile down the road,
more maybe."

Prince Andrei Dubelsky's "little house," as might have been expected,
was a sizeable Regency mansion in a small park, and approached up an
avenue of well-grown oak trees. Why he had bought a house almost in
Wales, when contemplating sending Misha and Kolya to Eton, would
never be known; perhaps all distance in England had seemed to him too
inconsiderable to matter.

The reunion left nothing in warmth or emotion to be desired. Once
more Daisy was torn between her English feeling that she could not possibly be wanted on such a family occasion, and her acquired Russian
feeling that it would be unforgivable not to enter completely into it all, to
embrace everyone, to laugh, cry, sing, leap, partake of every possible emotion as if it were an obligatory Christmas cake. Varya was laughing hys-
terically, the Prince was weeping openly, Ella was dancing, the twins
were devouring their mother as if they were a couple of wolves. The
samovar had been set in the hall and was already in action. The house
rang with sound.

When the kissing, the hugging, the weeping and the laughter had subsided a little, and the first brief outline of the travellers' tales had been
told, Daisy produced her hoard of jewels—signal for a fresh burst of
exclamation and extravagant cries. The Princess, garlanded and decked
simultaneously with every piece of jewellery that she or her forebears had
ever possessed, was alternately embracing Daisy or drawing back to gaze
admiringly into her eyes amidst cries of "My children! My jewels! What
miracles! What wonders! How inexpressibly happy I am! Andrei! What
marvels! This wonderful Daisy! How happy a day!" When the part that
Nikolai and Arkady had played in their preservation was told her, she
was almost overwhelmed with wonder and glory at their marvellous cour-

age and presence of mind. Seeing that Varya looked a little bit out of it all, the Princess immediately presented her with a ruby necklace, and Varya's dark eyes shone like stars. "Ah . . . how beautiful she is. Look, Andrei, at how beautiful a grown-up daughter we have!"

The Princess, though greyer and less glowing, was no less beautiful. The Prince, also grey and thinner than of yore, wore a suit that, as ever, appeared to be perfectly new. They both surprised Daisy by expressing their delight at the boys' having been sent to the choir school—they could hardly wait to hear them sing. What a fool I was to worry, she thought.

"Later," the Prince announced, "I shall send them to Eton, since it is near Windsor, I understand. King George," he added, with great simplicity, "is almost the only Englishman I know, and I should like them to be near him."

Daisy uttered an inward sigh. How would the Dubelskys *manage* in England, between Mrs. Potts and King George?

Suddenly, Uncle Georg was also in their midst, in his eighties now and supported by Ambrose, but still chuckling, still sardonic, still embracing everyone with warm tobacco-laden kisses. Uncle Sergei, it seemed, had characteristically lingered too long in Moscow; the date of his death was unknown, but he was certainly dead. Uncle Georg spoke of him as if, in a moment of carelessness, he had missed a train. "So like him, poor fellow." Uncle Georg and Ambrose had been discovered in a refugee camp in Austria, from which the good fortune of Ambrose's Swiss nationality had enabled their extraction at short notice. As it happened, his wife's money had all been invested in Switzerland, so that Uncle Georg was by no means short of cash, but he had managed to manufacture a source of displeasure even from this singular good fortune, and complained constantly about the unfavourable rate of exchange. He had already decided that the climate of Worcestershire did not suit him—it was damp; he would become rheumatic; there was no air here; the people of the west did not know what air was, and drank, without apparent distaste, the most abominable tea. At intervals he paused in his greetings to speak severely to his niece and nephew, as though they had invented the soggy climate of the west country expressly to plague him. They treated him with undiminished affection and he returned a stony gaze, occasionally hooding those long light eyes in unbearable weariness, yet rousing from time to time to greet Daisy, and even Varya, with an unmistakably lascivious wink. While there was life there was lust.

Varya herself was a changed being, gleaming and confident, no longer haughty. She was being gentle and graceful with her difficult old great-uncle, docile and charming with her parents. Even if it doesn't last, thought Daisy, they will know how delightful she *can* be. She felt regretfully that she herself had never understood Varya. We were too near in age, and in an odd way, rivals. I managed her badly, or didn't really manage her at all. All you can say is that I brought her back safely to those who can manage her well. Varya shot her a sudden look of brilliant affection. Landed on this safe family shore, she could afford to love. Daisy responded with mingled pleasure and sadness.

The hours passed, the talk never ceasing, the emotion ebbing and flowing, tears succeeding laughter, and laughter tears. After four years, it was hardly surprising. It came upon Daisy suddenly that she must go.

"Never! Never leave us!" the Princess said.

"I must, my father needs the car tonight."

"A car can be hired!"

"No, truly, I must go. I will see you soon. Yes, tomorrow. You must meet my parents."

"Yes, yes, yes, indeed . . . and that brave captain who came to your rescue. I must see him and all his crew. And every year I will give a great dinner for them all—in London, in Portsmouth, where you will."

"Yes, yes, tomorrow . . . no, the children did it all; they were splendid. Yes, good night, good night."

Driving out on the main road, Daisy felt curiously empty and flat. It's the reaction from all that feeling, she told herself firmly. But how odd it would seem not to kiss Ella goodnight, not to bully the twins into cleaning their teeth! She felt an overwhelming relief, now that this seemingly endless responsibility had been removed from her shoulders, and yet also, an equally strong sense of loss and of emptiness. A six years' habit of love and tenderness, of duty and obligation, had perforce suddenly gone from her: the picture of her life, as an essential part of the children's well-being, had now to fade. Where now?

Two men were walking behind a herd of cows, and she got out of the car to shut the Dubelsky iron gates and keep the cattle out. It was a large herd; she watched their great swaying quarters go by.

A shadow fell across the road; she was seized in an embrace.

"*Misha!*" she gasped, adding, inadequately, "I thought you were the *cow*herd."

"Why are you getting into the car with me?"

"Because I am coming wherever you are going."

"This is where your parents live."

"I know. I sent them a telegram. I was on the way to them. And then suddenly, there you were looking so beautiful."

Daisy felt unable to respond to this. The hard indignation of a wounded pride, the bitterness of that long painful ignorant wait continued to ride her. She took refuge in chat, as if Misha were someone met for the first time at a party and talked to perforce whilst the bored eye roved elsewhere. "Telegrams aren't always delivered in the country. It depends on whether a little boy from the forge is available. He may be harvesting potatoes."

"Nobody harvests potatoes in April," Misha pointed out. "You don't seem ecstatic to see me."

"I've worn out my ecstasy on seeing your parents. And leaving the

children with them. Why don't you join them, Misha? You would complete the joy. I am going back home." Her voice sounded, and was meant
to sound, cold.

"And I am coming with you."

Daisy contemplated his stubborn face. It was the same Misha, much,
much thinner, sadder perhaps, but the same ebullient Misha. Perhaps
more handsome than ever. He was regarding her with a kind of joyful
triumph. She looked very well and was prettier than he remembered her.
There appeared not to be a cloud in his sky.

Daisy was suddenly furious. "I suppose you remember how you left
me? Without a word, without a goodbye? I suppose you remember that
you have written not *one* letter, sent not *one* word, to tell me whether you
were alive or dead? I suppose you think you can come back out of the blue
like this, and take up exactly where you left off, as if none of all that had
happened?"

"But of course. Whyever not?"

She had started to drive now, too angry to wait to persuade Misha to get
out. How *Russian* of him—this unheralded arrival, this glowing assumption of welcome! They drove on in silence. The rain rattled on the windows of the open Morris, the hood shook as if in sympathy with Daisy's
shaken voice and shaking hands.

"It is, alas, finished in Siberia for now," Misha said. "For just now. I
shall learn to be an engineer." He said it as if it were as easy as learning a
new game of patience. "A marine engineer. In the ship, in that long time
in the ship that brought me to England, I became much interested in
marine engines. I have come back, like the bad penny, to find you. You
have not married?"

"What do you think?"

No, thought Misha, you have not married, and you have been too long a
virgin, my poor Daisy, with that put-on, hard, punishing voice. He felt
immense pity, and an awareness of having been in some way to blame for
those pretty lips being tightened against him, that resolutely turned
away profile. And yet, she had been ready enough to kiss him in the first
moment of surprise. Ready indeed.

An occasional drop of rain spat in at him. The April evening was damp
and cold. He put an arm along the seat behind Daisy. "I believe," he said,
"that you love me. That you remember me entirely. That you have
thought of me while I have been away. That you will now marry me."

Daisy drove on in silence, staring steadily ahead into the rain. *Thus
blindly with our blessedness at strife*, she thought suddenly, but cussedness
prevailed. He had behaved so utterly forgetfully and callously. "You
can't expect me to forgive everything, in a flash, as if these two silent
years had never happened?"

"Having wasted so much time, why should we waste more?" I had
forgotten, he thought, that she had such a beautiful long neck. Daisy

turned her head for a moment to contemplate him. He looked, and was, too large for a Morris car.

In a flash of clarity Daisy saw him for what he would be: the classic example of an unsatisfactory husband—moody perhaps, incalculable, likely to be intermittently unfaithful. He would always ache for lost splendours, for a world that had once been his oyster. No willing cheerful Sergeis or Ivans would be on hand to bring his horse round, to clean his car, to pick up his discarded clothes from the floor. For all the hardships he had undergone, would it ever occur to him to pick them up himself? No, it would not.

He would always feel himself a prince in a world where no one else would. Could he forget, could he adjust, become an exile with the degree of humility expected of exiles? No. He would never do any of these things. Chastened he might be, by the long hard years, and open-eyed as he had never been before. But he remained a bad matrimonial bargain and life with him would never be undemanding or easy. The trouble was that life without him would be impossible. She felt for him an aching and abundant love, a powerful desire to give him everything he wanted the moment that he wanted it, to give him all that she had of love and unselfishness, and a simultaneous determination to make him work his passage home.

Misha leant back in the car, regarding with satisfaction the sweep of Daisy's eyelashes, the soft curve of her cheek. He was no fool, and had swiftly become aware that his line of approach must now be different. Daisy was in her own land, had her own standing in this world, doubtless her own string of local admirers better situated than himself. He would have to put in some hard work, must even concentrate, for a while, on the task. He had taken too much for granted, thinking to go on playing the King Cophetua role that had seemed natural to him in Russia.

Unaware of any motive, Daisy for her part acted entirely from instinct—like a loving mother whose wandering child has given her a bad fright, who has to be scolded uphill and down dale before the inevitable finale of a warm embrace. Only, not like a mother.

Misha, with a serious look, tried a new tack. "If you are unwilling to marry me for my own sake, you would maybe marry me for Kolya's?"

The humility of this touched Daisy deeply, but she declined entirely to soften. Why do I play with fire, she wondered, and risk losing a being whom I love so much? Unable to think why, she yet continued.

The proximity of Misha was rapidly becoming too much for her. With relief she came to the outskirts of Werringham village; another half mile and she might have melted. And melt I will *not!* I wish he would go away, back to his parents, and allow me to build up my defences in solitude and calm. But equally, I'd kill him if he did.

No kind of calculation entered into these impulses, no notion of a strategic keeping of Misha at arm's length. They proceeded from pure rage, a rage whose pump she was at pains to prime by continued recollections of his desertion, failure to write and his general and hateful perfidy.

Comfortably aware that both of Daisy's hands were occupied with the wheel, Misha continued his advance. Daisy's anger amused him and lent a spice to the pursuit. He had no doubt as to its outcome. Everything in his garden was rosy, and he glowed with joy and delight. For this, he thought, for this I survived and lived and came home. For she, undoubtedly, is my home. And I am hers.

Daisy broke sharply in upon his thoughts.

"Take your arm away, please, Misha. This is my village, where I live." With an unwonted grinding of gears that betrayed a mind elsewhere, Daisy swung the car into a drive, outside a solid and handsome Georgian rectory.

Not bad, Misha thought. "And now," he said, aloud and rashly, "for the worthy pastor."

He had far better have held his tongue. "You'll stay for dinner?" Daisy asked coldly.

"If you please." Misha had had nothing since an early lunch and was exceedingly hungry.

"It's unfortunate, but this happens to be the feast of our local saint. St. Caradoc; he's Welsh. We eat nothing today except a very little dry bread. And boiled cabbage," she added, suddenly inspired. She could hardly wait to see that great big jaw drop. "And mind your P's and Q's."

"Mind *what?*"

Assuming a long face and an air of browbeaten meekness and signing to Misha to do the same, Daisy led him up the steps and into the warm and well-lit hall of her parents' house.

Mr. Pelham and his wife were entertaining some friends. They had just come from a committee meeting, and those who lived farthest away had previously been asked to stay to dinner. Misha hardly had time to notice a beautifully furnished room, with a fine Richard Wilson landscape over the chimneypiece, before he was led away.

Goodness, thought Mr. Pelham, a little wearily, *another* young man of Daisy's. How large, how travel-stained, and what *amazing* clothes. She is *too* good-natured. "Perhaps you'd like to wash?" he suggested kindly, propelling Misha through a hall hung with another choice landscape and a couple of Northcote ancestors in military red coats.

Dumbfounded, Misha followed him. Who could this urbane fellow be? Surely not Daisy's father? He perceived that his own suit, hurriedly purchased in Singapore, was all wrong.

"What's the fellow's name?" Mr. Pelham demanded of Daisy, returning to the drawing room. "I didn't quite hear it."

"Dubelsky."

"Ah, one of your Russian friends."

"Yes, one of them." Daisy looked flushed and upset, her father thought. She was naturally distressed at the children's leaving her.

"Pity we haven't any vodka. Does he drink sherry, d'you suppose?" he asked. "And you might warn him, gently, not to throw his glass into the fireplace. These are some of the good ones."

"Of course, Papa darling. How are you, Lady Fox?"

"I suppose he'd like dinner?" Mrs. Pelham ventured unenthusiastically, just before Misha's fair but still dishevelled head appeared round the drawing-room door. "A fine-looking man, but he looks half-starved, poor fellow," she murmured to her daughter. "I suppose they can eat pheasant? No, of course, it's duckling—that should be all right. Ring the bell, darling, or just go and ask Barton to lay another place."

On this errand, Daisy passed by Misha, traversing the drawing-room carpet with an unusually careful tread.

"Don't leave me," he besought her out of the corner of his mouth.

"You'll be fine. Courage! If the conversation flags, you can do a Cossack dance."

With a lowering glance, Misha addressed himself to a glass of sherry. Gloom clouded his brow, and he perceived at once that he would have to get himself an entirely different suit. And an entirely different haircut. Returning from her errand to the kitchen, Daisy embraced the company with a radiant smile. Misha received the impression that she was about to strip him naked with some devastating comment upon his appearance, character or race.

"I hope you can eat smoked salmon," she addressed him in tones of honeyed sweetness, but with a glittering gaze. "Monsieur Dubelsky," she added, speaking to Lady Fox, with exaggerated gush, "was simply *splendid* at dealing with wolves."

Misha permitted himself a sigh of relief. From Mrs. Pelham, who had addressed him with the kindly tolerance of the Edwardian Englishwoman confronted by the luckless foreigner, he had been detached by Sir Mordaunt Fox, to whose long tales of a visit to Batum in 1903 he was listening with a decent show of interest.

It dawned upon him that Miss Prim had departed forever into oblivion and left this sparkling, beautiful opponent, worthy of his fire. Winning Daisy might take longer than he had anticipated, but it would be worth it.

Daisy's mind was now, she believed, quite cool and collected. She would continue to be cross and standoffish with Misha for as long as she possibly could—or at any rate for two months. Or at least a fortnight. She stole a brief look at Misha's face as he stood talking by the fire. I must look at him clearly now, she thought, now for the last time while I can still *see* his face. Soon, I will cease to see it. It will just be a part of him. And that will be a part of me, and no more visible in a detached way than one's own face is. As he's so handsome, it's a great waste that his looks will no longer matter. He'll just be me. I'll just be him. We shall be one flesh.

To her surprise, this thought caused Daisy's heart to swell and her arm to move so sharply that most of her sherry leapt smartly from its glass and fell upon the Persian carpet. She gazed at it in astonishment, and caught her father's look, which said more clearly than words, Don't worry your mother, it will soon merge with the pattern. But Daisy was past taking anything in, gazing straight past her father with a look of incredulous joy on her face. He thought she must have gone very slightly daft and could not for the life of him think why.

Conversation continued. Daisy's glass was refilled. Her countenance, with some difficulty, recovered its stern remote look. Even this, she feared, might not totally deceive Misha. Better not overdo it and look too stern. An easy naturalness would disconcert him more. But with naturalness itself crying out to her to let love rip, that might not be so easy.

Dinner was announced. And now, Misha thought, for the dry bread.

The clear soup was delicious. So was the dry Chardonnay wine. He perceived that he had fallen on his feet. Whilst the formidable Barton, assisted by Nelly, was removing the soup plates, Misha continued to listen to his righthand neighbour, whose melancholy monologue was not unamusing, at the same time seizing Daisy's smooth hand below the table, since her back was still resolutely turned to him; she was talking with animation to the elderly man on her left. She turned on Misha a look of reproof. Before the blue blaze of her eyes, Misha's caution melted from him. There would be advances and retreats, and skirmishes and surprises; and in this little-known country she could lay ambushes for him as she had done tonight. But *this* war, at least, he knew how to win. His native exuberance rose within him.

"I drink," he said, "to Askold Mihailovitch."

"Please let go."

"Do you like that name?"

"*Please let go of my knee. In England, cela ne se fait pas.*"

"I don't believe you," Misha said, not letting go. "It is agreed between us, then, that our eldest son shall be christened Askold?"

Daisy's gaze was fixed on the silver bowl of narcissus in the middle of the table. She read and reread its familiar inscription as if it were the most absorbing piece of information that had ever come her way. "To the Honourable Edward Pelham," it read, "on the occasion of his marriage, September the fifteenth, 1893. From the tenant farmers of the Royham Estate." To her relief, the roast duckling was now coming round, and she would have something else on which to concentrate, and Misha would have another occupation for his hand.

Behind him Daisy was laughing; apparently convulsed with mirth at some joke made by her neighbour. But Misha knew very well that she was laughing in mockery of him, in affection for him, in exultant joy for them both.

"You like that name," Misha insisted. "I am very *certain* that you like that name."

Daisy's head was now low over her plate, as if she were a gourmet critically absorbed in a favourite dish. But there had been something in the bending of that long neck that, to Misha at least, had worn the aspect of assent, of a surrender leading to affirmation and joy. He trembled; his large appetite left him. Why all this food, why all these people? He felt like leaping to his feet, yelling, dancing, and going totally mad.

Daisy had turned again to her lefthand neighbour. On Misha's right hand came the incisive penetrating tones of an English gentlewoman determined not to be neglected at the dinner table. "Now, Mr.Dubelsky," Lady Fox insisted, "*you* will be able to tell me the difference between Lenin and Trotsky."

With a monumental effort, Misha began to comply.